THE COLE
PROTOCOL

THE COLE
PROTOCOL

TOBIAS S. BUCKELL

BASED ON THE BESTSELLING VIDEO GAME FOR XBOX®

G

GALLERY BOOKS

New York | London | Toronto | Sydney | New Delhi

G

Gallery Books
A Division of Simon & Schuster, Inc.
1230 Avenue of the Americas
New York, NY 10020
www.simonandschuster.com

First Gallery Books trade paperback edition April 2019

For information about special discounts for bulk purchases, please contact Simon & Schuster Special Sales at 1-866-506-1949 or business@simonandschuster.com.

The Simon & Schuster Speakers Bureau can bring authors to your live event. For more information or to book an event, contact the Simon & Schuster Speakers Bureau at 1-866-248-3049 or visit our website at www.simonspeakers.com.

Manufactured in the United States of America

10 9 8 7 6 5 4 3 2

Library of Congress Cataloging-in-Publication Data is available.

ISBN 978-1-9821-1171-7
ISBN 978-1-9821-1172-4 (ebook)

For fellow HALO fans everywhere

THE COLE
PROTOCOL

PROLOGUE

The Rubble, Covenant Occupied System, 23 Librae

Ignatio Delgado ducked behind a bulkhead next to a set of cargo containers, the red paint peeling off their ribbed metal surfaces, just as a burst of plasma hit.

The dull metal he hid behind glowed—hot tiny molten gobs dripping then spitting as they hit the cold deck near his feet.

"Melko?" he called out over the acrid sizzling.

The answer came after a worrying pause: "Still here."

His copilot made it behind the container. But that didn't change the problem coming right down their throats.

The hold stretched up all around them—the core of a mile-long asteroid, slowly spun up to provide gravity, and recently hollowed out. Delgado and Melko stood on the inside wall of the rocky cylinder. The cargo area's metal walls sunk into the rock and it was crammed with spare supplies from other asteroids.

Delgado pulled out his pistol and pressed the heavily engraved and personalized grip up to his cheek. His uncle had replaced the weapon's stock with some very rare oak back on Madrigal, and created a piece of art out of this standard-issue M6.

That was before the Covenant forces had glassed Madrigal. Before humans had fled to the safety of the asteroids trailing the gas giant Hesiod that the Insurrectionists who had been hiding there called "the Rubble."

Delgado kissed the scrollwork.

Firing around the corner of the bulkhead, he leapt for the safety of the next stack of cargo containers.

He caught a brief glimpse of his attackers—awkwardly tall, birdlike aliens with plasma pistols gripped strong in their talon-like hands. Their beady eyes stared right at him.

The spiny quilled mohawks on their skulls twitched. The sound of plasma shots hit the other side of the container and reverberated through the hold.

"Jackals," Delgado said with a wince. That was what most humans called these aliens, though they called themselves the *Kig-Yar*. They were just one of the alien races of the so-called Covenant. The ones who'd discovered humans hiding out near Hesiod in the Rubble after the destruction of Madrigal and, for some reason, chose not to wipe them out.

They were as greedy for spoils as their human nickname suggested. Ruthless piracy raids from rogue Kig-Yar weren't uncommon in the Rubble.

Melko Hollister leaned against the old container, his gray reservist's uniform specked with blood. "How many?"

"Three." Delgado looked at his old friend, worried. They'd flown their way around the Rubble's nooks and crannies together and helped each other stagger back from late night binges for years. They were close enough people often mistook them for brothers. "What happened to you? Looks like something ran you over."

"Think *I'm* in bad shape?" Melko coughed. "Should see the other guy."

Delgado kept his back to the container, gun aimed at the edge. "You killed one of them?"

"We turned the corner at the same time." Melko stepped back, chancing a glance around the other side of the container. He held his handgun in his right hand while his left clenched his stomach. "I fired first. I fired second. I fired the third time, too."

"Where'd the blood come from?"

"One of the other Jackals fired fourth."

Delgado shook his head. This had gotten out of control. He reached in his pocket and pulled out the instigator of all their troubles: a tiny chip, lying in the heart of a toughened case just smaller than his thumb.

The information inside never used to be all that special, back when the planet Madrigal was a thriving Outer Colony world. Back before the Covenant destroyed it, and the survivors fled to the drifting rocks of the Rubble. Back before the United Nations Space Command abandoned them all. And back before Delgado ended up here.

The location of Earth had been commonplace, buried in the heart of every ship making the long jumps back to the Inner Colonies and on to the homeworld.

"Here." Delgado handed the chip to Melko.

Now, as far as anyone here knew, this chip contained the only known navigation maps that could get someone back. All the others had been destroyed, rooted out by viruses, or the ships they were on mysteriously disabled and all info wiped clean. All this had happened in the last week or so.

It had radically changed things in the Rubble.

Melko slipped the black oval into a thigh pocket. "Jackals are getting pushy, trying to sneak in here for it."

They were. And Delgado didn't like it. Although the Kig-Yar here in the Rubble had been relatively peaceful, and even worked to help build the asteroid Habitats, deep down Delgado could never trust anything Covenant. Not after seeing the glowing remains of Madrigal from orbit as a child.

This just confirmed a deeper suspicion. The Covenant were never up to any good, and Delgado's people were probably at risk.

So, for Delgado, it was important the navigation data be kept from them at any cost.

Delgado gauged the distance to the airlock from their cluster of containers. "Make the run, Melko, I'll hold them off. When you get on board *Distancia*, blow the locks and make a hard run for it, in case there's a Jackal ship waiting. Start calling for help the moment you punch out." He held up the scrimshawed gun. "Me and *Señora Sies* here will hold them back."

"You can't . . ." Melko started.

"If I try running to the ship after you it'll slow everything down—they'll be able to come running in too. At the very least, this splits them, and confuses them. They'll be expecting us both to make a run for it."

He hoped.

Melko grabbed Delgado's arm. "Okay. But the moment you hear me cut free and the emergency overrides shut the doors, you bug out of here and keep clear of the Jackals."

The asteroids of the Rubble were all connected to each other by flexible docking tubes. Once *Distancia* was away, Delgado planned to use those to get out of this storage facility and into the larger asteroid complex.

There were bloody smudge marks on Delgado's forearm. "No problem there."

The sound of something crawling on top of one of the containers made Delgado look up.

"I guess it's time," Melko said. He handed over his plain handgun. "You'll need the extra firepower."

"Thanks. Hey, *mijo*," Delgado said. "See you on the other side. In three," and held out three fingers. Three . . . two . . .

On one Melko leapt forward and threaded his way through the maze of containers that stood between him and the airlock. Delgado quickly followed.

The Jackal on the top of the container ran forward, focused on Melko. It looked down, spotted Delgado aiming up at it, and raised its curved firearm to shoot.

Too late. Delgado pulled the trigger three times and the large, birdlike alien screeched as the shots hit home. Purple blood made a faint cloud in the air, and as the Jackal fell forward, an oval energy shield flickered on from a bracelet strapped to its right hand.

Delgado had made it across a corridor to a gap in the containers.

The other two Jackals would turn the corner any second. He dropped the empty magazine out of his handgun one-handed, keeping Melko's handgun aimed forward. He slid another magazine out of his pocket awkwardly with the fingers that still held *Señora Sies*, wiggling the tip in until it clipped, and then shoving it home against his chest.

He kept both up, aimed and ready, and as the Jackals turned the corner, he let off a withering burst of shots. The aliens slid to a stop and ducked back behind the container, but not before firing back.

Metal splashed around Delgado, searing his ribs.

But as he clutched at burned skin with a hand, he heard the thunderclap of explosive decompression from the other side of the containers. Air rustled, and then roared past as it was sucked out into the void past the open airlock Melko used when he'd cleared out.

The Jackals shot clear of the corner, triple-jointed legs jerking and their oval energy shields flaring as they ran at Delgado.

He emptied his magazines uselessly against their violet translucent shields and stood ready with gritted teeth as they lowered them to bring energy pistols to bear on him.

A gray blur dropped down from a set of containers stacked four high behind the Jackals. Massive boots struck the fused rock floor, leaving large dents in place and tossing up shattered rock.

Delgado stared as the massive gray statue with the gold-faced helmet shot the nearest Jackal in the torso with a full round of submachine-gun fire, point blank. Then it yanked the butt of the gun up hard into the other Jackal's long, jagged-toothed jaw as it turned to face the sudden threat.

The Jackal flew back, purple blood slinging up in a long arc above it in the air.

The limp body of the alien landed at Delgado's feet with a crunch, then slid past him, slamming into the container at his back as the Jackal's blood rained to the ground.

A long trail of slick purple wetness pointed back toward the tall, armored soldier that stood where the Jackal had been. The armor-plating, chipped, scarred, and dull with wear, shifted as it removed its helmet.

It was a woman.

She ran a gray-gauntleted hand over her tightly tied-back hair, surveying her handiwork. "Now that I've done you a favor," she said in a Slavic-accented voice, "I don't suppose you could return it and tell me where your friend is headed in that little spaceship of yours?"

Delgado felt something sticky and wet spreading down his side, and patted at it. His fingers came up red with his own blood. He shook his head and staggered, then slumped to the ground. *Señora Sies* and Melko's gun skittered away from him as he let go of them.

"Damn." The woman thudded her way over and crouched by him. She unfolded a small med kit and pulled out a can of biofoam and some field dressings. She had very blue eyes for such an efficient killer, Delgado thought.

"What the hell are you?" he asked, as she ripped his shirt open to spray the foam. It stung as it sealed the wound.

"A Spartan." She wrapped tape around his torso to hold the bandage on.

"I've heard rumors about Spartans out here. But figured if you really existed you'd be all off in the Inner Colonies now, fighting the Covenant for the UNSC. What are you doing out here, behind enemy lines?"

Satisfied with her emergency medical work, the Spartan leaned back. "Some of us get more bizarre assignments."

There were always rumors that Spartan soldiers were around, sneaking about and causing trouble. But then, people also blamed gremlins in the equipment for causing random, unexplained trouble. One didn't believe it. Spartans were like boogeymen to the Insurrectionists.

"You're after the navigation data too, huh?" Delgado realized, wondering if the navigation data was the whole reason they were here, or if they somehow had gotten abandoned in the Rubble.

The massive Spartan smiled. "If the Jackals get their claws on that chip everyone will suffer." She leaned forward and placed a small pin into his open hand. The gauntlet was surprisingly careful and precise as she folded his hand into a fist, the device inside it. "If you ever want to hand it over, just trigger this beacon, we'll come calling. We'll certainly protect it better than you're doing right now."

Delgado shook his head. He didn't trust the Kig-Yar. But the UNSC was far from loved out here, too.

She sighed. "A shame." She scooted back and picked up *Señora Sies* and tilted it in her hands to examine it.

Delgado held his hand up, and she gave it back to him. "Nice piece."

"My uncle spent three weeks on it," Delgado gasped. His side still hurt.

"He's talented."

"He was."

The Spartan cocked her head, listening to her earpiece. "Your backup has arrived."

"Wait." Delgado tried to stand, but gave that up the moment he shifted and felt the pain rush up through him. "Who are you?"

The Spartan stood, looming over him. "My name is Adriana. Spartan One-One-One."

"Ignatio Delgado." Delgado held up his hand again. "Thank you."

Adriana shook his offered hand, carefully. "You're welcome, Mr. Delgado. Just remember this. I was not here, and I certainly did not help you. There are no Spartans going bump in the night. Understand?"

Ignatio didn't, really. He was feeling quite dizzy. But he nodded anyway. It seemed prudent, sitting on the floor in front of this titan in her suit of armor.

Very prudent.

"Well then, Mr. Delgado." Adriana let go of his hand and pulled her helmet back on. The voice that came out from the helmet sounded powerful and amplified. "Good-bye."

She leapt up onto the nearest container, then thudded off, leaving Delgado to wait for his rescuers.

PART I

CHAPTER 1

O ut of the cryogenic darkness came a deep, crisp-sounding, but slightly amused voice. "Wakey, wakey, Professor."

Jacob Keyes sat up and took his first deep breath. The gel mat underneath him flexed as he coughed out medical-tasting fluid from his lungs, gasping for a second breath of air in between the dry retching.

"Lieutenant," Keyes coughed, his lungs protesting at his insistence of talking before they'd had a chance to clear themselves out fully. "Lieutenant Jacob Keyes." In the classroom he was Instructor Keyes, but back here on the deck he wanted the proper rank accorded. He'd worked hard to get there in the years before he'd been assigned to teaching due to injuries.

He sat inside a long pod, one of many laid out in a row. The rest of the crew of the *Armageddon's Edge* were just starting to crawl out of their own pods.

The crew members helped each other out, cracking jokes as some violently coughed up the fluid that they had breathed in to prevent their bodies from being damaged by the cold of the frozen sleep. The on-duty officer squatted next to Keyes. A thin Navy lifer, Edgar Sykes was a pale man in his mid-fifties, with short-cropped gray hair and dark brown eyes that squinted with amusement at the chance to give Keyes some grief.

"How was your date with the Admiral's wife, *Lieutenant*? Been a while since you were put on ice?"

Some of the other crew, already standing and pulling on clothes, glanced over with grins. Keyes had been in the classroom too long; he didn't get the joke.

"I'm sorry?" Keyes asked. "The Admiral's wife?"

Sykes pointed at the pod. "A frosty bed?"

Oh, Keyes thought. That's what the crew called the pods now. They'd just been called "freezers" the last time he'd shipped out. "Not something you forget easily," Keyes rasped, rubbing his arms for warmth. The chill of the cryogenic pod permeated every last cell. Even worse than the chill, however, were the old injuries from his time on the *Meriwether Lewis* that flared up. The deep gouging plasma burn to his thigh, the shattered-then-rebuilt hand that he clenched and then opened again. They had sidelined him, and kept him in front of wide-eyed non-commissioned officers, playing the role of a classroom drill sergeant.

He carefully shifted himself to the side of the pod. The injuries had healed enough over time. Enough that on most days, now, they were only a faded memory, a twinge when he tried a little too hard in the gym. But the freezer seemed to bring it out more.

Sykes reached out a hand to help him as he noticed Keyes's careful movement. Keyes looked at the man. "You asking me out on a date?"

That got a few chuckles from the crew. Sykes nodded. "Alright, Keyes. Welcome aboard *Armageddon's Edge*." He turned to the crew. "What the hell do you think *you're all* looking at?"

Eyes darted back as the crew resumed their tasks, and the chatter faded.

A smartly pressed gray uniform lay on the side of Keyes's pod. He pulled it on, checking to make sure the double silver bars signifying Lieutenant were clipped on.

It felt good to be back in uniform, especially on deck.

As time passed from his service aboard the *Meriwether Lewis* he felt that the chances of being involved on the bridge of a ship again were slipping further away from him. It stung.

Still, at forty, Keyes made sure to get up early for his ten-mile run, and he hit the weight room at least three times a week. He was terrified of getting soft.

He'd learned, back when the *Meriwether Lewis* had been boarded, that it gave him an edge. Even if the edge today remained his ability to outrun his students in physical training, it was still useful in that it earned their respect.

Service was service. If the Navy needed Lieutenant Jacob Keyes to serve out the next couple of decades teaching navigators how to fly their ships, then that was what they needed him for.

Everyone had their place, their role to play.

With the alien forces destroying planet after planet, with people giving their lives just to slow them down, Keyes felt there was no room for self-pity.

He reserved those darker moments for thinking about things like his sister, out there on the Outer Colony of Dwarka.

Wondering about her fate ever since the colony had gone silent, too far away for the UNSC to even try to defend.

When he'd gotten the orders to leave Luna, he'd only taken the time to visit his daughter, Miranda. The last time he'd had orders to ship out somewhere he hadn't had family of his own. He was just an eager, young man. Now it felt like he had to tear himself away. He'd grown accustomed to picking her up every day and bringing her back to the small on-base apartment they shared.

He'd kissed Miranda good-bye and let her know she'd have to stay at the dorms in her school, just like all the other children with family on duty.

She was a good Navy kid—she actually perked up at the news and asked what ship he was flying out on.

Someone cleared their throat behind Keyes. He turned to find a man standing there in full pilot's kit, helmet slung under one arm. The pilot saluted. "Good morning, sir. I'm Petty Officer Jeffries. I'm taking you dirtside."

Keyes leaned forward and tugged at the pilot's bedraggled uniform. "I hope you don't fly as sloppy as you dress." Some ships, like the *Armageddon's Edge*, ran a little off kilter. Captain's prerogative. What mattered to many at command was their battle performance, and Keyes had heard the *Edge* had limped back to Earth with pride for a full refit after it had paired with another ship to take out a Covenant Destroyer.

Still, Keyes felt it didn't hurt to make a point.

"Sir?"

"If you can't bother to fasten your buttons, keep your insignia on straight, and follow procedure, why should I feel safe getting in your bird?"

"Sir, because my uniform doesn't have to drop soldiers off in hot zones. Sir."

Keyes relented a little. "Okay, Jeffries. Let's see what you've got waiting for me."

Petty Officer Jeffries approached a green, battle-scarred Pelican dropship squatting next to two others in the *Armageddon's Edge*'s tight storage bay. The sides had been splashed and gouged by energy beams. Keyes followed the pilot as he walked under the high rear wings and engine nacelles up the ramp into the belly.

Jeffries walked past the webbing, storage bins, and the seats lining the walls to climb up into the cockpit. "You can strap in behind me, sir," Jeffries said. "You don't have to ride back there. I don't want to get lonely on this trip. There's room under your feet for your kit bag."

The ramp groaned as it slowly closed, the hold of the dropship darkening.

Once it clanged shut and sealed, Jeffries tossed his helmet aside. "Don't have to stay airtight on this milk run. Not exactly leaping into combat today, are we?"

No, thought Keyes, flashing back to the times he'd been in combat. They certainly weren't. Combat was men strapped shoulder to shoulder in the back, while you weaved and ducked a Pelican through anti-aircraft bursts. Your palms would be sweating and your breath heavy in the confined space of your own helmet. Combat was when the cockpit you were sitting in smelled of blood, and fear.

Keyes clicked back to the present as Jeffries flicked and tapped the console in front of him, bringing the Pelican to life. In the copilot's seat Keyes kept an eye on things. Jeffries ran the systems check with a bewildering rapidity that could only come with practice and familiarity. There was a photo of a brunette with two boys taped to the side of the cockpit window. Keyes pointed at it. "Your kids?"

"Yes sir. You have any?"

"A daughter," Keyes said.

The four engines wound themselves up, a kick that shuddered through the entire frame of the Pelican.

"Gamma 54 to *Armageddon's Edge*, preflight check is green, systems nominal, flight plan filed. Permission to fly?" Jeffries sounded bored.

"Gamma 54, hold tight for the trapdoor," came the breezy response from the bridge.

The ship's bay doors opened to reveal the planet beneath. Thin, long clouds covered the unfamiliar green-and-brown-colored continental shapes. Keyes hadn't had time to read up much about his destination. He'd gotten his orders at lunch, and been bundled off and frozen in an *Armageddon's Edge* cryogenic pod by dinner.

"What brings you out all the way from Luna to see the wonderful skies of Chi Rho, sir?" There wasn't a lot of room for a Pelican to move in the *Armageddon's Edge*'s bay, but Jeffries gunned the four thrusters and the Pelican hopped up and forward, and then, just as abruptly, spun and dove through the bay doors.

Jeffries was looking back over his shoulder at him, showing off that he could get out of the ship's bay without even paying attention. Keyes didn't give the pilot the satisfaction of a flinch. But Keyes was impressed. The dangerous stunt showed Jeffries could fly blind. And damn well, too. "Orders, Petty Officer. Orders."

"We go where they tell us, right?"

"You know it." Keyes glanced up through the shielded glass, catching a glimpse of the medium-sized ship that had taken him all the way from the home system. Craters pocked the ship's surface, and burn streaks crisscrossed the arrowhead-shaped nose of the ship. Despite a refit, the scars remained from the ship's last encounter.

Armageddon's Edge dwindled away as Jeffries thundered them down in a long arc toward the atmosphere. The Pelican shook and shuddered as heat built up from atmospheric reentry. Streaks of glowing red filled the air.

"Do you know if there are any training stations for patrol craft here, Jeffries?" Keyes asked suddenly.

Jeffries checked a monitor, then glanced back. "Training stations? Here? Sir, Chi Rho is for repairs and drydocking. Support for the front line. There's no training out here. All you have to do is head out a few days and run into a Covenant long-range patrol—you'll get all the training you need."

"I thought so." Keyes looked out through the red haze. Chi Rho was an Inner Colony world. Not as developed or as large as the mother planet, but still home to hundreds of millions of people on its primary continent and Earthlike surface.

But Chi Rho was the closest Keyes had been in some time to that somewhat gray, invisible line where planets turned from the Inner Colonies to the Outer Colonies.

With worlds scattered so far from each other, and travel being a long and sometimes dangerous affair, news traveled slowly, and most of it came through UNSC channels of late. Every citizen knew that the Covenant were slowly destroying human planets from orbit, world by world. Only the UNSC stood in their way, fighting for every bloody inch.

And even the UNSC's official bulletins indicated that most of the Outer Colonies had been destroyed—glassed with incredibly powerful energy weapons, the likes of which the UNSC had never seen.

Every day for the past nine years, since the first encounters with the aliens, the front line had moved closer to Chi Rho and the outer edge of the Inner Colonies.

Keyes knew this was not where you trained green pilots.

But his orders, strange as they were, said that he was to get out to Chi Rho at full speed for a training exercise.

Even a follow-all-commands Navy lifer like Keyes knew the orders were a load of crap. A cover for something else.

And that something else might involve getting back aboard a ship, Keyes found himself daring to hope. Maybe even the recently patched up *Armageddon's Edge*.

CHAPTER 2

Jeffries dropped out of his flight plan pattern and came in low over a large park, the tops of the trees whipping about in the fury of engine backwash. Birds scattered in their wake, rising to the sky in flocks of green and blue.

He angled the Pelican back, flaring the craft out for a spectacular, bone-jarring landing that had Keyes grabbing the arms of his chair. Again, Jeffries was showing off.

The engines whined down as he cut them, and dirt slowly settled back to the ground. Keyes considered giving Jeffries a hard time for the unusual approach, then decided against it.

He wasn't this man's bridge crew. Just let it go, he told himself.

"I'll be here waiting for you when you get back, sir," Jeffries said. "Taking you to your next location."

Keyes unsnapped himself from the copilot's seat. "Where are we going next?"

"Don't know, sir," Jeffries said, twisting back. "My orders are to wait for you to come back, and presumably you'll know where we're going next."

Keyes walked up to the front of the cockpit and looked out the window. "What is all that?"

Out around the dirt patch they'd landed in, rows and rows of small wooden stakes had been sunk into the ground. Beyond them, what looked like young stalks of corn poked up through the tilled soil.

But right near the woods, which Keyes could tell had been recently cut down, a large sign proclaimed the area as the *Bacigalupi Memorial Nature Preserve.*

"Victory Gardens," Jeffries said. "Victory Farms is more like it, I guess. Anywhere you can grow crops and food, no matter the surface, we're using it. The Outer Colonies used to grow most of the food, so we're experiencing shortages here. I'll drop the ramp for you."

Keyes walked to the back of the Pelican as daylight filled the inside. The ramp lowered to reveal a Warthog waiting for him, along with a completely dust-covered and annoyed-looking private in olive camo, a battle rifle slung under one arm. The private looked tiny compared to the bulky, armored, oversized all-terrain vehicle. Keyes had always liked the Warthog's metal tusks on either side of the tow winch, which were ostensibly metal guards.

The private saluted. "Lieutenant Keyes?"

Keyes nodded. "That's me."

"Private Tom Gerencer. I'm your ride the rest of the way, sir." The marine hopped into the driver's seat of the massive vehicle. Keyes followed. "Sorry about the drop-off point, but our main sites are overrun by tent cities. Traffic's snarled, so it's more of a pain than it's worth. Better to drop you straight in."

"Tent cities?" Keyes stared at the marine sitting next to him. Had things really gotten this bad? He felt like his stomach had been kicked. Keyes and his neighbors often shuttled to Earth to visit relatives or to enjoy some fine dining and sightseeing. Meanwhile out here large numbers of people were living hand to mouth. Was the UNSC censoring so much that not even a whiff of all this had reached Earth? They must have been. This was dire stuff.

Gerencer nodded. He drove them down the dirt road, spinning the large, grippy balloon tires as he gunned the Warthog toward another dirt road through the preserve. "Outer Colony refugees, sir. They keep piling up at spaceports. Nowhere for them to go. We've shut down arenas, parking lots, even whole streets for them. Running out of tents, food, and a lot of people are running out of patience. It's ugly out there, sir. I've pulled a shift or two patrolling."

"Patrolling?" Keyes asked. "What's the UNSC doing police work for?"

"The refugees are a drain, sir. We're planning an extended battle here, a few surprises for the Covenant if . . . or when they arrive. With the refugees on the surface, they're just costing us food and sitting out here like targets. Every ration they get is a ration we won't have when holding the line. How long brass will put up with all this chaos out here, I don't know."

They roared on past several massive JOTUN robotic combines, and then into a gap in the wooded area around the recently created farmland.

"Almost there," Gerencer said as they bounced over ruts and gaps in the dirt.

With a final roar the Warthog leapt out into a small ring of trees. The marine idled them over a well-worn patch of mud.

The ground rumbled underneath, and the edges rose around them as they slowly moved down a long shaft.

"Welcome to Camp Patmos, Lieutenant." Gerencer grinned. "From here we plan how to open up a can of whup-ass on the Covenant every hour of every day."

Rows of Warthogs lined a metal cavern wall. Lurking behind them in the shadows were the marines' tank units, looking like squashed but hulkingly armored four-legged spiders dominated by two pairs of fore and aft treads and a long cab at its core. The barrels of their long cannons pointed menacingly at Keyes. Any Covenant landing on Chi Rho were in for a fierce fight. There were enough Scorpion M808B Battle Tanks for a full division.

"Lieutenant Keyes!" a strong voice shouted. "How good to see you."

Keyes let his eyes adjust as he peered deeper into the gloom of the oversized hangar. A doorway between a pair of Mongoose quad bikes spilled light, and someone stood in the doorframe.

Keyes hopped out of the Warthog, right leg tingling slightly. He briskly walked over, and swallowed. Even on a silhouette, it was hard to miss three stars on a uniform. Keyes knew who this would be. Only one vice admiral on Chi Rho. A man who'd volunteered to come out to the front, and agreed to take on any colony defense, no matter how long the odds.

"Vice Admiral Jean Mawikizi. Sir! It's an honor." Keyes snapped a smart salute. Mawikizi had fought intense lost battles on three planets, getting lifted off each one under protest as they were being glassed.

The stringy, yet short, dark-skinned Mawikizi returned the salute with a smile. "I pulled some serious strings to haul you out here this quick, Keyes." He held the door open for Keyes, and it banged shut behind them once the lieutenant stepped through. "Walk with me."

The rough rock-tunneled corridor stretched out in front of

them. Mawikizi led Keyes down past offices, shouldering past privates and officers who stood to attention as he walked by.

Keyes glanced off down a subcorridor, seeing barracks in the distance. All well below ground, and recently constructed. Mawikizi spotted his glance. "They yanked me out of retirement in Burundi to run a battle fleet that's been getting pushed back almost every day. I'm drawing the line for that group here on Chi Rho. A last stand. We're burrowing down as deep as we can. They're going to have to come on down and flush us out man by man."

"Sir, what about the refugees? And the gardens? I never imagined it was this bad."

Mawikizi opened the door to his offices. "It's that bad. We've ordered local colonists to share the burden, but they believe the refugees had their chance to fight and survive. They're happy to give them land, but the locals here come from survivors of what used to be a rough planet. No handouts, just self-sufficient families spread out across the continents. They're not thrilled about being ordered to share . . . it's not their culture. Been some dust-ups, so we can't trust locals or refugees to police. We're trying to figure out where to move them to before the Covenant attacks. And before they get too comfortable here."

The vice admiral's offices had windows and a balcony that looked out over a massive shaft leading deeper into the ground. No doubt at the bottom Pelicans and other support craft lay stored, waiting to spiral up and out into battle when needed. "But when will the attack come? That's the question. The Covenant started glassing planets nine years ago. They could hit us next month, or another couple years down the road. In some ways, Lieutenant Keyes, we're all dead men walking and we know it."

The outer offices were filled with the hum of smooth-working administration—privates murmuring into headsets, officers poring over holographic battle readouts; this was the center for a lot of frontier decisions.

Keyes threaded past desks to the inner office, and the hum of activity disappeared with the thick blast-proof door creaking to a thud as Mawikizi shut it.

"Keyes, this is Commander Dmitri Zheng."

Zheng, waiting by the conference table in the corner of the vice admiral's office, stood up and shook Keyes's hand. He was taller than Keyes, with sharp cheekbones, piercing gray eyes, and a shaved head. He looked about the same age as Keyes.

"Zheng's a frigate man, just coming forward to the front." The vice admiral sounded tired, Keyes thought. Five years of being back at the top must have worn him out. The man looked gaunt as he sat down at the small conference table. "Okay, gentlemen, let's get down to business."

Mawikizi opened a letter-sized envelope and slid the contents across the table to Keyes. "Every shipboard Navy CO has to read this. It just went out recently. The order is spreading around to all vessels and all UNSC as we speak."

Keyes pulled a plastic sheet out and read it.

UNITED NATIONS SPACE COMMAND EMERGENCY PRIORITY ORDER
   098831A-1

ENCRYPTION CODE: RED

PUBLIC KEY: FILE /FIRST LIGHT/

FROM: UNSC/NAVCOM FLEET H. T. WARD

TO: ALL UNSC PERSONNEL

SUBJECT: GENERAL ORDER 098831A-1 ("THE COLE
   PROTOCOL")

CLASSIFICATION: RESTRICTED (BGX DIRECTIVE)

THE COLE PROTOCOL

To SAFEGUARD THE INNER COLONIES AND EARTH, ALL UNSC VESSELS OR STATIONS MUST NOT BE CAPTURED WITH IN-TACT NAVIGATION DATABASES THAT MAY LEAD COVENANT FORCES TO HUMAN CIVILIAN POPULATION CENTERS.

IF ANY COVENANT FORCES ARE DETECTED:

1. ACTIVATE SELECTIVE PURGE OF DATABASES ON ALL SHIP-BASED AND PLANETARY DATA NETWORKS.

2. INITIATE TRIPLE-SCREEN CHECK TO INSURE ALL DATA HAS BEEN ERASED AND ALL BACKUPS NEUTRALIZED.

3. EXECUTE VIRAL DATA SCAVENGERS (DOWNLOAD FROM UNSCTTP://EPWW:COLEPROTOCOL/VIRTUALSCAV/FBR.091)

4. IF RETREATING FROM COVENANT FORCES, ALL SHIPS MUST ENTER SLIPSTREAM SPACE WITH RANDOMIZED VECTORS NOT DIRECTED TOWARD EARTH, THE INNER COLONIES, OR ANY OTHER HUMAN POPULATION CENTER.

5. IN CASE OF IMMINENT CAPTURE BY COVENANT FORCES, ALL UNSC SHIPS MUST SELF-DESTRUCT.

VIOLATION OF THIS DIRECTIVE WILL BE CONSIDERED AN ACT OF TREASON, AND PURSUANT TO UNSC MILITARY LAW ARTICLES JAG 845-P AND JAG 7556-L, SUCH VIOLA-TIONS ARE PUNISHABLE BY LIFE IMPRISONMENT OR EXECUTION.

Keyes looked back up at Mawikizi. "Admiral Cole thinks we're taking some serious hits." He thought for a second and realized that since Cole's major victory at the Battle of Harvest four years ago, there'd been no big victories.

"The order is spreading throughout the UNSC. Keeping Inner

Colony and Earth locations secret has become a top priority, particularly here near the front. And that, Lieutenant Keyes, is where you come in.

"I sat in on the board when they sidelined you. I voted for you to stay on your ship. I am most sorry about the medical disqualification from active duty."

"So am I, sir." Keyes massaged his leg.

"It is a waste to me, just a waste, to leave you in a classroom back on Luna. You are a good tactician, Keyes. I have read your papers and looked at your training. More important, you charged boarders on the *Meriwether Lewis* with nothing more than a pistol and a barbaric yawp. I like that, Keyes. You stand strong when you need to."

"Thank you, sir." Keyes was still waiting to hear what came next. A rush of adrenaline was building. He might be getting back on a ship!

At the least, maybe a staff position advising fleet movements and strategy on Vice Admiral Mawikizi's team. He'd have to move Miranda out from Luna to a closer Inner Colony. Not here, too close to the front, but close enough he could easily visit her on leave.

"So, we have an offer for you, Keyes." Mawikizi glanced over at Commander Zheng, who'd been watching the exchange in silence.

Zheng tapped a button hidden in the table and a scale model of a frigate flickered into existence in front of the three men. Like any other frigate it looked like a bulky rifle with its magazine removed. Only one with two barrels, one on top of each other in front.

Unlike the dull gun-metal gray of most, this frigate was midnight black. Toward the bow, the numerals FFG-209 had been overlayed by the computer. Farther back, near the center, was the frigate's name: *Midsummer Night*.

"She's a light frigate." Zheng stated the obvious. "With a few tricks up her sleeves." A faint smile cracked his stony exterior as he said that.

"*Night* is a long-range stealth ship," Mawikizi said. "Like a Prowler, but she packs more of a punch."

"But it's frigate-slow," Zheng finished. "She also has the ability to deliver a large complement of marines and orbital-drop shock troopers, giving her a wider variety of mission abilities."

"Which will come in handy," said a fourth voice from behind them. Keyes twisted in his chair, surprised that they'd been snuck up on so easily.

"Major Akio Watanabe, of the Prowler Corps. ONI," Zheng introduced the addition.

Keyes hadn't heard the door open. But then, that was a spook for you. The Office of Naval Intelligence didn't believe in announcing themselves to the world; they really liked sneaking up on people.

A point of professional pride, no doubt.

Keyes still found it creepy and annoying.

Watanabe slid into a vacant chair. He wore long sleeves and a high-collared form of gray uniform. His dark black eyes seemed to look through people into the distance. "I arrived . . . just in time, I see." He looked around. "I take it, Vice Admiral, our agreement is still in effect?"

Mawikizi looked truly disgruntled. He sighed. "I stand by my word, Major Watanabe."

Zheng tapped a button, and the scale hologram of the *Midsummer Night* faded away. "The ship begins her shakedown cruise today, Lieutenant Keyes. We'll be helping enforce the Cole Protocol for the first three days, getting a feel for the ship."

Zheng turned to Watanabe. The major nodded. "After that,

there will be sealed orders for the bridge crew that will be available to me after the quick shakedown cruise."

Keyes frowned and turned to the admiral. "Sir, we'll be working for ONI?"

Mawikizi pursed his lips. "Only initially. A professional exchange for helping us stealth the frigate."

"It'll be a brief mission," Watanabe promised. He glanced at Zheng, who'd folded his arms. "Then I'll be out of your hair and you and the vice admiral can play with your new little toy."

Keyes looked over at Mawikizi. The old Burundian looked like he'd found bird crap on his freshly polished staff car. Then he looked at Keyes and grinned. "Zheng and I'd like you to be on the bridge. We're planning for very long recon and long-range Covenant harassment, taking down targets of opportunity, and just causing general hell. We want you because of your excellence in long-range navigation and your tactical skills, as we'll be using the *Night* in ways frigates aren't usually used. We need someone who can really work with Zheng to think outside the box."

"How long-range?"

"Very," Mawikizi repeated. "I know you have family, but we don't have a lot of time for you to make a decision."

Keyes leaned forward. "I won't lie to you, sir," he muttered. "It's a hard thing to ask me to leave my daughter." Raising Miranda had been the brightest point of being stuck in the Academy.

Now that he was faced with a potential position on a ship, Keyes wondered if he'd just been focusing on what he couldn't have, and not on what he really had.

"I know," Mawikizi said. "I know."

"On the other hand, defending our worlds from the Covenant is the best form of fathering I can think of," Keyes finished. "I'd be honored to serve aboard the *Midsummer Night*. Thank you for giving me the option." Technically they didn't have to ask. It had been a courtesy because he was medaled and taken off the line.

They'd made a good choice. There was a lot more bite left in this dog, Keyes thought.

"I have one favor to ask, if I may," Keyes continued. "The Pelican pilot who flew me here. I'd like him transferred to the *Midsummer Night*."

Commander Zheng looked at Vice Admiral Mawikizi, who shrugged. "I don't see why not. You know the pilot?"

"Never met him before. But he's a hell of a flyer and if we're going to be doing unorthodox missions, he might come in handy. His name is Jeffries."

"Consider it done." Mawikizi stood up, as did Keyes and Zheng, then finally Watanabe. The vice admiral shook Keyes's hand. "Glad to have you aboard, Lieutenant."

"Thrilled to be aboard, sir."

And he was, Keyes realized. Thrilled to be back on the line.

Jeffries waited for him, his legs propped up on the controls of the Pelican. When he heard Keyes board the dropship he sat up. "Know where we're going, sir?"

Keyes smiled as he stepped up behind the pilot's chair, looking at the Warthog that had dropped him off barreling away down the fields. "Yes, Mr. Jeffries, I do. Hail *Midsummer Night*. They'll give you coordinates."

"Yes, sir."

"Also, do you know anything about Commander Dmitri Zheng?"

"Zheng?" Jeffries thought for a second. "He's been all over

the rumornet lately. He was from one of the Outer Colonies. Captained a frigate for a short while."

"A short while?" Keyes didn't like the sound of that.

"He rammed a Covenant destroyer."

"Sometimes that's the only option you have . . ."

"That was *after* he'd been ordered to retreat. The only reason he wasn't court-martialed was because he disabled it long enough for another ship to finish it off with a MAC. They fished him out of the debris."

Keyes mulled that over. He was going to be serving with this man. Maybe he shouldn't have jumped to saying "yes" so quickly.

"You know why he did it, sir?" Jeffries continued. "Rumor has it he's mad with grief. Covenant burned his homeworld, while he was out on a patrol, seven years ago. Never been the same since."

"Okay, that's enough," Keyes said. The conversation was sliding into innuendo; he didn't need to be poisoned against his future commanding officer. There'd be plenty of time to get to know Zheng once aboard. And maybe this was why Keyes had been called back in, to add a bit of strategy and calm into Zheng's style. "Oh, and one more thing, Mr. Jeffries?"

"Sir?"

"When you fly me, a commanding officer, out of a military installation, you *will* follow the flight plan you were given. Failure to do so, including dropping out of radar range near tree level, means they have every right to swat you out of the sky like a bug. We are, after all, on a world near the front. You yourself indicated that to me." The steel in his voice surprised even him. "In the event that we were to be shot down for violating the flight plan, I would personally hunt you down from beyond the grave, soldier, and make your life a miserable thing to behold. Do you get me, soldier?"

Jeffries kept his gaze dead ahead through the windshield. "Yes sir."

"Lastly, you *will* don your full flight gear. Were this Pelican to be holed, while *I* might be gasping for air, I fully expect you to be able to fulfill your mission—even if your mission is as meaningless as being my personal, full-time chauffeur. We clear, Jeffries?"

"Crystal, sir."

Keyes clipped himself into the copilot's chair and listened to the Pelican's engines warm up. He was bridge crew on a stealth ship, with a mystery mission from the ONI in three days.

It was good to be back.

"All right, Mr. Jeffries, take this bird up."

Keyes leaned back in his chair, enjoying the sensation of thrust. Three days to shake out the frigate and chase civilians to enforce the Cole Protocol seemed straightforward enough. A nice way to ease back into ship life.

CHAPTER 3

Ignatio Delgado walked slowly toward his copilot's funeral dressed in a full suit, a tie uncomfortably snug around his neck. The painful plasma burns on his torso still hurt but he felt compelled to attend.

The parks existed on the inside of a hollowed-out asteroid; look up and you were looking down on the treetops of the other side of the park.

Maria Esquival intercepted him near a grove of tiny trees.

"Hey, Nacho." She grabbed his hand. Only Maria called him by that nickname, because only Maria knew him from back when he was a grubby little kid running around the surface of Madrigal. Back then she'd been a scrappy tomboy from just down the street with her hair pulled back in a functional ponytail. "You really shouldn't be here."

"He was my best friend."

Maria squeezed his hand. "I know. But they still don't want you here. You have to respect his family's wishes."

In the distance, the Hollister family had their backs to him. All dressed in black, surrounding a small urn, they were adding his ashes to the ground near one of the trees that gave the habitat its name.

They blamed Delgado for Melko's death. The copilot had succumbed to his wounds before anyone had gotten to *Distancia*. An unnecessary death, his family thought. They could care less about protecting the data that led back to Earth. They'd fought for self-rule from among the depths of this system for generations. Let the aliens have Earth, let it burn. They didn't care.

"Come on," Maria said, guiding him away.

"Do *you* think he died in vain?" Delgado asked.

Maria kept moving him along. "It's not for me to say, Nacho. But I've known both of you long enough to know that you both stood by each other to do what you each thought was right. So pay them no attention. They're grieving."

Maria had been with Delgado when their parents had rushed them to the large fields outside Nueva Lima, bundling them aboard a fat cargo ship as their crying parents told them they'd be on the next ship following them.

They'd been crammed into the hold with all the other scared children, trying to figure out what was happening. Delgado had been fourteen. Maria had been planning her *quinceañera*.

They'd held each other when the air outside turned white-hot, and the cargo ship shook and rattled. And when it had reached orbit, the shocked pilot's voice filled the hold, telling them that the entire surface of Madrigal had been "glassed."

All because of the war between the UNSC and the Covenant.

They strolled along, heading toward a man, who appeared to

be waiting for them by one of the habitat's famous large oak trees. His dark eyes taking in the funeral in the distance. He wore casual overalls, and a cap.

Maria stopped. "My brother needs to talk to you, though he refuses to tell me about what."

"Don't take it so personally, Maria. It's council business."

Nine Security Council members were voted into position by the citizens of the Rubble. They handled the entire structure's defenses, along with the AI Juliana.

Diego and the Council had chosen Delgado and Melko on short notice to protect the navigation when the Nav data started disappearing. With their years of piloting cargo throughout the Rubble, they knew it all inside and out. The council felt secrecy was their best option. With their volunteer defense forces and open nature, trying to put the chip under iron-tight guard would raise attention and create a big target.

But after this latest mishap, Delgado was convinced someone on the Council was leaking the location.

"You slumming it, Diego?" This was not the usual, tightly tailored man that Delgado expected.

Diego grimaced. "Keeping a low profile, Ignatio." He kissed his sister on the cheek, and she left the copse of trees to walk alone across the manicured grass toward the funeral.

"What do you need?" Delgado finally asked, watching Maria.

"You seem convinced that someone on the Security Council is leaking information about the location of the navigation data. You've been sniffing around, kicking up attention, trying to figure it out." Diego started walking out from the park toward the large airlocks at the end of Oaks Central Habitat. "When we decided to use you to move the data, and keep it safe, we were figuring on your keeping a low profile. That was the whole damn point, Ignatio."

"*Someone* is leaking it," Delgado said. "Those Jackals knew exactly where it was. This was the second time they made a play to get at it, and they were damn close. If I hadn't decided to move the data earlier than the date I gave the Security Council, those Jackals would have had it. You know, whoever leaked that murdered Melko. And I want them to pay."

They passed by the giant rolling axle of the join between the docking tubes and the asteroid's slow-spinning hub.

"I understand what you're doing, Ignatio. But the only people who knew where the navigation data was are the Security Council members. To suggest that one of us leaked it is serious."

"I know that," Delgado said as they walked into a massive, clear tube. From here they could see other asteroids connected to Oak Park. The connected structures faded off into the distance like a giant's tinker toy set.

Artificial gravity faded away, and the two men grabbed the railings running along the tube as they hung in the air. In the center of the docking tube, pods zipped along with goods and passengers moving from rocky habitat to habitat. "A lot of people wouldn't mind handing over the chart data to the Kig-Yar. They're offering us power, money, and Covenant technology for it."

"And what about you, Diego?" Delgado asked. "You in favor of that?"

Diego slowed down and came to a stop in the busy tube. He looked off at the looming orb of the gas giant Hesiod in the distance. "I think that if we hand over the chart data, our usefulness to the Kig-Yar is over. That's why I've worked so hard to keep the data concealed. That's why I asked you to help me do it. Most of the Council agrees."

"Most?" Delgado seized on the word. Diego was being surprisingly moderate for an old Insurrectionist.

Diego handed him a cigar, letting it hang in the air thanks to the lack of artificial gravity. Delgado looked down. "A Sweet William? I didn't realize there were any left."

"A Council member gave me one of these. Hinted around that he could get me more, said he had a smuggling operation out of Charybdis IX with one of his ships. He says that the UNSC Navy has been getting ready to crack down on slipspace jumps by citizens. They want everything to be militarized." Diego practically spat the last word. "This Council member has been shipping weapons of some sort he purchased from the Covenant for brother Insurrectionists back in the colonies, but he's worried that whatever is destroying the navigation data throughout the Rubble may get to him. He wants to give it to the Kig-Yar before something happens. He claims he's making his last smuggling trip now. Afterwards, he wants to give the Kig-Yar his ship, and the navigation data aboard it. I'm getting this secondhand, but it looks like he's trying to bribe a majority Council vote for selling the navigation data."

"You're going to let that happen?"

"I had Juliana hunt for a likely candidate among recent ship activity." Diego smiled referring to the Rubble's AI. "She came up with one. The ship's name was *Kestrel*. It is the only known ship that could still be in the colonies and able to make it back. It hasn't returned to dock, as far as we can tell. All our other smuggling ships have been destroyed, or had their data erased. We're truly cut off from the rest of humanity."

"Your Council member could have been lying; he could have just found some boxes of Sweet Williams."

"Maybe," Diego said. "But Juliana thinks the *Kestrel* is our ship."

"So what do you want me to do?" Delgado handed the cigar back by bumping it back through the air at Diego.

"Find out more about the *Kestrel*, Ignatio. See if they were really working for a Council member. Find out if they've snuck back into the Rubble. Because if you can connect them to our Council member, then I can move against him. There are better things to be trading for those weapons. Like . . . medicine instead of damned cigars." Diego crushed the cigar, and the pieces of tobacco flakes hung in the air between them. "And since I'm giving you this lead, please work hard to keep it quiet."

"I can do that." Delgado brushed the crushed cigar out of the air between them. "What's his name?"

Diego sighed. He looked very reluctant to be giving out a name of a fellow Security Council member. Maybe he was having second thoughts. He turned and looked out of the tube. The entire collection of tubes and asteroids housed the remains of Madrigal's proud colony: its people.

It was called the Rubble because that's what it had once been. Detritus, rubble, rocks, and slag left over from the creation of the solar system, trailing the gas giant Hesiod.

"You've done a lot for me, Diego, I appreciate everything," Delgado said. Diego had taken in both Maria and Delgado when they arrived those years ago, after Madrigal was destroyed. Diego had joined the Insurrectionists years before Madrigal was glassed, and he'd been the only person waiting for them after they'd fled the planet. Delgado owed Diego a lot. But before everything changed, Diego planted bombs in passenger ships, spaceports, and on stations. He'd smuggled and pirated, and everything that implied. Delgado always felt a sense of awkwardness, accepting what his hard-working parents, had they lived, would have called blood money. There was a tension in his friendship with Diego. But then, maybe that wasn't fair. Since the fall of Madrigal, Diego had thrown himself at the idea of the Rubble. Delgado changed the tone of his words. "So please give me the name. I won't kill the man. I'll bring him to justice. We're not the rabble we used to be, we've changed since the Fall of Madrigal."

Back then, the Rubble had just been a massive Insurrectionist military base, quartered and scattered throughout the asteroids trailing the gas giant in a trojan orbit.

But in short time, using spaceships, raw materials, and anything they could lay their hands on that hadn't been destroyed by the Covenant, they'd built the Rubble that they were now looking out on. It was something to be proud of.

"I know." Diego turned back to him. "Doesn't make it easier. The man you're looking to link the *Kestrel* to is Peter Bonifacio."

Delgado looked down the length of the tube. Bonifacio did a lot of smuggling back before the Covenant glassed Madrigal. Now he was reduced to occasional sneaks back to the Inner Colonies, though even those trips had become too dangerous as he lost ship after ship to both UNSC and Covenant forces. Delgado had moved stuff from asteroid to asteroid for the man, who always paid late. How he'd managed to get on the ballot to be voted onto the Security Council Delgado had never understood.

"Consider it done," Delgado said. Halfway around the clear tube a series of streamlined transit cars sped up, moving passengers inside from one habitat to another on a maglev track.

"Good. Thank you. And Delgado? You'll need to be careful."

Delgado nodded. The two men shook hands, and then floated to go off their separate ways. Diego with sadness in his eyes. Delgado with fire and vengeance.

CHAPTER 4

Keyes rode the copilot's seat as Jeffries expertly guided a Pelican full of orbital-drop shock troopers into the inky depths of space between the *Midsummer Night* and the tattered-looking civilian cargo hauler *Finnegan's Wake*.

Finnegan's Wake had been slowly edging its way toward the periphery of the Ectanus 45 outer system ever since it left Chi Rho, getting ready for a jump. Zheng had shadowed the freighter long enough to make sure it wasn't an in-system trip.

It wasn't. The ship, unaware it was being followed, had headed off well clear of this system's ecliptic plane.

A surprise shot across the bows from the *Midsummer Night* convinced them to not try accelerating and to allow *Midsummer Night* to match speed so they could sling the Pelican over.

Jeffries came in nice and easy, passing over the hull to the other side of the civilian ship and then slipping the Pelican into the cargo ship's hold.

"Check your equipment!" the ODST platoon commander Canfield shouted. "Look sharp."

In the Pelican's hold ODSTs stirred, unclipped their safety belts, and lined up. They'd been bugging Zheng about not getting a chance to board the previous three civilian ships the *Midsummer Night* had stopped, so the Commander had finally agreed to let them get some action in.

"They're still running a check on the ship's registry," Canfield called out from the back. "But we're ready to rock, sir."

"Sure you don't want to wait for their full report, First Lieutenant?" Keyes asked.

Keyes kicked himself for the rookie attitude he'd had just forty-eight hours ago, when he'd thought he had an easy three days ahead of him. True, this was a shakeout, prior to a real-live mission with possible action thanks to the ONI spook and his mysterious sealed orders.

But that hadn't stopped one exploding pipe and a radiation leak, and several crew from ending up in the infirmary. Two of the point guns on the starboard hull were out. A number of on/off magnets on the MAC, in essence a railgun, were failing, preventing them from getting the full power of the massive cannon.

The *Finnegan's Wake* didn't know it, but at the moment, thanks to a partially shut-down reactor that the engineers were working on, they could've easily outrun the *Midsummer Night*.

"Hell no, sir, I'm all for going in," Canfield said. He vibrated with energy. Keyes had a feeling Canfield wanted some action, and now. He'd have to keep an eye on him, make sure Canfield didn't get overly rough with some civilian.

"Okay, Canfield, let's get this show on the road, then." Keyes unclipped from his seat, and Canfield stepped forward, waiting for his cue. Keyes nodded at him. Time to give the civvies something to gape at. Impress upon them the absolute *seriousness* that the UNSC was taking about the Cole Protocol. And that included sending an officer to oversee the boarding.

Canfield spat chew out on the grated floor of the Pelican and shouted, "Lock and load Helljumpers!"

Keyes turned to the cockpit. "Drop the ramp, Mr. Jeffries. Hard and quick, as long as it's clear."

"Dropping the ramp, sir."

The ODSTs of the 105th, or Helljumpers as they were also called, clad in black vacuum-rated armor, mirror-faced helmets and all, streamed out. They scattered through the hold of the freighter and its containers, picking targets. They were quick and quiet, with no chatter, and focused on the whole process.

Keyes strode down the ramp into a canyon between the containers. He glanced in through the tough, scratched window of one of them. Nothing to see but labeled boxes.

The captain of the freighter and three of his crew stood with their arms folded at the edge of their bay, watching the ODSTs.

"Sir, are you the captain of this ship?" Keyes asked.

The ascetic man nodded a shock of blond hair. "We did nothing wrong. We've made the jump to—"

Keyes held up a hand. "Your ship is leaving UNSC protected space, Captain. You had the choice to make alternate arrangements for this cargo, or request to join a convoy where your navigation would be handled by Navy communications AIs. Either way, we need to wipe your nav data and check the ship out."

"This is a violation of our rights as merchants. We need to move our cargo now," the captain insisted.

"Sir, there is a *war* on," Keyes snapped. "In case you haven't noticed, there are aliens forcing their way toward the Inner Colonies. Cargo can wait." ONI was stretching it, targeting civilian ships, but they just couldn't risk nav data falling into Covenant hands.

The captain glared at Keyes, boiling with anger. "And here we lose another right."

Keyes turned to Canfield, who had sidled over. He looked eager to get his men kicking in doors and checking over cargo. "Do your thing."

"Fascists," the captain spat. Keyes kept an eye on the man. He seemed overly keyed up and angry.

Canfield's helmet twisted and Keyes heard the crackle of his radio in his earpiece. "Okay, Helljumpers, move out, Oedant—"

Keyes didn't hear the rest of Canfield's orders. The container they stood next to exploded, throwing Keyes clear and smacking his head against the deck.

The scene of Helljumpers scrambling for cover faded away as a thick cloud of smoke and unconsciousness rolled over Keyes.

CHAPTER 5

our more explosions rocked the inside of the cargo bay. Debris flew through the air and clattered off the walls, then rained down to the floor. A thick haze of smoke filled the air, making it nearly impossible to breathe. Keyes lay on his side, blinking away the blood trickling down his forehead into his eyes.

He tried to get on his hands and knees to stand, but he couldn't quite manage it.

An ODST Helljumper grabbed his arm. "Come on, sir, you just got your bell rung."

The man was right. Keyes could hardly focus on the grating of the floor right under the Helljumper's boots. He leaned against the Helljumper's body armor, struggling to keep under his own power.

The thick haze was starting to clear. Keyes let the Helljumper set him down against the side of the container where they'd come in. Keyes could see the high tail of the Pelican around the edge of the container in front of him. The other wounded ODSTs sat by him, armor ripped open or dented from container shrapnel.

Several of the bodies just lay still, flat out on the floor.

Keyes swallowed and rubbed his sleeve over his face to get the blood off. He could feel the warm trickle of more coming. "Where's Canfield?" He wanted to find out what the veteran ODST commander was doing.

"Canfield's dead, sir." The soldier who'd dragged him to safety was checking people for injuries, spraying biofoam into wounds to try and stabilize things. They needed to evacuate quickly before they lost more soldiers.

"Dead?" Keyes blinked more stinging blood and sweat out of his eyes. "Who's in charge?"

Keyes was overwhelmed with the thought that the entire cargo bay had been a trap that he had led good men into.

"Faison, sir."

Keyes felt for his earpiece and realized he'd lost it in the shock-wave. "Someone toss me their helmet ASAP. I need a heads-up and comms."

A wounded soldier threw his helmet over, and Keyes slapped it on his head, wincing when it touched. Whatever hit him had glanced off his skull, giving him a head wound and most likely a concussion.

"Faison, this is Keyes, give me a sit rep."

"Shaped charges on the containers, sir. Insurrectionists no doubt. Three of them attacked us when the explosions happened."

"Any survivors?" Keyes had hoped that they'd captured them alive, to get some information out of them.

Faison cleared his throat over the air. "One. He's with the

wounded. Sir, they *were* shooting at us. We thought it prudent to return fire."

"I understand that," Keyes said. "I was hoping for intel—like how many more surprises might be waiting. You're securing the ship, checking for others?"

"Yessir." Faison sounded a bit annoyed. "Of course, sir. And an emergency beacon has been triggered to bring the *Midsummer Night* in with reinforcements. We'll move right on through every inch of this boat, sir."

"I'm sure you will," Keyes muttered.

"And if you don't mind, sir, I don't need someone second guessing my orders and looking over my shoulder. All things considered, sir, you're Navy, I'm the marine. Let's stay out of each other's way."

The loud roaring in the cargo bay had grown a bit more noticeable. Keyes looked at the soldier checking the wounded over and ignored Faison's disdain for a more immediate concern. "Son, where are we losing air from?"

"Everywhere. The explosives punched holes all over this little tub," came a response.

"Wish I were a marine right now," Keyes said, looking around at the ODSTs. "I'm not in vacuumproof armor."

"We'll think of something," the Helljumper said, glancing over at the Pelican.

Keyes tapped his earpiece. "Jeffries, Keyes here. Acknowledge."

Silence.

With a grunt Keyes got to his feet and stumbled over to the container. He leaned against it and slid around the corner.

He stared at the gaping hole in the side of the Pelican.

"They pulled him out, sir." Another Helljumper tapped Keyes

on the shoulder. "We pumped him full of foam; he's in bad shape. But *Midsummer Night* should jockey in here soon. We'll have them transferred over."

Keyes looked at the line of wounded and dead ODSTs. These were the best of the best. Ask for volunteers to hold a line and kick ass, they were the first with their hands up. Happy to face the long odds, happy to face the enemy in the eye.

All dead from a routine boarding.

From a trick.

Keyes knew there could be more. He turned to the one *Finnegan's Wake* crewman still alive. He was lying on the deck with the wounded. A Helljumper sat near him, keeping a pulse.

Keyes looked around the cargo bay. *Think laterally*, he told himself. This wasn't a typical fight; he needed to think a step ahead.

The Helljumpers were combing the ship for more Innies. They'd need transport off the ship once they'd combed it, since the Pelican they'd come in on was holed. Keyes triggered the *Midsummer Night*'s ship-to-ship channel and tried to make contact, but got nothing.

Keyes bit his lip. "Commander Faison, Keyes here. Did you trigger the beacon calling the *Midsummer Night* in?"

"Faison here. No, sir."

"Then who did?" Keyes felt a cold stab of fear. They could all hear the beacon just by flipping to the emergency channel. A steady series of digital beeps tapping out a number code that, when translated, told any UNSC listening: men down, need backup and medical assistance with all possible speed.

"I don't know, sir," Faison said, annoyed. "We're in the middle of sweeping the ship . . ."

"Commander, I'm pulling rank. I'm ordering you to stop the

sweep, get a response from every single marine under your command. I want to know who set the beacon off."

"Yes*sir*," came Faison's clipped reply in Keyes's ear. "Don't suppose you want me to interview any of the dead, sir? Could be somewhat difficult." The Helljumper's passive-agressiveness was turning into anger. Faison obviously wanted to kick back. And hard.

"No, Faison. We'll do that here." Keyes turned to the Helljumpers standing around him. He couldn't see any expressions behind those dark blue faceplates. He had a feeling that there wouldn't be any smiles. But knowing exactly what was going on in a battle was extremely important. And while they might not respect the man right now, Keyes would make sure that even the ODSTs would damn well respect the rank. "Pull the chips on any soldier's helmets, check the footage and audio, look to see if anyone triggered a beacon."

They all stood silent. Then one marine managed a "Sir . . ."

"Don't stand there and stare at me," Keyes shouted, the crack of a whip in the back of his tone. The words echoed in the cavernous bay. "*Just do it!*"

They jumped to, pulling chips out of their fallen comrades' helmets and checking the footage. Keyes looked at the soldier who'd tossed him his helmet, and the man shook his head. Not him.

As they worked, Keyes switched frequencies and continually called out to the *Midsummer Night*. Nothing. They could talk inside the freighter, but it seemed nothing was getting out.

One by one, the Helljumpers all reported their beacon results: nothing.

"Faison?" Keyes called out over comms.

"Nothing here, sir. No one standing did it."

"Nothing on the wounded or dead."

"Sir?" Faison wasn't questioning Keyes this time, or annoyed. He wanted to know what Keyes was thinking.

"The Pelican is down. If any of your men find a way to talk to the *Midsummer Night*, have them tell Zheng to stand off for now. That we have things under control."

"I'm on it, sir." Faison went quiet.

Keyes took a deep breath and another wave of dizziness hit him. They were losing too much air from the cargo bay. He had maybe another fifteen minutes before he'd start gasping.

"Sir?" Faison was back. "We're being jammed. Nothing's getting out. There are some pretty hefty blast doors between us and the cockpit. We can start working on blowing those out to see if we can gain access to this ship's comms."

"No," Keyes said. "They'll have more surprises. Not worth it right now. Get back and let's regroup, figure out what to do."

"You have a plan?" Faison asked. Keyes smiled inside his ODST helmet. He sure as hell had a plan. But Keyes wasn't going to broadcast it over a suit radio, not when the Insurrectionists aboard already showed a capacity for messing with their communications so easily.

"No, Commander. I just want to regroup, take care of our wounded, and get ready for the *Midsummer Night* to come in. Get every ODST back to the cargo bay ASAP. Move it."

He motioned one of the Helljumpers over. The man's tag read MARKOV.

"Sir."

"This armor really vacuum proof?" Keyes asked.

"Yessir."

"How long can the air hold?"

"Fifteen minutes, sir." Good, that hadn't changed in his years off.

"Alright, Markov." Keyes looked around, then lowered his voice. "We need explosives. We're going to widen one of these debris holes in the hull large enough to shove one of these containers through. Say nothing over comms, ask for anything you need in person and quietly. Grab as many battle rifles as you can, a pair of field goggles, and all the ammo you can hang onto. Move it."

Markov took off, and Keyes walked over to a puncture in the far side of the hull from the cargo bay doors. The ragged edges whistled as air leaked out the gap.

Keyes walked back toward the wounded. "Listen, as everyone comes in relay this in person. Not over comms, understand? I need all these cargo containers searched and cleared out. Put the dead in one, the wounded in another."

Helljumpers flooded back into the cargo bay. As word of the order spread, each man started pulling their comrades toward the empty pair of containers.

Markov came back with a pair of battle rifles and extra ammo magazines tucked into every pocket of his armor. Keyes looked him over. "Strip your armor, son, and hand me those rifles. Then I want you in the container with the wounded."

"Sir?"

"I'm going to need to get out there in front of the containers."

"There's other armor," Markov protested. He pointed a black-gloved hand at the rows of dead men.

Keyes got up close to the man's helmet. "You want me to use body armor that may have been damaged in the explosion, that may have caused their injury or death? We don't have time to check them over."

"Markov, strip your armor down, now!" A Helljumper with squad leader paint on the shoulder of his body armor had walked up behind the two of them. Faison.

Markov removed his armor, and just as quickly Keyes started buckling up.

"No plan, huh?" Faison said out loud. "Sure doesn't look that way from where I'm standing."

Keyes finished snapping up. He was now another black-clad ODST Helljumper for all appearances. He slung the pair of battle rifles over his shoulder and checked to make sure the ammo was all secure.

He looked at Faison. "I lied. I have a plan. They blew us up at the boarding, and they've set off the emergency beacon that's bringing in the *Midsummer Night*. Because we obviously didn't set it off. What do you think is the next step? I'm willing to bet this whole freighter is ready to blow the moment our ship gets close enough. So for now I want you to get this gap lined with explosives. I want a hole big enough to shove a container through. Wounded are in one container, dead in another. Any walking and fit Helljumpers I want jumping outside and throwing themselves clear of the freighter."

"We're blowing out of here?"

"Literally." Keyes held up a battle rifle. "When you're in zero-gravity training, rule number one about firing a gun! Make sure you're braced or you're intending to go flying."

"Newton's third law, sir!" Faison nodded his head. "For every action there's an equal, and opposite, reaction. You want us to use our weapons like pocket rockets, sir?"

"Now you're talking my language," Keyes said. "Yes. We're all going to jump ship and use our weapons to maneuver, but me first. I can get far enough clear of this jam to warn the *Midsummer Night* what's happening, we don't want them shooting at us by mistake."

"And we're not using the bay doors because?" Faison asked.

"When terrorists set off a bomb, it's often designed to create panic so they can do real damage when people start to flee. And what's the natural escape route here? Can you guarantee me that there are no weapons outside covering it?" Keyes asked.

"Bay doors . . ." someone muttered.

"Exactly. Plus, it's pointed the wrong way. We have only fifteen minutes of air. We all need to head straight for the *Midsummer Night*. I want ODSTs hanging onto the container with the wounded, so they can navigate it as best they can away from the ship using their guns. Leave the dead tagged with a beacon, we'll pick it up after-action."

Faison shook his head. "This is crap, sir. We're risking our lives to jump clear of a ship with limited air when we should be taking the fight right to them . . ."

"I'm not asking for your feedback, Faison," Keyes said firmly. "This is an order."

For a moment they stood and glared at each other, then Faison backed down with gritted teeth.

It only took another two minutes before the Helljumpers had the containers sealed, explosives primed, and were ready to rock. It had to be done quickly. If there were Insurrectionists still lurking around on the ship, somehow, it wouldn't take long for them to realize Keyes had figured out what they were up to.

The ODSTs had performed well, organizing the whole thing with quiet efficiency. The wounded waited inside a cargo container that had been dragged to the hole and the other Helljumpers got ready for their departure.

"Let's do it," Keyes said, from a safe distance.

"Fire in the hole!" Markov pressed a remote.

The explosion rocked Keyes back, slamming him against the container behind him. Fortunately, this time he had on a helmet. Molten metal rained down, sizzling as it hit the cargo bay floor.

Four Helljumpers rushed to the edge with Keyes. He felt the suit kick over to internal air as the pressure dropped. They grabbed his arms and legs.

"You sure about this, sir?" one of them asked.

"Get on with it," Keyes said.

They wasted no time asking him again; all four held him between them like he was a battering ram. They ran toward the side of the hull at a sprint, and then threw Keyes through the center of the ragged hole. One of the rifles caught on an edge and was ripped free.

But he still had the other.

Keyes flew out in a cloud of crystallizing vapor.

Out of the corner of his eye he saw a series of muzzle flashes. Something struck him in the back, spinning him out of control. Stars cartwheeled around him. No more bullets struck; he was probably already far enough away that the black armor was too hard to spot. He'd only been visible because of the cloud of vapor ice around him.

"*Midsummer Night* this is Keyes, come in."

He waited for a moment. There was no reply.

Keyes grabbed his remaining battle rifle and tried to gauge his rate of spin while he breathed slowly to remain calm. He fired against the direction of his spin until he'd stopped and he could see *Finnegan's Wake* off like a toy in the distance. He looked around.

He couldn't see the *Midsummer Night* out there, but he'd cleared the freighter in roughly the right direction. He just needed to get farther away.

He tried to radio in again as he lined up a shot that would move him farther out in the right direction, but not fire bullets right back at the freighter where the ODSTs would be following. "*Midsummer Night*, this is Keyes, come in."

Again, no reply. Keyes fired the rifle off, a burst of fire aimed below the freighter, a few seconds above to compensate, moving him farther away into the quiet darkness. Keyes's heart sped as he thought about how little time he had left. If Zheng had moved away, or to the other side of the freighter . . . Keyes willed himself to remain calm, and follow the plan. Life was full of what-ifs and they had no place in an emergency.

Keyes emptied the battle rifle's magazine, and ripped through the spares as fast as he could.

In the far distance the *Wake* looked about as small as his thumb. He could see two specks of red metal falling away from it, and hoped it was the two containers and the rest of the ODSTs getting clear of the freighter.

"This is UNSC Frigate *Midsummer Night*," Zheng's voice suddenly crackled in Keyes's ears. "Identify yourself."

"Lieutenant Keyes, sir!" Keyes grinned. "The rest of the ODSTs are jumping clear of the freighter. We were attacked. Wounded and dead are in the two containers that were just shoved out. The freighter is most likely a big trap, sir, probably rigged to blow when you got close."

Keyes raised field glasses up to his helmet. Recognizing the model, the helmet's heads-up display accessed the device and the view of the distant freighter zoomed. He could see a steady stream of Helljumpers using their weapons to propel themselves away from the gray craft: a swarm of black dots drifting out in the vacuum. "Well done, Faison."

The two containers became visible, the tiny figures of Helljumpers hanging onto them, their guns aimed at the ship. Once the first group cleared the ship, the Helljumpers hanging onto the containers started firing their weapons to get the bulky boxes moving outward.

In the distance *Finnegan's Wake* collapsed, sections of the ship straining against the ribs of its bulkheads and then caving inward. The Insurrectionists hiding on the outer hull had realized that the ODSTs were abandoning ship on the double, and were blowing it up while they could still take out what UNSC forces they could.

"Helljumpers empty your magazines!" Keyes shouted, even as Faison screamed for them to do the same.

The freighter blew out in a white-hot fireball of debris, the brightly colored shockwave of gas and debris stripping the containers of the Helljumpers clinging to them.

In the bright light, and under magnification, Keyes saw the outlines of Helljumpers splayed out and spinning as they were tossed away from the vicinity of the destroyed freighter.

Keyes stared in horror, forgetting to breathe. They hadn't gotten clear in time, and because he insisted on going first, taking the risk of any Insurrectionist fire on the way out, he might be the only one to survive.

"Scramble recovery vehicles!" Zheng shouted as a shockwave of glowing gas slammed into Keyes.

In the wake of the fireball came debris, and Keyes felt himself thrown farther away as a constant pitter-patter of chunks of the ship, along with even larger pieces of deck plate and machinery, flew past.

A numb feeling of shock filled him.

His first mission back was a failure. He wasn't fit to be out here at all, and he had gotten some extraordinary men killed because of it.

CHAPTER 6

A structure the size of the Rubble, with its hundreds of habitable asteroids with artificial gravity all connected by docking tubes, had a lot of places a man could get a drink. Eddie's in the Rock was one of hundreds, and on any given ranking of the bars, it lay somewhere in the lower ten.

Delgado knew that any ex-smugglers who would know anything about the *Kestrel* wouldn't be anywhere trendy, or frequenting the larger habitats where slamming beats of flip music blared out from behind the doors built to look like industrial airlocks.

No, they'd be holed up in one of the outer habitats, far from the core, where the asteroids were still being mined or hollowed out. Where the bar door was an actual airlock, in case some massive piece of construction equipment broke a hole in the rock while baking it and all the air blew out.

Delgado had spent the better part of his day ducking in and out of the dark holes drilled into the sides of these habitats near the edges of the Rubble, places hastily equipped with permacrete and grating inside. Dressed up in a cheap pair of clean pants and a *Distancia* leather jacket, he had meandered through habitats without artificial gravity, and others where it was half a standard gravity to make it easier on the construction crews.

Eddie Underwood looked up as Delgado walked into his bar. "*Distancia*, right?" His artificial right hand, a fake pink against Eddie's white upper arm, jerked a bit as he cleaned a glass out with a clean rag. Eddie's in the Rock was a dive, but one with an owner obsessed with cleanliness.

"Yeah." Delgado had shuttled mining supplies from one freshly finished habitat to another, as well as mining crews in a hurry to get from one end of the Rubble to the other. He was a known quantity in this crowd.

Delgado sat at the bar. A crowd of heavy-set miners lined the counter, and toward the back scattered groups drank loudly in booths or played gravity ball on a table. A lean bodybuilder or heavy-crew worker sat alone in a booth in the far corner with his back to the door. "Heard about Melko Hollister?"

Eddie nodded. He gave no indication how he felt about it, which Delgado could take. "What'll you have?"

"Here to ask a favor." Delgado leaned on the bar near a corner post that ran up to the raw rock ceiling. Hanging over the bar was a stone arm. It was Eddie's. He'd lost it while working on a crew, falling into liquefied rock with his hand out to try and catch himself.

He'd retired after that. He had his lost arm jackhammered out of the cooled rock and started the bar.

Eddie hadn't said anything, so Delgado continued. "I know it's soon, but I don't have any crew. I'm looking for anyone in search of a ship to work on."

"Maybe I know someone," Eddie said.

"Looking for a whole crew," Delgado replied. "Willing to pay a solid finder's fee. I've got a chance for a cheap lease on a ship with a slipspace drive, a one-time run sort of thing. I need the sort of crew that can handle slipspace jumps without getting frozen. Particularly one with recent experience. Particularly anyone who's gotten back recently from the Inner Colonies?"

Eddie leaned forward. "Ya know no one is smuggling any-more. All the navs have been Purged." Purged. Eddie capitalized the word with his voice. It was the topic of discussion throughout the Rubble. How they were getting cut off from being able to slip the occasional ship out and back over enemy lines. What little news of the outside world they'd gleaned, what supplies they'd managed to haul back, had all come to a halt. People were scared. Some speculated it was Insurrection-ist hard cases, sealing them off from the UNSC. Others blamed the Kig-Yar, pointing out that the Covenant had, after all, de-stroyed Madrigal. They feared the Rubble would be next. Some claimed that the UNSC was cracking down on all nonmilitary travel.

"There may be a ship or two still straggling in," Delgado mut-tered. "Some that might still have nav data and help me out."

"Like the crew from the *Kestrel*?"

Delgado froze. "I wasn't specifically looking for information about them . . ."

"Huh . . . Well you're not the only one. Miss Universe over there is, too." Eddie jerked his head toward the booth in the shadows where the massive man sat. He shifted, and Delgado noticed the triceps flexing under the person's shirt. He had to assume Eddie meant there was a woman in the booth with the guy.

It wasn't a bodybuilder sitting there. It wasn't even a man. It was the Spartan, Adriana. He recognized her face. The last time he'd seen her, she had been surrounded by iridescent gray metal, and she'd worn the immensely powerful armor as if it had been a second suit of clothing.

Now she wore a clean pair of pants and a tight, long-sleeved shirt in the manner of the off-duty miners in the bar.

It didn't camouflage the fact that she was well over six and a half feet tall and dominated the booth.

It *couldn't* camouflage the fact that she could, quite obviously, break any man in the bar in half. And many of them seemed to sense it and keep well clear.

Delgado sat back down in the chair, and Eddie sighed. "You know her."

"No, not really, Eddie. Not really." Delgado didn't try too hard to sell that. He slid off the chair and approached the booth. "Can I buy you a drink?"

She didn't bother to turn, but waved him into the booth. "Hello Mr. Delgado," she said. "Hunting for something, are we?"

Delgado glanced around the bar. "Maybe. But the chances of me finding it are somewhat ruined now that you've arrived asking the same questions."

There were people paying too much attention to them near the other side of the bar. "I'm sorry," Adriana said.

Five men walked over before Delgado could suggest that they get the hell out of there.

"What the hell are you two doing asking about the *Kestrel*?" the leader of the little group asked.

"Hey, guys, come on." Delgado held up his hands, placating them. "Let's stay calm."

"Shut up." These were large, muscled miners, their eyes glassy from being too far into the drink. "This freak's been nosing around about stuff that's not her business."

Adriana looked at the group. "I'm just asking a few questions. No reason to make this anything it's not."

"What we don't need, is some Earth-lovin' she-hulk skulking about our bars, asking about things that ain't none of her business," another man snapped.

"Hey now," Delgado said.

"Hey now what?" The leader reached over and grabbed Adriana's shoulder. "Now listen here!"

She shrugged his hand off and pushed it back. The stout miner staggered slightly, and for a moment, the whole group paused.

Then the miner surged back, grabbing at Adriana's shirt collar again. "You—"

This time she grabbed his hand and twisted it. "Don't touch me." She didn't ask this, she stated it. Like it was a fact.

A second man swore and lunged for her as well. "We'll do whatever the hell we want."

He grabbed for her arm, but she grabbed his instead and jerked it.

Now she had both men by an arm, twisting their hands back around. "Now listen to me," Adriana snapped. "If I want to ask after the *Kestrel*, or anything else that strikes my fancy, what makes you think you could stop me?"

The air in the bar suddenly broke, and the faux politeness dropped. "None of that stuff ain't none of your business, bitch!" another miner screamed. He threw a punch.

Adriana let go of the two arms she held and grabbed the punch out of midair. She pulled the man toward her and slammed his head into the table.

The table gave way and splintered where the man's head struck it. He fell through the destroyed wood onto the floor in between Adriana and Delgado.

A fight erupted, the whole bar streaming their way in, Delgado cursing as he pushed his way back farther into the booth. He hadn't wanted to get involved, but the entire bar had already assumed they were working together.

Adriana ripped the remains of the table out of the ground with a grunt. She held the large pedestal that had anchored it into the floor out in front of her with one hand, keeping the angry men at bay as she tapped her ear. "Yeah, okay, let's bug out."

An explosion of brick, grating, and debris blew past Delgado.

As the dust settled, he spotted one of the miners pulling a gun on Adriana. Delgado whipped out *Señora Sies*, and the men all froze.

But they weren't looking at him. As the dust cloud in the booth wafted away, they all stood looking at the giant gray suit of powered armor that had just burst its way through the wall of Eddie's like it was balsa wood.

"Don't move," the deep voice from behind the gold visor snapped. A large rifle in the Spartan's hands covered the crowd.

No one moved.

This new Spartan grabbed Adriana and Delgado and pulled them back through the debris. Delgado's feet scraped against the jagged remains.

While the far back of Eddie's was buried into the hard rock, this section had apparently been right next to a maintenance corridor.

A few of the bar's patrons tried to peer around the hole in the bar to see where they were going, but the armored Spartan fired the rifle at the bricks, and the faces ducked back into the bar.

"Delgado, look at me," Adriana ordered, and Delgado turned to her voice.

Something very large smacked the back of his head and he fell to his knees in front of her, then passed out.

CHAPTER 7

Delgado woke up on a cot. He sat there, rubbing the back of his head and wincing. He was in the cramped crew quarters of a freight ship—bulkheads, grated flooring, flickering tube lights, and grime and grease was everywhere.

"You're up."

A giant machine had been welded into the back of the crew quarters. The voice came over the sounds of a maintenance pod whose arms sparked electricity as they carefully removed the suit of armor from a Spartan with almost midnight black eyes.

The Spartan scratched his stubbly head and pulled on pants and a shirt. "Itches," he said. "I'd like to take a shower, but we have to deal with you first. Adriana refused to leave you knocked out on the ground for those miners to eat alive."

Delgado stood up and stumbled. The Spartan grabbed him

firmly by the arm and hauled him back up. Another giant of a man who stood so tall he blocked the lights above. Delgado blinked. "What do you want with me?"

"You know who we are, right?"

"Spartans. The boogeymen of Insurrectionist children everywhere," Delgado grunted.

His head still throbbed, but he was feeling scrappy despite the fact that this mountain of a human being next to him could probably break him in half like a stick. But if they were going to kill him, they would have done it already. This gave Delgado a sudden boldness as he straightened up. Delgado smiled.

"Don't be spoiled, don't start a fight. Always be careful, here at night. Because the Spartans might come, in suits that weigh half a ton. And they'll steal from you all you gots, just like they did from Colonel Watts."

The Spartan cocked his head. "What?"

"Just a kid's rhyme," Delgado muttered. "Yeah, there are a lot of rumors about you guys. Like the one about how you super soldiers took out Colonel Watts and the rebels' whole network had to scramble to find a new leader. And there are other rumors, too. You know, a lot of people would be quite flattered that the UNSC created an entire special division of super soldiers just to come after them. But it's all been different since Harvest fell, hasn't it? The aliens sure bloodied your noses."

"Yes, yes they have," the Spartan agreed.

"Suddenly the idea of fighting for the right to your own survival isn't such an alien idea."

"True," the Spartan said. "But then, the UNSC never glassed an entire populace, so it's not exactly fair to compare the UNSC/Covenant fight with the UNSC/Insurrectionist fight, is it?"

The Spartan had a point.

"What's your name?" Delgado asked.

"Jai. Spartan double-oh-six."

"You like your numbers. You have last names?"

The Spartan didn't even answer, just pulled Delgado along into the freighter's cockpit, stooping to avoid hitting his head on the bulkhead.

Another man, too massive not to be a Spartan, sat in the pilot's chair. Adriana lounged near a navigation console. She spun her chair to face the two of them. "Mr. Delgado. You've met Jai, our team leader. In the pilot's chair is Mike."

From the windows of the cockpit Delgado could tell they were still in the Rubble, but not hanging off a dock connector. They were moving slowly through the intricate maze of tubes and asteroids.

Jai sat down at a communications console and swung around to face Delgado, who found a jumpseat.

"You were right, back there. We used to go after Insurrectionists. But that's what we were trained to do . . . We live, breathe, and eat this stuff, Delgado. We serve humanity, we exist to protect Earth and all her colonies."

"Huh . . . Nice sound bite." Delgado crossed his arms.

"That's no sound bite," Mike growled.

Jai held up a hand. "We have given everything over to this, Mr. Delgado, don't dismiss our entire lives so casually. I take it you are an Insurrectionist?"

Delgado shook his head. "Not exactly . . . A lot of people on Madrigal were neutral, even loyal to Earth. But when Madrigal was being glassed, it wasn't the UNSC that scrambled freighters and everything they had to evacuate people from Madrigal and try to hide them here."

It had been the rebels. Even though Madrigal refugees and

regular miners fast outnumbered them here in the Rubble, there had always been strong respect for the Insurrectionists. Even Delgado. He owed his life to them.

Jai leaned forward. "Then understand; we're not here for a fight. But we are here to try and stop the Covenant from taking any more colonies. Or Earth.

"For a while top brass and ONI agents have been worried about the Covenant's progress. As a result, earlier this week the Cole Protocol went into effect. All UNSC ships have to jump randomly before making a jump to their next destination. If Covenant forces appear, they have to destroy all navigation data that might lead the Covenant back to Earth."

"Just back to Earth, huh?"

"And to the colonies, that's inferred. However, months before the Cole Protocol went into effect, ONI put together several Prowler Corps missions to get back behind enemy lines—including this team. We have a list of places where navigation data might have survived, and our mission is to make sure it's all destroyed.

"In the case of the Rubble." Jai leaned further forward, intense. "We've been stuck here for almost a month. Every day we're here, we're not destroying data or checking over our targets elsewhere, and the greater the chance of the Covenant stumbling across the location to an Inner Colony, or Earth."

"What Jai's getting at," Adriana interrupted, "is the question of whether you really think the navigation data will be safe here in the Rubble?"

Delgado looked around the cockpit at the three Spartans. "I'm not giving it over to you. You have to do your jobs. I have to do mine."

"So . . . we noticed you didn't tell the Security Council that you ran into a Spartan," Adriana said.

He looked up at her, startled. How did she know that? What all were the Spartans into? How much of the Rubble had they gotten bugged? "Why would I? You're not good at keeping a low profile, it seems, with your dramatic attempt to sneak around and ask questions failing so spectacularly."

Jai folded his arms. "You picked a stubborn one to save, Adriana. I don't know."

"Don't know what?" Delgado asked.

Mike shook his head. "Let him be, Jai. Let him be."

A moment passed between the three Spartans. A decision. Delgado shivered. He'd bet anything his life had just been on the table.

Jai stood up. "My team thinks you're one of the good guys, Delgado. I don't know. Mike, we passing the ship yet?"

Mike turned back around. "Yes. Let me flip us around."

Delgado frowned as the Rubble rotated around the ship. The freighter's cockpit shook a bit as distant thrusters farther down the hull fired.

They drifted past one of the larger habitats on the edge of the structure. Docked to it was a ship that didn't look all that different from the Rubble itself—a Tinkertoy assemblage of parts of varying age, shapes, and function.

It slowly passed by, and then Jai turned to Delgado. "It's hard to trust people who do business with the enemy, Delgado, and that's a Jackal ship. Also known as: the enemy."

"Yes . . . that's a Jackal ship," Delgado said. "But most Kig-Yar are like us. Rebels. Asteroid dwellers. And they're helping us."

The Covenant had once seemed an implacable foe. A force of nature. When the conglomeration of aliens first made contact ten years ago, at the planet Harvest, the images of destruction relayed back were horrific. Covenant ships and their plasma weapons destroyed the surface of the agrarian world until nothing was left.

Madrigal had not lain too far from Harvest. And after the destruction of Harvest they'd readied themselves for the inevitable. And readied, and waited. Until 2528, when the Covenant stumbled into orbit around 23 Librae and destroyed Madrigal, the survivors fleeing to the Rubble.

When the Kig-Yar came back to 23 Librae, looking to mine the asteroids around Hesiod, they found the Rubble. Everyone had girded themselves for another one-sided battle. But instead the odd, birdlike aliens had furtively begun trading with the humans. They'd even established refuges on some of the outer asteroids.

So as the Rubble heard snatches of rumors and data about the Covenant destroying all humanity, they had to second-guess what was happening. After all, they were still alive.

And yet . . . it had taken the Covenant three years to get around to attacking Madrigal. Delgado knew the Rubble might still be on the list.

"The Jackals are helping you by violently hunting for the navigation data?" Jai asked.

"I know," Delgado muttered. "I don't particularly trust them either."

"So you know," Jai said, "the moment you hand over the data, the Covenant will deal with the Rubble the same way they did Madrigal."

Delgado had no reply. He stood with his arms crossed, staring at Jai. "Maybe. It's our problem, not yours. The UNSC isn't running things here."

"All right," Jai said. "But we'll be watching you."

The freighter thudded into dock under Mike's control. The air inside shifted, and Delgado's ears popped. Adriana led Delgado down to the airlock, where the door had already opened.

Delgado hesitantly walked through. He bit his lip. They

wouldn't shoot him in the back, would they? They had honor, and a code, didn't they?

Adriana leaned against the rim of the airlock. "Good-bye, Mr. Delgado. Try to stay out of trouble."

He turned and looked back at her, the tall, dangerous Spartan without her armor. The freighter's airlock door lurched, and started to slowly close, rust scraping off the surface as it did.

"And don't forget, there were no Spartans here." She said it seriously, without a sense of humor.

After the freighter left, Delgado looked out one of the airlock portholes at the distant Jackal ship.

The Spartans were right. The moment the Jackals got their hands on the navigation data they'd probably sell it to their brothers in the Covenant. He was going to have to figure out how to secure the navigation data. There were way too many people after it. If the Rubble was going to survive against the Covenant, it needed to be safe.

CHAPTER 8

Jai watched the last sliver of light fade away as the airlock shut. They were back alone in the freighter *Petya*. He folded his arms as Adriana walked back up at him.

"We should have kept him," Jai said as she passed.

Adriana paused and looked him eye to eye. "We've had this discussion. If you'd like to order me to go get him, *Petty* Officer Jai, I will follow your commands."

He stared back at the intense blue eyes. "Would you?"

She sighed and left him leaning against the wall. The freighter shuddered as Mike disengaged the airlock and coasted away from the asteroid.

Gray Team, Jai thought to himself with a small amount of frustration.

He'd ask what he'd done to deserve being put with the other two, but he already knew. It had started when he was six. He'd been snatched away from a life he only dimly remembered and taken to a military training facility on the planet Reach, along with seventy-five other children.

Jai remembered being herded into an amphitheater after waking up from the chill of coldsleep by a tough, gristly looking Naval drill instructor in fatigues. Every child had had an instructor standing next to them.

And then, up front on a raised dais, a woman with dark hair and gray-blue eyes cleared her throat. Beside her stood a man with medals that they would all come to respect and fear: C.P.O. Mendez. But it was clear this woman was in charge. All the big Navy men in the room responded to the crack of her orders with a nervous jump.

The woman had looked at the crowd of nervous children and told them "As per Naval Code 45812, you are hereby conscripted into the UNSC Special Project, code-named SPARTAN II."

Conscripted.

Jai hadn't liked the sound of the word. It felt wrong. And when he'd heard it, he stood up and tried to leave. The heavily muscled drill instructor next to him had grabbed him by the shoulders and shoved him down.

Shocked, Jai continued listening as the woman said, "You have been called upon to serve. You will be trained . . . and you will become the best we can make of you. You will be the protectors of Earth and all her colonies."

He'd been six, damnit.

His life in Bhuj in an orphanage hadn't been much better than the hellish boot camp that followed the next morning, all orchestrated by C.P.O. Mendez, but Jai had roamed the streets on his own time back on Bhuj. He'd scrapped with other urchins, stolen food, and found all the best boltholes in the city to hide and watch other people from.

It had been his life, and even as a wiry six-year-old, Jai had decided conscription didn't figure into his plans.

After the first night of boot camp Jai met Adriana, who'd been out that night sneaking around.

"Are you leaving?" she'd asked in awkward English.

"Yes," Jai said. "I need something to pick a lock with."

Adriana had handed him a sliver of metal from under her tongue, a paperclip stolen from somewhere on the base.

Jai had picked a lock and they'd snuck out from the barracks, using the shadows until they'd broken for the gates.

He got halfway up the fence before the guards turned the electricity on, and Jai had dropped to the ground with Adriana, both writhing in the dust and screaming.

"Good evening," Mendez had said, walking up to look down at him. "I don't recall giving you two permission to leave base."

Neither of them said anything; they just stared at the forest off in the distance.

So the next week Jai used a blanket to help them climb, and the guards caught them on the other side. And after that, it was sprinting across the barren space around the camp. They were hunted down in the forest, but he and Adriana split up and eluded their pursuers for days. They came after him on the roads past the forest, hunting them down in large teams by Warthog and Pelican.

But no matter how much Mendez punished him with extraordinary runs, push-ups, latrine cleaning duty, no matter how hard he tried to break him, Jai and Adriana always planned the next attempt.

The men who had to catch the young Jai paid the price too. The tougher he trained under Mendez, the harder he fought when captured. Guards got shattered kneecaps, lost eyes, fingers, and toes. They'd started tranquilizing him from a Pelican at the end, waiting until he burst from the forest and shooting him down from the safety of the sky.

Until one day, five months in, the woman asked for him. Catherine Halsey. Always watching them from a distance, always scribbling her notes down.

Jai had sat in front of her desk, C.P.O. Mendez by his side.

"What do you want?" Halsey asked, suddenly looking up from her desk.

"You called me here," Jai had said defiantly.

Halsey chuckled. "I did. Do you want to leave, Jai?"

"Yes!"

The woman who'd had him snatched away from everything studied Jai like he was a strange bug under a rock. "You understand what you were told, when you first arrived?"

"You stole me. You want me to fight for you. Fight for Earth. It isn't even my home planet," Jai said. "I don't want to be here."

Halsey nodded, and suddenly looked tired. As if she didn't want to do what came next. But then her spine snapped straight. "Okay, Jai. You see this?" She'd picked up a small dart. "Some of you don't have what it takes. Some have folded. Some just aren't ready to be protectors of the colonies. And that's okay. This dart will induce selective neural paralysis. The next time you break out of the forest, the guards in the Pelicans will shoot you in the head with one of these, and you'll wake up in a city. You won't remember any of this."

A crawling sensation in the back of Jai's mind told him that this was a lie. A memory eraser? It didn't sound quite right, nor did Halsey's eyes look right. There was a deeper pool of weariness and sadness there. Jai had no doubt the dart would erase something.

Halsey must have noticed Jai shift. She amended her words.

"You may also lose more than that. There are no guarantees. The process is messy, and it's worse with a child because they have so few memories to lose."

Jai swallowed and stared at the dart.

"Of course," Halsey said, steel in her voice. "You could just continue your training, and your duty."

"Why?" Jai asked.

"You're an orphan, right, Jai? State Dorm Five-Five, bed number sixty-eight? And you want to go back to that?"

Jai nodded.

Halsey sighed. "You think they remember you there? We called; no one had even noticed I transferred you. No one there cared enough to even check your bed until I called, and you've been gone for months, Jai."

Jai stared back at her. It shouldn't have hurt to hear that. He kept to himself, why was he surprised they hadn't noticed?

"No vendors remember you; your hiding places in the city have been taken over by rats. No one has even noticed you were gone. You had no family, no friends, nothing. You left no imprint on the world when you were taken, Jai. You're fighting so hard to leave, when there's nothing for you to go back to."

Jai shook his head and bit his lip.

"But here, Jai," Halsey continued, driving her words home, "you have people who notice when you try to leave. Mendez who trains you. And even though you don't have family, I find it interesting that you keep seeking out Adriana to make your escape with. Would you miss her if you left? Would you be happy if we just erased your mind with a single shot, and erased your name from our computers, and Adriana just . . . forgot all about you?"

Jai stared at her, his mouth dry. He didn't say anything, but inside he felt like he'd been destroyed. She'd picked him apart, like he was some simple puzzle. Mendez could break their bodies, but Halsey could break their minds.

"I'm giving you a final offer, Jai," Halsey said. "The guards are around the forest tonight—if you escape we'll delete you from our records and it will be like you were never here. But if you are in your bed tomorrow morning, I offer you a family, Jai, and a place to make your mark and be remembered. We have special things in mind for you and the others. Very special things. I swear to you."

Jai stared at her. And he had believed her.

Adriana had also returned to the barracks that night looking shaken.

But they broke out again, of course. They made it out past the fence using a tunnel they'd dug together a week before. There were caches of food and simple weapons in the forest, buried under trees.

But they'd both stopped well clear of the edge of the forest.

"What'd she tell you?" Jai asked.

Adriana had tears streaming down her cheeks. "I can't tell you."

"But you're not going to go, are you?"

"No. I like this too much to go," she'd said, with that odd Adriana smile that Jai was now always comfortable seeing.

"Me either."

They'd both sat on a log and watched the Pelicans crisscross the sky outside the forest, and then turned back for the barracks.

Mendez didn't comment on Jai's dusty boots the next morning, just threw a ten-mile run at him with a small grin.

When Jai had returned, Mendez introduced him to another quiet kid with even browner skin than Jai's and tight curly hair who stood outside the barracks running in place next to Adriana, both of them holding heavy wooden logs over their heads.

"At ease! Jai, Adriana, and Mike," Mendez said. "You are now a team. You will eat together, run together, drill together. Fight together."

"Sir!"

When Mendez left, Adriana and Jai had turned to Mike. "What did you do?"

Mike smiled. "I stole a Pelican," he said, innocently. "Then blew it up when they got me."

And all those years ago, all three of them had shaken hands. Gray Team trained to be isolated, slipped into distant fields for missions where there was little, if any, oversight. And after the physical augmentation, and as they became lethal killers, the ONI branch began to use the three loners for long-duration missions way out of reach from command.

They were ghosts that could wreak terrific damage.

Which was why this latest mission made sense. Supplement ONI Prowler Corps efforts to destroy all information that was left behind enemy lines.

But the same attributes that made Gray Team an incredible asset made it hard for Jai to be its commanding officer. Gray Team was . . . different. Adriana and Mike accepted Jai's leadership, but they'd been trained to think for themselves and act on their own.

So Jai had been frustrated to find out that Adriana let the Insurrectionist Delgado live after the Jackals made a play for the last known navigation data in this bizarre asteroid creation of theirs. She should have focused only on the data.

But she hadn't.

And now, they had once again let him go.

But as Adriana pointed out, had they destroyed that last bit of data and left the Rubble, then they wouldn't have known about another ship coming back from Charybdis IX. So their delay had helped. They might have left the Rubble without fully finishing their mission.

But Jai still felt they should have kept Delgado aboard. He was, after all, working with Insurrectionists. And Jai had killed his fair share of Innie terrorists.

Now Adriana felt they had a duty to help make sure the people living here were safe. Covenant-collaborating Insurrectionists, no less.

Jai walked up to the cockpit of the old freighter. Mike sat at the controls as the Jackal ship slowly drifted past their field of vision.

"One Shiva nuke," Mike muttered.

"You think Adriana's right? That these Covenant will turn on them?"

"They always do," Mike said. "The Covenant always attack. Always destroy it all. Why would they stop now?"

"I don't know," Jai said as Mike boosted them out away for the fringes of the Rubble, where they could lurk. "We've never seen anything like this before. Jackals trading and working with humans to build asteroid habitats?"

But then, that was what Gray Team was for. They couldn't call back for orders, they were the UNSC in absentia. The three of them had to figure out what this all meant, and what to do next.

"One Shiva?" Jai turned and looked at Mike.

Mike ran a hand over his shaved head. "Put it in the right place, yes."

"Put it where?"

"Inside."

Jai looked at him and then laughed. "That would do the trick, Mike. That would do it."

And he imagined that if Adriana and Mike were right, and they usually were, they would end up having to do it.

"How many Shivas do we have left in the holds?" Jai asked.

"Enough," Mike said.

"Enough to what?"

"Cause a lot of trouble here in the Rubble," Mike said. "When the time comes."

"I haven't made any decisions about that yet," Jai said.

Mike shrugged. "When you decide, the nukes will be ready."

Jai left the bridge. Those two were just way too sure of themselves. Then again, so was he. He smiled to himself. They were cursed with each other.

"Wait a second," Mike shouted.

Jai turned back around, annoyed. "What?"

Screens lit up with warnings and scrolled text faster than Jai could read. Mike tapped away at the keyboards, his fingers flashing over the keys as he started swearing.

"What is it?" Jai repeated.

"Something's leaping in through our communications dishes. I can't stop it; incursion alerts all over."

Jai felt his stomach flip. Mike was the systems expert, had always been. He'd figured out how to steal that Pelican when he'd been conscripted into the Spartan II program because he'd been flown into the camp on one, and that single session of watching how the pilot flew was enough for him. He had a gift with machines and computers that Jai envied.

Now Mike looked flustered. "Hit the kill switch. Now!"

Jai ran to the center of the cockpit and pulled up a plate of metal. He yanked out the red handle inside and the entire freighter abruptly plunged into darkness.

"What just happened?" Adriana shouted. "Was that the kill switch?"

"Yeah." Without any power the artificial gravity had failed. Jai hung near the kill switch, a manual circuit breaker Mike had installed during the long slipspace journey to this system.

Just in case, he'd always said. You can't hack into a ship if someone yanks the power cord loose.

The *Petya*, their home for the last several months, coasted along in the dark.

Mike twisted onto his back in the starlight and moved over to one of the windows. "We're not going to hit anything for twenty minutes or so," he said. "That'll give us time."

When it came to the ships and hardware, Mike called the shots.

Mike spun in place to face them. "Jai, get clippers and snip the wires going to any comms arrays. You have eighteen minutes before we go bump. Adriana, you should suit up. If someone was trying to get into our systems they might try a less virtual route and show up outside."

"On it." Adriana kicked off the edge of the cockpit door and back down the dark center of the ship toward the bunks.

Jai followed, leaving Mike in the cockpit.

Fifteen minutes later, after crawling around the guts of the *Petya* to trace wiring, Jai had two of the arrays cut. Adriana had cycled out the lock in full armor and coasted up the belly of the freighter and just ripped the last array off the ship and flung it clear.

As Jai pulled himself out and shoved himself through the air into the cockpit, Adriana exited the airlock and followed. With full armor, she seemed to take up the entire cockpit.

"There's no one out there; didn't spot anything moving toward us either," she reported.

"That's both reassuring and worrying," Mike said. "Plug her back in."

The *Petya*'s emergency lights flicked on. A bit late, Jai thought, but then it was an old tramp freighter, just barely able to struggle from slipspace point to slipspace point until Mike had insisted they snag it. The team had spent a whole week under his direction, refitting a faster, military-grade slipspace unit into her.

But Jai had to agree now, it had been worth it. There was more space in the cargo area for the weapons they'd accumulated, which made Adriana very happy. Mike as well; he'd picked up a few extra Shiva nuclear warheads, and stocked up on just about everything else he could get his hands on.

The primary lights flicked on as Mike tapped at screens and guided the ship's rebooting. Jai realized everything had fallen deathly silent as fans and pumps whirred back into life. The entire ship's steady background hum slowly trickled back.

Artificial gravity returned. Adriana and Mike twisted like cats and landed on their feet.

"All right, let's see what we've got." Mike moved back to the controls and *Petya* shuddered as he adjusted their trajectory with thrusters. They passed by one of the flexible, clear docking tubes stretching half a mile between two asteroids.

Inside people hustled from point to point on their business, hardly even noticing that the freighter had come within a mile of striking it.

One of the screens to Mike's right flickered, and a woman appeared on it, her skin a ghostly skein of numbers and calculations. The effected look of many AIs. It seemed to look around the cockpit. "Neat trick," it said through the cockpit's many speakers. "But before you cut the power again, know that I infected a number of your external stellar navigation sensors. They don't have much broadcasting power, but I have a lot of comms equipment trained on your guys throughout the Rubble listening for them. Plus I already disabled your slipspace drives, so you really do have to listen to me."

Mike checked a screen, then swore and turned to Jai, who reached down for the red handle.

"Wait, wait, please hear me out," the AI on their screen said. "I have an offer for you. I can get you the Rubble navigation data, but I want to cut a deal."

Jai froze and locked eyes with Mike, who shrugged. Jai looked back up. "A deal?"

The AI nodded on the screen. "You're Spartans. The best of the best of the best." It smiled. "There are a lot of lives at stake here, soldiers. I will help you get that navigation data, because I want you to protect it. But you can't leave right away. And that's the deal."

"We have to stick around?" Jai asked, a bit incredulously. "Why?"

"Because the lives of everyone in the Rubble are at stake, Spartan. And I am going to need you three to help save them in the very short days ahead. We will be their deliverance, and you three their paladins, my very own knights in somewhat shining armor."

Mike shook his head and held up seven fingers by his thigh for Jai to see.

An artificial intelligence usually lasted seven years before it legally had to be put down. After seven years they often started to go through stages of instability. They became rampant: convinced of their godlike power and ability. Rampant AIs were destructive, dangerous, and somewhat insane.

But rampancy was not inevitable, just statistically likely. An AI older than seven years was playing a dangerous game. Out here in the Rubble, they must have felt it prudent to keep the AI running this long in order to keep the system together.

"Come on!" snapped the AI, yelling at them. "I can see your fingers, Spartan. I am over the age, yes. Maybe I am rampant. I damn well deserve to be."

Adriana turned to look at Jai, but he waved his hand. Let it talk. See where it went.

"They unpacked me from storage to run the Rubble the year after Madrigal was glassed—they couldn't handle the course corrections manually to keep asteroids connected to each other. They needed the constant and genius-like attention of someone like me.

"That kept me busy, growing all this out, until the Jackals came. Since then, well, I've been planning for the end, Spartans. And now it's here. Yes, I am Juliana, the goddess of the Rubble. Your experts may suspect me of rampancy, but a benevolent goddess may be exactly what you need right now. And this one happens to be very, very attached to the idea of saving the people of the Rubble."

Mike shifted. "Doesn't sound rampant to me." He was mollifying it, engaging it, Jai saw. Maybe even validating it. And Jai felt not pulling the plug had been worth it. This unsettled AI, somewhat frazzled by the chores it had been given in keeping the Rubble going, might be a very useful ally indeed.

Juliana looked down, suddenly tired, a flash of sadness crossing her face. "I . . . think, right now, my preoccupation with the tricky, immense, complicated task of saving the Rubble's citizenry is all that does actually keep me from the depths of rampancy. It's been eating away at the edges of me for two years now."

"And you want us to help?" Adriana prodded.

The AI looked back up. "In return I'll give you even more than the data you want. The Covenant forces here are up to a lot more than just setting up shop in a few of the Rubble's asteroids. I have details. You'll want these." She had a coy smile.

Adriana and Mike looked over at Jai, who smiled back at the AI.

"We don't have much time," Juliana said. "We need to help each other *now*."

They had a rampant Insurrectionist AI demanding their help, with a promise of greater secrets. Adriana's pet Insurrectionist running around. And a crippled freighter.

Jai smiled. This was just the sort of situation Gray Team thrived on.

CHAPTER 9

Vadam Keep, Yermo, Sanghelios

Early in the predawn light of the day after Thel 'Vadamee's ascension to kaidon of his keep, he woke to the faint scratching sound of three pairs of feet.

They were on the roof outside his window, moving quickly and getting ready to vault the lip of his windowsill into his room. Thel wasted no time getting up from the chair that he had sat in all night, waiting for this.

As the first assassin broke through the window, Thel pressed the button on the thick bar of metal in his hand that had been lying casually by his side. The energy sword flicked into being with a crack of ionized air from the handle as the twin half ovals of blue plasma appeared.

The first swipe of the angry-sounding sword dug deep into the assassin's chest, spearing him on the tip of the concentrated plasma. To his credit the assassin did not scream.

Thel barely had time to duck, though, as the next two assassins bearing energy swords of their own hit the floor in front of him. Their crackling energy weapons just barely missed Thel's head. But their overeager swings doomed them. Even as their energy swords passed by him, Thel was coming back up to a full stand, slicing the sword arm of the nearest assassin clear off his body.

The last assassin backpedaled, looking for room to defend himself, realizing that this was not a simple job anymore.

There was a lot of space in the master room. The assassin stepped back over the large stone slabs of the room's floor, his eyes darting from door to door, wondering whether he could make a run for it. Or at least, how he might use the space to his advantage.

Thel remained in front of the window, watching the assassin. To be honest he had expected more than this. The Vadam elders had voted him kaidon based on his abilities as a leader, fighter, and zealot. The keeps worked on a system of meritocracy—only the most capable would be voted as kaidon upon the death of the previous one.

But for those who felt that their vote had been ill advised, or who had second thoughts, it was both a cherished right and a tradition to send in assassins to test the true merit of that ruler's martial abilities.

It was another layer of meritocracy. A kaidon who could not defend himself from assassins was not a true ruler.

This was classic Sangheili thinking.

The assassin tested the first door, and found it locked. The four-inch-thick kafel wood would not break easily, and the assassin had to have known that with just a glance. The second door was just as locked and solid.

Now he turned and looked at Thel, realizing that he was as good as dead, and ran straight for the window where Thel stood. A last stand.

Thel pulled a plasma pistol out of his holster and shot the assassin straight through the head. The assassin tumbled to the floor right in front of Thel's feet.

Now which elder, Thel wondered as he turned around to look out over the solid rocky walls of the ancient Vadam keep, was brave enough to order this?

The massive moons of Sanghelios, hanging over the peaks of the mountain, offered no answers for Thel.

He turned and stepped over the corpses, and unlocked the door with the key hung by brass links around his neck. Several of his personal guard stood outside, weapons drawn.

"Gather the elders," Thel ordered them. "In the stone hall."

"It is not even morning yet," one of them protested.

Thel rounded on him. "Who is kaidon?"

The guard snaked his long head downwards. "I swear on the blood of my ancestors I shall not question you again."

Thel looked his guards over. Lean and tall, their muted brown skin was almost all hidden by sturdy armor. Covenant armor. Their long-necked heads were sheathed in chain mail, and their large eyes gleamed in the flickering light of the hall.

They were all well built, powerful, overly trained since birth, specimens of Sangheili warriors.

All poised to do Thel's bidding.

They split off to go rouse the elders, as Thel walked through the stone corridors and tight spaces.

This was a tense but glorious day that Thel had worked toward his whole life. The lineage of Vadam, in the long history of his kind, was relatively young—founded by a distant ancestor during the first exploratory age, when Sangheili ships plied the dangerous oceans, risking terrific tides due to the multiple suns and moons the planet danced with.

From the sides of Kolaar Mountain the Vadam keep looked out toward Vadam harbor, thirty miles away. They'd huddled against invaders throughout the ages here, and it was also from this well-defended location that they'd lashed back.

The Prophets themselves had even tried but had been unable to properly destroy Vadam, among many others. They'd been too buried into the crags and cliffs of their mountains.

Great Sangheili had built Vadam's power up through the generations. Thel wanted to add his own name to the Vadam Saga, etched into the living rock of the walls under the mountain.

"They are waiting for you," a guard said outside the stone room, as Thel walked down the steps that took him ever farther down into the depths of the mountain's bedrock.

In the distance, the thunder of the river shook the stone under Thel's feet. An underground water source, and power source, that no enemy had ever managed to get to.

Thel entered the stone hall, and looked up at the curved timbers rising a hundred feet over his head. Then he looked down at the long table in the center of the room. The elders, most of them with their cloaks wrapped around them against the morning cold, stared at him with large, unblinking eyes.

"My blood," Thel said, as he walked to the head of the table. "You voted me for kaidon, and yet it seems one of you did not believe in his vote, and did not believe in me, for three assassins broke into the High Room just minutes ago."

With that said, Thel shrugged his own cloak off, and stood naked before them. "Kaidon . . ." one of them whispered, shocked.

"As you can all see with your own eyes, they failed to even

scratch my body." Thel glared at them all as one of his personal guard rushed to his side to pull the cloak back on. "I killed two of them, but left the last one alive so we could discuss the matter of who sent him."

A lie, but it was a telling lie, as Thel saw one of the elders stiffen, then let out a long breath.

Koida, Thel remembered his name. Koida 'Vadam. Thel felt the faint kick of disappointment.

Any of these elders could have sired Thel. It was not the Sangheili way to let a child know its father, as Sangheili took sires based on their fighting prowess. Sangheili only truly could know who their mothers' brothers were, and so were raised by their uncles to learn the fighting arts.

Many of these elders had once been great warriors. And several of Thel's uncles sat before him.

Koida, thankfully, was not one.

"I am Thel 'Vadamee." Thel stressed the "ee" that signified his military service. "If you voted me for kaidon, surely you knew I could defend myself?"

Koida leaned forward, his wrinkled hands on the table before him to steady himself. "You have spent your last years fighting the lesser races of the Covenant, not Sangheili. I feared you had weakened, and would not make a strong kaidon of the keep."

Thel shook his head. "The only ones who grow soft, it seems, are elders who cluster in their small rooms, plotting against their kaidon. Had you been strong, you would have waited in my room to attack me yourself."

The elders murmured agreement, and Thel walked around the table, grabbed Koida's cloak, and pulled him up from his chair. He pushed him toward the nearest massive wall, where the Vadam Saga stopped.

"There are the words of our lineage, Koida," Thel said. "Where is your name on that wall?"

Koida shook his head sadly, his wrinkled, faded brown skin bunching as he did so. "It is not on the wall."

"We Sangheili are only as good as our deeds. We are born and live in the common rooms, beginning life equal to each other in the eyes of the keep, and rise according to our ability. You should have voted against me and stood your ground, or killed me yourself. Your cowardice is not a trait I want spread through the lineage of Vadam."

Koida's eyes widened fully. "I will fall on my sword, kaidon, but please do not revoke the blood of my line."

"I did not quench it," Thel said. "You did."

Koida leapt forward, suddenly finding courage, and Thel pulled his energy sword out. The blue plasma leapt out, and Thel swung the blade through Koida's neck.

The elder's head rolled across the floor, and purple blood gushed out, splattering the Saga's chiseled words. It was the closest the elder would get to having any part of himself on the wall.

Thel turned to his guards. "The Koida line shall leave. They are no longer Vadam. They have until sunrise to do so. Any of Koida's line still here after that will meet the same fate as he did. I grant them mercy, because Koida at least found his spirit right before death. Had he taken a knee and begged, they would all be dead."

"It is our honor," the guards said, and left to spread the order.

Thel turned back to the elders. "I have been looking over the state of Vadam." The harbor brought in profits, the buildings reached from the valley under the keep out across the land, and Vadam's serfs were happy and working hard, hoping to rise and distinguish themselves and gain a position in the keep. "I am happy with your guidance. The lineage is strong."

"Vadam *is* strong," an elder agreed, perhaps hoping to gain favor and notice.

"But I am no figurehead," Thel continued, ignoring the interruption for the moment. "I will take a close interest in all our investments and activities. Those who work for only their own gain, and not that of Vadam, risk my wrath. Am I understood?"

They all did. "Yes, kaidon."

"Good." Thel flicked the energy sword off, and slid the handle into the depths of his cloak. "You were right to elect me kaidon. I have news for you. I have been given a promotion, and command of a ship that is part of a fleet created by a High Prophet himself. We have discovered a new human world."

"We pity the poor creatures who are about to be destroyed by your mighty hand," one elder said.

"What is the name of this world?" another asked.

"The humans call it Charybdis IX. I leave you all now in stewardship of Vadam." Thel eyed the elders. "I hope it is in the most capable hands."

They all rushed to reassure the new kaidon that, indeed, it was.

CHAPTER 10

K eyes walked into the chart room of the *Midsummer Night*. The whole bridge crew sat around the tabletop chart, nodding as he entered. His fellow junior officers were all here: Lieutenant Badia Campbell ran ops, Lieutenant, Junior Grade, Rai Li on weapons, and Lieutenant Dante Kirtley ran communications.

"Heard you got hit pretty hard, Keyes." Badia Campbell looked up from her notes. The jovial note in her voice sounded slightly forced.

A piece of deck plate had slammed into Keyes while he floated toward the ship, but he had waved on the medics that had been sent to pick him up—he thought the others needed it more. The explosion had killed some twenty Helljumpers. And although the container with the wounded had been badly damaged, it had been recovered, and many survived. Other Helljumpers had been concussed, or suffered internal bleeding and injuries from their proximity to the shockwave.

But more people had made it out than Keyes initially had even hoped for. And many were treating him with a newfound respect, something above and beyond just his rank and his reputation of being well learned.

And that added respect included the bridge crew all around the chart table looking up at him. Keyes hadn't had much time in the first forty-eight hours to get to know them. They'd all been running around, checking on repairs and trying to figure out why things weren't working.

But on the bridge all three of his fellow officers had been crisp, together, and on top of things . . . though Campbell sounded tired and a bit short-tempered with the people reporting to her.

Keyes would've been too. Ops was taking the brunt of the work to get things running smoothly.

"Minor head wound," Keyes said.

Rai Li smiled. "I personally think your skull's too thick for debris to get through."

They all laughed, breaking the ice. This was the first time they'd all sat in a room together. They'd been busy with their duties, and then reporting to Zheng, who had been very hands-off so far with the crew, trusting only his officers.

That hadn't sat well, a lot of nervous crew wondered why Zheng had been given a ship after sacrificing his last one in a suicidal dash. They whispered that he'd been caught sitting in the captain's chair, staring out at space, crying silently to himself. Everyone tiptoed around the man.

The shakedown problems didn't leave a lot of time to size each other up. But the *Finnegan's Wake* incident had now run them through a critical event, and everyone aboard had stopped bickering over petty things. The ship seemed to have pulled together. After the somberness of the past twenty-four hours, it was nice to smile.

"Should have seen Kirtley's face when Zheng hailed you and you answered. He was knee-deep in his console, upside down, no less, trying to figure out if something had gone wrong with our equipment," Campbell said.

"Well, we've had so little luck on equipment so far." Kirtley shook his head. "I know we need to refit and build these ships as fast as possible to face the Covenant, but we need to be a little bit more careful about build quality . . ."

The door opened and Commander Zheng walked in, Major Akio Watanabe close behind. They all stood to attention, but Zheng waved his hand. The exuberant mood the officers had shared died. Even they were beginning to be affected by Zheng's reputation. They only interacted with him formally, as they were now. It made him hard to gauge. And Keyes's efforts to talk to the Commander had been rebuffed with the hasty excuse of being too busy.

"As you were," Zheng said.

They sat back down. Except Watanabe, who held onto a small box and continued to stand behind Zheng. If Zheng was standoffish, Keyes thought, then Watanabe here was almost as mysterious, staying in his room alone for most of the trip so far.

"Good to have you back, Lieutenant Keyes," Zheng said. "We dodged quite a bullet, there. The ship owes you."

"Thank you, sir." Keyes ducked his head, somewhat embarrassed at the attention. This was wildly outgoing for Zheng. "What about the captured Innie? Has he talked?"

Everyone turned to Watanabe.

"Well, he has admitted to being an Insurrectionist, yes."

Watanabe looked down, as if in thought. "I haven't gotten much else out of him."

Kirtley murmured, "I'd hate to be *that* guy right now."

Watanabe snapped his head up and stared at the two of them. "Mr. Dante Kirtley . . . do you think I brought aboard a portable torture chamber?"

Kirtley didn't answer.

"I know we're the boogeymen," Watanabe continued. "But don't be ridiculous. You torture a man, he'll tell you anything to make it stop. Anything you think you want. He might even, if you're pushing hard enough, believe whatever that is with all the will that he has left."

Akio Watanabe unbuttoned the top of his sleeves. He pulled them back to reveal scars running from his wrists all the way up to his elbows. A fast unclip of his odd, high-necked collar revealed horrible scarring around his throat. "If I tortured them, I'd be no better than them."

He sat down and rebuttoned his uniform slowly.

"I'm sorry," Kirtley started to say, but Watanabe cut him off.

"If I'm overloyal to the Prowler Corps, and by extension, the UNSC, it is because they rescued me from hell itself. Now, let's not ever talk about this again."

"Of course, sir," Keyes said, eager to get everyone past it. "So no information out of him."

"Sadly, not much. The Insurrectionists use cell tactics, and the man we captured doesn't know too much other than the details of this mission. I'm using a mild sedative to relax him, and a lie detector he doesn't know about. So I'm just chatting with him. With the detector and random conversation for calibration, we may yet learn something, but don't get too hopeful."

Rai Li shook her head. "Doesn't make sense, what they did."

"Really?" Watanabe cocked his head. "We've just ordered that there be no more non-Navy travel. They can't resupply each other, they have no communications ability. They're isolated. We've incidentally dealt the Insurrectionists all across the colonies a killing blow, as a complete sidenote to the war against the Covenant."

"We should have done this years ago, then," Kirtley said.

"What kind of martial civilization would we be where civilians weren't allowed to travel unless by the military, where all communications between worlds were controlled by us?" Watanabe asked.

"We'd be a functional one, without uprisings. Orderly." It seemed obvious to Kirtley. Keyes had to admit he agreed somewhat.

"Ah." Watanabe shrugged. "Maybe. At first. But don't forget, these Insurrectionists knew what frequency to jam. They have sympathizers in the UNSC, they could be anywhere. It isn't as simple as killing this or cutting that. People facing an invasion, no matter what we'd like to believe, behave in a variety of different ways. Some ready for battle, some try to bargain, others look to what advantages they can gain in the short term, and old wounds still run deep."

"In the meantime," Commander Zheng said, "we need to focus on the next leg of our mission."

Watanabe held out the box. "And now it is time to unseal our orders. Commander Zheng, your thumbprint please?"

Zheng pressed his thumb against the screen. Then Watanabe did the same.

The pad lit up, and Watanabe handed it over to Zheng, who read it.

"Would you like to brief them, Captain?"

Zheng looked up with a frown. "You know the particulars?"

"I'm the one who suggested this operation." Watanabe steepled his fingers together. "It's a situation I've been following for a while now. We haven't had the resources, until I became aware of this ship."

"Then go ahead, Mr. Watanabe. It's your show."

"During my . . . recovery," Watanabe started, "I was on loan from the Prowler Corps to the data gathering and analysis section of a certain ONI branch that I'm not at liberty to name. It was there I started coming across reports of Covenant weaponry turning up in civilian hands throughout the colonies."

"But that isn't unusual." Campbell leaned forward. "Marines who've tangled with Covenant forces bring them back. They can hock them on the black market."

Watanabe unfolded his hands and leaned back in his chair. "That's true. But according to regulations you're supposed to turn them in to ONI, and not everyone is so . . . rules bound. With the Cole Protocol being rolled out, you'll note that bringing a Covenant weapon back to any UNSC installation or Inner Colony location is an act of treason under one of the attached sub-articles. They might not be weapons, but drones, or bombs, or have beacons in them that will let the Covenant map our locations."

"That'll have a chilling effect on the pawn shops near military bases," Li said.

A strained smile quirked on Watanabe's lips. "One imagines. However, I'm not talking about the usual levels of black market collectibles. Until the Cole Protocol was put in place, we saw a *dramatic* increase in Covenant weaponry flooding the market. My fellow analysts and I came to believe that somewhere out there, Insurrectionists or other parties may actually be trading with the Covenant. Or, alternatively, they are being co-opted by the Covenant somehow, instead of merely being destroyed."

The ONI agent stood up and tapped the chart table. A hologram of a plasma pistol appeared. "A shipping container was found in a routine board-and-search late last week on its way to Charybdis IX. It contained three thousand fully charged plasma pistols on board, and a thousand plasma rifles."

"Enough to arm a significant number of Insurrectionists," Kirtley said. He folded his arms.

"Correct," Watanabe said. "Now, this was a slow freighter, and ONI agents from Charybdis IX intercepted it well before it got to the planet. It had another week of travel yet to get to orbit. Our orders are to head out to Charybdis IX and meet with ONI agents there. We're going to find out who's receiving these guns, where they come from, and why the Covenant is acting in a whole new manner with this gunrunning."

They all sat in silence, digesting the mission. Commander Zheng stood up. "Well, it sounds like this is going to lead us to Insurrectionists. And I don't know about you all, but I'm ready to repay them for what they just did."

"Yes*sir*," they all chorused. Except Badia, who glanced down at the floor and closed her eyes. Keyes wondered if she was thinking about all the dead from the last engagement.

"Then let's get to it. Keyes, lay us on a course straight for Charybdis IX . . . after our random jump, of course." Zheng leaned back, watching them all with calculating eyes.

"Of course, sir." Keyes looked around at the bridge crew as they stood up. They were on their way to forming a comfortable team in a surprisingly short time.

And judging by the tiny smile Zheng had on his lips, he felt the same way. Maybe Keyes had read his standoffishness wrong; maybe Zheng was just eager to get back to the fight. No matter which, it was still a good thing to see a ship's crew coming together.

Keyes had a feeling it would be important. Insurrectionists and Covenant working together left a very bad taste in his mouth.

They'd need to be at their fighting best on this ship in the days ahead.

But whatever Zheng may have had in mind, Keyes noticed that the other officers seemed eager to get out of the chartroom and back to their duties, at a safe remove from the Commander.

CHAPTER 11

Keyes moved down the corridor quickly, crewmen snapping to attention as he passed. He had just laid them into a geosynchronous orbit over Charybdis IX, right above the capital city of Scyllion. A Pelican was being prepped to take Akio Watanabe dirt side. Things were moving along.

He paused at a corridor. The hangar bay would be *this* way.

He was still getting a feel for the frigate: adding to the ship's speed meant reconfiguring the normal layout of a ship of this class.

"Lieutenant Keyes," buzzed a frantic voice in his earpiece. "We need you at sickbay, now. It's Jeffries."

Keyes turned around, then turned around again. Medical no longer lay at the heart of the ship, but farther off to the starboard.

Keyes broke out of his fast walk into a half jog. If Jeffries died, he'd never forgive himself for asking for his transfer.

"Lieutenant!"

It was Faison. He stepped out of the corner of a junction from behind a bulkhead.

"Yes?"

Five Helljumpers tackled Keyes from the side.

He went down, shocked. Then self-defense training kicked in. Keyes fought his way free of the hands holding his legs and kicked the nearest Helljumper in the head.

The kick sent the man down, but not before another behind Keyes put him in a chokehold.

Sputtering, Keyes managed to swing and dish out a black eye. He ripped free of their holds again, but three more Helljumpers joined the fray.

They came with duct tape.

Keyes found himself being trussed up and dragged into a nearby storage room, the door locked behind them. "What the hell do you think you're doing?" he shouted.

The Helljumpers surrounded the furious Keyes, who was then raised up onto a table with a solid thump. Faison walked over and viewed the results. He nodded. "Good."

"Hoo-ah," they replied.

"Lieutenant Jacob Keyes." Faison leaned over and looked him in the eyes. "Do you know how many Navy brass have pulled rank on me in the middle of combat action?"

"I have no idea, Mr. Faison."

The Helljumper smiled. "None, Mr. Keyes. At least, none that have lived."

Keyes knew that the Helljumpers regarded themselves as tougher, more willing to fight, than regular marines or Navy men. They were certainly far crazier.

Faison pointed at one of the men. "Chesnik, do it."

A buzzing sound came from Keyes's right. One of the

Helljumpers whipped out a huge Bowie knife—and cut the sleeve off Keyes's uniform. A smarting pain shot up his shoulder. He twisted to look. Chesnick was holding a portable tattoo machine, a long metal penlike tool with an ink reservoir on the end. Chesnick leaned in and pressed the needle into Keyes's arm and started etching a careful swoop.

Keyes stopped struggling, leaning back as the needle continued its smarting journey over his arm. "You're all crazy," he said. "Guess I won't have to court-martial you, though." He took a deep breath.

"Well, aren't we lucky," Chesnick replied, and then leaned back. "Done."

Faison pulled out a huge knife of his own from an ankle sheath. It had the words "Bug-Hunter" traced on the blade. He sliced the duct tape off.

"You'd make a hell of a marine, Keyes," Faison said. "You saved a lot of our asses out there."

Keyes shook his head. "Should have seen it coming earlier."

"No," Faison said. "Anyone else would have stood there and let us do our job, and we'd all be dead. We owe you, Keyes. You ever need a favor from a Helljumper, no matter where, you just roll up your sleeve and ask."

They opened the door, and it seemed like half the ship's Helljumpers were waiting in the corridor.

"You're not bad for an officer," said Markov, just outside the door. "But if you ever take my armor again, it's your ass."

"By the way, next time, try not to scream so much," another Helljumper shouted while laughing.

The center of the corridor became a gauntlet, with Helljumpers pushing Keyes on through all the way down the line, many of them slapping the newly inked tattoo and laughing as he winced.

At the end of the line Akio Watanabe waited stiffly.

"If you don't mind, Lieutenant Keyes, now that you're done playing with your new friends, I have a favor to ask."

Keyes had a wide grin on his face from the relief that the Hell-jumpers weren't actually going to kill him and a bit of pride from their actions. "Of course, Major Watanabe. What is it?"

"I'd like you to come dirt side with me. There are not a lot of people I implicitly trust. The nature of the job, you know. Judging by your actions, you seem like a man I could trust with my life, implicitly. I would count most of the bridge crew as trustworthy, given my research on them, but to be honest, Mr. Keyes, I think they just plain don't like me. How that would play into a split second's hesitation to back me up in a dangerous situation, I'm not sure . . ."

"You're a cynical man, Major." Keyes did not like Watanabe's judgment of his fellow officers. A force was only as good as the man next to him. It was who you fought for, when it came down to it, but that bond started with a fundamental trust. A trust that Watanabe did not have.

"Comes with the job." Watanabe's smile wasn't so much a smile, but bared teeth. "Will you come anyway?"

Keyes nodded stiffly. "If those are your orders, of course."

Watanabe grabbed Keyes's arm and looked at the lettering. "The ODST tattoo. They must really like you. You know what it means?"

"No." Keyes shook his head, pulling his arm back. Watanabe kept his grip on the arm. It was surprisingly tight.

"The kanji stand for 'bastard,' or 'bad ass,' depending on who you talk to. Lieutenant?"

"Yes?"

Watanabe let go of Keyes's arm. "Make sure you visit the ship's armory before we leave."

CHAPTER 12

Scyllion burned.

Jeffries lazily swung the Pelican above the tightly clustered skyscrapers of the city, and through patches of billowing, black smoke from burning piles of furniture and barrels on the roads.

"Food riots," Watanabe said, hanging on to webbing and looking out the back of the Pelican with Keyes. Jeffries had already lowered the ramp for a hot drop.

Keyes walked to the back and looked out. "I never thought I'd see anything like that in the Inner Colonies."

"Hold tight, sir," Jeffries shouted back. The Pelican slowly banked around a set of towers.

Watanabe looked out at the random pillars of smoke mingled among the concrete, steel, and mirrored windows of the city. "It started as a corporate mining town. The whole thing was laid out and designed to keep all money in the corporation. You worked for them, paid rent to stay in an apartment they built run by a division of the mining company. You shopped at company-run stores. You traveled on the company line. It is an example that used to be taught in business schools."

"So what's happening now?" As Jeffries straightened the Pelican out the city fell away behind them, towers glinting as the sun sunk down behind the city skyline, its orange hues streaking the clouds. Scyllion looked as if it were made of gold due to the sunset filtering through its windows.

"They had a monopoly: they started raising prices dramatically. People became trapped. Once here, the price of living exceeded their company pay, putting them further and further in debt with no way out.

"It became a problem when a rival company tried to get mining rights and was barred by the puppet government the company had funded here on Charybdis IX. So the new company funded dissatisfied and trapped workers back in '25, hoping to shake things up politically a bit, and Scyllion's police shot a few of them during a protest march. Since then, Insurrectionists have been a huge problem here. Scyllion's corporate masters are now spending more money on trying to get everything they can off planet and back to colonies closer to Earth to protect their assets. ONI recommended that the UNSC implement martial law last year.

"We just don't have the troops and ships to spare," Watanabe finished.

The Pelican flew over the edges of Scyllion, passing over a long snaking river. Warehouses lined the banks, and large container ships lay at dock next to concrete wharfs.

"Here we are," Jeffries announced in their earpieces. The Pelican slowed, its engines swiveling to redirect thrust.

They landed on a pad on top of one of the warehouses. Watanabe let go of the webbing and walked down the ramp. Keyes followed him.

The Pelican revved up and lifted off, leaving them on the suddenly quiet rooftop pad.

A woman with long hair and grubby gray overalls stood waiting for them at the stairwell leading down to the warehouse.

"Corinthia Hansen," Watanabe said. He shook her hand. "Lieutenant Keyes, this is our ONI contact on the ground here. She's been coordinating tracking the influx of Covenant weapons and trying to get them off the street to be examined and destroyed. She was also responsible for intercepting the Insurrectionist ship."

"Good to see you, Major Watanabe." She looked at Keyes. "What's the Navy here for?"

"Peace of mind. A line to further resources back in orbit if we need it." Watanabe looked around the pad. "Your report said you had crew uniforms and fifteen agents?"

"Downstairs, in the Hogs. You can change en route, we're short on time."

"Why the rush?" Watanabe asked. "I thought we had more time?"

"Yeah, in case you didn't notice, the city is rioting. It's only a matter of time before the crowds downtown decide that there might be food or resources out here. The Insurrectionists agree— they're coming in early to take the guns. So let's get rolling."

Keyes raised an eyebrow. In his experience changing plans on the fly added to the potential of things going wrong.

CHAPTER 13

═══════════════════════════════════════

Scyllion Warehouse District, Charybdis IX

Civilian Warthogs waited in a line for them on the lower floor of the empty warehouse, as well as three large trucks pulling containers. Hansen had them get in the back of the truck in the middle.

It was full of stacked crates, with just a four-foot empty gap near the doors. Or at least Keyes thought so, until Hansen walked to the wall of crates and pressed her palm against them.

The crates swung aside.

Inside was a fully furnished mobile command center. Screens hung from the walls with information, and ONI agents stood in front of them, murmuring into microphones.

At the back agents in black body armor checked their weapons and eyed Watanabe and Keyes warily.

The ONI mobile command center jerked into motion, and Keyes grabbed a wall.

Hansen pulled a gun out from her waistband and handed it to one of the agents. "We're hoping we can help you out, Watanabe, and get them to give up what system the weapons came from. But I'm pretending to be crew of that ship, so it's dicey. Our main goal is to give these Innie creeps the crates, and then see where in the city they end up. Give them a few days to talk around the crates, give us some intelligence, then we can roll in and bust them. Because the last thing we need are the mobs that are out there right now getting their hands on Covenant weapons."

She walked away from them both to go check on one of the monitors.

Keyes leaned over to Watanabe. "I get the feeling you're not exactly wanted here. They seem to think they've got the whole thing figured out."

Watanabe shrugged dramatically. "Between your crew and these agents, my not being wanted around places seems to be a character failing of mine, I'm sure."

Hansen looked back down the center as Keyes laughed. She waved them over. "Here's an example of the product."

She picked up a hefty Covenant plasma rifle and gave it to Watanabe. Unlike the utilitarian, industrial human weapons, the Covenant device was smooth and aerodynamic, almost organic. The plasma rifle consisted of what looked like two large semi-automatic weapons welded together: one on top, the other beneath. The pair of curved bodies were mated via the trigger guard, and then at the front with a second guard.

"They're not quite right," Keyes said. "What's that on the side?"

From what Keyes knew in briefings, Covenant plasma rifles had a small temperature gauge on the side. This had been replaced with a counter with the numerals "380" glowing on the tiny display. Someone had already tested the weapon.

"Good eye," Hansen said. "Yes, these guns let you know how many shots are left. There is also this."

She reached over and took the bulky weapon back from Watanabe. A quick, firm press near the front of the plasma rifle caused the casing to click, and a tiny targeting reticule popped up.

"What we have here," Hansen said, "is a Covenant weapon that seems modified for human usage. The counter, you'll note, doesn't use any form of Covenant numbering, but rather our own."

The truck ground to a halt.

"The Insurrectionists are already here," someone reported from a monitor.

"Good." Hansen tapped her earpiece. "Everyone knows their places, let's get it done."

She walked out the back with the plasma rifle in hand.

One of the agents at the monitors waved them over. He pulled a stool out from the wall. "We can hear what Captain Hansen there is saying, and see through a buttonhole camera."

Keyes and Watanabe stood by the agent's shoulder. "What's your name, son?" Keyes asked.

The agent glanced back. "Smith, Josh Smith, sir."

"Good to meet you, Smith." On the screen Hansen moved close to a trio of men wearing simple gray coveralls, just like herself. The man in front had a military cut, and scarred cheeks from some sort of explosion, and was whip-thin. "Who are we looking at here?"

Smith tapped another monitor lower down on the wall to reveal a set of files pertaining to the operation. "The man in front, that's Jason Kincaide, a known Insurrectionist. Mid-level sort of guy. The other two are just heavies of his."

Hansen approached Kincaide, and they shook hands. The sting was on.

But in the back of the unit, someone held up a hand. "We're getting reports of disturbances four blocks away. Can someone bring up the live sat imagery?"

One of the larger screens flickered. Keyes walked away from Smith's station and looked at it.

There were thousands of people milling about.

"I can get street cam shots," Smith said. He minimized the video of Hansen and Kincaide meeting each other and exchanging code words, and pulled up a small window showing a street corner.

The rioters had a large battering ram, made from a chopped-down tree. They were smashing in a door to a warehouse while the crowd shouted encouragement.

"This could cause a problem," Watanabe muttered.

"Maybe," Smith said. "We'll see if they keep moving down. Anyone call this in?"

"Yeah, but they're more focused on downtown," came the reply from another agent. "This is a low-priority area."

"If they were a military branch we could have over-ridden that," Smith muttered. "Shit. They're moving at us."

The mood changed inside from operational calm to nervousness. The mob could be seen on several screens as more doors were kicked in or smashed open.

"We're going to have to call it off." Smith tapped another screen. "Hansen, we've got a mob breathing down on us; we're not getting out of here if we delay things. Nod once if you're going to break it off and jet, or twice if you think we should round these jokers up as well."

Hansen straightened, and then nodded twice.

"Go, go, go!" someone shouted from the back.

A ramp dropped from the side of the container and hit the

ground, kicking up dust. The ONI agents leapt out into the warehouse, rifles up and aimed at Kincaide and his men.

Kincaide shook his head, but kept his hands up near his chest. "You sons of—"

One of the agents hit him on the side of the head with the butt of his battle rifle and the Insurrectionist dropped to his knees.

"This won't be the end," Kincaide shouted. "There are more where I came from. We'll find you in your homes, at night, and kill you there. We won't stop until this world is ours, as it rightfully should be."

He got another jab in the head for his shouting. A trickle of blood ran down his temple, and he looked dazed. Within seconds, they had his arms zip-tied behind his back, and the three Insurrectionists were shoved quickly into the trailer.

"Let's *move* it!" Smith yelled at everyone. "They're about a hundred yards up the street."

"You heard the man—pull that ramp back in, let's roll," Hansen shouted. She walked toward Watanabe. "Well, I guess that's that."

"I'm sorry." Watanabe stepped aside to let her stalk back down the center of the trailer. The agents up front pulled the ramp back up and dogged it shut with a loud slam. Engines belched as they started up.

"The damn situation is what's messed up, Watanabe. We're all pulling overtime and doing our duty. It's next to impossible to run ops while the city is falling apart. How are we going to face the Covenant when we don't even have our own crap in gear?"

Keyes grabbed ahold of the back of Smith's chair as the trailer jerked into motion. "They always used to say that if an alien menace threatened humanity, we'd put aside all our differences, band together to face it as one."

Watanabe shook his head sadly. "They were wrong. When you look at wars, even ones where it looks like people were united, there are always factions and jockeying. At the close of the Rain Forest Wars Neo-Friedenists turned against hardliner Friedenists in Delambre when the UNSC got in close. The Neos hated UN control, but they tried to then negotiate for a surrender that left them in some sort of power. You read Elias Carver's work?"

Keyes nodded. "Carver's a pessimist."

"Hundreds of religions. Competing corporate-backed colonies. Political persuasions of every imaginable variety breed in the shadows, and there is a lingering resentment at the UN for trying to keep all the colonies under an Earth government. The colonies, Lieutenant Keyes, are a powder keg. The Covenant advancing on us doesn't make the mixture any less volatile. And the enemy can always try to exploit that, if they have really good intelligence. That's why these guns are worrying. They're a fuse, Keyes."

The ONI convoy drove through the giant warehouse doors.

"I'd give anything to know what factions exist among the Covenant," Keyes said.

"Yeah, but they're aliens, and we can't assume they think or work like us, because so far—" Watanabe started, then turned. Keyes heard it too, a jetlike roaring swoosh.

The front of the command trailer erupted in a fireball. The whole unit lifted off its wheels, and slammed back down to the ground, grinding into the road as it came to a slow stop. Keyes pitched forward, slamming into a chair.

"Get down!" Hansen shouted. "RPGs!"

Fire raged in front of Keyes, licking its way up the walls. A monitor exploded from the heat, shooting glass shards everywhere. He crawled back toward Watanabe, who had pulled his sidearm out and was looking back down at the door leading out.

Someone on the other side of the flames fired a gun three times.

"Was that us or an Innie?" Keyes crawled over to Watanabe.

Another RPG struck the trailer, blowing in the side of the wall. Burning fragments struck Smith, who started screaming as he was enveloped in flames.

Keyes ran forward and threw the man to the floor, getting him to try and roll the fire out. The flames kept him from getting near, and after another second of screaming, the charred Smith finally slowed, whimpered, and died next to the tiny flames he'd started on the carpet.

Watanabe and Hansen hauled Keyes to his feet. Watanabe kicked at a weakened section of the wall that had been melted by the explosion. It caved outward, and they jumped into the street.

A large crowd of rioters watched the burning trailer, not sure what to do next.

PART II

CHAPTER 14

Habitat El Cuidad, Inner Rubble, 23 Librae

The moment Delgado stepped out of the airlock he knew something was wrong. Five very burly men stood waiting for him. Their shaved heads gleamed in the artificial lights of the inner asteroid, and they wore expensive, well-tailored suits. Delgado also noticed the telltale bulges of holsters just underneath their left armpits.

"Ignatio Delgado?" one of them asked.

"Yes, that's me." Delgado stared into the eyes of the nearest heavy. He didn't see any way to get out of this. The five men had covered all degrees of escape. He was hemmed in.

"There's someone that would like to see you."

They led him across the open expanse of hangar and into the back of a roomy, plush, tube car that waited at the lip of the docking tube leading out from the asteroid.

Inside sat a thin, sparse-looking man with jet-black hair and dark green eyes. He set down the computer pad that he had been reading, folded his arms on his lap, and swiveled slightly to regard Delgado.

"Mr. Delgado," he finally said after a long pause, no doubt calculated to make Delgado somewhat uncomfortable. "You would not believe how hard you are to track down."

Delgado blinked. He'd been hard to find because he hadn't been around. The Rubble Security Council had asked him to move the navigation data once more.

"I had sensitive business to take care of," Delgado said. The door to the tube car shut behind him. The tube car moved over and gripped a long sliver of track that led down and away from the hangar asteroid where Delgado had docked the *Distancia*.

"I know that," said the man. "I was one of the members who voted to send you out to secure the navigation data today."

"I'm sorry?" Delgado frowned.

"No, no," the man waved in the air. "Entirely my fault." He reached out a hand.

Delgado reached over and shook it tentatively.

"I am Peter Bonifacio, and I hear you've been asking about me, Mr. Delgado."

Delgado stared into the eyes of the man who, most likely, had caused Melko's death. He bit his lip. "I don't think so. You must be mistaken. I've been far too busy with the Security Council's orders. As you must know."

If Bonifacio, this short, intense-looking man, was really desperate to get his hands on the navigation data, he was hiding it pretty well at the moment, Delgado thought.

Bonifacio lit a cigar. A Sweet William, Delgado realized with a kick in his stomach. "No, it's certainly you, Delgado," Bonifacio said. "Asking all sorts of very interesting questions. So I thought, maybe it's time I asked some questions of *my own.*"

Delgado watched Bonifacio inhale a long drag of the Sweet William, and then let it out into the tiny, cramped interior of the bubble car. A haze of smoke lingered around them.

Bonifacio leaned forward. "What do you know about the Exodus project?"

The tube car moved on past pedestrians floating their way to and from asteroids.

"The what?" Delgado asked.

It felt like Bonifacio was studying every pore on Delgado's face. "What about the Kig-Yar—why are you asking about them?"

Delgado shook his head, pulling back from Bonifacio, offended. "I have my reasons."

"Mmm," Bonifacio grunted. "It's a strange coincidence that the Kig-Yar attacked a place that only the nine Council members knew about . . . and you."

"You're accusing me of selling that information?" Delgado leaned back in. "I was *shot* protecting the data. My copilot *was killed.* How dare you suggest I gave anything to them?"

Bonifacio looked out the window at the depths of space passing them by. Ahead, the tube pierced the center of another asteroid habitat. They passed into the heart of it, curved green farmland stretching up on all sides around them.

"We are all innocent until proven guilty, of course, Mr. Delgado," he said. "But in your case, this is such a sensitive matter that a few Council members and I have decided that for the safety of the Rubble, you will have to be detained while we investigate certain concerns regarding your loyalties."

Delgado clenched a fist. "My loyalties are to the Rubble."

Bonifacio chuckled. "Oh, I'm sure you're just a living, breathing patriot. So I've heard. But the Council would like to hand over security of the data to me now.

"So where is it, Delgado?"

"Lodged deep, deep up your ass, Bonifacio." Delgado grinned.

Bonifacio's face steeled. "There was no call for that," he said.

Delgado shrugged and leaned back in the chair. "If we're playing games, I might as well have some fun too," he said.

Bonifacio quickly hauled back and punched him in the stomach, not even an inch away from a still-healing plasma wound. Delgado felt like he'd been stabbed, and the pain doubled him over.

"It's such a shame," Bonifacio hissed. "We started off on a nice foot, and then you had to go do that."

"You're such a charmer," Delgado grunted, holding onto his stomach and leaning against the seat in front of him. "You like this on all your first dates?"

"You're in a lot of trouble," Bonifacio said. "Because as of this moment, you're under arrest for suspicion of leaking the location of the navigation data."

"The Council will not stand for that," Delgado said. "They all worked hard with me to keep that data safe when we realized it was being destroyed."

"For all we know you could be part of some conspiracy to destroy the data. You and your friend Diego. Who incidentally, did most of the exhorting us to 'trust' you." The tube car slowed, and Bonifacio leaned back. "And the Council signed the warrant." Bonifacio pulled up his pad.

Delgado looked down at it. Then back up. "How?"

"A nice benefit of being a trusted, elected Security Council member. Now, I want the location of that navigation data, Delgado."

"And how long will you be able to get away with this? Eventually the Council will realize it's not a normal arrest when I don't actually show up in a proper holding facility, Bonifacio."

The smuggler sighed. "True, but we have enough time for what I need."

"Until the *Kestrel* gets in?" Delgado ventured.

Bonifacio quirked a small smile. "And to keep you from spreading that damn name around."

"It's coming in from Charybdis IX, right?" Delgado said, trying to prod more information out of the man. "I hear the UNSC Navy is sewing everything up, so it's obviously a last-hurrah smuggle. A ship full of luxuries that soon people will pay a premium for . . . and then you no longer need the navigation data. Right?"

Bonifacio said nothing, but looked out the window.

Delgado nodded. The silence said a lot. "So you'll sell us out to the Kig-Yar? Give them the data?" Delgado growled.

"Are you some weepy Earth sympathizer?" Bonifacio snapped, suddenly irritated. "Because you seem really hung up on this idea that I'm trying to steal the data to sell it to the Kig-Yar. Even if I am, who the hell cares what happens to Earth? They could care less about us."

Delgado shook his head. Bonifacio hadn't come straight out and admitted anything yet, but at least he was getting chatty. He pressed the issue some more. "The Kig-Yar will attack the moment we sell that data. They're just here to scavenge it."

Bonifacio shook his head. "That's where you're wrong. They're risking a lot to be here, to help us build these asteroids. And they will reward us. They think of this as home just as much as we do."

"How do you think they will reward us?"

Bonifacio smiled. "Don't you worry yourself about that right now." Delgado gritted his teeth. The smuggler had now all but admitted he was working with the Kig-Yar. That he was the leak in the Council.

The tube car slowed near an industrial looking section of the asteroid, where metals were being processed from the raw slag forwarded by other mining companies still operating in the outskirts of the Rubble.

They stopped in front of a large warehouse half dug into the ground. Bonifacio leaned forward as one of his men snapped a pair of handcuffs on Delgado. "Welcome to your new home for the next few days."

CHAPTER 15

Keyes stared at the faces of the rioters, reading the rage and the desperation of the crowd's mood. So far they were just watching the ONI survivors. The trucks and trailers the ONI team and Keyes crawled out of lay broken across the road, burning from the RPG hits. The asphalt had melted underneath them in some places, and the warehouse windows reflected the dancing flames.

"Behind us." Hansen whirled around and shot at the corner of the burning trailer. Someone ducked back behind it.

"We need to get out," Watanabe told Keyes.

The crowd muttered, and triumphant shouts increased in the distance as several of them dragged an ONI agent out from the remains of a trailer. The man struggled, but the ten people holding him were too strong.

They shoved him to the ground and started kicking him. They could hear his screams.

"Can't we do anything?" Keyes asked.

"It's just the three of us, and hundreds of them over there," Hansen said. "I can't even get a shot clear, there're too many of them."

"Damn it." Keyes turned so that he could glance back and forth between the crowd and the trailer. "Pelican 019, this is Lieutenant Keyes." He pulled his side arm out of the holster, but didn't point it in either direction, just kept it at his side.

"I take it you're ONI?" The Insurrectionist on the other side of the trailer yelled at them. It sounded like Kincaide. "You think you're so smart, sneaking around. But we have you now! We'll beat you down like your friend over there."

The screams from the ONI agent had stopped. The crowd moved away from the limp, broken body. Keyes felt sick, then nervous as the mob screamed in his direction.

Hansen dropped a magazine out of her gun. It hit the asphalt at the same time as a new one clicked home. She didn't respond to Kincaide's rants.

"Jeffries here, sir," crackled the voice in Keyes's earpiece.

"Can you get a read on my location?" Keyes tried to keep his voice calm. Something about the pent up rage of the crowd unnerved him.

"Yessir."

Hansen pointed at a nearby door to another warehouse. They backed over to it.

Keyes held his hand up to his ear. "Get ready for a hot pickup. We're coming up to the roof. Got a mob after us, and we lost the Insurrectionists we were after. They were using RPGs on us, so come in fast and low and keep your eyes open."

An Insurrectionist peered around the corner, and ducked back again as Watanabe fired at him. "These are company agents," Kincaide shouted into the air. "Any one of you grab them I'll give you weapons. Free guns."

A pair of rioters heard that and ran down the street at the trio. Watanabe and Hansen shot in unison, and the two men pitched forward into the road.

Hansen turned around and shot the doorknob several times, then kicked the door in. "Inside."

They moved in, Watanabe and Hansen staying by the door as Keyes looked around for a way up. A few more gunshots cracked out—they convinced the mob to stay back. Meanwhile, Kincaide was screaming at the mob to attack.

Still, even rioters didn't want to charge head on into gunfire. Keyes could see that through the shattered windows of the door. They were holding back as the two ONI agents shot just above their heads.

Looking the other way, Keyes spotted a service elevator.

"Sir, I'm a minute away," Jeffries called in. "Get to the rooftop."

"To the roof," Keyes shouted.

They ran to the elevator, pulling the cage shut. It lurched up, just as the door they'd come through shattered, rioters pouring through, Kincaide with them.

He raised a Covenant plasma rifle, and as the elevator rose to the next floor, a burst of plasma hit the elevator doors beneath them, blowing them out into the shaft.

Smoke rose up with them as they climbed toward the top floor.

The elevator lurched to a halt, and once the doors opened Hansen shot the control panel several times. The foyer led to a doorway out onto the roof, and past the stairs leading down the warehouse's floors.

They could hear murmuring and footsteps farther down the stairwell as they passed it to kick open the door.

As Keyes ran onto the flat roof, he saw the running lights of the approaching Pelican wink off. The craft swooped by, blinding them with a sudden glare of a spotlight that then shut off almost as quickly as it had been flicked on.

"That you coming out on the roof, sir?" Jeffries asked.

"Better believe it," Keyes grunted, sprinting away from the stairwell.

"Coming back around for the land, deploying the ramp," Jeffries reported.

The Pelican banked and disappeared off into the night. Then it appeared again. Jeffries was throwing it full speed right toward the top of the building, skimming just over the rooftops in a near suicidal dash.

Keyes had to admire the skill.

From the street level the bright flash of a rocket launch lit up an alleyway and a rocket streaked for the Pelican.

"RPG!" Keyes shouted, but Jeffries had already kicked the tail of the Pelican out, crabbing it around in midair to face the rocket and present a smaller profile.

The rocket streaked by, missing but bathing the Pelican in an eerie orange light.

A second rocket flashed and leapt up from underneath the Pelican. It slammed into the belly of the craft, gutting it. Debris rained down out of the Pelican, and a second explosion inside rippled throughout the craft's body.

It hung in the air, engines wailing, but not moving.

The third rocket slammed into its tail, and the Pelican dropped out of the air into the street below, sinking from eye level in an inferno of boiling metal and parts.

Keyes threw himself at the ledge of the building, firing his sidearm into the street, but the Insurrectionists had already melted back into the shadows.

The flaming wreckage burned itself against the back of Keyes's eyes as he waited for some movement, any movement, near the ruins of the Pelican.

"Lieutenant." Watanabe grabbed him and yanked him back from the edge.

Chips of concrete stung Keyes in the face as gunfire hit the lip of the building. Watanabe locked his eyes. Keyes stood in front of Watanabe, frozen, as Watanabe grabbed him by the face to look right at him. "There's nothing you could have done, Keyes."

Keyes numbly ejected the spent magazine from his sidearm and slid in another. "I'm the one who transferred him aboard the *Midsummer Night*."

"He was a good soldier and a good man. Jefferson flew hard, and now he's down and we need to focus."

Keyes stared at the ONI spook. Jefferson? What the hell was that? Watanabe was supposed to be a man of details, observant. But Jeffries hadn't rated his attention, apparently. But then, that was a spook versus enlisted. They didn't care about the man standing next to you. They had their own agendas.

"Keyes, you listening? Can you raise the ship?"

"I can try," Keyes said.

By the stairwell Hansen fired three shots, and someone screamed.

Keyes moved away from the lip of the wall and closed his eyes. He flipped frequencies on the earpiece, and then looked up at the stars in the night sky. One of them was the *Midsummer Night*, parked in geosynchronous orbit. It hung directly over the city.

"*Midsummer Night*, this is Keyes." He waited a moment, then repeated it.

A response came through, crackly and faded. "Keyes, this is Kirtley. Glad to hear your voice. What's your situation?"

"Pinned on a roof," Keyes reported. "Jeffries was hit by RPG fire; the Pelican is down. We've got Insurrectionists and a mob ready to tear our throats out."

"Listen, hold tight," Kirtley said. "There are ODSTs on their way."

"They won't get here in time," Keyes said.

"Major Faison had it out with the captain, said you guys needed boots on the ground for support if a mob was moving in. They left early, before you called Jeffries. You need to hold out twenty minutes. Copy that? Twenty minutes?"

Twenty minutes. Might as well have been an eternity.

But it was a chance. "Tell them to space out and watch out for rockets," Keyes said.

"Will do. Good luck, Lieutenant."

Keyes ran over to Watanabe and Hansen. "ODSTs are on their way. Twenty minutes."

Watanabe and Hansen glanced at each other. Watanabe held up his side arm. "Last mag."

"Same here. Keyes?"

"I'm on my last mag too."

The three of them looked down the empty stairwell.

"Twenty minutes, huh?" Hansen said.

"Twenty," Keyes repeated.

"Well, I'm game to try it," the ONI agent said, and steadied herself against the wall for a better shot.

CHAPTER 16

Scyllion Warehouse District, Charybdis IX

"They're not trying to push up the stairs hard enough," Hansen said, ten minutes later.

So far Keyes had only fired warning shots. The rioters would peek around a corner and fire off a round, and he would too, and then there would be silence until the next rioter nerved up enough to try doing the same thing.

"She's right." Watanabe stepped forward, trying to look down the stairwell. He jerked back as someone fired a shot.

Plasma exploded against the walls of the foyer.

"They've got the Covenant weapons now." Hansen shuffled back from the doorway.

"So why aren't they rushing us?" Keyes asked. He scanned the rooftop. "They're up to *something*."

Hansen pulled a wicked-looking knife out of her boot and put it on the ground. "Keyes, go left, Watanabe, right. Just start

— 129 —

checking the edges. Don't pop your head over, just listen for anything. I'll hold this point."

Keyes and Watanabe took off at a crouch for the edge of the roof. Keyes skirted it, slowly moving against the concrete lip. The edge came up to his head.

On the other side of the building, he could see Watanabe doing the same.

Keyes made his way down one whole side of the building. His thighs burned from the awkward waddling by the end, and he paused to stretch them out.

Watanabe had stopped as well.

But he wasn't stretching his legs. He had his gun out.

Three men leapt over the lip near Watanabe, with Kincaide vaulting the edge just behind them. The ONI agent charged them from the side, shooting down the first man, then the second.

Keyes couldn't risk firing, he'd just as likely hit Watanabe at this distance, so he sprinted at the group.

Kincaide used the third man, a rioter, as a shield. He shoved the surprised civilian into Watanabe, then shot them both several times with a plasma rifle. Keyes felt sick as he watched Watanabe fall. The man may have been ONI, but he was crew and a fellow soldier, and Keyes realized he was screaming.

Keyes had his pistol up without a second thought. As Kincaide seemed to turn in slow motion, Keyes pulled the trigger.

He'd been aiming for the chest, but the first shot hit Kincaide in the shoulder. It spun the Insurrectionist back, and he struggled to bring the heavy plasma rifle back up to aim at Keyes.

Keyes shot him in the chest, then stomach, grazed his side, and then ran out of ammunition. He slammed into Kincaide, grappling for the alien rifle.

"Damn . . . UNSC . . . pig," Kincaide spat, still trying to force the rifle up into Keyes's ribs. "Go back to Earth. You don't belong here."

The memory of the explosions in the cargo bay of *Finnegan's Wake*, the flaming Pelican Jeffries piloted going down, wounded ODSTs gritting their teeth and bearing the pain as they waited for help, all filled Keyes's mind. He grunted and kept forcing the plasma rifle down until it was aimed at Kincaide's feet.

He pulled the trigger, and a burst of white-hot plasma destroyed the Insurrectionist's leg and threw Keyes back, still holding onto the rifle.

Concrete bubbled where they'd stood, and Keyes felt the legs of his uniform burning. He patted the fires out quickly, and looked back at Kincaide.

The man had lost his left leg, blown clean off at the thigh. He'd been shot in the shoulder and chest.

Yet he now had a small pistol in his right hand, lifting it up to point it at Keyes with determination in his glazed eyes.

Without hesitation, Keyes blew the Insurrectionist's head off his body with a burst of plasma.

His hands shook. He'd never shot a man before. He'd shot at people, fired warning shots, practiced in drills, but never actually looked at someone in the eyes who was about to kill him, and beat him to the draw.

Watanabe groaned, and Keyes crawled over to him. The plasma rifle had ripped through the ONI agent's left torso, leaving a crisped mess.

Keyes gagged at the smell.

"This is bad," Watanabe muttered.

"Don't move," Keyes told him. "Stay still, don't close your eyes."

"It hurts."

Keyes bit his lip. "Just hang in there, Akio. They're on their way. We just need to hang in there."

Hansen fired three shots at someone in the stairway trying their luck. Watanabe grabbed Keyes's forearm and grimaced, then let go.

Keyes looked down at the limp, dead body of Major Akio Watanabe.

He stood up and grabbed Jason Kincaide's headless corpse, dragged it to the lip, and shoved it over. He heard the distant thump, and a crowd of people shout in surprise.

Keyes walked to the ledge and looked down. A fire truck had been commandeered, the ladder pushed up to the roof. Several hundred rioters milled below, many with plasma rifles.

"Listen up!" Keyes held up his newly acquired plasma rifle as he shouted. "Anyone else tries storming the roof, I'll blow their damn heads off too."

He fired the plasma rifle twice into the base of the ladder, and watched with satisfaction as metal slumped and the ladder slid off the side of the building, falling over toward the crowd.

Rioters scattered as it struck the street in their midst.

"Now," Keyes snapped the word out, in full drill sergeant cadence. He may as well have been talking to a crowd of new recruits. "UNSC marines are about to arrive any second. If I were you, I wouldn't want to be standing around here in plain sight, lest they get the mistaken impression you're *hostile*, and act accordingly."

Keyes turned around and walked away from the edge.

"Look," Hansen said, pointing up.

Stars in the sky grew larger, twinkling brighter and brighter, until they could be seen streaking toward the building.

"The cavalry has arrived," Keyes said.

CHAPTER 17

Scyllion Warehouse District, Charybdis IX

Twenty single occupant exoatmospheric insertion vehicle pods came in high, ripping through the atmosphere, still glowing hot from reentry. Parachutes popped, enough to slow the human-sized capsules down a bit. Then at the last second rockets flared, lighting up the night sky in flames and thunder as all the SOEIV pods slammed into the reinforced structure of the roof.

Concrete dust hung in the air, and chips off the roof clattered down as the pods split open and ODSTs leapt out with their battle rifles drawn.

From the corner of the roof, in a pod that leaned precariously near the edge, one ODST hopped out. The SOEIV shook, and then fell off the edge onto the street below.

The Helljumper pulled his helmet off. It was Faison. "Miss us much?"

Keyes pointed at Watanabe, and Faison paused. "Damn. Didn't like the spook, but still . . ." He pointed at two ODSTs and detailed them to wrap up Watanabe's body. Keyes looked away and swallowed the lump in his throat. He'd seen too much death for one day.

"They're firing RPGs around. It's probably too risky for Pelicans," Keyes said. "They took Jeffries out."

"We heard about them coming in," Faison said. He looked around. "But don't worry, we've got it in hand, Lieutenant. You saved our asses back on the *Finnegan's Wake*, now it's time for us to even up."

"I don't want to see anyone else die down here," Keyes said.

"Magnus! Jeremy!" Faison shouted. A pair of very tall and bulky Helljumpers ran over. "Grab four spotters, get your gear in place where you two can do your thing. Start marking targets. But stay in the shadows."

"Yes, sir."

"And someone," Faison said into his mic, still hanging from his ear, "please start tossing grenades down that stairwell." The mob had retreated when Keyes threw the body of Kincaide over the wall, but there were gunshots coming from the corridor and the street as the mob worked itself back up.

Two svelte ODST shadows meandered over to the side of the doors and skipped grenades down the foyer and into the stairwell.

"Fire in the hole," one shouted, just before a fireball gushed out the door.

There were screams from the depths of the warehouse.

Keyes switched frequencies to the marine's open chatter. He could hear the spotters with their night vision and thermal gear muttering. "See the one out by that window?"

"Yep, marked him."

."Okay, I got one on top of the building. North-north-west. Near the water tower."

"Sneaky. Yeah."

Keyes followed Faison over to an edge, where he held his helmet over the lip for a second, then pulled it back over and reviewed the cam footage.

"Look at that," Faison said. "All this excitement scared off the rioters. So, anyone left is an Innie."

"Perimeter secure," a Helljumper reported. "They're not shooting at us yet."

"Okay," Faison said. "Bring on the decoy and let's play find-the-RPG-launchers."

A Pelican with its running lights on came in slowly, passing them overhead, and swooping around. "Take out your targets," Faison said.

The two snipers, Magnus and Jeremy, were the focus now.

Crack. The sound of an SRS 99 carried over the rooftop. "Got Mr. Window." The pair of snipers had crawled onto the top of the small structure above the foyer, a building on a building. It gave them unobstructed line of sight to the surrounding streets and buildings.

"Mr. Water Tower is . . . clear of the lattice . . ." *Crack.* "And he's most definitely not going out to party tonight."

"Moving location." One of them jumped off and sprinted across the rooftop, the long barrel of the sniper rifle bobbing. He set up on the corner of the building, the edge of the gun resting on the concrete lip.

"While you're huffing about, Mr. Street Corner is sighting on the Pelican . . ." *Crack.* "And down."

Crack. "That's the last one."

Faison made a circling motion with his hand. "That's how we do it, gentlemen. Bring the other Pelicans in."

Two Pelicans descended out of the clouds and came in hard, slamming onto the roof. Hansen and Keyes ran up the ramps and buckled in; the Helljumpers followed.

The Pelicans dusted off, engines screaming as they zigzagged their way out of the neighborhood. An occasional zap of plasma-rifle fire rang in the distance.

As the ramp shut, Faison staggered his way forward to Keyes and handed him him a cigar.

Keyes eyed the flaked exterior. "A Sweet William?"

"Nothing but the best, sir. A victory smoke."

"A victory smoke?" Keyes looked over at Watanabe's body. "We lost two of our own down there. Those rioters have *Covenant* weapons, now."

"Sir, any day you come back from a mission alive, it's a victory." The Helljumper grinned. They were a different breed of soldier, Keyes had to keep reminding himself. They had to be. Packing yourself into a heatshield pod, braving the flames of reentry over a planet, and parachuting down into the middle of action, surrounded . . . that was a bit above the call of duty for a normal marine.

Keyes handed Faison back the cigar. "I don't smoke. It's against regulations."

"Sir, I've seen you standing with a pipe, in the chart room, looking over maps."

His grandfather's pipe. It was an heirloom, and Keyes kept it on him. It comforted him to have it in hand. An old habit. "And I don't smoke it. But tell you what, marine, when I see a victory, I'll smoke one with you. This wasn't a victory, it was a cluster—"

"It wasn't a complete loss," Hansen said. She stood at the center of the Pelican, balancing as the craft shook and shuddered its way higher and higher. "The reason Kincaide was so set on eliminating us was that he realized he made a mistake. He told me the name of the next ship making a smuggling run while he was trying to bid up the price of the weapons. Said he'd done business with them."

"And the name of the ship?"

"The *Kestrel*. These Covenant weapons, they're a problem, Keyes. We need to figure out why the Covenant's doing this. And we damn well need to stop it."

"Hoo-ah," one of the Helljumpers agreed.

Keyes folded his arms. The *Kestrel*.

They'd hunt it to the edge of the galaxy if necessary, as far as Keyes was concerned. Someone was going to have to pay for all the deaths on his watch.

"Sir," the pilot of the Pelican shouted back into the hold. "Sir, the *Midsummer Night*'s hailing us."

The pilot's voice had cracked slightly.

Fear.

Keyes walked calmly up behind the woman's chair, even though he could feel the kick in his stomach.

The pilot's helmet twisted back. It had the name Carson stenciled on it. The Pelican bucked a bit as it passed over clouds, still gaining altitude. The craft was pitched up, aiming for the black of space. "The sensor stations at the edge of the system think something's coming in. Something big," she said.

"Covenant?" Keyes asked.

"Know of any other fleets planning to wing by this place?" Carson returned to getting them to orbit, and Keyes stumbled back down the steep angle.

"Are there any Navy ships scheduled to arrive?" he asked Hansen.

She shook her head. "Cole is still out near Harvest. Mawikizi's main fleet is spread out around Ectanus. There are three destroyers picketing—"

"The *Night*'s main attribute is her stealth," Keyes said, his mind rapidly running through some rudimentary plans on how three Destroyers and the *Midsummer Night* could face this Covenant fleet. So far only Admiral Cole and his battle group had ever scored a meaningful victory against the Covenant. And it was a loose secret within the Navy that Cole had thrown three ships against the Covenant forces for every ship of theirs he destroyed. *Midsummer Night* and the three other frigates would be facing long odds. "If it's Covenant, we'll have to utilize that stealth for a defense."

With stealth, and the single MAC gun aboard the *Night*, a series of hit-and-runs could perhaps harass the Covenant into chasing them, and lure them into a situation where the three Destroyers would only face one or two Covenant ships.

Hansen shook her head. "If the Covenant are coming for Charybdis, your one frigate will make no difference. Keyes, it's vital you follow up on the *Kestrel,* find out what the Covenant are really up to. It's what your ship was designed for. We can't waste it on a last stand."

"But—"

"It wouldn't be a wise use of resources." Hansen bit her lip. "And the UNSC, every day, has fewer and fewer resources to spare, Keyes. We've been fighting the Covenant now for almost a decade. As of now, we've pretty much lost all the Outer Colonies. You need to find out what is going on. You need to go after the *Kestrel.* Before the Covenant get all the way in-system and trap you."

It didn't sit well with Keyes, abandoning people to a doomed defense. He stood next to the ONI agent in silence as the Pelican broke free of the atmosphere.

"After you drop me off at the orbital depot, tell Zheng to get clear. I'll transmit the orders. You'll find that I outrank you both."

"Yes, ma'am," Keyes said.

Hansen sighed. "And when you find your real victory, Lieutenant, make sure you smoke one of those Sweet Williams for me."

"We're coming in!" Carson announced from the cockpit. "And fast. Captain Zheng wants us back on board ASAP."

Through the cockpit windows the long spars of a Navy orbital depot slowly rotated. Carson twitched the Pelican until it slammed against one of the spokes.

As the back opened, Keyes stood straight and saluted. The ODSTs inside followed his example, not sure what was going on.

Hansen saluted back, and then left the Pelican.

"Okay," Carson shouted. "Hang on!"

CHAPTER 18

═══════════════════════════════

Thel 'Vadamee burst through a corridor at a full run and aimed a plasma rifle down its length. Nothing.

There had to be more humans aboard this destroyer than the pitiful few who'd tried to hold off the boarding party. The angular ship with its sharp corners and boxy layout reeked of a larger contingent of humans.

The Sangheili did not reholster his gun. A drawn weapon demanded blood, and one didn't draw a weapon in Sangheili culture unless you intended to use it, even if it was just a gun. So now it would remain out in his hand.

Thel crossed another bulkhead and turned to his right. There it was, that scent again: a pungent smell. The humans. They must have retreated to a core area, deep inside the ship.

Throughout this system his fellow Sangheili hunted down human ships to destroy them, and the flagships of the fleet would now be raining the full strength of their energy weapons down on the surface of the planet. It was sterilization. A mandate for destruction handed down by the leaders of the Covenant, the three High Prophets.

But Thel and his handpicked team were off on a side mission.

To his right a team of zealots padded along with him, keeping a full 360 degree path of fire at the ready in case of an ambush. Their long, leathery necks craned around, their eaglelike eyes scanning the awkward nooks and crannies of the human ship for the enemy.

"Cowards," Jora 'Konaree hissed. Jora was one whose blood always ran hot, always ready for the fight and eager to rush a position. He sounded disappointed and frustrated to not have a direct fight to engage in. "They flee in front of us like panicked forest creatures before the flame."

An apt metaphor, thought Thel, considering that Covenant ships rained fire down on the human worlds. "Be cautious," Thel warned. "They are small creatures, but they are not unaware of their disadvantages."

The humans would ambush them, soon enough, in some sort of last stand. He'd heard a few rumors from other Sangheili who'd boarded human ships looking for information that they would fight hard, almost honorably.

Or, at least, Thel hoped so. Hunting them down like vermin would be . . . demeaning to everyone involved.

From past dissections of human ships of this class, they knew the control center would be close to the front of the ship. A daring and brash position that Thel appreciated.

They broke through the doors by tossing a sticky grenade at the seam. The grenade thudded into the gap and stuck in place. It glowed a sickly blue, then exploded. "Forward," Jora shouted.

The other three zealots—Zhar, Saal, and Veer—followed Jora and Thel through the ruined remains of the doors. Zhar, careful but constant and steady; Veer, a bored expression on his face but eyes darting everywhere, looking for details and oddities for his war poems; and Saal, like Jora, looking for anything to kill.

They were Thel's own small force, a band of fighters that had seen many enemies fall at their feet.

Jora rushed through the room. "They abandoned their own command center," he growled. Then he leaned over the alien computer consoles and tapped at them. The only response was sparking and fizzing: the consoles had been shot up before the humans abandoned them. "Useless!"

He unsheathed his energy sword and fired it up in frustration. The two crackling, curved blue flames of energy rose up on either side of the hand holding the bar. Jora plunged it into the heart of the machine, sparks flying and metal oozing out around where the sword pierced it.

The screens above flickered and faded.

Jora pulled the sword out and cut the whole console in half, the energy sword cleaving it cleanly down the middle. "Savages with starships and toy weapons, Shipmaster," he hissed at Thel, who watched the display of anger without any emotion.

The barking chatter of human gunfire ripped through the cockpit, and Jora's armor flared. "Blood," the zealot swore, as he ducked for cover.

Zhar calmly turned and lobbed grenades down the corridor.

"So they finally attack." Jora's mandibles split open as he roared a challenge down the corridor.

Thel, though, already ran down the corridor at the attack. The humans had cornered them here. A smart move. Thel leapt through the smoke and chaos of the explosion, his armor dinged, nicked, and its energy shield flaring due to human bullets. He shot the first human he saw as he landed back on the deck.

The second human, flush against the wall, spun to bring his rifle to bear. Thel was too close to shoot him: he snapped the butt of the energy rifle into the short alien's face and watched it slump to the floor.

Weak, very weak. The human's insubstantial armor of olive clothing did little to protect it.

Jora barreled through, sword high, and cut the third marine in half, but not before the man got off several shots, near point blank. Jora stumbled, and clutched at his armor.

Thel threw grenades around the corner, angry. Jora might act a little crazed, but he was a hard fighter. Thel did not want to lose him. Thel waited for the explosion to dissipate, then rounded the corner, firing at anything that moved.

Within seconds Thel and his boarding crew stood in the odd crimson pools of human blood. Twenty men lay dead in the corridor, their bodies twisted, contorted, missing parts, or just plain destroyed.

"There is nothing here for us," Thel relayed back to the *Retribution's Thunder*. "We are returning."

A shame, thought Thel. The humans had thwarted their mission to find data about their homeworld by destroying their computer systems before he'd even boarded.

Twenty Unggoy filled the large, open space of the hangar bay. The Unggoy, like the humans, were short, bred too fast, and were individually weak. The Unggoy, however, wore triangular methane tanks and breathing masks over their flattened, squashed faces. Thel found them useless for intense fighting, but in large enough numbers they were very effective, so he'd left them to guard the boarding craft.

The Unggoy were a part of the Covenant, and thus were to be used in the war against the apostate humans. But that didn't mean Thel had to go out of his way to include them in the heart of his missions.

As they jumped up into the long, pipelike snout of a boarding craft, Jora groaned. Thel and the others pretended not to hear.

"Back on board," Thel ordered the Covenant forces in the hangar.

The Unggoy grumbled about being moved about randomly, and about being forced to wear their heavy tanks and their itchy masks, but did as they were told. They streamed back up into the mouth of the boarding craft, stepping past their fallen brothers who had died as the humans tried to defend the ship.

The boarding craft yanked away from the gash it had made in the side of the destroyer, shields flaring as it did so. Thel watched as the bulky, blocky destroyer fell away from them.

Streaks of carbon ran along the side where they had fired at the human ship. Most of the damage clustered near the ship's engines.

"It is strange," Jora grunted. Everywhere the hiss and occasional wispy stink of methane filled the air in the boarding craft due to the lines of Unggoy staring straight ahead, trying not to be noticed by any of the five Sangheili.

"What is?" Thel asked as the destroyer dwindled into the size of an eyeball. He nodded at Saal, who murmured into a mouthpiece.

"The Prophets have demanded we destroy their ships, burn their worlds, and allow no heretic to live." Jora held his side, and Thel noticed a trickle of purple blood seep through his fingers. "Now we search for information and sneak aboard their ships?"

"The Path is strict, Jora—it brooks no deviation, no remorse. We are zealots. We serve the Way. These are our orders. We do not question them." Thel saw the tiny destroyer suddenly light up as a long sliver of a plasma beam ripped into it. It exploded, chunks flying off in all directions, superstructure glowing hot and failing.

"You do not wonder why our orders changed, Shipmaster?" Jora asked.

Zhar, from nearby, looked up. "The Prophets, in their infinite wisdom, want to shorten this war. Maybe the Hierarchs did not realize these vermin were spread out in so many different places, like some weed. Now they urge us to seek the source."

"You think we have failed to find their homeworld?" Thel asked.

"We keep finding more and more developed worlds to destroy," said Zhar. "Like the one we just visited. What was it the human Saal tortured called it?"

"Charybdis . . ." Thel said. "The aliens called it Charybdis." His split mandibles struggled with the word. It was an afront for lesser species to name an entire world. That was a right reserved for the powerful.

Saal ran to them, his eyes wide with astonishment. "Shipmaster! Encrypted signal from *Infinite Sacrifice*!"

Thel walked with him to a communications niche. A holographic image turned, startling the Sangheili zealot. *Speak of the Prophets*! Here one was. One of the Hierarchs themselves.

The image was of a tired, ochre-skinned, and hunchbacked creature slouched over a floating antigravity chair, its head bowed with the weight of an enormous gold crown its long neck could barely support. "Thel 'Vadamee," it hissed. "You are to report to me aboard the ship *Infinite Sacrifice*. I have studied your intrusion attempts aboard the human ships. I have a new mission for you."

The Hierarch leaned forward, and the image flickered away.

Thel turned to Saal. "That was the Prophet of Regret. He has been following the fleet, observing the destruction of this latest human world. He has a new mission."

"What is it?" Jora looked a bit awed by the thought a Hierarch had noticed them.

"I do not know, but whatever it is, I am sure it will bring us honor," Thel said. He looked at Jora's purpled hand. The zealot would need medical attention soon, probably from one of the Huragok. That Covenant species was obsessed with fixing anything. Yet even letting a Huragok work on you was a grave dishonor. It was the same as letting a *doctor* put his filthy claws on you. Thel sighed. Blood was your essence, your nobility. To spill it meant to lose honor, and Jora had lost honor with his eagerness and carelessness. Now he would have to let a doctor—a Sangheili warrior so low as to make his living slicing and causing other Sangheili to bleed without honor—tend to his wounds. That was a deep shame.

Jora would be eager to prove himself again after this slip.

Thel looked back at the glowing remains of the human destroyer. It would be an honor to help find the world the pink, fleshy humans came from.

And to reduce it to nothingness.

CHAPTER 19

Covenant Cruiser *Infinite Sacrifice*, Charybdis IX

The Prophet of Regret hunched forward, head bowed with the weight of his crown. The wrinkled wattle of his throat shook as he looked around the room at the many holographic screens that flickered in the control room buried deep in the heart of the *Infinite Sacrifice*. An honor guard of Sangheili surrounded the Hierarch, ready to kill anything that moved to attack the hierarch.

Thel was surprised to see the Hierarch himself here, but Regret had always seemed to spend as much time as possible around Sangheili warriors.

Regret admired the Sangheili martial prowess, rumors said. While most of the San'Shyuum floated about the holy city of High Charity and focused on their lives, Regret traveled with Sangheili battle fleets to see them in action.

It was rumored that the Hierarch carried a sidearm of his own underneath the silk robes draped over his lap, and had killed acolytes who dared ask too many questions on the spot.

One of the Minister's honor guard, a distant cousin with obligations to Thel's bloodline, had told Thel that the Prophet of Regret had come to his throne through machinations.

That may have been true. Thel had his doubts—everyone was prone to gossip. And so what if it were true? The Sangheili were sent forth into battle by the mixed Council of Masters, a group of Sangheili and San'Shyuum masters who dictated war needs. But most of the fighting was done by Sangheili as the San'Shyuum remained on High Charity, the mobile world and heart of the Covenant. That was the nature of the Covenant itself—the Sangheili defended the Prophets, defended the holy objects. Meanwhile the Prophets deciphered the holy relics, doling out the technology they found and adapting them for Covenant use. Their eventual hope was to unlock what the races would need to do to join the Great Journey. Much like the mysterious race of the Forerunners had done all those thousands of years ago when they disappeared from this area of the galaxy, leaving only their artifacts behind. It didn't matter to Thel how the Prophet of Regret came to be one of the three hierarchs, because Regret was here, monitoring the fleet and talking to him.

Regret nudged the floating chair he sat in closer to a grand conference table that swooped up from the floor. He threw a plasma rifle onto the table in front of Thel. "Pick that up," he ordered.

Thel froze. If he picked up the rifle, he would have an unholstered weapon out in the presence of a Prophet. The honor guard would be obliged to kill him.

Was this some way of punishing him for failing to find data leading to the human homeworld aboard the destroyer? Thel met the honor guard's captain with large, brown eyes. The Sangheili shook his head in a snaking motion. It was okay.

Thel picked up the plasma rifle. "What would you like me to do?"

"Look closely at it," Regret said, sounding suddenly annoyed. "What do you see?"

For a moment, Thel saw nothing. It was just a normal plasma rifle. Then he spotted the small readout on the side. It scribed an alien symbol at him. Human script.

"You see it, do you not?" the Hierarch said, looking intensely at him.

"What is this?" Thel dropped the rifle back on the table, feeling unclean. It was forbidden to alter the technologies that the Prophets handed down. They were the holiest of gifts.

"It is blasphemy. Heretical human creatures touching and altering the holy gifts of Forerunner artifacts like our energy weapons . . . or anything else," hissed the Hierarch. It navigated the floating chair around the table and pointed a hand and jointed finger right at Thel. "And I want you to find who is responsible for it. Find them out and destroy them. They have been found in Kig-Yar black markets on High Charity. Supposedly they come from a system the humans call 23 Librae, by way of Kig-Yar–run ships. One of my loyal deacons aboard a ship of theirs died transmitting this data to me. Ungrateful pirates."

The Hierarch's voice had risen to a scream, even as Thel listened. He remembered 23 Librae, he had fought there, on a world the heretical creatures called "Madrigal."

Thel dropped to a knee and fist in a bow before the Hierarch. "Your will be done, Hierarch."

Regret cleared his throat noisily; large fishy eyes gleaming as he stared at Thel. "Of course you will, my Sangheili warrior. Of course you will. That is why I asked you here. You will leave while we continue destroying Charybdis IX and go to 23 Librae to hunt down this heresy."

He pivoted his chair, and said over his back, "You will take your own ship, but you will also have additional forces at your disposal. I have tasked Jiralhanae to accompany you aboard the Kig-Yar raider *A Psalm Every Day*. They will help you with whatever you may encounter. And keep the Kig-Yar Shipmistress well in line. I've come to distrust their greedy natures more and more of late."

Jiralhanae? Thel blinked his large eyes, but dared not question the Prophet. The Jiralhanae were barbarians who considered themselves the equals of Sangheili.

The Jiralhanae had once attained space flight and high levels of technology. But by the time the Covenant came across them, they'd bombed themselves back into a state of barbarism.

Why the Prophets regarded them so highly was beyond Thel.

They had no culture. No refinement in their fighting. No thought about their bloodlines, copulating at will with no foresight or plans.

They were not noble.

But Thel bowed his head. "I thank you for your gift of troops and ships," he said out loud. And he thought secretly to himself: I do not have to use them on this mission, they can simply come along and watch true warriors do their duty.

He had just recently become a shipmaster, something he'd longed to attain ever since he'd stood on the stone walls of his keep and looked up at the stars and wondered what amazing things might be waiting for him up there. Now, with another ship and more troops under his command, the dream of becoming a fleetmaster seemed within reach.

With a promotion like this, Thel would need to send a message home to the keep elders. He would have more wives brought to the keep. It was time for Thel to create more alliances on the homeworld. It was time to expand the rooms, and father more children to pack the common rooms. The line of Vadam would be continued in strength.

The keep's poet would add a line to the family saga, celebrating Thel's furthering in rank. Thel would be the most renowned Vadam yet.

The Prophet of Regret waved his hand. "Come with me, Shipmaster."

Thel loped behind the antigravity throne that Regret drove across the room to a massive wall-sized projection of the planet they'd come to orbit.

"They left only three ships to protect it," Regret mused. "You know why we fight these creatures?"

"They committed a grievous sin," Thel said. "They destroyed Forerunner artifacts."

He shivered as he said that.

The Forerunners had left traces of the time they spent in the galaxy scattered across worlds and in space. These mighty demigods of the galaxy had been the forefathers of all the Covenant knew, and they'd just . . . disappeared.

But they'd left clues as to where they'd gone. A Holy Journey, to another plane of existence, using the technology of the Halos.

So the Prophets taught, and the Covenant existed for finding the Halos, and following the Forerunners on their holy path.

But these humans, they'd found Forerunner artifacts, and instead of venerating them like all other species, they had destroyed them.

Thel vibrated with religious rage. For that, the humans would pay.

"It is important their heresy and desecration be punished," Regret said. "So anything that distracts us from this holy duty, that itself, is unholy. And must be stopped. Like these blasphemous weapons."

"I understand, Hierarch," Thel said. "I will stop at nothing."

Regret sighed. It spoke into its chair to the fleet commanders throughout. "Destroy this planet, and all on its surface."

On the screen, plasma roiled and grew on the sides of the Covenant cruisers as the ships prepared to rain fire down upon the world the humans called Charybdis IX.

CHAPTER 20

Zheng stood on the bridge of the *Midsummer Night*, his hands behind his back. Keyes watched him pace as the screens lit up.

All the bridge crew were on duty, and the junior officers stood at the back, looking on.

"I called you all here to watch this," Zheng announced, suddenly pausing in place to turn and face them, "because it's important to remember why we fight."

Keyes swiveled his chair. Zheng had been averse to talking to the entire ship before this, slightly nervous. Keyes bet that Zheng knew what his reputation was. Or maybe Zheng was still damaged from whatever it was he was dealing with. Either way, he'd kept his distance, even from his own bridge crew. And everyone had been happy to keep their distance from him as well. Until now. Zheng looked animated. Angry. For this he'd asked Kirtley to broadcast his address to the rest of the ship. It was an interesting change.

"Some of you joined because you had no other options, some because you were looking for adventure, and others because of patriotism. And since the first contact at Harvest, many of you out of a desire to fight the Covenant.

"But as days pass, and the dreariness of daily life, cramped in this ship with your fellow sailors mounts, I know it can be easy to forget that we are, first and foremost, a weapon." Zheng looked out over the officers on deck. "A weapon to strike back against all our enemies. External . . . or internal. Because if we don't do our best, this will be a small taste of what is to come."

Behind Zheng the screens lit up with images broadcast from Charybdis.

Keyes found his eyes drawn to the nearest, a scene from low orbit taken by a satellite. Far below, the sleek, sharklike shape of a Covenant cruiser passed over the patches of land, and as it did so, everything underneath it glowed.

The screen flickered off, jumping to a new scene: a shot from the top of a skyscraper in downtown Scyllion. What looked like shimmering rain fell from the sky, but wherever it touched the city exploded into actinic flame.

Buildings melted, slumping over and then bubbling down into a lavalike mix of asphalt and concrete and shattered glass. The camera wavered as blue haze began to build up near it, and then it melted and static filled the screen.

Another live feed, from far outside the city, showed the blue waterfalls of plasma strike the river, sending up a giant cloud of steam as it was vaporized.

"They're attacking," someone said in a shocked voice.

Keyes looked to the screen everyone pointed out, and saw tiny dots rising up to harass the bulbous-nosed Covenant cruisers.

They were about as successful as minnows attacking sharks,

Keyes thought. Plasma darted out from the sides of the cruiser over Scyllion, swatting the tiny Charybdis defense fighters out of the sky like annoying insects.

Maybe if they'd been more coordinated, Keyes wondered. Could a force of tiny craft distract a Covenant cruiser long enough for someone to slip something through their defenses?

He realized he was trying to avoid the death and destruction in front of him with academics, and forced himself to continue watching.

One by one the screens turned to static, and Zheng waved at them. "This ship we're chasing, it looks like it's going into Covenant territory, and we know it's Insurrectionist. Working with Covenant. For all we know, they led the Covenant to Charybdis."

Keyes raised an eyebrow. That was quite an assumption for Zheng to make. If the *Kestrel* had led the Covenant to Charybdis IX, they'd gotten a lot of their fellow Insurrectionists killed here today, not just UNSC.

Innies might be ready to die for their cause, but like this? Keyes thought back to what Jeffries had said about Zheng when they'd first met. Zheng had lost his entire family to the Covenant. Zheng had even been impatient about Watanabe's mission.

Now Zheng seemed to have been electrified into fiery, angry motion. "There will be a reckoning," he shouted to the bridge crew. "We will throw ourselves against whoever was responsible for all this."

And behind Zheng the remaining screens shut down, leaving the last few images of the burned world flickering across everyone's eyes. Keyes spotted Badia Campbell staring at the screens. She looked queasy.

Zheng turned back to the empty screens, surveying them for a long moment, and then said softly, "That is all."

CHAPTER 21

Covenant Cruiser *Infinite Sacrifice*, Charybdis IX

The Prophet of Regret watched the surface of Charybdis IX melt from the firepower of his ships with grim satisfaction and heavily lidded eyes.

He shouldn't have chosen to smoke in his private quarters before coming out, but before attacks like this Regret always found a good smoke calmed his nerves.

Energy rolled over the square buildings that the humans loved to cluster near one another on the ground. That made it all that much easier for the Covenant to destroy them.

Regret grew bored of watching the destruction of the planet, and turned the screen off.

"You are dismissed. Go. Weed out the Heretics. Leave no stone unturned!"

The Sangheili zealot blinked, and then bowed in that sinuously graceful Sangheili way. "Your will be done, Hierarch," he said, and then left to pursue his mission.

Regret sat in the control room, listening to the buzz of the ship's bridge crew.

The matter of the Kig-Yar smuggling weapons rankled the Prophet. Only the San'Shyuum, the leaders of the Covenant and its pinnacle species, could alter holy technology.

To let other races control technology was a dangerous path. The Covenant's cohesion was grounded in their shared need for Forerunner technology. It was their unified religion, their political structure, and the hub of all commerce. To pull out one major tenet of the Covenant meant risking the entire thing crumbling. And Regret had not worked the last ten years of his life to watch the Covenant die. He'd helped it face one of its biggest threats, with hardly anyone any the wiser, right before his ascension to Hierarch.

Together, Prophets Regret, Truth, and Mercy had been aboard the massive Forerunner dreadnought that sat in the heart of High Charity, powering the entire moving world with just a fraction of its engines' power.

The dreadnought had come to life as the Oracle at its heart had muttered blasphemous, world-changing accusations at the Prophets. All triggered by the Oracle encountering information about the humans. This machine had accused the Prophets of mistranslating Forerunner documents, and misunderstanding the Great Journey.

It claimed the very tenets of their religion were false.

And then the Oracle had attempted to launch the dreadnought. They had disconnected it just in time.

In that moment, Regret felt, they had saved the entire Covenant.

Without the Halos to search for, the Path to walk, and the worship of the Forerunners who left their mark all over the galaxy, the Covenant would fall apart.

And the Hierarchs would not let that happen.

So they turned that conflict into the annihilation and genocide of the humans. There was no room for negotiation or settlement. Humanity would be the first species they had encountered that they hadn't tried to absorb into the Covenant, as it was the source of the Oracle's confusion. Destroy them, and the Covenant would be able to continue its holy search to follow the Forerunners safely.

Nothing could detract from that. Not even these counterfeit weapons.

Regret didn't care that they'd been modified. The San'Shyuum happily pilfered Forerunner technology and modified it as they saw fit. What Regret cared about was that the weapons had been modified for humans, and that they'd been tampered with without the Prophet's approval.

And Regret wouldn't stand for that—not from the Oracle, or from whoever was making those weapons.

Regret turned the screen back on and looked down on the burning of Charybdis IX and watched.

This was for the good of the Covenant, he told himself.

Regret had only made one major mistake, he told himself. When the humans were first discovered Regret had assumed the world they'd been found on was their homeworld.

But after destroying it, they'd found out that the humans had scattered across many worlds.

It made destroying them all a lot more difficult, tiring, and time-consuming than Regret had anticipated.

CHAPTER 22

The humans called it 23 Librae. For the Covenant it was no more than a series of coordinates, another star in a long series of stars that Kig-Yar ships scouted out under their Ministry of Tranquility contracts. The Covenant hoped to find Forerunner artifacts in these various systems.

It was in one of these many human places that the Kig-Yar had found signs of a massive wealth of Forerunner artifacts, the Prophets said. They also said that instead of studying them and learning of the glorious truths contained in them about the journey all species could prepare themselves for, the stupid creatures had destroyed them.

Cosmic vandalism, mused Thel, as the two ships skipped out of slipspace next to the one planet 23 Librae had in its habitable zone: the orbit not too close to the sun where it would boil its atmosphere off, or so far away that it would freeze.

"Start scanning the planet," Thel ordered his bridge crew. "Engage all sensors. Make the sweep through. Last thing we need is for the Kig-Yar to lay claim, or the Jiralhanae to best the Sangheili in a task personally assigned them by a Hierarch!"

Madrigal.

Retribution's Thunder fell into orbit around the planet that had once been inhabited by the humans. Just off to their starboard side the Kig-Yar ship that the Hierarch had assigned to them, *A Psalm Every Day,* accompanied them.

Thel's lower mandibles twitched. The Kig-Yar Shipmistress had come in too close. They could have collided thanks to her aggressive piloting.

But neither the Kig-Yar nor the Jiralhanae aboard would listen to Thel.

They hadn't so far. He'd asked them to keep their distance, but they acted as if he were going to cheat them of any discovery, or any chance to get into battle.

Thel felt he would have been better off alone than saddled with *A Psalm Every Day* dogging his every move.

Then again, maybe that was the Hierarch's way of keeping an eye on him. Thel had a general feeling, from what he knew of politics on High Charity, that the Prophet of Regret was very crafty.

Yes, this one probably didn't just outright trust Thel, but wanted some verification. *A Psalm Every Day* was here to monitor him.

Fair enough.

"Nothing there," Jora grumbled from his station as initial results from the systematic scans began to scroll through the holographic display. "It is as we left it, Shipmaster. There are no signs of activity. Our quarry could not have come from here."

The entire surface of the human planet had been destroyed. Melted with plasma.

Zhar grunted. "Their structures have deep roots. Is it possible they survived deep underground?"

Thel shook his head. "I participated there." Thel considered it briefly. "I personally saw to the destruction of their warrens in the capitol. I doubt it will become useful again in this Age. You may tell the Jiralhanae they may check the capitol for spoils . . . with my leave. Meanwhile, send a probe to finish the sweep, then let us move on."

"To where?" Jora asked. He threw the words out almost like a challenge.

Thel eyed Jora. "This is a *system*. There is more than one place to hide. These are Kig-Yar we are dealing with, remember."

Zhar frowned. "Asteroids?"

Thel smiled. Zhar, ever the analytical. Hardheaded, but a hard thinker. He knew that the Kig-Yar, after leaving their homeworld, had chosen to settle out among the asteroids of their home system. It was what had made them so hard for the Prophets to ferret out while battling them when the Kig-Yar had initially resisted joining the Covenant. "Yes. We will seed the asteroid belt with sensor buoys. We will leave no stone unturned."

Zhar nodded. "It will be done."

Thel leaned over. "Veer, would you do me the . . ." his voice dripped with sarcasm, ". . . honor of contacting *A Psalm Every Day*?"

Veer nodded, and the three-dimensional image of Pellius appeared in front of Thel. The Jiralhanae stood eye-to-eye with Thel. Behind the giant, furred chieftain sat the Kig-Yar Shipmistress, Chur 'R-Mut, her lanky arms draped over her chair's arms. He grinned his needle-sharp grin and the quills on his head twitched.

Pellius curled his lip slightly. "What do you want? We're preparing to land and search the destroyed capital city."

"You will not find anything there," Thel said, and explained what he'd already told his bridge crew.

The Jiralhanae chieftan looked disappointed. For a second. "You still search, though?"

"Yes."

"Good." And then the image faded away.

"Jiralhanae," spat Saal from his weapons console. "Uncivil and untrustworthy."

"So they are," Thel agreed. "The Prophets in their inscrutable wisdom have assigned them to us. They are here to stay. Zhar move us out."

Without seeding the system with navigation buoys the ship's own long-range scanners weren't good enough to root out a hiding enemy. Unless something was moving around.

To catch sneaking ships, they'd need to lay some traps.

Thel settled into his chair, getting ready for the slipspace hop they'd have to make to the asteroid belt, when Veer straightened in his chair.

"Shipmaster," Veer hissed. "Our long range instruments are detecting multiple signals. They are not even trying to hide!"

Thel hid his excitement before them. "Where?"

"The gas giant."

Not where he'd been expecting. But nonetheless, they had something!

"Take us there," Thel ordered.

Retribution's Thunder poked a hole through space and time as the ship made the sudden leap from Madrigal to a trailing orbit just behind 23 Librae's sole gas giant.

This was a great location, Thel thought. Gas giants tended to have small rocky clusters both in front of their orbit and behind them—it was a natural place to hove his ship to and spy on whatever was going on near the gas giant.

Retribution's Thunder's screens lit up with contact symbols. Alarms wailed as the crew scrambled for damage control and fire stations, and Thel realized he hadn't been the only one with that particular idea.

"Situation?" Thel barked.

"They are everywhere!" a Sangheili shouted from the deck. "We are surrounded."

Thel whipped around at the outburst to look at the unnamed and slightly unnerved Sangheili. "Get off my bridge!" Thel turned to Saal. "Take his console. What do we face—numbers and weapons strength?"

"My honor, Shipmaster," Saal replied quickly.

Thel watched the shamed Sangheili slink off the bridge, disgusted that someone so incompetent could end up on *his* bridge.

"Human contacts," Saal reported. "But they do not appear to be warships. And they are not moving to engage."

"Tell Pellius to hold his fire and follow our lead." Thel stood up and walked toward the screens, a long shipmaster's cloak pulling off the chair with him. His ancestors had worn thick, doarmir-fur cloaks like this at sea to stay warm and dry on long voyages.

Thel had made his by hand during a long recuperation in the Vadam Keep after a training accident the family had tried to hide. Thel remembered the shame of seeing his own blood spilled on the sand of the training ring in the courtyard, due to his own mistake. He recalled the faintness and the tall snow-capped mountains that rose above Vadam Keep as he pitched to his side.

The family had a recently promoted shipmaster in their

bloodline, and they had been loath to lose that particular honor. They'd secretly called for a doctor in the night and held Thel down by his limbs as he was operated on.

Thel kept the cloak as a reminder to himself that he could make grave mistakes when he let his guard down.

Mistakes like letting an inexperienced minor Sangheili aboard the bridge who panicked at the thought of being surrounded by human warships.

"Make sure that coward gets his rations revoked," Thel said to Veer, letting his mind dwell on that particular incident now that he knew the ship was not in danger. "Maybe with a hunger in his belly he will find the hunger in his soul that he needs to be a real warrior."

"A well thought-out solution, Shipmaster," Veer said, and leaned over to send out the command.

"Saal, report." Thel gathered the cloak around. Be sharp, he reminded himself. Keep your mind open, and think sideways instead of walking forward into a pit-trap.

"I . . . I have to show you," Saal said.

A complex set of scans appeared on the screens. Thel narrowed his eyes, then opened his mandibles in shock. "These are all asteroids," he said. "They are all connected."

There were hundreds of connected worldlets.

"This is unlike anything I have ever seen the humans do," Thel said out loud. "There was nothing like it when the human world here was destroyed."

"Perhaps they built it after that?" Zhar suggested. He looked intrigued by the scans. "You have to admit, that demonstrates some strong blood on their part, to remain here and build after the Prophets ordered them destroyed."

"Strong indeed," Thel agreed.

"But it does them little good ultimately," Jora said. "Their blasphemy still cannot stand, and they must all still die."

"What bothers me," Thel grumbled, "is that they have gone this long unnoticed."

"I think I know why," Zhar said. He tapped his console, and before the bridge crew the long-distance image of a Kig-Yar freighter appeared.

It was docked against one of the many asteroids in the superstructure.

A human structure.

"What new treachery is this?" Thel hissed. The Kig-Yar, pirates and scum, worked under contracts given out by the ministries. They were hardly loyal fighters; they had little nobility. But they usually remained in line due to the dual methods of Unggoy Deacons aboard their ships, as well as the contracts and payments the Prophets offered them.

Thel could hardly believe what he saw.

"Brace for impact!" Saal warned, just as the *Retribution's Thunder* shivered, throwing Thel from his feet against a pillar.

So the humans had found them and were attacking, Thel thought as he sprang for his shipmaster's throne.

The second impact stabbed through the heart of Thel's ship, a violent, metal-boiling line of light that just missed the bridge. But this wasn't human. Humans employed kinetic or explosive ordnance, not plasma.

A Psalm Every Day was preparing a second volley. It was very obvious that the plasma salvo was from another Covenant vessel.

Their own escort.

"Traitors!" Thel seethed. "Evasive maneuvers!"

"I have a firing solution," Jora yelled, turning to Thel. "Permission to fire, Shipmaster?"

"Fire at will! Saal tactical slipspace, now!"

But getting past the shock of being fired upon by their own escort had cost them critical seconds. Even as *Retribution's Thunder* fired back, another salvo of blue plasma ripped through the heart of Thel's ship.

He could feel some of the engines firing, but they had been too slow. Sangheili double hearts could take far more acceleration than Jiralhanae or Kig-Yar, but the incredible random high-speed evasive maneuvers Thel had braced himself for didn't come.

"Status," Thel snapped.

He did not like the returning reports. They were venting precious air into space. The number of casualties was rising. Long range communications were down. Life support was failing. The last volley had taken their core engines offline, and their ability to generate plasma had gone with it. While most of their sensors were still operational, they could go nowhere and do nothing.

Pellius appeared in hologram before Thel. The Jiralhanae looked pleased with himself, his large teeth bared. "A mighty shipmaster Sangheili, helpless before me. I shall savor this moment for the rest of my life."

Thel stared at Pellius and wondered where the Kig-Yar Shipmistress had gone. She was nowhere to be seen on the bridge. "It will be a short life."

"Not as short as yours. Good-bye, Shipmaster." Pellius faded away.

"He has released boarding craft and Spirits!" Saal reported.

"They will not have the *Retributions' Thunder*," Thel said, staring at the spot Pellius had faded from. "Alert the crew. Get in protective gear and draw the boarders in deep. Rig every section to explode. We will leave nothing to salvage!"

"Shipmaster! *A Psalm Every Day* has engaged their slipspace drive!" Zhar said. "They're leaving!"

"Leaving?" Jora growled.

"The humans are not likely to go anywhere as are we. He will report whatever his feeble mind can concoct when he reaches High Charity."

"They get the glory for reporting this structure and the humans hiding here," Zhar concluded with frustration.

"Cursed cowards," hissed Jora.

"The Spirits are approaching to attack!"

"Where are their boarding craft?"

"They are hanging back."

In the distance, the outer hull shook and shivered as Spirits flew up and down the length of the ship, strafing it.

Thel broke the arm off his chair in frustration. "Those who wish to escape the ship may do so now."

It was a rhetorical statement. But it did serve one purpose: to weed out any dishonorable Sangheili who might falter by your side.

Thel pressed his mouth parts firm against each other as they waited in silence for a handful of dishonorable crew to desert. Maybe they were serfs who had risen far enough to work simple duties aboard the ship, or Sangheili who'd managed to hide their lack of real blood.

He waited for that, and for the Kig-Yar to get bolder and try to board the ship.

One of the screens showed Sangheili trying to escape aboard Spirits from inside *Retribution's Thunder*'s hold, and the Kig-Yar–run ships fell on them en masse, overwhelming them. Plasma ripped out and filled the space around the ship, and it wasn't long before the cowardly died in the vacuum at the hands of traitorous Kig-Yar.

A fitting fate, Thel thought. "Fire the empty escape pods," he ordered.

They watched those get destroyed, and it strengthened their resolve to fight. To run was to die.

Now the Kig-Yar felt that they could risk boarding, with what seemed like most of the crew of the ship gone.

Thel waited. Waited until Kig-Yar swarmed the hull and trooped through the heart of his ship, and then gave the order.

Explosions ripped through the interior, section by section. The smooth, bulbous lines of his ship flexed and twisted, and fire gushed out from in between the cracks, roiling up through the corridors.

The air in the bridge heated up, and then rushed out. Thel found himself panting for air that no longer existed, and then a secondary explosion turned the cockpit inside out.

Thel hurtled through the air and struck a bulkhead.

CHAPTER 23

The *Kestrel* was a svelte smuggler of a ship, more engine than cargo bay. Even then, civilian engine technology didn't hold a candle to what the *Midsummer Night* had at its heart.

The *Midsummer Night* had been shadowing the *Kestrel* for almost a week. UNSC sensor buoys had been put on high alert on the edges of the system, and caught the *Kestrel* preparing for its jump into slipspace. These were the same sensor buoys that had detected the inbound Covenant.

Dmitri Zheng had thrown the *Midsummer Night* on a ripping course out to follow it. Badia Campbell at ops reported nervously that the ship's reactor was struggling to keep up.

But the ship had been shaken out. No more pipes blew, or components failed. She'd gotten up to speed, closing in on the Insurrectionist ship like a shark slipping up from the depths on its prey.

On their way out, they'd all continued to watch broadcasts from sensor posts scattered throughout the system of the Covenant ships moving over Charybdis IX, glassing the surface.

The mood onboard had remained somber and determined. The crew had been itching to fight, and now had to turn tail and run.

No one liked it.

But they had a mission, and they'd all had friends and family fall to the Covenant. Despite Zheng's anger, many had gotten used to the dull pain of human loss. Casualties mounted; they had for years. It had become a part of life for many.

Now they were deep behind Covenant lines, hopping through what had once been the Outer Colonies, sticking close behind the *Kestrel* as it seemed to randomly jump into Slipstream space.

"We're close," Keyes announced. The last three jumps the *Kestrel* had taken made a line on the star charts that Keyes could use.

Assuming that the jumps continued in their pattern, Keyes had run the charts. He posted the result to the bridge crew's screens.

Zheng took a look and frowned. "You think they're headed to Madrigal? That planet was glassed by the Covenant."

"It could be where they make their drops," Keyes suggested. He paused as his sensors showed the smuggler making another jump.

He was right. The last several slipspace jumps took them to the outer edge of the system, and then the *Kestrel* began curving its way in-system.

The *Midsummer Night* followed, invisible and silent. They coasted with the *Kestrel* all the way into the depths of the system.

"It isn't Madrigal," Keyes announced several shifts later, reviewing the navigation data left by a junior officer.

"Then what is it?" Zheng asked. "Where are they headed?"

Keyes had astronomy data up on his screen with possible paths of the *Kestrel* mapped out. "There's a gas giant, farther out. It's called Hesiod."

They followed the *Kestrel* as it fell into an orbit trailing far, far behind the gas giant, but slowly catching up to it.

"There we go," Keyes said, upping the magnification on the view ahead of them.

"Asteroids?" Zheng said.

"Trojan asteroids," Keyes said. "Most gas giants have asteroids sitting just ahead and behind their orbit in stable L4 and L5 positions."

"Makes a good hideout," Rai Li spoke up from weapons. "The rebels at Eridani used the asteroid belt there and it made it hard to hunt them down."

The *Kestrel* slowed as it slipped into the cloud of rock.

There was something wrong, Keyes thought. Dirtsiders heard the term "asteroid field" and thought of a large collection of rocks floating near each other.

The truth was that asteroids lay millions of miles from each other. A slow-moving ship could thread through them easily enough on their way through a system.

But *this* collection of asteroids looked just like a layperson's idea of an asteroid field. Hundreds of asteroids had been moved within a mile of each other.

Keyes magnified the image even more, putting it up on a wall screen the whole bridge could look at. The hundreds of irregularly shaped rocks jumped into view.

"Looks like some of them are built up," Dante Kirtley said. "Plus, I'm starting to get a lot of direct-line comms chatter. They're trying to keep it focused and quiet, but I'm hearing it. Looks like we got ourselves an Insurrectionist hiding hole. And behind Covenant lines, no less."

But something glinted between them. Keyes upped the magnification even further, and everyone on the bridge gasped.

The glints were long, silver lines. As Keyes jumped the magnification up again, the gossamer lines resolved themselves into tubes.

"They're all connected," Li said. "With docking tubes."

"If each of those asteroids is fully inhabited, this isn't just an Insurrectionist hiding hole," Zheng said. "It's a floating metropolis . . . behind enemy lines."

They coasted in closer, staring at the spectacle of an asteroid field towed in closer, connected together, and hollowed out. Ships moved in between the rocks, and occasionally a burst of flame from a guidance rocket adjusted an asteroid, presumably so that it didn't break one of the tubes.

"Freeze that," Li suddenly snapped. Keyes stopped the drift on the image. "Zoom."

He saw it too, now.

"Is that a Jackal ship?" Kirtley asked.

"That's Jackal," Li confirmed. She tapped her console and put a window up next to their live image of a Jackal ship taken from the combat camera of a Navy ship. Unlike the usual Covenant-made ships, the Jackal-made ships looked like last-minute scrap yard projects—girders, rockets, and capsules haphazardly joined together around a core unit. These ships were not made to even kiss an atmosphere, but remain in space.

Zheng cracked his knuckles and stared at the screen. "Bring the crew up to ready, ops. Weapons, unlock missiles and arm a nuke. Comms, make sure you're scanning and getting everything that's going on."

Li, Kirtley, Keyes, and Campbell got to work.

"Lieutenant Campbell, set up preparations to destroy our navigation charts, as per the Cole Protocol."

Campbell paused, considered something, and then spoke up. "Sir, does it make sense? The *Kestrel* obviously has charts, and I'd bet other ships in this . . . complex have charts as well. We're not making it any harder for Covenant here to find charts, are we?"

Zheng looked at the screen. "You're right, Lieutenant. That thing out there, that's just one giant Cole Protocol violation, isn't it? But orders are orders. Ready the purge. Just in case."

"Yessir."

"Okay, Keyes, bring her in nice and easy. We just want to swing nearby, nice and quiet, and see what intel we can pick up to bring back with us. But if things get hairy, be ready to get us the hell out."

"Aye, sir," Keyes responded. Then he spotted movement. "They have patrols, it looks like. Moving around the perimeter."

"Let's see how stealthy this frigate really is, Keyes." Zheng leaned forward in his chair.

The *Midsummer Night* moved closer to the tangle of docking tubes, asteroids, ships, dust, and debris trailing the massive orb of Hesiod.

CHAPTER 24

Pineapple Habitat, The Rubble, 23 Librae

Thel 'Vadamee and his bridge crew sat on the far end of a large cell. It was a crude thing: a hole dug out of the rocky interior wall of a hollowed out asteroid, with bars of metal over the front, some of which were hinged.

Thel had seen medieval keeps with similarly built jails back on Sanghelios. In museums.

He'd woken up with a horrific headache pounding the side of his temple where he'd struck the bulkhead. Not an honorable battle wound, or a way to end a fight, Thel thought miserably as he looked out through the bars.

The Kig-Yar had combed the remains of the ship, carrion sniffers that they were, and found the bridge crew alive. The rest of the crew had fought to the death, destroying the ship in the process.

Thel sincerely wished they'd just left him for dead on his

destroyed ship. But the Kig-Yar had some plan in mind for them, using the Sangheili as hostages.

Jora crept his way over. "I am beyond shame, my shipmaster."

Thel had been told Jora rushed the Kig-Yar with no weapon, and they'd shot him several times in the leg. Now Jora was dragging the useless limb behind him on the cell floor.

"I have snapped one of the legs off those useless cots made for humans."

He handed it to Thel, who tested the sharp end with a finger. Jora had worked hard to get the long piece of metal sharp.

"Please," Jora begged. "I have no honor left. I am crippled. I cannot face my keep."

If the Sangheili masters found out that they'd been captured by a lesser race like the Kig-Yar, or that they'd failed so horribly in a *holy* mission handed to them directly by a Hierarch, there would be dire consequences.

Jora's entire bloodline could be killed off. They'd hunt down his nephews and behead them. The genetic proclivities of failures, the planetary heads of Sangheilios thought, could not be allowed to continue on.

But if Jora did the right thing, and killed himself before the Kig-Yar could get any use out of him, or further sully his name and by extension, his line . . . well, his keep might fall in stature, but at least the line could try to struggle back up from its loss of honor.

"Please," Jora whispered. "You have been like a cousin to me. Please do me one last favor. I have not the strength to do it myself."

"Come and kneel," Thel said.

The other zealots in the cell faced away. It was embarrassing to see that Jora could not even dispatch himself, but needed the hand of another.

But Thel remembered how Jora had thrown himself against

the Kig-Yar. That had to count for something, he thought, as he stepped behind Jora.

"May the Great Journey await you, may your enemies writhe in hell, and your line continue forward, and gain honor," Thel said to his boldest fighter.

And then he slammed the spike into the back of Jora's head.

Jora slowly toppled forward with a sigh.

"May your scattered body go," Veer murmured, turning back around, "beyond the limits of your mind. . . ."

"Beyond the limits of our worlds," Saal said the next line of the death benediction.

"To the places our ancestors dream and sang of," Zhar sang.

"And the Prophets speak of," Thel finished. The survivors clasped forearms. "You all remain alive—why?"

"We want to study how to destroy the humans hiding here," Saal said. "The Kig-Yar spoke of ransoming us to our keeps. But Thel, you are kaidon of your keep now. Would you pay for one of your own captured like this?"

Thel snorted. "I would sooner bleed on the ground than do it. You know this."

"Exactly," Zhar said. Thel could see his tactical mind working. This was good. Set Zhar on a problem and he was like a warrior— he'd tussle with it to his last breath.

Saal laughed. "The Kig-Yar are idiots who pay no attention to us. They should have known to kill us where we lay; no Sangheili in his right mind would pay a ransom. That is a Kig-Yar game."

Zhar turned to him. "And that is how we will destroy them. They are too far away to find this out so quickly. And our suspicions were right; we have heard Kig-Yar say as much. The Jiralhanae who betrayed us are returning with the Shipmistress to High Charity where they can claim this find for themselves."

"And find favor with the Prophets," Veer said. "But how is it that we're in a human cell *here*?"

Thel understood what he was getting at. "The Prophets will not like it."

"Humans and Kig-Yar, working together," Veer mused. "There were humans here talking to the Kig-Yar who dragged us in."

"They called the one human Bonifacio," Saal said. "You could smell his fear of us in the air."

"All we need to do is get out of this cell," Zhar said.

Saal walked over to Jora's body and pulled the spike free from his head. "I have yet to see anything spying on us. This all looks like it was recently welded together on short notice to contain us."

Thel snorted in appreciation. "Roll Jora's body onto a cot and cover it. Eventually they will want to know why he doesn't move. Make sure the covers they gave us drape over where the metal leg used to be."

They had a weapon now. And a plan. Of sorts.

Four Sangheili free would be a force to reckon with.

And Thel did not, one way or another, intend to be recaptured.

Now all they needed was an opportunity.

CHAPTER 25

Ignatio Delgado pulled at the handcuffs attached to the long chain until he was at the very end, and got a drink of water from a sink.

It was a long drink. He used his body as a shield as he picked at a cotter pin holding one of the taps in place. He palmed it and stood up.

He was being held inside a dingy factory. The dust seemed to cling to everything. Even the light beams from the windows seemed to ride in on floating clouds of dust.

Bonifacio's five pet heavies sat at a table with a deck of cards that fizzled and popped and lit up their little corner of the warehouse.

The card game paused as he watched. The men gathered the cards up quickly, all five rushing to get things cleared off.

One of the men stood up and trotted over as Delgado finished drinking water out of his hands.

"What's going on?" Delgado asked.

The men had ignored him. Bonifacio had yet to return. He'd had no food, but he could drink out of the sink and use a bucket they'd left for him.

"Your time is up," one of them grunted. "The *Kestrel*'s back."

That meant Bonifacio had no reason left to leave him alive when he got back from wherever he was.

The question was, since he was handcuffed here under Council's orders, how was Bonifacio going to properly get rid of him?

"The thing is," another heavy added. "She's got company."

Delgado looked around. "Company?"

"A UNSC stealthed frigate. Some new design. It's poking around the edges of the Rubble."

"How do you know?" asked Delgado.

"Same way we know anything about them. We have someone aboard. They've been using a tight-beam laser to cast out messages to us, like where the ship is, what it's up to. They're getting ready to help us take care of the problem.

"Once we know that's solved and the *Kestrel* is safely at Mr. Bonifacio's private dock, then we take you back to the Council." The man grinned.

Delgado did not believe what he said for a second. Delgado imagined they'd be on their way to take him back, and hand him over, but somehow there'd be a terrible tube car accident. Or airlock accident. That's how people like Bonifacio worked.

Four of the men were called away, leaving one heavy to sit by himself and forlornly guard Delgado.

The lone guard only lasted about three minutes before he

unfolded a small screen and started watching something on it. The sounds of tinny gunfire and screams from the movie echoed in the empty factory walls.

Delgado retrieved the cotter pin he'd been hiding. He started using it to fiddle with the lock on the cuffs. The guard stared intently at the screen.

CHAPTER 26

There was an art to deciphering patterns, Keyes thought, looking at all the contacts the ship's radar was showing him on a screen. And despite all the training he gave in his life he felt it wasn't something you could analyze. Seeing patterns came to those with intuition. You looked for the gaps and cracks that opened up.

The *Midsummer Night* had slipped deep into the Insurrectionist structure. He couldn't help but be amazed by it all.

All these asteroids, all these connections. What a tremendous achievement.

"Say what you will about them, this is a pretty slick operation," Lt. Dante Kirtley muttered from comms. He was bent over, looking for stray chatter. "They've routed most of their communications through physical lines, there's almost no wireless leakage. Makes all of this pretty quiet out here, Commander."

Commander Zheng checked the information they were all sending him. "The Jackal ship, Lieutenant. Don't forget about the ship. These Insurrectionists are probably working with the Covenant—that's how they've managed to achieve all this. I'm not inclined to be as charitable."

The radar contacts Keyes was following shifted with the ship, as if orbiting it, but from a very long distance.

Keyes puffed the thrusters, gently moving them along a random line. The bulk of the cloud of freighters, personal ships, drones and other small contacts all shifted slightly.

A slight sense of claustrophobia washed over Keyes, but it was quickly quenched.

"Commander, you better take a look at this," Keyes said, putting the contacts up on a forward screen. "They're adjusting their position based on our adjustments. I think we're not as stealthy as we think we are." Out of the corner of his eye Keyes saw Badia Campbell swallow a pair of pills with a pained look on her face. She looked stressed.

Zheng double checked the time-lapsed information, then nodded. "I think you're right, Lieutenant."

Campbell at ops disagreed. "We can damp our engines down further, alter our course and coast through. Lighting up full to jump out of here will just blow our cover. We won't be able to get back in this deep ever again."

Keyes disagreed, but didn't say anything. The bridge crew had been tight. He wasn't going to risk second-guessing anyone just yet, even if Campbell was being jittery. The decision was Zheng's anyway.

Zheng mulled it over for a second, then tapped the pad. "I don't like it. Keyes, light us up and let's blow clear. We'll observe from a distance. We can drop some drones and double-check the stealth there; maybe something is going wrong. It's still a new ship."

Keyes had a rough line plotted out already. He double-checked it, and checked the engines. Ready to come on fully hot.

They'd rip right through that school of slow Insurrectionist freighters to safety, Keyes thought, tapping the navigation console and getting ready.

But then something in the heart of *Midsummer Night* exploded and the air in the cockpit rose in pressure, making Keyes's ears pop.

"Ops!" Zheng shouted, turning to his side. "Report!"

Keyes fired the ship's main engines, looking to throw them clear while Zheng and Campbell figured out what had happened.

But the engines wouldn't fire.

Keyes turned to Campbell, about to ask for a report. But Campbell leapt clear of her station and pulled out her sidearm. "Campbell, what the hell?"

He hesitated for a second, not sure what was happening. So did everyone else.

Badia Campbell pulled the trigger. She shot Zheng twice in the side and stomach as he started to get out of his chair. The loud crack of the gunfire stunned everyone into moving.

Keyes jumped forward at her without thinking, as did Kirtley and Li.

Campbell turned and shot Li low, getting the weapons officer in the leg. As Campbell raised her gun, she shot Kirtley in the shoulder, spinning him around. Keyes smacked into her before she could pull the trigger again.

They rolled over the decking, Campbell twisting to get free and kneeing Keyes in the groin as he wrestled to grab her gun.

He finally pinned her against the bottom of her console, using all his strength to hold her down. "Why?" Keyes asked.

"You heard Zheng back on Charybdis," she said. "He said he would destroy them. I couldn't let that man in among the Rubble. He's too dangerous. You know what he *did with* his own ship, lost his whole crew, just for the smallest chance to get his revenge. I can't let him do that to us."

She was amped up on something, preternatural strength exhausting an already recovering Keyes. Sweat beaded her entire face, and her pupils were dilated. "We will win, Lieutenant Keyes," she hissed at him. "One day, we will be free."

Her vicelike grip on the gun twisted, and Keyes fought her. But the adrenaline and drugs in her system left her crazed. She twisted the gun up between them until the point of the barrel jammed up against her chin.

"Badia, please . . ." Keyes hissed, his arms shaking from the effort of trying to pull the barrel away from her chin.

She pulled the trigger. The sound, this close to Keyes's face, was more than deafening, it washed through his skull and left it ringing. A red mist hung in the air underneath the console. Her jaw slackened, and her eyes glazed.

Keyes rocked back, holding her limp hand and the gun. He closed his eyes, unwilling to look at the mess of blood and brains spattered across the deck.

"Medic!" he screamed, trying to process what had just happened. But as he looked around, he realized the whole bridge crew had been shot by Campbell as she'd leapt forward. Campbell didn't need help. But they did. He turned around to see Zheng crawling up into the Commander's chair, holding his stomach with one bloody hand, spitting even more blood clear of his mouth.

Li had hobbled back to her weapons console, and Kirtley had cracked open a first-aid kit and rushed back to Zheng's side.

"Engineering!" Zheng croaked. "Update. What happened?"

Kirtley sprayed biofoam on Zheng's wounds. That would sterilize the wound, and the hardened foam would act as a firm bandage, seeping into the wound and holding everything together. It would do until the medics got to the bridge for something more thorough.

There was a haze of swearing in the background, along with the clanking of crew running from place to place, as engineering crackled back in reply. "We've been sabotaged. Lieutenant Campbell, or someone working with her, put explosives on the goddamned fusion core coolant system. It's a mess, sir."

"Can we fix it?" was all Keyes wanted to know.

"Sir, she knew her business. The fusion core is going critical. We can stop it from blowing us up to hell, but we're not going to get the engines back very quickly here."

Engineering got into spacesuits and opened the back of the ship. They started flushing everything out to the depths of space; the lack of air began extinguishing most of the fires and let them get to work on the damaged cooling system. But this was also venting heat and radiation into space.

They were no longer stealthy in any sense of the word.

They were as good as dead in the water. Keyes reoriented the *Midsummer Night*, realizing that they had only thrusters to work with.

"We have thrusters," Keyes reported, a bit relieved. He scanned his console for the largest asteroid. If he could get them to it and use it as a shield of some sort, he could buy them some time to fix the engines.

"And weapons," Li grunted.

Commander Zheng groaned as he shifted. "Comms, set condition red. Battlestations." Kirtley moved back to his console and tapped away, one-handed. More blood had begun to stain his uniform.

Emergency lighting flickered on and the sirens yelped.

"Missile crews stand by. Get the MAC ready," Zheng ordered. He glanced over at Keyes. "Where are you headed, Lieutenant?"

Keyes explained his strategy quickly as they continued thrusting their way back into the rebel structure that Campbell had called the Rubble. He finished with, "We can just go right through the structure, buying time for us to get the engines fixed."

"Belay that," Commander Zheng snapped. "Steer away from the structure, get us out into the open."

"Sir, with all due respect, we can't outrun them. Lying about in the open like this . . . we're too vulnerable," Keyes said.

"Don't repeat the obvious to me, Lieutenant," Commander Zheng said. "I've already had one of my core bridge crew shoot me. Now another is heading the ship deep into enemy territory. Please forgive my inability to trust your judgment right now. I don't want to hand the enemy my ship on a damned platter. Take us out and away. Now."

"Yes, sir," Keyes said. He didn't like it. Not a bit. But he saw Zheng's position. And he had his orders.

The *Midsummer Night* ponderously turned about, into a net of freighters and small ships moving in toward it around the very edges of the Rubble.

Keyes flipped through the scans until he found the biggest Insurrectionist ship, and then wound the *Midsummer Night* through the weave of docking tubes and asteroids out toward it.

Keyes wanted to move them close to one of the Insurrectionists' big ships. He wanted to get the rest of the smaller ships attacking the *Midsummer Night* to stop for fear they might fire on their own ship by accident.

A slim chance. But Keyes would take it.

"Incoming!" Keyes shouted, as the world lit up.

"Countermeasures deployed," Li reported. The twinkling chaff Li had enveloped the ship in confused a handful of the missiles. The others penetrated the screen. The ship shuddered as they struck the hull.

A second wave of missiles streaked in, and Keyes had the ship thrusting as close to one of the smaller asteroids as he could, almost grazing it. Missiles struck the asteroid, throwing up dirt and dust.

"Good thinking," Li said.

Keyes looked over to Zheng, who had narrowed his eyes. "We're not stopping, Keyes. Full thrusters, get us clear."

The moment they cleared the asteroid the next wave of missiles struck. The ship shuddered and shook; damage reports started streaming in.

They were taking a hell of a beating.

And still Commander Zheng, now doubled over and clutching his stomach, had them limping their way out into the open.

This was suicide, Keyes thought. He wanted to speak up, say something. But he didn't. An order was an order, damn it, and Zheng was a good commander.

A fast-moving blip ripped across the screen before Keyes could even call out.

The explosion slammed Keyes's face into his console. When he sat up, blood dripped all over the screen.

"That was a mass-driver slug," Keyes said, wiping the blood away with the edge of his palm. "Pretty much like a MAC; though in this case, they use it for mining operations."

"It hit near engineering," Zheng said.

"They fire it again, we're dead," Li said. "We're barely taking the hammering from their missiles."

Zheng closed his eyes, fighting some inner pain. "They're

working with the Covenant. I have no choice but to enact the Cole Protocol. Keyes, destroy the navigation data, databases, logs, and anything related to them. You have the bridge. I need to get down to engineering."

Zheng painfully left his chair and shuffled out of the cockpit.

Keyes accessed the Cole Protocol instructions. He found the virus needed to scavenge through the ship's systems as a second line of defense. This was it, he thought. Once he started this, they were stuck here, no matter what happened next. He'd probably never see Miranda again. Never see another Earthrise over Luna.

Another missile strike shook him out of those thoughts. They were dying here. He had a duty. Getting rid of the data might well protect Earth and the colonies.

Keyes triggered the program, swallowing his nervousness as he began shutting down the nav station.

Lieutenant Li was coordinating fire response, trying to keep the Insurrectionist forces busy and at arm's length. But judging by the more and more frequent explosions on the hull, it was a losing battle.

Kirtley caught Keyes's eye. "They're hailing us. They want to talk to the Commander."

"He's on his way to Engineering."

Kirtley shook his head. "Engineering hasn't seen him yet."

Keyes frowned. "Where the hell is he?"

Li swore, and Kirtley looked frustrated. Keyes checked the progress on his virus. It was done. This ship would never get back to the Inner Colonies or Earth.

"They're saying they have more mass-driver shots aimed at us if we don't kill the thrusters," Kirtley said.

"Patch them through, then, I'll stall," Keyes said.

Just as he finished saying that three distinct explosions threw the whole ship sideways a few hundred feet. Bulkheads groaned. Metal screeched all up and down the ship.

"What was that?" Keyes asked.

"Nukes," Li said. "Our own Shivas."

Kirtley leaned forward. "Got Zheng now. I'm putting him through to the Insurrectionists."

Zheng's voice had dropped almost to a hoarse whisper now. "This is Commander Dmitri Zheng, of the UNSC Frigate *Midsummer Night*. I have just unleashed our Shivas. Remember, I could have dropped these into the heart of your structure, but chose not to. We have honor. I'm ordering my crew to stand down. I demand that you treat them fairly. That is all."

As he faded away, an engineer's voice came from comms. "Sir, someone needs to get down here. The medic says Zheng's bleeding out. He doesn't have long."

Keyes stood up. "I'm on my way."

The last time he'd rushed through the ship, he'd gotten somewhat lost. By now he knew his way down the corridors, leaping through bulkhead doors and swinging into the next section with accomplished ease, sliding down rails and leaping up stairs in other sections.

Engineering was a chaotic mess of steam, slagged metal, and activity. They'd repressurized the section, but the chief of engineering was at the center of a maelstrom of human activity.

Near the engineer's operations center a medic crouched next to Commander Zheng, who sat in a pool of his own blood.

The medic met Keyes's eyes and shook his head.

"He hand-loaded the Shivas himself and shot them off, wouldn't let anyone near him," the medic said.

"If you want something done, you got to do it yourself. You

can't trust anyone," Zheng said from the floor. He held up a bloody hand. "Keyes . . . come closer."

Keyes crouched next to him and the medic, and Zheng grabbed Keyes's hand slippery tight. "Didn't think I'd let any Insurrectionists get their hands on some nukes, did you?"

"No, sir," Keyes said.

"I want you to know, I didn't ram that Covenant ship for revenge, like they say," Zheng whispered.

"No one said that." Keyes glanced at the medic, who just waved his hand to indicate that he keep listening.

"Yes they do. I rammed that ship because we had no other choice. It would have killed many, many more. I had to look at the big picture. I had to step outside the box and do what I could with what I had."

"I understand, sir."

"Maybe, Keyes. Maybe. Just remember, don't trust any of these people, Keyes. Covenant, rebels, hell, keep an eye on your own crew. Look for the big picture. You take good care of my ship. Make sure they treat the crew well once they take them prisoner."

Commander Zheng squeezed Keyes's hand, and started to breathe heavily.

"Move aside," the medic said, as Zheng slumped over. "Defib!"

Keyes looked at his bloody hand that Zheng was gripping as the medic tried to revive the Commander.

"Sir, Li here," the comms piece in Keyes's ear buzzed. "They're boarding. The ODSTs want to know how to proceed."

Keyes swallowed. He was next in line. He was now in charge of the ship. All these lives. The mission. It had all been handed to him. This was no classroom, this was all the real front-line mess he'd been hoping to get.

Well, he'd gotten it all right.

They had no navigation data. They were outnumbered. Damaged. And dead in the water.

"Tell Faison we follow Zheng's orders to stand down. Spread the word." Keyes felt numb as he stood up. "Give me directions to the nearest incursion. I'll go meet the Innies myself."

It was all on him, now.

PART III

PART III

CHAPTER 27

Thel sat in front of the bars, his legs folded underneath him, watching the two guards. It was a modified warrior's crouch, one that let a Sangheili rest with his legs beneath him, but in a manner that allowed one to leap up and forward in the blink of an eye. He'd spent long hours practicing with fellow students in the sandy training courtyards of the Vadam keep, learning the pose; now it came as second nature.

The short, shuffling Unggoy that guarded them carried a plasma rifle too large for its frame, and Thel caught the trace whiffs of methane that leaked from around the guard's mouthpiece. The Unggoy—an annoying lesser being—was careful to remain as close to the far wall and as far away from the bars as possible, rightly fearing the Sangheili's long limbs.

But that didn't stop the Unggoy from taunting them and

puffing itself up. "Look, you mighty Sangheili. Look you not so mighty now, eh?"

Thel growled from somewhere deep in the back of his throat.

"You ignore the Unggoy, yes. Throw us to die at your feet. Don't care when other races take advantage of poor Unggoy. No more. Wait until you are taken to Metisette, then see you our might."

Thel looked over at Zhar. "Might?"

"Unggoy *might* is a contradiction in terms," Zhar grumbled.

"So think you," the Unggoy hissed. "Just you wait. Just you wait."

"What's this Metisette? That is the second time I have heard that word," Zhar observed. "The Kig-Yar who locked us in here mentioned it."

Thel took a deep breath. "It is the human name for a world around the great gas giant." His calves burned somewhat, now. But he waited still.

Just under his feet, hidden by his crouch, was the long spear of metal. Using the edge of the bedframe, and their own strength, Thel and Saal had taken turns sharpening it further. They'd also cut rudimentary barbs into the spike by shaving out sections of the crude weapon.

Now it was a case of choosing the best moment. Thel didn't want to waste their one attempt.

This cell, they had determined, was in one of the far edges of what Zhar had heard the humans call "the Rubble." Though the Kig-Yar and humans were working together, this was mainly a human creation.

Before Thel's thoughts meandered further, the walls shook and debris began breaking loose. The bars of metal holding them in started bowing and screeching as they were tortured into slightly different shapes.

Lights flickered, and Thel still remained absolutely still, like a helioskrill imitating a rock back on the home planet, just watching for a meal to unsuspectingly walk by.

As the cell plunged into darkness, Thel felt his weight lift off as the antigravity generators failed. He picked up the spear, the end of it tied off to several lengths of tightly braided sheet strips, and listened.

He could hear the Unggoy's panicked breathing and the hiss of the methane tank as he struggled in the air.

The spear flew out from between the bars and made a wet, crunching sound as it struck the Unggoy. Thel gave the impromptu rope a quick yank, and the screaming Unggoy was pulled right into the bars.

Zhar and Saal waited there. Their long arms snapped the Unggoy's neck and quieted it.

Saal retrieved the plasma rifle as Thel pulled the makeshift spear out of the Unggoy and shoved the body away. Bright blue blood hung in the space, expanding into large globules as the Unggoy slowly spun in the air.

"Get the lock," Thel ordered.

After bracing himself against the far wall, Saal fired at the lock three times. Plasma blew the device away into a cloud of molten metal rivulets that flew across the room, sizzling against Unggoy skin and slapping into the wall.

The four Sangheili pushed the cell door open and floated out as the lights flickered back on.

They hit the floor, along with dried metal beads and the Unggoy's limp body. Blood splattered the floor a split second later.

Zhar looked around the room, blinking as his eyes adapted to the overly bright human lights. "They brought us in over there." He jutted his mouthpieces in the direction of a corridor.

Thel moved with the spear, taking point.

The Kig-Yar still here would deeply regret jailing him, he thought, as he turned a corner and spotted one of them standing by an airlock door.

Thel sprinted the length of corridor, caring little for stealth. The Kig-Yar spun, a protective shield flaring up by his forearm, but Thel struck so hard the Kig-Yar's head smashed into the bulkhead behind him, and he drooped to the ground.

Saal peered in through the window briefly, then pulled back.

"More inside," Saal grunted. "But they seem preoccupied."

Thel looked at the door controls, regretting his impulse to kill the Kig-Yar guard so quickly. The collection of buttons that the humans used to control things stumped him. But he managed to tap a large green button that cycled the door open.

The Kig-Yar all turned and found themselves facing Saal with the plasma rifle aimed right at their heads.

"Remember us?" Saal said, and pulled the trigger. Long Kig-Yar faces exploded as Saal calmly shot all four in the head over their screeches of fear and rage.

"And that," Veer said, stepping over the bodies and closing the airlock door of the ship behind them, "is why you never imprison Sangheili; you execute them."

The walls and seats were splattered with bright purple blood. Thel looked around with satisfaction. "That is a good start," he said, a pleased rumble in the back of his voice. "Throw the bodies out."

Now it was time to find out what the Kig-Yar, humans, and Unggoy were up to.

And make them all pay.

CHAPTER 28

The *Petya*'s alarms sounded. Jai bolted for the cockpit, where Mike was already strapping in. In the far distance a bright flash receded, a glowing ball of excited trace gases in the vacuum of space that had been disturbed by an explosion's shock wave.

"That's a Shiva," Mike said, reading off the monitors. "Probably three, actually."

"Nukes? Who's nuking the Rubble?" Adriana asked.

"Us," Mike said. "There's a UNSC ship in system. Some sort of stealthed ship."

"Prowler? ONI coming around to check up on us?" Jai wondered.

Mike shook his head, half of which was covered in shaving cream—he'd been in the head when the alarms flashed. "Would have piped us a message by now. No, this is fleet. Looks like a frigate on the long-range."

"One of our own," Adriana said.

"Getting the crap kicked out of it," Jai said.

Adriana nodded. "Look at all those ships surrounding it. What the hell were they thinking?"

"Arm us up. Let's get in there and see if we can help," Jai said.

"Too many ships," Mike said. "I don't have enough explosive surprises to get those guys off its tail. Plus, I'm seeing a bunch of them moving in to board it. That's a death trap, Jai."

Jai hit a console with his fist, leaving the imprint in the metal.

"Easy, cowboy," a female voice that wasn't Adriana's said.

Jai whirled to find Juliana's image appearing at navigation, her large eyes regarding his.

It's just a simulation, he told himself. Those eyes can't see, like they almost seem to right now.

The AI spread her arms. "I can help your UNSC friends; you can't. Mike is correct. They're surrounded. They fell into a trap. One of their bridge crew was a sympathizer who signaled the ship's location. They're being taken to temporary holding cells."

"And after that?" Jai asked.

"After that, well . . ." Juliana folded her arms. "If they followed instructions, I doubt they have working navigation data. Which means they're no major threat. They'll be left to live. If they aren't, I've threatened to stop working for the Rubble. They need me too much to ignore that. It all falls apart without me."

Jai glanced at Adriana over the top of the AI's image. Adriana smiled back.

"I will look after this," Juliana continued. "I'd like you to go look after Ignatio Delgado. I've sent Mike the coordinates."

"Adriana's pet Insurrectionist? Why?" Jai walked over and sat in front of the AI.

"He's in a spot of trouble. And we need him because, while I can spy on him and monitor his movements, he's been quite canny about keeping the navigation data hidden even from me. I think he fears you might hack me." Juliana cackled at the thought, then stopped abruptly, looked around, and continued. "I think at this point, Delgado may give you the data for safekeeping."

"Why is that?" Mike asked, eyes narrowed.

The AI smiled and shrugged. "Call it a hunch," she told the team of Spartans. And then she flickered off.

Jai frowned. "I don't feel like being some AI's errand boy."

Mike raised his hand. "Yeah, she's also holding back on us."

"How's that?" Jai moved to his side.

"The ship the dockworkers were passing rumors about, that was coming back from the colonies, was the *Kestrel,* remember? Well, it's out there now. The chatter is that the UNSC ship came in after it. Took me a bit to find her . . ."

Jai slapped him on the back. "Damn good. We go for the *Kestrel,* knock her engines out when she docks."

"And Delgado?" Adriana asked. "He's the next navigation puzzle."

"Once that smuggler's out, we snatch Delgado for the AI." Jai smiled. Everything was coming to a head now. It was time to move. Mike stood up and nodded. Gray Team was on the same page.

"Your pet AI? Jai, I think maybe it just likes you," Adriana said as she turned around to go back to where their Mark IV MJOLNIR armor waited on brackets. Jai and Mike followed.

"You're just jealous," Mike said, as they stopped in front of the armor. "But then, we both seem to be making friends out here. Shame Jai doesn't seem to have the social knack."

"Idiots," Jai said. "We're not supposed to be making friends."

"But it's so much more fun." Mike grinned.

Adriana chuckled, then looked at the armor waiting in the

gloom for them. "Get the feeling we're going to be spending a lot of time in our second skin?"

Jai reached a hand up and caressed the gray exterior.

Yes, he did have that feeling. Things were past that tipping point where you felt you could still back away and lie down in the grass and just observe.

No, someone had tossed grenades into the anthill. It was time to jump in and participate.

Back in action.

CHAPTER 29

Thel grumbled happily. They'd taken the Kig-Yar shuttle out farther away from the Rubble, slowly scanning the area until they'd found a larger Kig-Yar transport ship on its way to Metisette.

They boarded it, fast and quick, before the few Kig-Yar on board had even realized what had happened.

On board were several hundred Unggoy. The Kig-Yar had been in charge, but didn't have the numbers to run their own ships. Now the Kig-Yar were dead.

But the Unggoy had run the ship for the Kig-Yar. That made them useful. They were willing to work for Thel and his crew, or so the cowering Unggoy Deacon said as Thel stood on the purple-stained bridge. "It would be the Prophets' will," the Deacon yelped.

"It would be," Thel said from behind the Unggoy. "We are on a direct mission from a Hierarch."

The Unggoy waddled about, shifting its mouthpiece, to face Thel. It looked up and spread its arms out. "I do not question. I serve. That is our fate," it moaned.

Thel couldn't care less for Unggoy self-pity. "Tell your crew this ship flies where we command, or we will slaughter every last one of you. Saal will go down to engineering and watch over you. Veer will roam the corridors."

Veer growled, and the Unggoy backed up. "Sirs! We will do our ship duties! Doubt us not."

Thel turned to Veer and Saal. "Be wary. The slightest notion the Unggoy are playing games, hold nothing back."

Veer and Saal grunted affirmatively and walked out of the cockpit.

The deacon turned to go, but Thel held up a hand, and the Unggoy froze.

"What is down there, Unggoy?" Thel asked. He pointed at the image of the planet on a screen at the front of the cockpit.

It was Metisette. Its sickly, yellow-orange–colored atmosphere swirled; thick, cold storms lashed the icy surface.

The Unggoy stared at them, saying nothing.

Thel turned back to the screen and folded his arms. "Zhar, my closest advisor, didn't want to come here. He wanted to turn this transport right around to attack the Kig-Yar ship docked by the humans, and take that right back to High Charity so we could warn the prophets about the Jiralhanae treason."

"A noble choice," the Unggoy said.

"It is not," Thel said. "We were captured, and jailed. When we return, we will be lucky if we hold our titles, if not our very *names*." The Unggoy trembled at Thel's anger. "What is your name, Deacon?"

"Pipit," the Unggoy replied.

Thel folded his arms. "Pipit, one of my ancestors, a kaidon of Vadam, lost a war to one of the keep's bitter rivals. The new kaidon put my ancestor in the cellars, jails where the defeated were left in the most dishonorable manner imaginable. They were fed scraps, and visited by the invaders to be mocked and laughed at. The most honorable among the jailed killed themselves or each other.

"The kaidon escaped after weeks of starving. He had become so thin he could pull himself through the bars of his window looking out over the Vadam keep cliffs. He scaled the cliff, and swam down the river, all the way to the valley.

"The kaidon walked for many days, eating vermin and scraps, becoming lower than low, until he came into the vast deserts that lie in the interior of all our lands. And out there, after wandering for many years, built his strength, his hardness, and made allies from other wanderers. They were the least of the least, yes, but with a will to fight, and a will to live no matter the odds.

"With this new tribe, my ancestor returned to Vadam keep and scaled the walls. He killed his enemies all, throwing their bodies to the river. It is said that it ran purple with blood for a week. And when the kaidon was done killing his enemies, he opened the jails and killed the Vadam who had been cowardly enough to remain alive in them. That was my kaidon. That is *Vadam*. Our blood was forged in the desert, confirmed in the keep that day, and purified through Kaidon Ther's experiences. So it is carved on the Vadam saga wall."

Thel looked over at Zhar, who asked, "Shipmaster, do you have a point to retelling a stanza of your family's saga?"

Thel sat down in the shipmaster's chair at the center of the cockpit. "I can hardly turn my back on my lineage, can I, Zhar? I will not return to High Charity with a lost ship, knowing we were locked up by Kig-Yar, and little knowledge of what is happening here. I would be no better than the jailed Sangheili that Ther executed for being useless."

"It was a suggestion. An option," Zhar said.

"But it is not an option, as we are Sangheili." Thel now turned back to Deacon Pipit. "So you understand, Unggoy? We are here to stay. I ask you, again, what is on Metisette?"

"Dreams," Pipit sighed.

"Do not play word games," Thel growled. "Be plain."

"When commanders need fighters, Unggoy are ordered to breed and expand. Then we die in great numbers. Unggoy, you all say: do this, do that. Some dream of free," Pipit explained. "And though we hate Kig-Yar, this one named Reth, high commander, says to those Unggoy that they can come to Metisette. Come, build a home. Help change this moon so it becomes a place you can live where the methane is free in all the air. Breed free."

Zhar started to laugh. "And you believed this . . . Reth?"

Pipit looked up, beady red eyes squinting in anger. "Kig-Yar always betray, yes, but the opportunity . . ." The alien shrugged.

Thel looked down at the fatalistic little alien. "So Metisette has methane in the air that you can breathe."

"A place for Unggoy," Pipit said. "A safe place, where we can live without interference, without controls on our population that are imposed from on high. Where we can walk around without these chafing harnesses and breathing tanks."

"An Unggoy paradise," Thel muttered. "Where you can breed until you overrun the entire place." The Unggoy were well-known to reproduce like mad. During peacetime the Prophets monitored their population closely; the Unggoy had never cared for that. And even though they hated the Kig-Yar, it made sense that the Unggoy had jumped at the chance in this strange sequence of events to gain a world of their own.

Thel scratched his lower mandibles.

Saal called Thel over the intercom. "They have our infiltrator harness here," he said. "In their storage bay. The Kig-Yar stole it from our ship!"

Thel stopped scratching as he thought about the news. "We have a change of plans. Take the armor down to the Kig-Yar shuttle. Get the shuttle warmed up as well. We are going down."

"Into that murk?" Zhar protested from nearby.

"Yes. Zhar, the Prophets unleash the Unggoy to breed whenever there is a war; they stop mixing antibreeding hormones into the methane supplies. Now we have a renegade Kig-Yar breeding Unggoy. I think this 'Reth' is creating an army on the surface of Metisette for himself."

"So we are going to see for ourselves?" Zhar snorted.

"I want to talk to Reth," Thel said simply.

"Why?"

"If he is in charge of Metisette, he knows what is going on with the humans and the Kig-Yar working together. And he knows about the betrayal of the Jiralhanae. Reth knows things we need to know."

"And he is surrounded by hundreds of Unggoy," Zhar noted.

The deacon cleared his throat. Thel turned to him, and Pipit said, "Not hundreds."

Thel waited a moment. "Thousands?"

Pipit still bobbed his head. "Tens of . . ." but already the alien had shaken its head again.

"Hundreds?"

Now Pipit nodded eagerly as Zhar swore.

Reth had quite an army at his disposal. This would make getting to him a lot more difficult.

But Thel smiled. "We have our infiltrator harness back." That gave them an edge. They were not just Sangheili, but well armed, well armored, and also invisible Sangheili.

Like his ancestor Ther, the ancient kaidon, Thel would come back against great odds, swarming into the middle of his enemy before they even knew what had happened.

"Get us ready, Zhar," Thel ordered. "We are going down there. Pipit, Veer will take over while we are gone; you will help him. Give us the coordinates to Reth. And if you deceive us, Veer will be here to make sure you suffer immediately for it."

Pipit nodded and, in a voice that seemed to crack, gave Zhar the necessary coordinates.

"Thank you, Deacon." Thel looked around. "You will also need to have an Unggoy pilot meet us at the shuttle, Deacon. Talk to the Unggoy down there on Metisette, tell them you had an accident aboard, and need to be resupplied with methane for Unggoy to breathe."

With that done, Thel stalked off the bridge with Zhar close behind.

"Three of us against hundreds of thousands of Unggoy," Zhar said.

"The little ones will cower with fear and run from us in floods," Thel proclaimed as they thudded down the corridors.

Zhar laughed. "You are confident."

"I am Sangheili," Thel said. "This is what we are."

They crammed into the tiny shuttle. Spec ops armor lay on the benches where Unggoy would have lined up and sat. Now there was only one Unggoy, a terrified pilot who remained strapped in and staring at the Sangheili in terror.

Thel felt the warmth that came to him when he had a direct plan. "Take us down, Saal."

Once they'd broken through the worst of the deceleration in the upper atmosphere of Metisette, Thel unstrapped himself and walked back to don his spec ops armor, and helped Zhar with his. The shuttle shook and rattled its way through the thick atmosphere, but they remained balanced on their feet easily enough.

Once suited up, Zhar flicked the armor on, and faded away into invisibility.

"It works," Thel said. Then tested his own.

Zhar and Saal switched places. As Saal struggled into his armor alone and Zhar flew the shuttle in, Thel walked up to the edge of the cockpit to look down.

Nothing but thick orange clouds and haze—at least until they broke out under the clouds to fly over a jagged, ice-cold landscape whipped by constant storms.

Zhar banked them slowly through the orange murk toward a massive crater. As they flew across it the sides reached up like distant mountains, and Thel could see a massive lake at its center.

In the distance stood what looked like a keep, straddling a giant river of liquid that tumbled over the edge of the crater down to its floor. The keep was ramshackle, made out of parts of old, ruined ships that had been rudely deorbited and landed near the lip of the immense waterfall.

But it stood high with additions that had been built in between the spaceships' hulls, with tubes and domes that hung like carbuncles pocking the rock faces and rising above the river. Thel saw that it could house hundreds of thousands.

Elevators ran down along the sides of the thousand feet of waterfall to structures around the giant lake.

Metisette wasn't a world one could breath in. Its mostly

nitrogen atmosphere would leave Sangheili, or Kig-Yar, or most races with nothing to breathe.

The liquid on the very cold Metisette was methane. Thel watched as a stream of it fell off the lip of the crater. Methane mist hung strong in the air all throughout the natural valleys and low areas of the crater, thanks to the falls.

"Giant reactors heat the land all around the crater," the pilot spoke up, pride suddenly more powerful than its fear of the Sangheili. "It makes more of the mists."

Zhar skimmed the lake and approached the falls. The shuttle hit the mists, and then rose up near the falls, pressing Thel against the seat.

"We pop over the edge and land, Zhar," Thel shouted. "Make sure your armor is tight, Saal. It will give us air until we are inside the structure. If Reth is breathing and Kig-Yar are in there, then we will be okay.

"If there is only methane, we go in as far as we can before coming back. Zhar stays with the shuttle, hiding, as this Unggoy has the other Unggoy load up our shuttle with tanks of methane."

Thel watched the remains of a large Kig-Yar merchant ship appear over the lip, and Zhar arced over it into a large landing area marked out in plasma-melted rock.

As soon as the shuttle touched rock, the three Sangheili activated their camouflage and flickered and vanished. Zhar sat across from the Unggoy who was supposedly piloting the shuttle, and Thel and Saal jumped out the back of the shuttle.

The Unggoy pilot had not lied—the land here was bitterly cold to Thel, but it was tolerable. Like an arctic waste. Not nearly as cold as the rest of the moon.

Silent ghosts moving through the orange murk that hung in the air, they maneuvered across the field, keeping well clear of the

Unggoy who waddled out across the landing pad toward the shuttle, barking and shouting in their language.

Thel kept an easy lope going, covering the ground so fast that any Unggoy who noticed a wavering in the air would surely shake their heads and dismiss it as a trick of the light.

They slipped in through a series of giant airlocks, where Unggoy still had to wear their harnesses and tanks.

Thel looked around. "This is Kig-Yar territory," he whispered to Saal. It made sense that the lesser aliens were here in a repurposed old ship, mounted near the lip of the falls. It made for a commanding view, because although the Unggoy felt like this was their world, Thel would imagine that the Kig-Yar saw it differently.

Saal found a lone Unggoy, and an empty room in the back of what had once been the large hangar bays of the Kig-Yar ship.

It didn't take long to get the Unggoy to give up the location of Reth.

"The cockpit room, at the very top."

Saal snapped the Unggoy's neck and they took the emergency maintenance tubes up through the ship. Thel panted heavily and his mandibles were wide open, his tongue flicking the air, by the time they arrived at the top.

Four Kig-Yar guarded the cockpit's doors, but two of them were looking out the windows down to the launch pad, bored, their plasma rifles slung over their backs.

They never had a chance to turn and see what attacked them. The two Sangheili were in their midst in a split second, firing point-blank into their faces with their own plasma rifles.

The other two Kig-Yar had a second to squall loudly before they met the same fate, and Thel blew the cockpit doors apart with a grenade.

Inside the carpeted, lavishly furnished room sat a single

Kig-Yar, his large eyes staring at the shimmering flaws in the air before him. Thel shut his invisibility off.

"Sangheili," the Kig-Yar hissed. "Damn you, what have you done? Do you know who you cross?"

"You are Reth?" Thel asked.

"Yes," the Kig-Yar said.

"You let Unggoy breed without control. You pretend to be a voice of the Prophets here. You are a heretic." Thel raised his plasma rifle and struck Reth in the head with it.

"Pick him up," Thel ordered Saal. "Let us return to the shuttle."

A loud warble echoed across the corridors. Thel looked around. "That sounded like an alarm."

Saal walked over to the front of the cockpit, Reth slung casually over a shoulder. "It is. We should call Zhar, have him fly up here. We can get outside onto the top and get him to pick us up there."

Thel stepped forward to stand next to Saal and looked down. Saal murmured into the air, talking to Zhar.

"Zhar needs just a minute. Too many Unggoy inside the shuttle."

Hundreds of feet below in a courtyard formed from the superstructures of three or four mothballed spaceships, thousands of Unggoy streamed out. The crowds ran to surround the building they were in.

"They cannot enter," Saal said. "Almost all of them have no harnesses or air. The methane mists out there let them breathe. Where are their harnesses?"

Thel looked at the unconscious Kig-Yar on Saal's shoulder. "The Kig-Yar either have not made them many, or are keeping them under lock and key."

"But why?" Saal asked.

"Because they cannot leave Metisette, or even attack this Kig-Yar structure in the center of their own keep, if they have no tanks."

"Doesn't help us right now," Saal said, looking at the quadrangle fill with Unggoy. "Enough Unggoy seem to have harnesses to cause *us* trouble."

Thel turned and looked back down the corridor, hearing the sound of Unggoy screeches. "It tells us who's really in charge of all this."

"The Kig-Yar."

Thel looked back at Reth's limp form. "Yes. That one in particular. Wake him up. We may have to put a gun to his head. What is Zhar's progress?"

Saal cocked his head, listening to an update from down below. "Zhar is closing the ramp and warming the shuttle up."

"The timing will be tight," Thel said. He walked over to the doors with his plasma rifle up and ready. "Be ready to blow the windows out when he gets airborne."

"My honor," Saal grunted. He set Reth down and slapped the Kig-Yar's face. "Wake up," the Sangheili zealot growled.

CHAPTER 30

Keyes watched his people being herded toward gates. They huddled together and stared down at their feet as they moved forward. Men in gray uniforms, rifles slung at the ready, moved about the edges, pushing the crew back into line toward the five checkpoints the rails led everyone toward.

The *Midsummer Night* had been docked with an asteroid. From the cargo bay they'd all been herded out at gunpoint, down a long corridor in the endcap of the habitat, and walked out into the interior.

But the tall rails, all enclosed in chicken wire with razor wire wrapped around that, effectively prevented them from walking out into the habitat until they'd passed through five stations. Humorless-looking officials stood by small podiums in the stations with computer pads.

"Stay *single* file," a guard shouted.

The lines formed up, people jammed against each other, wondering what came next. They were face-to-face with the enemy: Insurrectionists.

Captured.

A woman in a black uniform with yellow trim walked up to a dais mounted over the gates. She brushed back a long lock of black hair, then folded her arms at the small of her back in a sort of parade rest.

When she spoke her voice was amplified so that the entire crowd could hear her. "Welcome to the habitat Asuncion," the woman said.

Keyes leaned back and looked up at the far side of the asteroid's interior, far on the other side from where he stood. Patches of gardens and trees could be seen. It was odd, seeing something almost pastoral in a megastructure like this.

"And welcome to the Rubble," the woman continued. "My name is Maria Esquival. I am here to help orient you to your new situation."

Keyes was surrounded by his remaining bridge crew. Lt. Dante Kirtley had folded his arms and was watching the woman, but Junior Grade Rai Li checked out the crowded crew, looking worried.

Behind Keyes loitered a handful of ODSTs, with Faison standing in their midst. He raised an eyebrow at Keyes.

Maria Esquival continued her speech. "After the destruction of Madrigal, as we escaped into the asteroids and rocks here, we had some very tough decisions to make about who we would become: refugees struggling to exist, fighting over scraps? Or a civilization?

"We chose civilization. We worked hard to build the Rubble. We worked hard because we knew we had something to build. A world like nothing the UNSC has ever known, with its strict hierarchies and militaristic command."

Keyes looked over at Dante, who rolled his eyes. "More Insurrectionist bullshit," the comms specialist muttered.

"Free of the trappings of being a colony, we reinvented ourselves from the ground up. The Rubble is a technocracy. All of its municipal functions, all its laws, are voted on by our members. Some of us are Insurrectionist, some of us are refugees from Madrigal. Others are miners who were here from the beginning. Some are smugglers who made it here from the Inner Colonies. All are welcome.

"We mean that. All are welcome to have the right to vote. This includes you, crew of the *Midsummer Night*."

Esquival paused to let that sink in. In the crowd, Kirtley leaned back toward Keyes. "They all vote on everything. Like even security? That'd be insane."

"Because we believe in freedom, the Rubble invites you to join our democracy. You have a choice in what happens next to you. You can choose to turn your back on the imperialist nature of the UNSC. Many of you may have come from Outer Colonies. Colonies that fell to the alien Covenant while the UNSC took their time to enact methods of dealing with the aliens. Colonies that you know were not as well protected as they could have been, because the UNSC's loyalties are to Earth first, the Inner Colonies next, and the Outer Colonies last. Here in the Rubble, you are equal among all."

Rai Li sniffed. "How many crew you think are going to buy that crap?"

Keyes looked out over the crowd of heads. How many crew were survivors of border colonies, or had family in the Outer Colonies?

He thought of his sister for a second, a twinge of pain at the thought of her dying without UNSC protection, out there alone in the Outer Colonies.

Or maybe, Keyes suddenly thought, maybe they'd survived. Just like the Rubble had.

The idea captured him for a second, and then Keyes shook himself. No, he had to remember what the Covenant was really about. The Rubble was some strange anomaly . . .

"Too many." Keyes rubbed his jaw, thoughtfully. "And can you blame them? We have no options. We're stuck out here. Behind the lines. They might as well start trying to find allies, figure out what the new game is. We're refugees, now."

His eyes burned. He hadn't slept since they'd been boarded, running from place to place to make sure things went smoothly.

Now it was over.

Everything was over.

He'd read about POWs in past wars, unlucky bastards who'd been the first shot out of the air and stuck in a camp for the length of a war.

If he lived, he'd be one of those footnotes.

Maria Esquival cleared her throat. "But, as you are UNSC, and have a checkered background, there are some concessions that have to be made when integrating you into the population of the Rubble.

"You will have to swallow a motion tracker, in the form of a pill. This will let the Rubble's AI monitor and track your location. You will have to report for counseling and you will be assigned a case officer who will review the integration process. However these things are a small price to pay for your freedom."

Keyes wished he had his pipe to fiddle with. He had to leave it aboard the ship, along with any other personal effects or objects as they were moved to Asuncion.

"Those of you who wish to become citizens, have only to ask when you reach Processing. You will be split off to a separate location. Those of you still loyal to the UNSC, who refuse the pill, we will, of course, be forced to jail you."

With that, Esquival turned around and left her perch. The large lines staggered forward.

"A lot of them are asking for citizenship," Faison said from behind Keyes.

"Can't blame them," Keyes said. "One can understand what's going through their minds."

"You're not going to do anything about it?" Faison asked.

"We're trapped. We have nothing. What do you want me to do? They're doing the rational thing."

Faison grabbed Keyes by the shoulder. "Either we're soldiers or we're not. Defeat or not, we should never forget that, Keyes. Give them a speech. Say *something* to counteract all that, because whatever this is you're doing right now, this isn't leadership. Where's the man who had us all jump out of that freighter?"

Say something.

Keyes cleared his throat, then jumped up onto the railing. He wobbled for a second. "Crew of the *Midsummer Night*," he shouted.

The snaking line paused. And Keyes suddenly felt like a blank sheet of paper. Nothing came to him.

Faison punched his shin, and Keyes sucked his breath in. "Crew of the *Midsummer Night*, we have had a hard blow, I know. Some of you, after hearing all this, will have a hard choice to make.

"Just know this. No matter who we are, or why we give our service, we all joined to fight a common enemy. The people here, although they fled the destruction of their own world, think that the Covenant can be allies. The same creatures that destroyed their world. I think this is an illusion. So I hope that you will, if the time ever comes, stand by my side again if the need calls for it. With no hard feelings. I will not be joining their citizenry. I remain ready to fight the Covenant and protect humanity, as I swore to do when I joined the fight. As did you all."

Keyes got back down.

There was only silence. Rai Li finally shook her head. "That was an awkward speech."

"Doesn't matter," Faison said. "What mattered was that he gave it." And Keyes knew he was right; he was stumbling toward being the leader they all wanted . . . and needed.

Keyes grabbed Faison by the shoulder. "By the way, why are so many ODSTs at the front of the line? They look like they're going to be citizens."

Faison nodded and looked Keyes in the eye. "Well, of course. You know the Helljumpers: first in and all *that*." He gave the last word in emphasis.

Then he winked.

Keyes got it. He could still trust Helljumpers to be Helljumpers. Faison was just making sure he got men out into the general populace in case they needed them out there.

"You've got company," Lt. Kirtley said.

Maria Esquival and several black-clad men pushed through the crowd of crew toward Keyes.

"Lieutenant Jacob Keyes, I gather?" Esquival said.

"Yes ma'am," Keyes replied.

"No more speeches."

Keyes laughed. "I thought we were all equals here."

Esquival tilted her head. "You just announced you gave up the right to citizenry, right?"

"Yes . . ."

One of the black-uniformed men punched Keyes in the stomach. Faison stepped forward, but Keyes waved him back as he coughed.

"Then I'm pleased to report I'm under no obligation to treat you as a citizen, Lieutenant Keyes." Esquival smiled. "The problem is, you have a position of power over your men. Such speeches, while admirable, are given from that position of power. Many possible citizens might feel compelled to go to jail who wouldn't otherwise."

"It'll all end," Keyes said. "When the Covenant gets bored of whatever game it's playing here."

Esquival sighed. "You're so sure of yourself. The war with the Covenant is something the UNSC somehow started back on Harvest, we're sure of it. This is not our war, we just got caught up in it. It's *your* war. While you all fight to the last man with your brotherhood of arms, we've built something here. I don't know if the UNSC has noticed, but the Covenant is comprised of a number of varying races. Many of these were allowed into the Covenant. We here in the Rubble are looking for ways humanity can *join* their ranks. As a junior race, perhaps. But we're adept, Lieutenant Keyes, we'll work our way up."

Keyes shook his head. "You conspire with the enemy."

Esquival sighed. "Take him and his bridge crew to the jails. Get them out of here."

They zip-tied his hands, and then led him off. Several junior officers started applauding, but it died out nervously after a few seconds.

CHAPTER 31

Somewhere Near Habitat Caribo, Inner Rubble, 23 Librae

Jai eyeballed the Insurrectionist smuggler in the distance. They'd been tagging along far behind it until it had docked.

Now he flew in the weightless vacuum toward it.

He struck the surface, absorbing the impact with his knees. Even as he rebounded, he threw a magnetic grapple at the hull to stay attached.

Adriana hit the hull next to him. She grabbed his leg with one hand to stop him from bouncing back off. She had a large plastic case tucked underneath the other arm.

Jai looked at her helmet. "What does Mike have for us today?"

"Electromagnetic pulse bomb. Mostly harmless—except to anything electronic aboard the *Kestrel*. It'll wipe it all clean," Adriana said. She opened the case and pulled out a large, disc-shaped device that looked like a landmine. "He's been saving this one."

With a thud the EMP attached itself to the hull. Adriana leaned over it and tapped out a code. "It talking to you, Mike?"

"We're live," Mike reported. "Now get well clear of that thing. The EMP pulse is strong enough to fry a whole ship. Usually our armor can recover from those bursts pretty quickly, but it will still knock out your MJOLNIR briefly if you're too close. I want to wait until we're all back aboard and well clear before—"

Jai spotted movement. "We have company. They're coming from the airlock."

Two black space suits, hardened-looking affairs, coasted quickly at them. A burst of flame from their backs jetted them down the hull even faster.

"Hostile or curious?" Mike asked.

Muzzle flash answered that; the two suits had machine guns in either hand.

Adriana bent down and leapt at them, pulling out her battle rifle and firing. Her rounds sparked and pinged off well-hardened material and the two suits curled up in a ball.

"They were expecting us," Jai said.

"We've been here a while, it's obvious *something's* happening," Mike replied. "Not too surprising they've rustled up a response of some sort. I'm jockeying *Petya* in closer."

"No," Adriana said. "Get ready to hit the EMP; we don't want to give these goons a chance with it. They've probably raised the alarm. We also don't want to give them time to get the data off the ship somehow."

She grunted as she smacked into one of the suits.

Jai leapt at the second one while paying out the rope on his grapple with one hand. He didn't bother shooting at the man until they collided. He ripped the rocket pack off the back of the combat space suit and threw it away, did the same with the man's two guns, then yanked himself back toward the smuggler with the line.

The black suit hung still, unable to move anywhere.

Adriana had smashed in the faceplate of their other opponent. The man's dying breath hung in the air between the two, a crystalline and fading cloud.

She threw the suit away, the motion pushing her toward the hull.

"Four more of them," she said. The glare of their packs marked them, flying right at them from the asteroid.

"Let's get out of here."

With all the strength available to them from the combination of their physique and the MJOLNIR powered armor, they crouched and leapt for the *Petya*, over a mile away.

Halfway across, Mike triggered the EMP bomb with a dramatic electric fireshow that crackled across the *Kestrel*'s hull.

It also left their chasers immobile, their electronics burnt out by the invisible wave of electrical energy the bomb had released.

Jai's heads-up display flickered slightly. "Cutting it close, Mike?"

"A little," came the response.

CHAPTER 32

The first trio of Unggoy to turn the corridor walked right into Thel's line of fire. Short bursts of plasma struck them in the center of their torsos.

Footsteps pattered behind Thel. He turned around and saw Reth trying to run away from Saal. Saal grabbed the Kig-Yar leader and dragged him back toward the windows and out of the direct line of fire.

"Do you two realize what you are doing?" the Kig-Yar asked.

Saal cocked his head. "We are kidnapping you."

Reth did not find it as amusing as Saal seemed to. "There are hundreds of thousands of Unggoy out there, all who are at my command."

"They are out there," Saal said. "But you and I know they cannot all get in here." And Saal chuckled.

"So you plan on doing what then?" Reth hissed. "You are meddling in extraordinarily important affairs."

Thel ducked behind the doorframe as more Unggoy spilled out into the far side of the corridor. One stumbled when he saw Thel duck back around with his plasma rifle. "Sangheili! Defend the Redoubt!" it screamed, and the back of its methane tank exploded from another accurate shot. Flaming debris struck other Unggoy, who lost their cohesive charge down the corridor and scattered, trying to pat the flames away before they got burned.

"That should hold them for a bit," Thel muttered. But then to his surprise, the Unggoy turned back toward him again.

These were some very determined Unggoy.

"They have something to fight for," Reth shouted. "Sangheili, you don't understand what's going on. You must free me. I can save your lives. I swear it."

Thel watched the Unggoy charge. There was little love between the Kig-Yar and Sangheili—Reth's kind resented the position Sangheili held in the Covenant. And the Sangheili regarded the Kig-Yar as little more than scavengers.

Thel suspected Reth was lying and would happily have them killed the moment they set their weapons down.

But Reth pressed on nonetheless. "You are the Sangheili from *Retribution's Thunder*, am I right?"

Why was Zhar taking so long? Thel shot another handful of Unggoy.

"Yes."

More came up the elevators and stairs and ran forward.

"It was a mistake. We should not have betrayed you to those Jiralhanae," Reth said in as soothing a voice as a Kig-Yar could. "But we needed you to not interfere! Not after all the work we've done so far."

Thel shook his head. "What is done is done. You have made your choices. Now we are making ours." Way too many Unggoy were rushing up to the top floor, flooding over dead bodies in the hall. Thel knew they were going to continue until he ran out of the charge in his plasma rifle.

"You go against the Hierarchs!" Reth shouted.

Saal backhanded the Kig-Yar. "We are on a direct mission *for* the Hierarchs. Do not dare blaspheme like that. As if you speak for the Hierarchs . . ." he muttered.

Thel saw out of the corner of his eye that the Kig-Yar looked stunned. "Which Hierarch?"

"The Prophet of Regret himself," Saal proclaimed proudly.

Reth shook his head. "Wrong Prophet," he muttered, the feathered spines on his head wavering in confusion.

Wrong Prophet? Saal and Thel looked at each other, and then Saal shouted, "Zhar is up!"

Sure enough a column of disturbed air rippled just outside the windows.

"Blow the windows out!" Thel ordered. He shut the doors and locked them against the Unggoy.

Saal used a sticky grenade on the thick windows. The blue light pulsed, and then Thel grabbed Reth to shield him as the explosion shook the room.

Glass shards flew out, and the thunder of engines filled the room, bringing the acrid clouds of methane mist with it.

Thel hoisted Reth onto his back. "You scream, struggle, or move about, you will regret it dearly. Now take a deep breath while there's still some air!"

He followed Saal out onto the lip of the window, looking at the slope of the repurposed ship stretching out before him. They didn't want to go that way. Slide off the edge, they'd have a very long fall.

Thel pulled himself and the weight of the Kig-Yar up, using

his hands and legs to crawl up onto the slope of metal above the windows. Saal scrambled up ahead, unencumbered, to the top of the ship, where the shuttle hovered, waiting for them.

They needed one last tactic to gain them some time. Thel pulled out a pair of grenades and let them roll down toward the slope of the hull. As they dropped by his feet he kicked them in through the window.

He scrambled up after Saal as fast as he could, the grenades' explosions blowing red flame and debris out of the windows underneath him as he ran.

The Unggoy pilot stood in the back of the shuttle, eyes wide in stunned surprise as he watched them run toward him. Zhar gently touched the top of the old Kig-Yar wreck with the shuttle and Saal and Thel leapt aboard. The tips of other grounded ships poked out of the thick, ruddy mists all around them like towers.

"Take it up!" Saal shouted forward, and they accelerated away, the structure dwindling at the top of the falls, the crater lake falling into the distance.

CHAPTER 33

Habitat El Cuidad, Inner Rubble, 23 Librae

Despite being left alone, Ignatio Delgado had still not managed to free himself.

The thing was, trying to use a sliver of metal to pick the lock of a pair of handcuffs was a challenging proposition. And Delgado couldn't even get the sliver to reach the keyhole.

With a loud sigh the one guard in the warehouse stood up and folded up whatever he'd been watching and pocketed it. "Alright, Delgado, things are settling down. Time to get you moved out."

Delgado nodded, filled with a sense of foreboding. This was it, then.

The guard noticed the look on his face. "Come on, Delgado. It's not like that."

"Really?" Delgado looked the heavily muscled man up and down. "How is it, then?"

The man shrugged. "All Bonifacio and the Security Council know is that the data keeps getting found out. Better to keep you on close watch."

Delgado shook his head. "Then why are you doing this? Why the hired muscle, the empty warehouse?"

"It keeps you under his eye. He doesn't trust you, Delgado. You're a wild card, man." Delgado was unshackled from the chain, then handcuffed to the man's right wrist.

With a shove, Delgado was pushed forward.

"What's your name?" Delgado asked.

"Owen."

"Your real name?"

"What do you think?" "Owen" asked, looking down at Delgado as he herded him outside to a waiting tube car.

"Where are we going?" Delgado asked.

Owen smiled. "One of Bonifacio's working ships."

Delgado frowned. "Working ships? He have a lot of broken ones?"

"Look." Owen leaned in close, almost whispering. "Relax a little, Delgado. Bonifacio's going to be in a foul mood because his smuggler ship, it just got fried."

"What?"

Owen was laughing. "The best-laid plans . . . Someone really doesn't like Bonifacio. They fried his ship. It's structurally intact, but nothing inside it works; the data got wiped out."

Delgado swallowed. The Spartans had struck again. "So now Bonifacio needs me."

"Pretty much."

The tube car stopped after making its way between a handful of coupled asteroids. Owen opened the door, and Delgado quickly followed him to avoid being yanked along.

Peter Bonifacio stood near an airlock, along with a handful of Security Council members. Including Diego Esquival.

Owen unlocked the handcuffs, and Delgado massaged his wrists. "What's this all about?"

"Where's the navigation data, Mr. Delgado?" one of the suited Security Council members asked.

Delgado stood still for a second. "Safe. As we agreed on."

Diego pursed his lips. "Bonifacio presented evidence to the council that there are Earth-first elements within our population that have attacked any navigation data that might lead ships of any sort back to Earth or the Inner Colonies. The data you have needs to be transported to its final destination, where it will be better safeguarded."

"Final destination?" Delgado looked around at them. "What final destination? The Kig-Yar? Come on, you know where that will lead."

"We're moving it to the Exodus Project," said one of the councilmen, an older man with scars across his face. "It's final. We've all voted. So please, Mr. Delgado, give up the data. You've served the Rubble well. It's time to hand it over now."

"What the hell is this Exodus Project?" Delgado snapped.

"It's just a big emergency plan," Diego said. "We can't talk about the particulars."

"And it needs nav data?" Delgado looked at Diego.

"Yes." Diego nodded, and spread his arms. "It really does, Ignatio. Please, trust me on this. Trust the Council as the Rubble's elected leaders."

Delgado looked at the other members. They didn't look like they meant him any ill.

But was it the right choice, whatever they had in mind? Delgado took a deep breath. It wasn't his decision to make, was it?

The Rubble had elected the entire Council for a reason. The Council had hired Delgado.

He was no longer keeper of the data.

"Okay," Delgado said. "It's aboard *Distancia*. I have to key everything open."

Diego laughed. "In plain sight, huh?"

"The best place." For a quick moment, everything felt okay. Maybe even normal. Delgado relaxed slightly.

The sensation was shattered as Peter Bonifacio stepped forward. "I'll take him over to *Distancia*, then meet the rest of you at Exodus. The *Distancia* only has a light guard on it. It's an easy target. My guards aren't just Rubble Defense volunteers, they have actual fighting experience." There was accusation in his glare, and Delgado saw a few nod in agreement. It looked like Bonifacio had been knocking Delgado's ability to keep the data safe.

Diego came forward. "I go with you." He and Delgado shared a glance.

Bonifacio shrugged. "I'd be delighted to have you aboard, Councilman, as well as anyone else who wants to come. Keep in mind, my ship's quarters are cramped. This way." He held out his hand, indicating that they should go first.

His guards had already cycled through the airlock into the ship Bonifacio had waiting for them.

It was a cramped ship, a converted tug of some sort. It had probably once grappled dirty asteroids and pushed them into new orbits to be harvested by the miners and their processing plants. Now it was Bonifacio's personal transport. Quick enough, Delgado thought, looking around the extended cockpit once they'd come in through the airlock. But still a bit over the top. Who had a personal ship just for transport in the Rubble? It was part of Bonifacio's desire to preen and make a point of showing how special he was.

Bonifacio got inside, gave the order to leave, and turned to Delgado. In the darkly lit cockpit he looked birdlike, his eyes pools of beady darkness. "Someone fried my ship, everything electrical was shorted, and several good men guarding it are dead. That *costs*. A lot."

"I'm sorry to hear it," Delgado said, eyeing the three large guards now surrounding him in the tiny cockpit.

Diego chuckled, and Bonifacio turned to him. "This amuses you? The future of the Rubble is laughable? I'm working hard to make sure we have a future, despite your meddling."

"A future?" Diego shook his head. "You're full of shit, Bonifacio. You care about future profits, not the future."

"Yeah?" Bonifacio reached into his pocket, hands trembling slightly, face red. "Were you all so high-and-mighty when the Covenant first came? Tell Delgado the real story, and how you all, in your democratic glory, turned to *one* person when it all came to a head."

Diego didn't say anything.

Bonifacio shook his head and pulled out a Sweet William. He pointed the cigar at Diego. "They tell you how the Kig-Yar contact *really* happened? I'll bet not. Because it doesn't make those men look good."

He lit the cigar and drew in a long pull, then laughed, cigar smoke puffing out of his mouth. "They crapped their pants when that first Kig-Yar ship swung by the Rubble, scanning us, checking everything out. Wanted to know what to do. Attack it, or try to pack up and run to some other part of the system? And if attack, how? But they were taking so long to deliberate, I did something else.

"I hailed it. And I offered to trade. Sent them a manifest of everything I could imagine we had in our storage areas. I explained we weren't UNSC, that we hated them. That we were rebels. Because, really, even other species have to know about trade, right, Delgado? Economics, that's universal. Everyone wants to better themselves."

"That was the real first encounter?" Delgado asked. "So it's the second where their ship appeared and offered to trade and set up in the Rubble?"

"A month later. Some sort of Kig-Yar big shot named Reth had a box that could translate their speech into ours. Like they've been studying us," Diego said. "And they wanted to trade."

Bonifacio nodded. "We took guns off them to sell to our brothers, where we could smuggle them back to the colonies, in exchange for goods. The Kig-Yar, in turn, wanted slipspace drives."

"Slipspace drives?" Delgado frowned.

"Turns out the Kig-Yar are pretty low on the Covenant totem pole." Bonifacio smirked. "They're not allowed to build drives for their own ships. Its engineering is all done by the ones they call Prophets. Closed boxes for the Kig-Yar. See, they're not the monolithic juggernaut the UNSC makes them out to be, this Covenant. They have divisions and inequalities. And where those exist, we have what you call a market, Mr. Delgado. Combine the engines with Earth's location, and the Rubble will do more for the Insurrection than any other place in history."

"But what happens when the Kig-Yar slip up and we're all found out?" Delgado asked. "The Covenant will be back to glass us."

"We leave," Diego muttered.

"Ahhh, exodus, exodus, exodus," Bonifacio waved his cigar around. "Diego, we have spent so long building all this. And you want to run away from it?"

"I don't," Diego said. "But it's irresponsible to not have a backup plan."

"I'll tell you what's irresponsible. Irresponsible is promising the Kig-Yar slipspace engines, taking their payments of nifty little weapons and shipping them back to the colonies, but then pretending to warehouse those engines until you've got them all gathered up. When you never intended to hand them over."

"Damn it, Bonifacio," Diego shouted, "the council voted to proceed with the Exodus Project. It's a backup plan. Once we have enough slipspace engines installed, then we'll hand the rest of them over."

"The Kig-Yar know what you've been doing anyway," Bonifacio said dismissively.

"What?" Diego stared at Bonifacio.

"You can't take an asteroid habitat as big as the Exodus Project and hang it way back off the Rubble, and not expect them to miss it. Plus, they really want their engines. They haven't believed your official excuses for not getting as many delivered to them as promised—not in the slightest. They are our allies, our business partners. We stand a chance to live on. Let the Covenant and UNSC fight, while we make money and trade instead."

Delgado stared at both men. "The Exodus Project is a giant habitat?"

"He's pretty much told you what it is," Diego said, annoyed. "The largest rock in the Rubble was held back from the beginning. The surface was coated to try and stealth it. Back at the start, it was an emergency in-system retreat: get as many civilians in it if the Covenant came back in force and try to sneak out to the Oort cloud far on the edges of the system where no one ventures.

"Now the Exodus Project is being outfitted with slipspace drives. A lot of them. The idea is not to hide in the system, but to head out away from the UNSC, and the Covenant. Just get into the stream and keep going until we're well away from all of this."

"That's audacious," Delgado said. "How many citizens can it hold?"

"It's big," Diego said. "Big enough for a million citizens."

"And you've hidden it away, all this time?" Delgado couldn't believe it. In the Rubble, where everything was voted on, the Security Council had pulled off something significant: a major secret.

The tug fired a series of thruster bursts and slammed into a docking collar.

Bonifacio grabbed Diego by the shoulders. "Look, Diego. I know you and I don't exactly agree on everything. But I'm a Council member, just like you. I want to see the Rubble continue and prosper. I'm not your enemy. You know that, right?"

"I know that," Diego said. "I'm sorry."

"I want that data on Exodus protected, but not out here in the Rubble where people are attacking it—whoever the hell it is that's doing that. Understand?"

Diego nodded.

"Good." Bonifacio pulled Diego tighter. "Now tell Delgado here to let us onto his ship so we can get it and do our duty."

Diego looked at Delgado. "Give him what he needs."

Delgado bit his lip. "You sure about this?"

"Yeah." Diego sounded subdued. "It'll be okay. And we'll need to talk to you about the Exodus Project. You can't repeat any of that to anyone."

"I can keep a secret," Delgado said, as the airlock doors opened.

Diego laughed. "I know. And after this, we'll make everything right for you. You took shots for us. They can't forget that."

They trudged out from Bonifacio's tug down an access tube to a set of quiet docks that Delgado had chosen. The rock ceilings sloped fifteen feet overhead, and only four or five docking collars led into this small chamber, as it was an old mining depot.

Delgado crossed the silent chamber to the airlock where *Distancia* was docked. They all crowded into the airlock and cycled through and in.

Delgado took a deep breath, pulling in the smell of metal, oil, and sweat. *Distancia* had once hauled miners out from Madrigal orbit across the system to the Rubble. Now she ferried cargo in and around the Rubble, from one end to another. Quicker than tube cars, as he didn't have to route through each habitat, pausing for traffic.

It felt good to be back aboard.

Maybe if Bonifacio was telling the truth, and he was really just a maverick Security Council member, then Delgado could just go back to ferrying things about the Rubble. Like before Diego had called, talking about the disappearing navigation data, asking him if he'd take on hiding it for the council, as he knew the Rubble the best. And he was the only person Diego personally trusted.

Going back to ferrying sounded good, Delgado thought, as he walked the small group over to the safe hidden under the floor grates of the tiny kitchen on the ship, halfway toward the cockpit.

It opened on his fingerprint, and Delgado pulled the oval container of hard plastic that held the chip out. He offered it to Diego.

Bonifacio reached out a hand, and Diego shook his head. "I think I'll be the one who keeps it on his person until we get it to the Exodus."

"I was afraid you'd say that," Bonifacio said.

Delgado turned around, eye to eye with the barrel of a very large pistol in Bonifacio's hand. "Hand it over to *me*, Delgado."

Diego swore, and was hit in the ribs by one of Bonifacio's men.

"Thank you," Bonifacio took the navigation data away from him. "Thank you very much, Delgado. I'd hoped to just take it and promise to meet you two aboard the Exodus and never show, but Diego had second thoughts. You're rubbing off on him. Either way, Reth is really, really going to appreciate this."

CHAPTER 34

The Kig-Yar named Reth screamed, a primal roar of pain and horror that echoed throughout the corridors of the ship, all the way up to the cockpit, where Thel sat poring over Kig-Yar estimates of human strength in the Rubble.

Zhar stood up, but Thel held up a hand. "I ordered Saal not to do this. I will go."

For a moment Zhar remained up, then he folded back down into his chair. "What—"

"That is my concern, Zhar." Thel walked out of the cockpit, past the Unggoy clustered in the halls. They chattered nervously and cleared a path as Thel strode by.

Thel walked to Reth's cell. The Kig-Yar had been strapped to the wall, his arms and legs splayed out in a large X by strong straps.

On the other side of the energy bars, Saal stood in front of the Kig-Yar. As he leaned forward, the horrendous screams began again. "Why are you really here in this system?" Saal bellowed. "What is it you seek to gain?"

Reth spit purple blood and screamed.

Thel shut off the containment system, and stepped into the alcove. "Has he said anything new to justify continuing this interrogation? Maybe something different?" Thel asked softly.

Saal spun around, turning off his energy sword. Purple blood stained the hilt in his hand and dripped from his fingers. "No, honor. He has not. He's still sticking to his story. That a Hierarch commands him to have done all this."

"Have you forgotten your orders, then?" Thel stared Saal straight in the eye, neck bared, as if daring Saal to try for it.

Saal backed away from the implicit challenge of confidence, moving closer to a wall. Reth gurgled in the background.

"I wanted to break him of his heresies," Saal said. "What he's saying *cannot* be true."

"It is a poor soldier who insists on seeing things not as they are, but as he wants them to be. One day reality hits, and his illusions fail him, and he dies stupidly. What honor is there in that?" Thel stepped closer to Saal, cornering him, dominating his space.

Saal straightened. "But if the Kig-Yar is right, then one Prophet ordered him to come here and do this, and another ordered us to come here and—"

"It is not up to us to pick apart what the Prophets may or may not have ordered, Saal. It is also not up to you to decide what orders of mine to follow."

Thel patted his waist, where his own energy sword was clipped, and kept his eyes locked on Saal, who finally looked toward the ground.

"I have failed you, honor," Saal said.

"You have." Thel sighed.

"I have lost nobility. I will do what is right." Saal's energy sword flared into being.

"You will not take your life," Thel said. "You will scar your forearms with the mark of disobedience."

Saal closed his eyes and shivered. "Please . . ."

"It is an order." Thel stood up straight and high over Saal. "Now leave."

Saal walked out of the cell with his head low from shame. Thel walked over to the slab of a bed and sat on it, facing Reth.

"Sangheili are insane," Reth hissed. "What is the mark of disobedience?"

"He will use his energy sword to burn marks into the skin of his arms. Crossing lines all up and down, where all can see and know him for what he is. It is shameful. Death is preferred. But for now, I need all my fighters. He can kill himself later, and we will destroy the body so that his lineage will not suffer. If he performs well in battle."

Reth shook his head. "Sangheili . . ."

"We are strong, Kig-Yar. That is why we sit at the right hand of the Prophets."

Reth laughed. "One day that shall pass."

"Not as long as we remain strong." Thel stood. "But Saal's worries do trouble me. You still claim that it is the Prophet of Truth who sent you here?"

Again Reth laughed. "You should worry. I speak the truth. And it was Truth who sent me here. He doesn't believe that the Prophet of Regret has come even close to the human homeworld."

Thel leaned closer. "But this here is not the human homeworld."

Reth blinked, focusing his memories. "When that Kig-Yar ship took back recordings of these humans begging to trade for their lives, Truth realized he had found a way to easily find the core of their infestation."

"These heretical weapons," Thel said.

"Humans have rebels among them. Something Truth wants to use. The weapons are traceable. We could map the entire human population if we got these rebels to smuggle back enough of them. Sadly, the humans have a new directive that has killed this opportunity."

"They destroy data on their ships before they are captured, yes," Thel said.

"But we still have a chance to get the location of their home-world from them here. There are opportunists who will sell it to us. Once we have it, these habitats are ours to keep, the Prophet promised us. The Kig-Yar will hold a special place then, Truth has promised us."

Thel shook his head. "The Sangheili will remain by the side of the Prophets."

"You are too arrogant," Reth spat. "The Jiralhanae betrayed you. We are given this special mission by the Prophet of Truth. Both seek to minimize your kind. You have dominated things far too long."

"We are in the midst of a holy war with the humans," Thel hissed. "That is not the time for such things."

"But it is," Reth said. "We will use our Unggoy army from Metisette to destroy the humans here once we have the data that leads us to their homeworld. And we will be favored in the Prophets' eyes. Not you, Sangheili."

"You are an obnoxious creature." Thel broke the straps around the Kig-Yar and freed him.

"When we hand over the humans, we will be honored. The Prophets will look kindly on us in the final journey." Reth staggered over to the bunk and lay down. "We will be holier and more blessed than you, Sangheili. You will see. You will see."

Thel walked away, back to the cockpit, where Zhar looked up. He'd overheard their whole exchange.

"Do you believe him?" Zhar asked.

"I think Reth believes what Reth is saying." Thel sat down, suddenly tired.

"What games are we caught in the middle of?" Zhar asked.

"I do not know," Thel said. He toyed with the image of the Kig-Yar ship on his screen. It was the closest thing the Kig-Yar had to a true fleet ship, similar to the designs of refitted Kig-Yar raiders that had fought the Covenant from asteroid belts before the Kig-Yar were granted a place within the Covenant.

He wondered if the Kig-Yar had managed to put a slipspace drive on it.

It looked likely, though Thel wondered if the cobbled-together affair would make it through. It certainly didn't look like it.

But it had weapons. Thel made a decision.

"We will take that Kig-Yar ship. We will use it to destroy all this heresy. If the Prophet of Truth shows up and tells me to stop, then I will do so. Tell the others to prepare, and tell these Unggoy to ready themselves to be useful."

Until the Prophet of Truth himself showed up here, Thel had to follow the orders he was given. And since the Jiralhanae would be back with the High Prophet of Regret soon, Thel wanted his actions to show that he had done his duty.

Yes. The human habitats here would burn, just as their world Charybdis IX had burned.

CHAPTER 35

Delgado didn't even think twice—he grabbed the gun and kicked Bonifacio in the stomach. But in that split second Bonifacio's three men piled onto him, trying to yank the gun away as they smashed his ribs.

As he gasped from the pain, Bonifacio shouted, "Shoot them both and throw them out the damn airlock!"

But Delgado had the gun up and pointed at Bonifacio despite the pain of getting pummeled by the bodyguards. "Get away from me. Or he dies."

The three overly muscled men backed away, their guns now out and trained on Delgado.

Bonifacio smiled and held his hands up. "Now, easy, Delgado. Come on. We can work something out here."

"Screw you, Bonifacio." Delgado wasn't in the mood for his bullshit now.

"Give me a gun," Bonifacio snapped. The nearest heavy tossed him one. Delgado hesitated, not really wanting to fire a gun inside his own ship. That hesitation cost him, because now Bonifacio had a gun of his own pointed at Diego. "I'm going to shoot Diego if you don't hand that over."

Delgado thought about it for a second. Giving away the data would certainly endanger the Rubble. Bonifacio, it was now obvious, would not be taking this data to the Exodus Project. No, he was going to sell it to the Kig-Yar. All signs pointed to it. Delgado shook his head.

Bonifacio shot Diego in the chest. Blood sprayed and hit the floor as Diego collapsed, clutching the wound with a look of shock on his face.

Delgado leapt over to Diego as he shot at Bonifacio, who ducked out into the corridor and ran for cover.

Delgado waved the gun at the bodyguards. "Back up. Back up." They were hired help—their hearts weren't into the idea of a close-range shoot-out, luckily. Only Bonifacio was insane enough to fire inside a damn spaceship, Delgado thought. He grabbed Diego's collar and pulled him out of the kitchen and down the corridor.

Bonifacio fired down at him from the cockpit, the bullets sparking off the metal bulkheads.

Delgado fired back as he dragged Diego to the airlock. This was all messed up. Very messed up.

Diego moaned as Delgado pulled him into the lock and cycled into the habitat's lock.

A very loud bang startled him.

The airlock seal broke as *Distancia* abruptly cut loose, her engines firing.

Air whistled out of cracks in the warped airlock. Red alarm

lights blinked, and Delgado kicked at the door leading into the habitat.

It wouldn't open, of course—with the outer seal broken emergency systems had kicked in. As long as the simple sensors on the outside detected loss of air the inner door was locked.

Delgado grabbed the emergency phone, and got Bonifacio's voice. "I just used an emergency Security Council code to override communications from your airlock," Bonifacio said flatly. "And I canceled the airlock's alarm."

The strobing lights shut off. It would look like a false trigger. A mechanic would be sent out at his leisure instead of an emergency crew.

"You bastard."

"Good-bye, Mr. Delgado."

"Go to hell, Bonifacio." Delgado slammed the phone against the wall until it broke.

Bonifacio had killed them. Almost as good as a bullet, Delgado thought.

He sat down next to Diego, holding a hand to his chest. Diego stared up at the ceiling, his breathing irregular and gasping.

"I'm sorry, Diego," Delgado said, looking down at his old friend.

Diego bubbled blood up from his mouth, but said nothing. Delgado closed his eyes and bit his lip.

Already the air seemed to be getting thinner. Delgado lay down, breathing shallowly.

Then he reached down into his right shoe and tugged out the small beacon Adriana had given him.

Delgado opened the casing and pressed the red switch. A small green light flickered on, and started pulsating.

He closed his eyes and waited.

CHAPTER 36

Reth lay curled up on the uncomfortable slab, thinking about the warmth and closeness of a Kig-Yar nest, and how far away such things were from him at the moment.

He hurt everywhere, thanks to his treatment by the Sangheili. Oh, they'd pay for this. Reth followed the orders of a *Prophet*. Who were they to treat him so cruelly?

The Sangheili thought they were lords of it all, but they were just thugs, Reth thought. Little different from the Jiralhanae and their violent approaches to everything in the world.

Soon the Prophets would listen to all Kig-Yar, Reth thought. Reth was here, working to find the secret of the human homeworld. It would have been his already, if not for the Sangheili meddling.

"Unggoy!" Reth carefully got off the bench, his limbs protesting, his steps dizzy.

The Sangheili would have to go. Things were so close to being finished. Soon his human agent would have the location to Earth for him. Once Reth had that, then the army of Unggoy he'd gathered on Metisette would be ready to be unleashed on the Rubble. The asteroids would make wonderful Kig-Yar nesting grounds.

"Unggoy, where are you? You must attend me. Are you not believers in the mission the Prophet of Truth himself gave to me, and thus to you?" Reth collapsed to the ground in front of the energy bars that kept him jailed.

Once he had the Rubble, he thought through a haze, and the location to Earth, the humans' Exodus Project would provide him the vehicle he needed to then bring the Unggoy to attack the human homeworld.

A daring plan.

A Kig-Yar plan.

A plan the Prophet of Truth had agreed to when Reth presented it after returning with the secret of the Rubble and the humans' desire to trade. He'd kept it a secret from his own Shipmistress, a violation that would have gotten him castrated if found out, but it had paid off handsomely.

"Unggoy!"

Now they'd been discovered, the Jiralhanae were returning to broadcast the news about the discovery of the Rubble to a different Prophet.

The Kig-Yar couldn't stop them. But they could move the plan up, so that they wouldn't look like traitors, trading with the humans.

No, it was time to destroy the humans and their homeworld and show the Prophets that it was the Kig-Yar, not the Sangheili or Jiralhanae, who were the most cunning and loyal and holy subjects of the Covenant.

The shuffling steps of two furtive Unggoy soldiers got Reth to focus on the ground in front of his long face.

"Sangheili kills us if we release you," one of the Unggoy protested.

"And you'll risk your chance at joining in the Great Journey because you're scared of these Sangheili," Reth hissed. His ribs hurt.

The Unggoy shuffled their feet again, methane snorting out from their masks as they looked back and forth at each other.

"Will you risk the Sangheili destroying the Redoubt, and all you've built on Metisette?" Reth asked. "Will you see all the Unggoy on that planet punished, when they've been following the right Path?"

They glanced at each other again. "Our nipple brothers would be all killed?"

The Unggoy sucked food from a shared tube, a nipple, Reth remembered. "Yes, your nipple brothers would all die."

That was enough to get them to free him. One of the Unggoy tapped at the controls for Reth's cell.

Reth smiled as the energy bars disappeared. He rolled out of the cell before the Unggoy changed their minds. "Quick, you must help me escape."

The two Unggoy grabbed him under his arms as he wobbled, prompting Reth to grunt in pain. Together, all three hobbled down the corridor until Reth had them stop near a service panel.

The Sangheili may have taken the ship by force, and cowed the Unggoy, but Reth still had some tricks of his own. He shut down the ship's computer system with an override password.

While the Sangheili raced to reboot the system, he had the Unggoy drag him to an escape pod.

Minutes later the cylindrical pod shot out of the ship, veering back toward Metisette at top speed, as the Sangheili coasted with a dead ship.

It was time, Reth thought bitterly while rooting around the pod for a medical kit, to show the Sangheili that Kig-Yar could fight.

CHAPTER 37

Mike flew the *Petya* through the Rubble, flipping the ship end over end for sudden deceleration, and weaving his way around docking tubes and asteroids.

In the confines of the airlock, braced against Mike's radical maneuvers, Jai swore. "I don't see why *I'm* in the airlock for the quick rescue, Adriana. He's *your* pet Insurrectionist."

"Shove it," Adriana muttered over the suit radio.

Jai stiffened. "Is that how you talk to rank?"

"When rank stops whining I'll modify my behavior," Adriana said. "Besides, I need to be in the medical bay in case Delgado's hurt."

"So we're trusting an Insurrectionist AI and rushing to help an Insurrectionist. You see anything wrong with this?" Jai asked.

Another voice crackled in his ear. The AI. Juliana. "Technically the Rubble is a collection of people with many different backgrounds. Only a small percentage of them are actually Insurrectionist as you understand it—"

"Can it," Jai muttered, as Mike flipped the ship again, making his stomach lurch. Mike fired the engines to dodge docking tubes. "Anything new about Delgado?"

"The airlock the signal emanated from is still throwing me error codes from the broken seal," Juliana reported. "You're still the closest ship. An emergency crew is outside the lock on the habitat side, but can't get at it, of course. I've broken the communications block on the airlock, but no one inside is responding."

Jai thought about that. A broken airlock and silence. "Doesn't sound too promising."

"No," Juliana replied. "It doesn't."

"Coming in on the lock," Mike shouted. Jai felt the *Petya* shudder like it never had before, and he was pressed against the side of the airlock despite the artificial gravity.

He was glad he wasn't looking at this from the cockpit.

Metal ground on metal as Mike forced the wrecked airlock against theirs.

"We're go on your command," Mike reported.

Jai faced the thick metal door with its yellow stripes and red warning symbols and notices. "Do it."

The airlock sprung open with a gust of air. Then the habitat's airlock ground open with a tiny puff of air.

Jai forced his way through the moment the gap was large enough.

Two men lay on the floor of the airlock's nonslip metal surface. Delgado, a gun in one hand and the other bloody, lay over the stomach of a man with a bad chest wound. Blood pooled the floor around them, freezing as the vacuum sucked air and warmth out even faster now that a bad seal was in place between ship and habitat.

Jai threw Delgado over a shoulder of his gray MJOLNIR armor, and picked up the other body as gently as possible, aware that he could be making the chest wound worse.

He cycled through back into the *Petya*, thudding his way past bulkheads into the tiny cramped offshoot to the crew quarters where Adriana stood ready by a large metal table.

She looked up. "Two? Who's the other one?"

Juliana flickered into being over a nearby shelf. "That's Diego Esquival." Her voice sounded muted, as if she were shocked.

Adriana shook her head as she checked him over, while Jai held him in his arms still. "He's dead." She pulled Delgado off Jai's shoulder and set him on the table. "But Delgado's got a pulse. Store the other man into one of the cryogenic pods."

Jai walked Diego's body around the table and to one of the three pods. Once he set it down and closed the lid, the automated systems kicked in. Diego was frozen in his last minute, for all the good it did him.

When he turned around, Adriana had an oxygen mask on Delgado and the computers reading his vitals.

Delgado stirred and opened his eyes, the oxygen taking effect. He tried to sit up, but Adriana put a hand on his chest to keep him in place. "You're back on the *Petya*, Delgado."

"Diego?" Delgado groaned, looking around. "What about Diego?"

Jai and Adriana glanced at each other, and Delgado saw it. He seemed to fall back in on himself, shaking his head and looking off into the distance. "Damn that bastard."

"What bastard?" Juliana asked from the corner of the room.

Delgado twisted to see her better, and his mouth fell open. "You!" Warring emotions crossed his face. Jai figured the man had wondered if the AI was not to be trusted, but that the revelation still caught Delgado off guard.

"Yes, me." Juliana grinned. The hologram folded its arms. "What happened, Delgado?"

"Bonifacio happened." Delgado all but spit the name out. "He took *Distancia*. He also shot Diego." Delgado bit his lip, and slowly sat, holding his knees to do it with a grunt.

"I knew Bonifacio was a sketchy man. I have watched him smuggle things into the Rubble. I know of ten different caches he uses. He's definitely running those Covenant guns to the colonies. He campaigned hard for that Security Council spot," Juliana said as Adriana and Jai watched the exchange. "But to do this?"

Delgado looked at the AI. "We have to catch him."

"He's not even trying to run," Juliana said. "Your ship is slowly coasting through the Rubble."

"Bonifacio thinks I'm dead. He's taking his time, so he doesn't alarm anyone." The group looked at each other, and Delgado caught the glances. He raised his voice. "Oh come on, I would not have done this. Why the hell would I risk my life to break an airlock? And do you think I shot Maria's brother? Really?"

Jai tapped the table. "Juliana, he makes a good point."

Delgado turned around to him. "And since when are you and the Rubble's AI all working together? When the hell did that start?"

"When the Jackals started getting too close to the data," Jai said, staring Delgado down.

Juliana was quiet, her eyes closed. "Okay Delgado. I think you are right. We have a big problem." She opened her eyes to look at the three people staring back at her, and the equations streaming across her holographic body suddenly flashed bright red. "Kig-Yar ships are withdrawing all throughout the Rubble. They're en route for Metisette."

"You told us the Jackals were up to something, like an invasion. Could this be it?" Jai said.

"Their encryption is good. I can't break it just yet. But communications traffic is up and that can tell me something. I've never seen activity like this. Delgado says Bonifacio is stealing the data. And this is happening at the same time as the largest movement of Kig-Yar ships we've seen since they first started arriving to make a presence on the Rubble. It has to be related."

"Damn," Delgado said. "We were right—all they wanted was the data. They're making a move now, right?"

Juliana continued. "*Distancia* is moving in the direction her flight plan indicated, but could make a break for it the moment it gets clear of the Rubble to wherever the Kig-Yar want it to. We have to get to it and stop Bonifacio. And prepare for whatever it is the Kig-Yar are up to."

Jai nodded. "Our first priority is Bonifacio." They had to focus on that; that was Gray Team's mission. Adriana met his eyes, then nodded. She agreed. "Once we have that secured, Juliana, you have our assistance."

The AI had her eyes closed again. Planning, running through the millions of threads spread all throughout the Rubble in a way no human could.

But she was an AI close to rampancy. Jai wondered how much they should follow her plans.

He'd have to revisit that once they had their hands on Bonifacio and the navigation data.

Juliana faded, becoming almost a ghost in the bright medical bay, then she appeared again. "Okay," she almost whispered. "I can pass the fix I have on *Distancia* onto you, but I'm going to need some of you to help me. One team goes after Bonifacio, the other I need to do something a little bit trickier.

"There's a Kig-Yar ship still in the Rubble. I can't crack their encryption, but if I can physically get into one of their systems, that would let me figure out exactly what they're up to. If it's a full-scale attack, we need to know for sure so that we don't make a big mistake. If we use non-Rubble attackers, then the Rubble can deny this little incursion was our doing if things turn out to be okay with the Kig-Yar."

Jai looked at the AI. "You want us to board a Covenant ship?"

"And plug me in, yes." Juliana nodded. "My higher functions. I'll be leaving a simple base copy to keep regulating the Rubble, of course. But the core me will go with the boarding party."

Juliana was rampant. Or just plain insane, Jai thought. He scratched his chin, then looked at Juliana. "We'll need a larger force. We need to free the crew of that UNSC ship that was captured. It'll have ODSTs aboard. Release those men and we have a force." Helljumpers weren't huge fans of the Spartans, but were somewhat like Spartans, Jai had to admit, but without the altered physiology and powered armor. And they were good fighting men; he was sure he could get them to storm a Jackal ship.

It was the sort of thing ODSTs would enjoy doing.

"I'm not the ruler of the Rubble," she said. "Only the Council can release them. Besides, most of those people are tagged with locaters. People will notice it if they start trooping out to help us."

"Do all of them have locaters?" Adriana asked.

Juliana smiled. "Not all. The ones who refused to become Rubble citizens don't."

"Then we can use some of them," Jai said.

"I won't open the doors," Juliana said. "That would draw attention. But if the cameras were to malfunction, you could break the crew out and get them to help you before anyone would really notice."

"That'll have to do." Jai turned around. "Adriana, Mike, you take Bonifacio. Delgado, you're with me, I need someone who knows the inside of these habitats."

Delgado swung his legs over the side of the table with a wince. "You sure you're going to break up your little team?"

Jai grinned. "Who else will be able to talk the ODSTs into coming with us? Mike, Adriana, get on the navigation data, and quickly. I'll take care of things for Juliana."

The *Petya* shuddered as Mike disengaged the ship. "I'll drop you off at the nearest working set of locks," he announced. "Then it's a full burn for *Distancia*."

Delgado stood up, wavering on his feet. "Do me a favor," he asked Adriana. "When you catch up to Bonifacio, make sure you shoot the thieving bastard for me. Preferably in the knee, or somewhere painful like that."

The *Petya* thudded into another airlock.

"I'll go release the others," Jai told Delgado. "You and Juliana need to scare up another ship for the attack."

Delgado and Juliana exchanged a glance. "We're on it."

Jai ran a systems check of the Mjolnir armor, and walked down the corridor for a pair of M7 submachine guns and extra ammo.

CHAPTER 38

Reth quickly strode through the hall of one of the Redoubt's grounded ships. There were ten old decommissioned ships that had been landed around "the Plaza," with the largest Kig-Yar ship towering over them all from the northeast corner. Docking tubes connected the ships like bridges high over the ground.

And if Reth chose, he could descend into the ground, where every day the Unggoy warrens spread deeper and farther into the warmed rock. The escape pod he had landed in still sat out on the landing pad of the Plaza, crackling and shimmering from the heat of reentry.

He'd lived in fear for several long minutes, convinced that the Sangheili would get the ship running in time to turn around for him, but they hadn't. The Sangheili had gotten the ship booted up and kept moving along their trajectory, headed for the Rubble.

Reth needed to order the *Infinite Spoils* away from dock along with all the other Kig-Yar ships, but he was reluctant to do so. Soon the *Infinite Spoils* would have human slipspace drives, something the Hierarch hadn't even granted Reth, but something that all Kig-Yar wanted: a slipspace ship of their own. But first Reth needed to take the Rubble, and any human ships with the drives, for the Kig-Yar. The humans had been stockpiling the slipspace drives they'd traded for to install in their own machine: the Exodus Project.

But when the *Infinite Spoils* got its drives it would mark something new, as long as the Kig-Yar could spirit it out of the Rubble before the Hierarchs heard of it.

Everything was about to change, Reth felt, as he took an elevator up into the tall, grounded ship that was the Kig-Yar refuge inside the Redoubt. There were many, many more guards around now than when the Sangheili had broached it.

He entered his room. The remains of the firefight had been cleaned up, the glass replaced so that he could, once again, look out over the Plaza, and the Redoubt as a whole.

The river of methane on the surface of Metisette rumbled underneath their creation. Its passage turned giant turbines, creating power for the entire complex. The Unggoy thrived here among the mists of methane reclaimed from the rivers and pools.

Shuttles were already descending from the reddened clouds to touch down on Metisette's surface. Kig-Yar were forming up in the square below the balcony, as well as Unggoy Deacons. All per his command.

Several of his key advisors hustled up behind him. They looked shocked at the wounds all over his body, and his hunched position. Reth paid the stares no mind.

"We have planned for the invasion of the Rubble for a long

time," Reth said, doing his best to straighten up against the twinges of pain the Sangheili had left him.

"Is it time?" they asked.

Reth smiled. "Yes," he said. "It is time. Send the orders. Gather the Unggoy out onto the Plaza. Give them their harnesses and masks. Prepare for the attack. We will take it all for our own, and once we have that data, we will continue to their homeworld as well."

The Kig-Yar in the room warbled happily. They had been waiting patiently as the humans developed asteroids that the Kig-Yar considered prime for Kig-Yar nests.

Now they would be rewarded.

"Go," Reth snapped. "Tend to your functions!"

The Kig-Yar advisors scattered out of the room, bumping into a slew of Unggoy that waited outside.

They were not rocketing into the Rubble just yet. But for all intents and purposes, the invasion had begun.

CHAPTER 39

Habitat Asuncion, Inner Rubble, 23 Librae

The first sign for Keyes that something was happening were the shouts from the guards who had been walking the corridor outside. Two of them ran full tilt past Keyes's cell. Keyes walked over to the bars as the guards dogged shut the thick, metal door leading to the corridor. They pulled out handguns and stepped back from the door.

"Faison?" Keyes shouted down the row of cells. "What's going on?"

"Don't know," came the response.

The guard on the left side of the door looked back at them. "Quiet!"

Keyes pressed his face against the bars to get a better look. As he did, the large metal door exploded inward between the two guards and bounced down the corridor. A heavy cloud of dust hung in the air, making everything hazy.

Something large and gray blurred through the door. The guards shot at it, but not before it smacked into them, knocking them both out with quick blows to the head.

The figure paused, and a golden faceplate scanned the rows of cells. Keyes heard Faison's incredulous voice: "Holy shit, a Spartan."

Dirt settled on the gray armor, then shook off as the Spartan thudded down along the cells.

"Who's the commanding officer?" it asked loudly from behind the helmet.

Keyes put a hand out through the bars. "That would be me, Lieutenant Jacob Keyes."

He still couldn't believe this. Had the Spartan come just for them? Where had he come from?

The Spartan stopped in front of Keyes. "Back up."

Keyes stepped back, and the Spartan gripped the bars and yanked them off their hinges, metal squealing in protest and more dirt falling from where they'd been set into the rock.

The Spartan tossed the door onto the floor behind it and walked into the open cell. "I have a proposition, Lieutenant Keyes."

By the entryway between the bent bars the face of an AI appeared. "We may have a way to help you get your crew back to where they belong as well. If you're interested."

Keyes leaned out of the open cell. "I'll listen to you both. You can explain what you're doing here and what's going on while you free my men."

The gold faceplate looked him up and down. "Of course. I'm Jai, Spartan double-oh-six, Gray Team."

Keyes shook hands with the large, gauntleted hand.

"We need an attack force," the Spartan said as he moved from cell to cell. "To get the AI Juliana into a Jackal ship and back out. To figure out what the Covenant are up to in this system, and whether they're readying an invasion force."

"You're a Spartan. You haven't tried going after the ship already?"

The gold faceplate shifted. "Those are long odds. Not something I want to try unless I absolutely have to, and am feeling extremely lucky."

"Fair enough," Keyes said. "You said you could get my crew out?"

A few more mangled bars clattered to the ground. Faison and his ODSTs had rifled through the pockets of the guards for key cards. Now they moved door to door, unlocking cells with less drama. A crowd of officers and crew now milled about.

Jai paused in front of Keyes, now that he no longer needed to free prisoners. "The ship we came in has navigation data. We can join its computers with your ship's by docking for a slipspace jump. It'll be awkward, but your frigate should be large enough to clamp us on."

Keyes looked over at Faison behind the Spartan. "Your men willing to jump a Jackal ship?"

"You kidding?" Faison said. ODSTs behind him nodded. "Beats rotting here."

The AI tilted her head. "Ignatio Delgado has a ship ready for you all. The alarms are shut down, but the guards change shifts soon. You'd better all clear out."

"She's your ship's AI?" Keyes asked Jai.

"No," Jai replied. "I'll explain later."

CHAPTER 40

Thel idly scratched at a small piece of charred carbon that had been flaking off his armor while the Unggoy before him trembled, wondering about its fate.

He finally stopped. "So Reth escaped."

"Lords . . ." The Unggoy shook as it started to speak. "Reth is devious. *And* he has commanded all within this system. You can imagine, most Unggoy are eager to please our masters. It is easy to be confused at times like these, when lords turn against lords."

Thel stood up from the pilot's seat. Saal looked up from his console. The Sangheili winced as he moved, the crisscrossing scars of his shame scabbing and causing him pain. Which was the point.

Saal refused to look at Thel; he kept his eyes cast down at the floor. Another sign of his shame, a refusal to meet another Sang-heili's eyes.

The message had gotten across to Saal, Thel thought. It was a shame it had taken so long to control him.

Thel leaned closer to Saal. "It will only bring shame if you do not perish triumphantly in battle."

Saal looked up, a glimmer of hope brimming in his large eyes. "I will redeem myself before you and my ancestors—by my blood I swear it," he said.

"I know you will," Thel replied. "That is why I ordered you to remain by my side for now."

Ahead, on their screens, the Rubble grew larger as they got closer.

"I want you to lead the charge on that Kig-Yar ship," Thel said. "The *Infinite Spoils*. It is powerful enough and large enough for what I have in mind."

"I'll destroy anything in our way," Saal said.

"Good."

Thel returned to the shaking Unggoy. "And you, will your soldiers do their job, by the Prophets? Or will they risk the chance of damnation by disobeying?"

"Sirs! They will fight. They have seen the error of their ways," it said.

"Then you will follow close behind Saal," Thel said. "Saal, get weapons for yourself and the Unggoy."

"My honor," Saal said, and left to go equip himself.

Zhar, still in the cockpit, scratched a mandible. "You think the Unggoy will really fight hard to take the ship?"

"Do they ever really fight hard?" Thel wondered. "I just need them to cause confusion while we do what needs to be done. With that ship, we can destroy this 'Rubble' and get things moving back in the direction they're supposed to be moving."

Zhar nodded. "And Saal will fight like an unleashed army to regain honor."

Thel grumbled happily. "Yes. Yes, he will."

CHAPTER 41

Delgado ached all over. His throat felt like someone had taken steel wool and shoved it down to his stomach, and he couldn't help stumbling a bit as he walked from the bridge down to the airlock of a decent-size freighter, not all that much different than *Distancia*.

But adrenaline kept him moving.

Juliana had run through a list of ships they could commandeer on short notice in the name of the Rubble Security Council and found this old bucket.

Delgado had moved and docked it near the prison.

He reached the airlock and flicked switches to power the door. Jai marched through first, with a quick nod at him. A long stream of UNSC Navy types trailed behind him.

The man immediately following Jai wore a standard orange prison jumper, but he had the air of command. He walked over to Delgado. "You're the pilot?"

"Yes."

"Excellent. I'm Lieutenant Jacob Keyes. They've asked me to run the ship. I hope I'm not stepping on any toes?" Keyes looked around the cockpit, and Delgado could tell the man knew exactly what he was looking for.

"No toes," Delgado said. "I'm happy to work with you."

"We need weapons," someone said.

Juliana appeared as a hologram over at the communications station. "And weapons you shall have. I need a few more minutes to download a version of myself into this ship. There's a high-capacity storage chip in the comms panel, Jai, Delgado. When we get to the Kig-Yar ship, you'll need to get that into the ship and plug me in."

It looked like some fifty people had invaded the freighter.

Keyes looked around. "This bucket have a name?"

Delgado looked at Juliana. "The *Mighty Sparrow*," the AI reported. "And no, I have no idea why. I'm downloaded now, though. Time to disconnect."

"Good." Delgado took the pilot's chair, and Keyes moved to stand next to him as Delgado cast off from the airlock. "Where to, Juliana?"

"Habitat Greenworthy for the weapons," the AI replied. She looked around at the cockpit. "So many determined men all around me. It's quite exhilarating."

No one responded.

Keyes cleared his throat as Delgado began moving the *Mighty Sparrow* through the Rubble toward Habitat Greenworthy. "The trick will be approaching this Jackal ship. If they get their shields up we'll be useless. By the way, do we have a name for this ship?"

"The *Infinite Spoils*," Juliana muttered.

One of the crew on deck, Dante Kirtley, who had seated himself near Juliana's image at comms, suggested a diversion. "You asked about tricks, sir. We need to keep their eyes on something else while we drift near."

"What can you offer us?" Keyes asked Juliana. "You said you controlled the Rubble when you were catching me up as we walked from the prison over to the ship."

Juliana thought about it for a second. "A very large industrial accident. I can cut loose one of the asteroids being mined. We can float it by their ship. It'll give them a scare but it won't hit."

"Excellent," Keyes said, folding his arms. "Add a lot of debris, we'll use it for chaff."

"Consider it done," Juliana said. "And because they built this Kig-Yar ship here in the Rubble, we'll be able to dock with them. No need for suits."

"What about just attacking the dock they're attached to? Why a ship?" an ODST asked.

"They have the dock airlock guarded," Juliana said. "Of course, a few feints from the docks will also serve to keep them distracted, so I think it's a good idea to attack from the docks as well as via a ship."

Now they had a plan, Delgado thought, as crazy as it was. And they seemed to have a leader, because even Jai, hardened Spartan though he was, deferred to Lt. Keyes's command of the bridge.

CHAPTER 42

The *Petya* had been hunting down *Distancia*, without the other ship even aware that there was a cat-and-mouse game going on.

Both were plain freighters, long ships with spars and cargo containers bolted to the main frames. But *Petya* had the advantage of being extraordinarily well armed.

Inside the *Petya*, Adriana watched Mike lean over the controls with the air of a predator waiting in the bushes, patiently biding time before striking. "He's edging out of the Rubble," Mike whispered.

That was all Adriana needed. Enough toying about. Jai was getting ready to invade a Covenant ship, while they were out here. They needed to move quickly to wrap this up and get back to support him. "Alright, let's hit him."

"We're done playing hide-and-go-ship?" Mike smiled.

"Definitely."

"You hail them, I shoot them."

Adriana looked at the screen showing their trajectories. "Shoot this jerk first. Hit the engines. We're not playing games. We can't give him a chance to turn back and do the right thing. He already chose his fate back at that airlock."

"Yessir," Mike said, with a sudden grin. Two distant thumps under her feet indicated missiles away.

Twin rocket trails flared in front of the cockpit windows as they sped ahead, and then slowly curved down.

"He sees them," Mike reported, as *Distancia* increased power to her engines to make a run for it. But the missiles closed the dark gap between the two ships and slammed into *Distancia*'s rear.

"Nice!" Adriana said, looking at the debris trailing off the stern of the *Distancia*.

"Crippled in one shot." Mike leaned back. "They're not going anywhere."

Adriana hailed the stricken freighter. "*Distancia*, this is *Petya*. We took out your engines, don't make us hole the rest of the ship. I'm coming aboard. You cause any trouble, it gets ugly. You cooperate, you live."

For a long moment there was no reply, leading Adriana to wonder if they weren't monitoring any of the standard channels.

Then finally, over a burst of static, a reply: "*Petya*, this is Peter Bonifacio, aboard the *Distancia*. I have to protest this extraordinary hostility. I am a member of the Rubble Security Council, on a top-priority mission. You are way out of line, whoever the hell you are."

"Shut up and get ready to open your airlock, Bonifacio," Adriana snapped.

"But what is this about?" Bonifacio whined over the radio.

Adriana didn't reply. Mike pulled them in over the *Distancia*'s spine, getting ready to dock.

"I will report this," Bonifacio radioed. "You can trust that . . ." Adriana muted the volume.

The *Petya* shuddered as the two ships docked, Mike grappling them into place. "Pressurizing the lock. You're go in twenty," Mike said.

Adriana pulled her helmet on and snapped it into place. "Once I'm in, you undock. Just in case. Hit them from a distance if it goes bad."

"You sure about that?" Mike asked.

"Damn straight. I'll find a way off."

"Ten seconds to full pressure."

Adriana turned and left the cockpit for the airlock. She flipped her battle rifle forward and stood in front of the door as the light on the airlock door flashed green. It slid open and Adriana walked through, wincing slightly as it then slid closed after her. There was always a sense of finality in leaving the safety of a base ship like this, a sense of stepping off the edge of a metaphorical cliff of some sort.

And now she was free-falling her way into a new situation, a new set of variables: whatever was on the other side of the large metal door in front of her.

But then, she liked the screaming flow of adrenaline coursing through her.

She liked the adrenaline rush even back when she'd first showed up at the Spartan training grounds, staring with all the other kids at the instructors. She hadn't broken out with Jai because she wanted to escape. She'd done it for the fun, that feeling of stepping off the edge.

The more dangerous, the more it felt like she was really someone. It beat the gray numbness of stillness, and sameness.

The world seemed to vibrate as Adriana watched the outer door open, her rifle up, her vision expanding into a sort of hunting state.

She burst through into the *Distancia*'s airlock where nothing waited for her but benches and metal grating.

The door closed behind her, and the *Petya* disengaged with a loud thump as Mike cleared away.

Adriana waited until Mike had time to get well clear, then banged on the inner airlock door.

It opened, and two gunshots cracked into the armor over her ribs. Adriana grunted and rolled through the crack in the door, firing back at the two men shooting at her. Always take the offensive, she thought. Don't get backed into a corner.

After dropping them she moved back into the airlock for a moment and checked her armor. Just dinged.

But her ribs ached from taking the impact.

"Hold on," a voice shouted. Not Bonifacio, another bodyguard of his. A handgun skittered down to stop in front of the airlock door. "I'm not going down like that, no way. I signed up as a bodyguard, that's it. I'm unarmed, now, please don't shoot."

Adriana moved her back against the corner and glanced at the gun. "Who else is there?"

"Just me."

"Bonifacio?"

"He's in an escape pod," the bodyguard said. His voice quavered a bit.

Adriana spun around the corner and marched up on the bodyguard, a slender man with a shaved head. He looked up at her, hands up near his chest to show he was unarmed.

"What's your name?" Adriana asked.

"Sean. Wha . . . What the hell are you?" The patch on his jumpsuit said S. WILLIAMS.

"You catching this, Mike?" Adriana murmured, amused. "Any pod launch yet?"

"No," came the answer.

Adriana looked down at Sean. "Why hasn't he launched?"

"Because you'll shoot him," the bodyguard said.

"Tempting, huh?" Mike said.

"So what game is Bonifacio playing, then?"

"He's hailing us," Mike said.

"Put him through," Adriana sighed.

Bonifacio's voice filled her helmet. "You're after the navigation chip, right?"

"Hand it over and live, Bonifacio," Adriana said.

"Maybe. I heard what you did to my crew, soldier." Bonifacio spat the last word. "I'm not stupid enough to believe you'll just play nice once I hand the chip over."

Adriana sighed. Now the man was getting seriously jittery and causing problems. "Bonifacio . . ."

"Here's the deal. I am leaving the data onboard, but I'll tell you where it is once I've cleared the ship in my pod."

"Oh, come on," Adriana said. "And then we find out that you lied and have the chip on you."

"We split the difference," Bonifacio said quickly. "Let me get far enough away in the pod that it would require some serious work for you to catch up to me. A good-faith gesture that you're actually going to let me go. I get to that point and I tell you where the data is."

"Let me think about it," Adriana replied, and toggled the mic off. "Williams?"

"Yes?"

"Did Bonifacio make a copy? And if you lie, don't imagine I won't make you pay for it."

Williams shook his head. "No, he didn't think you were on to him until you shot the engines out."

Adriana moved until her faceplate stopped an inch from Williams's nose, looking at his reaction. She waited until he finally closed his eyes. Satisfied, she flicked the radio mic back on. "Alright, Bonifacio, you cut loose."

Mike came on. "Adriana, you sure?"

"Jai is about to storm that ship without us, Mike. We don't have time—we need to move quickly and get back to him."

"Okay, he just shot clear."

Adriana walked over and stood by the pilot's chair of the crippled ship, and watched the tiny pod dwindle away on one of the monitors.

The pinpoint flare of its exhaust finally winked out.

Bonifacio's voice crackled. "It's taped above the edge of the airlock's lip, right where you entered." He laughed.

Adriana ran down to the airlock. She felt along the top of the rim of the entrance delicately, and found the chip where he said it was.

She pulled it free and looked at it. It wasn't much more than a tiny, stubby hardened wafer that sat in the palm of her hand. So much trouble over such a small thing, she thought as she slid it into a hip pocket.

"Got it?" Mike asked.

"Think so. I'm coming back to double-check," she radioed.

"I'm moving in."

She stepped into the airlock, and Williams moved forward. "What about me?" he asked.

"You stay aboard the ship." Adriana put a hand to his chest and pushed him back. "Someone will eventually be out for you."

"Eventually?"

"It'll give you time to think about the quality of the people you choose to work for."

The door slid between them, and Williams looked through a porthole at her.

Adriana turned her back to him and cycled aboard the *Petya*. She walked forward to the cockpit and handed Mike the chip. He plugged it into the ship's computer.

"It's good."

"Then let's get the hell out of here."

Mike looked at the monitors tracking the escape pod. "You sure you don't want to go after him?"

Adriana bit her lip. "Let him rot in his pod. It's going to be a long journey. I don't imagine whoever he was working for is going to be happy. People like Bonifacio might believe the Jackals are suddenly warm and fuzzy, but he's insane if he thinks the Covenant is going soft. He's a dead man, he just doesn't know it yet. Let's go."

"Strap in, then," Mike said. "We're bugging out."

The nearest chair groaned as Adriana sat in it. They'd reinforced the chairs to deal with fully armored Spartans, but the chairs still protested the weight.

Then Mike spun *Petya* around and fired up the main engine, speeding them toward the Jackal ship that Jai was going to be storming.

She hoped they got there in time.

Because she would be a little bit disappointed if they missed all the action, Adriana realized.

CHAPTER 43

The freighter *Mighty Sparrow* drifted ever so slowly behind the protective bulk of a stray asteroid as Juliana reassured some very worried Jackals that the asteroid would miss the *Infinite Spoils*.

An industrial accident.

A debris cloud of rock, water vapor, and metal shards all completed the messy illusion.

On deck, a tense Lt. Keyes eyed the screens, watching closely. Everyone in the cockpit was suited up, guns at their hips, ready for anything. He glanced over at Li and Kirtley, who had both managed to integrate themselves into the crowded bridge, helping out where needed.

"You have the mass driver primed to shoot their shields out, just in case this doesn't work?" he asked Juliana.

"Yes, but at that point we have to assume that even the Jackals won't believe that the attack on their ship was by escaped UNSC, if that comes into play."

Keyes doubted they'd believe this was the work of a lone UNSC vessel anyway, but Juliana wanted a door out, in case they found no plans by the Jackals for the Rubble.

Privately, Keyes felt the Rubble should just assume the Jackals had plans for invasion and strike first, intrigue like this be damned.

But it felt good to be back in action against the Covenant one way or another.

"Get ready, then," Keyes muttered. They were close.

"The Kig-Yar Shipmistress is relaxing; her computers are showing the rock won't hit. She's yelling at me for being careless," Juliana reported.

"All teams go, then," Keyes said. "Now or never."

Juliana's body flashed a sudden increase of the equations that decoratively flowed over it. "Airlock assault teams are go in ten, nine . . ."

Keyes turned to Delgado. "Fire it."

The pilot triggered the thruster sequence, and the entire asteroid rolled them around to face the Jackal ship. The thickest part of the cloud of debris lay between them and the Jackal ship as the *Mighty Sparrow* leapt across the several hundred feet, thrusters blazing.

"Four, three . . ." Juliana intoned.

"Brace for impact!" Keyes shouted.

"Two, one."

They struck, and the *Mighty Sparrow* screeched and shivered as its hull smacked against the *Infinite Spoils*. "ODSTs are go for intrusion," Keyes ordered.

"Moving out," Faison reported via radio, the banging of an airlock door coming over the channel.

"I'll be adding support," the Spartan, Jai, reported.

"We're locked in. Very nice maneuvering, Delgado," Keyes said. "Our hull is holding, minor leaks." He let out breath he hadn't realized he'd been holding.

Juliana cleared her throat. "The Kig-Yar shipmaster is complaining that we are deceitful, cowardly liars."

Keyes chuckled. "I take it she's figured out she's under attack."

In the distance, gunfire started up, with the return whine of plasma answering it.

"Yes," said Juliana. "I would say that she has."

"We have contact," Faison reported.

"Pull me," Juliana said. "We want to be ready to plug in the moment we get the chance."

"Okay."

Keyes leaned over and gently slid the chip, in reality a small matchbook-sized card, out of its housing in the station. Juliana's hologram flickered away, and he tucked it into his chest pocket as he left the cockpit.

A pair of ODSTs flanked the airlock, battle rifles at the ready. "What have we got?" he asked.

"Pretty small contingent of Jackals. We have the corridor in secured. Faison has us pushing them back toward their bridge."

The sound of grenades boomed out, bouncing around the walls.

"Breached the bridge," Faison reported. "There's still fighting outside the ship by the other entry airlock. You have a clear path to me, though. I'm sending Jai back to get you."

"I'll be here," Keyes said, as the echoes of the last blast finally dissipated, and the distinct sound of a wounded Jackal's screams followed it.

CHAPTER 44

Jai whipped out his submachine gun and peered around the cloud of smoke the grenades left behind. Jackals lay draped everywhere on the bridge, thrown clear by the explosions.

Nothing stirred in the haze, but Jai walked around, putting a round in the head of each Jackal for good measure.

"Bridge is secure," he reported.

ODSTs streamed in after him. "Bridge is clear," they confirmed.

They had plowed through the Jackals quickly on their way up to the bridge, Jai running in front. Five Jackals, unable to hide behind their energy shields, had died in the corridors. Same for the bridge crew.

But from the sound of battle chatter, the bulk of the fighting

Jackals had run out of the ship to fight the initial attack from the dock.

A good hundred or so of them had held their airlock against that threat, not even for a second imagining that they were going to get boarded from the outside. It was easy enough to keep them from getting back in.

The AI and Lt. Keyes had a flair for this, Jai thought.

"Spartan, can you head back and provide protection for Lt. Keyes?" Faison asked.

"On my way," Jai replied. He took one last look around the bridge. The ODSTs were throwing the dead Jackal bodies into a pile in the corner.

He double-timed it back down the corridor.

ODSTs snapped quick nods at him as he passed, some flat-out stared as he thudded his way back toward the *Mighty Sparrow*. He passed Li and Kirtley running toward the bridge with a pair of ODSTs guarding them.

Keyes waited in the airlock. As Jai stepped inside, his earpiece crackled. "Jai, this is Delgado."

"Go ahead," Jai said.

"I'm passing on a message from *Petya*. They report success, and are on their way back. That's all."

"Thanks," Jai said. He smiled inside his helmet. Adriana and Mike had taken care of business. "You ready?" Jai asked Keyes.

"Yes. And by the way, Spartan?"

"Yessir?" Jai looked down at him.

Keyes smiled up at Jai. "Boy, is it nice to see you out here with us."

So many things could still go wrong, Jai thought. But they'd stormed a Jackal ship, destroyed most of the nav data, and had control of the rest. So far, so good.

"Jai, Faison, Keyes," Delgado's voice burst over Jai's moment. "We have a problem. There's a ship inbound. Not ours. Covenant."

Keyes frowned. "Already?"

Jai put a hand on the lieutenant's shoulder. "Come, Lt. Keyes, we need to move quickly, then."

CHAPTER 45

Thel looked at the monitor, not quite believing what he saw: a human freighter, docked with the *Infinite Spoils*. And he was listening to the Kig-Yar battle channel, where they screamed about human attacks by their UNSC warriors.

Zhar looked over at him. "This Rubble grows stranger by the day, Shipmaster."

Thel shook his long head. "As strange as this may be, it cannot surprise you. The humans are heretics—it was foolish of the Kig-Yar to think they could enter into an alliance with them."

"Nonetheless, the airlock is occupied. What do we do now?" Zhar asked.

"Shoot the human ship," Thel ordered. "It will either move, or we will have to burn our way in."

Thel leaned back in his command chair, watching plasma leap out toward the human ship.

CHAPTER 46

Delgado grabbed the sides of his navigation chair as the cockpit shuddered. Air pressure dropped—the ship had been holed. He pulled the visor shut on his suit and sealed the gloves. It made operating a console clumsier, but it was clear this bucket was going to be full of nothing but vacuum soon enough.

The monitor showed the Covenant craft firing another round of plasma at them. Delgado winced as the *Mighty Sparrow* groaned. A large chunk of the cockpit ceiling caved in, and the glass all blew out.

This was bad. They needed to bug out.

"We're losing the freighter," Delgado reported. "Get your men out of this ship, Keyes. It looks like the Jackals have reinforcements."

"Get inside the *Infinite Spoils* with the ODSTs then," Keyes said. "Abandon the *Sparrow*, it's a lost cause. If we leave the *Sparrow* docked, they'll have a hard time getting through her. We'll fight our way out down the docks."

Delgado cleared out of the cockpit. At the airlock one of Keyes's men waited for him. Faison, if he remembered the name correctly. "I came back to make sure all my men were out," Faison barked, putting his black helmet on. Delgado could see the corridor he'd just run down reflected back in the visor. "Keyes and Jai are on the bridge, jacking the AI in. We're headed for the docks. I want to lead the breakout there."

"I'll go with you," Delgado said. Running with the leader of the Helljumpers had to be a safe bet.

They ran through corridors, Faison leading, turning the corners with his battle rifle up at chin level. Delgado followed, handgun out.

He was struggling to keep up with the marine, though. His legs hurt, his lungs hurt. Everything was one big ache.

Faison turned a corner well ahead of Delgado and plasma fire burst out. Faison dropped to the ground with a grunt, firing as he fell. The smell of burnt flesh filled Delgado's nostrils.

Delgado rounded the corner firing his pistol low, shifting his aim to hit a Kig-Yar running down the corridor in the feet. It howled, energy shield falling to the ground, and Faison shot it in the head.

"Damn it!" Faison shouted. He sounded angry, not hurt. Despite that, the floor was slick with his blood. The shot had been close to an artery, Delgado guessed. Even without the charring, Faison was in bad shape. "This corridor was supposed to be cleared."

"He could have been hiding until now." Delgado crouched in front of the marine. Faison's right thigh had been hit. As he cursed the Jackal, Faison used a knife to cut off long strips of cloth from his left pant leg.

Delgado helped him make a makeshift tourniquet, tying it off around Faison's upper thigh to reduce the bleeding. It was a blood-soaked rag by the time they finished.

Delgado wiped his hands on his trousers. "You need a medic."

Faison leaned his helmeted head against the wall and groaned. "I know," he grunted. "But if we call someone down we're putting them in risk."

Delgado sat down against the opposite wall. "What are you doing?" Faison asked.

"Waiting for help with you," Delgado said.

Faison shoved the battle rifle across the floor. "No, you keep moving. You'll have a better chance of getting out of here if you head for the docks. Keep your eyes open."

"There is no way I'm leaving you behind," Delgado said.

"Leave me your pistol," the marine said. "Take my rifle. I've been shot in the thigh and I've already lost too much blood. I'm not walking out of here, pilot. It's just not going to happen."

"You have men to lead. We can get them to come back via the docks for you," Delgado said.

"I'm not spending lives to save my own," Faison said. He shifted his position and winced, and then he yanked his helmet off, throwing it down beside him. "I turned the corridor too fast, I let my guard down, and I paid the price."

"And if I wasn't in such rough shape, I would have been right there beside you," Delgado said.

"Battle is random like that, sometimes." Faison gestured for Delgado's pistol, and Delgado tossed him *Señora Sies*. The marine examined it. "Fancy piece."

"It has a long history," Delgado said.

"I'll bet so," Faison muttered. "I'm sorry to have to ask for it, but you'll be better off with the rifle. Now go, quickly."

Delgado stood up, and grabbed Faison's wrist in an extended handshake. "You're a good man, Faison. For UNSC."

Faison laughed. "I bet it hurts to say that."

Delgado smiled. "Not really, soldier. Not really."

"Go," Faison hissed. "Please."

Delgado turned the corner with the battle rifle up and at the ready, his footsteps echoing softly off the walls as he left the ODST marine behind him in a pool of blood.

Once he was down the corridor he ignored Faison's commands and radioed Jai. "Faison is down. If you can get back to this location at any point, he really needs a medic. He'll need backup—we were ambushed."

CHAPTER 47

Keyes watched as Juliana appeared over the alien console, her form wavering and sparking.

"It's getting bad out here," he told her. "We have Jackals on the docks in solid numbers still holding out, and reinforcements at the door on the other side. We abandoned the *Mighty Sparrow*. Please tell me all this was worth it."

Juliana ignored him as her eyes flashed incandescent white and she dropped to her knees. "Strong security," she whispered. Then she opened her eyes wide. "But it *was* worth it. We're in real danger. All of us. Yank me, Lieutenant, and get me back into the Rubble. I have the data I need, and we need to act fast. The Kig-Yar are coming for us. The Rubble will need to make a stand. Get me out of here, Keyes. Now!"

Keyes pulled the chip and pocketed it.

"To the docks?" he asked Jai.

The Spartan's gold visor turned to him. "I need to make a detour. Your man Faison's hurt. Delgado asked if we could help."

Keyes nodded. "Get to him."

Jai thudded out of the room, and Keyes turned to the ODSTs inside the cockpit. "Let's get out of here."

CHAPTER 48

Infinite Spoils, off Habitat Tiago, the Rubble, 23 Librae

Thel stepped aboard the *Infinite Spoils* with a snarl. The human ship had clogged up their attempt to board, and they'd had to shuttle over on boarding ships, burning their way aboard the docked human freighter.

It left him in a testy mood. And with Unggoy milling about bumping into each other, Thel's mood had darkened further.

He leaned over to Zhar. "Have any of them figured out how to move this human ship away?"

"No," Zhar replied, looking over the Unggoy standing around the cockpit, pushing buttons and chattering to each other.

Thel sighed. "Leave five Unggoy here to cut the ship loose with plasma torches once we get through the airlock."

He stalked back to the airlock and made his way through after several Unggoy. They fanned out ahead of him into the corridors, their ungainly steps making far too much noise.

The Kig-Yar ship felt empty. No Kig-Yar had even tried to hold the airlock. Had the humans killed them all?

And if so, where were the humans?

Zhar followed him through. After the airlock closed, the sound of welding and cutting came through from the other side. A moment later a loud creaking sound filled the corridor, then silence.

"The human ship is cut loose. The Unggoy Deacon and Saal say they're towing it free and casting it off," Zhar said. "So far, no human ships have come to sniff around."

"Good." Thel looked around. "Unggoy toward the bridge. Zhar and I will secure the other airlock from the docks and eliminate any Kig-Yar there."

The Unggoy dutifully headed up the corridor.

Zhar patted the plasma rifle in his hands. "Let's go, then."

Thel's old friend took the lead, turning corners as Thel quickly followed behind, keeping him covered as they thudded down the inside of the ship through bulkhead after bulkhead.

Zhar turned a corner and flinched as human gunfire slapped into his armor. The old Sangheili fired downward, and the shots stopped.

The now dead human, its back against the wall, had been already wounded. A large shot to its thigh had bled the creature's strange red blood out onto the floor. Zhar had shot it once: clean through the head.

"It was sitting down," Zhar said. "Startled me. I barely got a return shot in."

"You are lucky it didn't have a more powerful weapon." Thel kicked away the handgun lying by its side.

"Indeed." Zhar actually sounded somewhat shaken. He squatted in front of the dead human. "I wonder why they left one of their own behind like this? Was it a trap?"

"Who knows how they think?" Thel said. "Who cares? They are heretics. They do not deserve names or life."

Zhar wouldn't stop worrying at some idea deep in his head. "I don't know, Thel. You're a true zealot, I know, and I would never doubt the word of the Prophets, but we've fought the humans for years and they show some capacity for honor. Look, they left behind one of their own, who was bleeding and dishonored, to spring a trap and die with honor. Don't you think that indicates something profoundly noble about them?"

Thel looked down at the dead alien and thought about it. "You think too much, Zhar."

As he said that, Thel saw something move quickly out of the corner of his eyes. Zhar snapped out his plasma rifle and fired, just as the large, gray-armor-clad human fired back with a rifle of its own.

Thel pulled out his energy sword as the armored human smacked into him, carrying them both rolling down the corridor until they struck a bulkhead hard enough to make Thel's vision blur and knock his sword loose.

"I cannot get a good aim," Zhar shouted, as Thel struggled to get a grip on the powerful human's rifle.

The loud human gun fired into the floor several times as they fought over it, and then Thel got the barrel in both his hands.

He stared at his reflection in the alien's visor and roared as he bent the weapon, straining to make it useless. The gold visor stared implacably back at Thel. There were no sounds, though the alien was straining just as hard.

What creature did not choose to show its face that wasn't a soulless and dead one? Thel roared again. "Demon! Heretic. Unholy alien!" He headbutted the gold visor, snapping the human's neck back with each whiplike blow.

The human threw him back and yanked a primitive knife from the chest of its armor.

The two warriors stood, staring at each other for a split second. Thel suddenly realized that they would both die, fighting to the very end, equally matched.

Equally matched with a *human*. Thel spat purple blood from his mouth. This was a surprise.

The human looked over at the other dead marine, shook its head, and then took off down the corridor.

"We follow it," Thel gasped, out of breath. He'd broken a rib with that impact.

"What *was* that?" Zhar asked, cautiously pointing his plasma rifle around the corner.

"I do not know," Thel said. "It was strong, though." He joined Zhar, turning around the corner.

"Looks like it was headed to the docks. Let's go."

Zhar had a small limp, and it hurt for Thel to run, but neither of them would allow these to slow them. Both Sangheili ran all out, grunting occasionally, to the airlock dock.

They got there just in time to see the gray-armored human disappear past the lip, running out into the large cavernous docking area where human tracers and Covenant plasma filled the air.

Kig-Yar corpses lay around the airlock.

Zhar took one side, Thel the other, forgetting about the strange new human for now. "It looks like the Kig-Yar were protecting the ship," Zhar said. "But were surprised by the attack from inside."

"The humans are moving out onto the docks, back into their habitats," Thel noted. "They have done us a favor. They cleared the ship."

He shut the airlock door with a laugh and walked over to Zhar and clapped him on the shoulder. "Guard this door, old friend. I will head to the bridge and get us moving. We will pick up Saal, and then we will see what our options are."

Zhar nodded.

"But you should also check to see what it was the humans were doing aboard when we get clear," Zhar said. "We do not need any-more surprises."

Thel thought about the pain in his ribs, and what had felt like a close brush with death, and nodded.

What *had* that human been?

CHAPTER 49

The sound of the ship's airlock doors shutting echoed throughout the spare cavern that the Kig-Yar had as a docking bay. The lanky aliens paused, looking over at the doors. Two of them ran for the lock, banging on the door, as loud clanks and hisses told everyone in the docking bay that their ship was undocking.

Delgado watched the panic spread through the Kig-Yar as they realized what had happened. The Kig-Yar had kept bunched up on the far side of the docks, close to their ship's airlock. That had made getting out onto the docks a dangerous exercise, but the Kig-Yar had realized that letting the humans get *off* their ship was better than trapping them in it. Now they were no doubt wondering who the heck was taking their ship.

Keyes, hunkered down on the far side of a shipping container they were both using as cover, waved Delgado over. The immense bulk of the gray Spartan Jai stood behind the lieutenant.

"I'm sorry to hear about Faison," Delgado said. The word had spread as they'd remained pinned down by the Kig-Yar. The aliens, with their energy shields and snipers, were doing far better now in the large, open docking bay than in the tight confines of the ship.

Keyes nodded. He looked tired, Delgado thought. These men were all his responsibility. The four dead in the open area of the docks were on Keyes. Now so was Faison.

"Jai has an idea," Keyes said.

The Spartan stepped forward. "You had them all suit up, Keyes. Everyone's vacuum ready. Only a few Jackals are equipped. If we figure out how to flush the air out of the entire dock . . ."

"We'd need Juliana for that," Delgado said. One couldn't just flush the atmosphere out of a habitat without extensive overrides.

Keyes pulled the large chip out of his pocket that held Juliana. "Jai will cover you; you just need to get somewhere to plug this in. Get Juliana back up and have her flush the bay. We'll pick off the stragglers."

Delgado almost reverently placed the AI's chip into his pocket. She'd been created to manage the mining operations of a Madrigal corporation, helping guide asteroids to processing plants around the system. She may have been commercial AI, nothing like the industrial strength thinkers the UNSC used, but she'd somehow managed to keep the entire Rubble together since the fall of Madrigal. Juliana had been a protector of the Rubble for so long she was almost like a technological deity, a god everyone in the Rubble looked to for help with their troubles.

And she fit in his pocket.

He scanned the docks. "Over there." He pointed Jai at a console used by supervisors to run the docks. "That should be doable." It was well away from the bulk of the firefight.

"So go!" Keyes said.

The rate of fire from the ODSTs picked up as Jai and Delgado made a run for it, ducking from one set of containers and large structural spars to another.

They stopped a mere fifteen feet from the console.

Delgado swallowed. From where he had been, the console looked out of the way. Up close, he realized it was in the open. Though far away from the Kig-Yar, they were good shots.

Jai realized it too, because the Spartan turned and held out a gauntleted hand. "Give her to me, I'll plug her in."

Delgado stared at the Spartan's hand. He'd be just handing over one of the most important assets the Rubble had.

How much *did* he trust these UNSC Spartans?

So far they'd worked toward the same goals. If you didn't start trusting someone at some point, he thought, then you'll never trust again.

This Spartan was offering to risk his life to get out in the open and try to save them all.

How much proof did Delgado need?

He took a deep breath and handed Juliana over.

Jai cupped the chip in his hands and darted out. For a brief second it looked like the Kig-Yar hadn't spotted them, that Jai would make it to the console and back before they noticed anything.

But as the Spartan stood and inserted the chip, plasma fire struck the wall overhead.

Delgado leaned out and wildly fired his battle rifle at the Kig-Yar.

Several plasma shots grazed Jai, but he kept the chip guarded until Juliana's form appeared over the console.

"Get back!" Delgado shouted. "She's in the system."

Near misses blackened the gray armor as Jai ran back to cover, firing his battle rifle as he did so. Three Kig-Yar fell over, dead. Delgado marveled at the Spartan's accuracy. At this range, across hundreds of feet of dock, all Delgado had done was harass the Kig-Yar.

Jai slammed his back into the container as plasma slapped the other side, boiling metal.

Delgado's earpiece crackled, and Juliana's voice filled his ear. "Thank you, Delgado, Jai. What do you need from me?"

"Blow the air out of here," Delgado requested.

Juliana didn't reply, but a second later all the airlocks feeding into the docks blew open with the bass warbling of emergency sirens and strobing warning lights. Air rushed out into the vacuum, thundering past, and the sound of plasma fire stopped.

It was over in a few minutes. ODSTs popped up and shot the few remaining Kig-Yar that were in full gear and still able to breathe and fight.

The other aliens died horribly, flailing around, asphyxiated, their long mouths open and frozen in silent screams.

Keyes and the ODST Markov looked out over the carnage once the docks repressurized. Keyes looked a bit horrified at the carnage. Markov looked slightly pleased.

Jai stood behind them, towering high, battle rifle in hand. "The *Petya* has caught up to us," he told Keyes. "I would suggest you use it as a temporary command center. It'll keep you from getting recaptured, at the least."

Keyes ran a hand over his silvering hair and nodded. "Thank you, Spartan. We'll need it. Juliana reported that this is just the beginning, the Kig-Yar are up to something. Juliana might as well brief us aboard your ship."

Jai slung his battle rifle and plodded off toward one of the nearby airlocks. After a moment, Delgado followed, both glad to be out of the dock full of dead Kig-Yar.

CHAPTER 50

===============================

Thel looked over the reports that Zhar had patiently gathered for him. The humans had dug around the Kig-Yar battle net, which had been poorly secured.

"These are details on where the Unggoy Redoubt is," Zhar said. "Including force strength, ships, how they will shuttle the Unggoy to the Rubble for an attack, and plans for an invasion of one of their habitats called 'Exodus.' The humans have the whole Kig-Yar battle plan for themselves now."

"Well, they are clever creatures," Thel said. He shut the display down. "You yourself admired that, if I remember correctly."

"This is troubling, though," Zhar said. "It means the Kig-Yar, Reth, may have been telling the truth."

Thel sighed. "That they plan to trick the humans out of the location to their homeworld?"

"Yes. And that he was doing a holy duty for a Hierarch. You

must admit the possibility, looking over those plans to attack the humans. These have been in place for years."

Thel rubbed the bottom of a mandible thoughtfully. "It is a possibility, now. I agree."

"Then we may have crossed the Hierarch," Zhar said. "You of all should know how that chills my heart."

"A Hierarch," Thel said, cautiously.

"What do you mean?"

"What I mean is that we were given a set of orders that put us in conflict with orders given by another Prophet."

Zhar shook his head. "These things border on heresy."

"Then do not speak of them ever again," Thel said. "But it does not change our situation."

"But—"

"So we shall also send a message to Reth," Thel said, trying to add a note of reassurance to his voice. "We will not approach or attack the Exodus asteroid that the Kig-Yar want. We will attack the other human parts of the Rubble, working to destroy the humans there."

Zhar swallowed. "Will that be enough to convince the Prophet of Regret that we did what we were asked?"

Thel grumbled. "We will destroy the Rubble. We will grind it to pieces from this Kig-Yar ship. How will they doubt our zealotry, then, Zhar? We offer Reth our agreement to leave their habitat alone, and maybe we will come out ahead."

"Maybe?" Zhar left the cockpit in a dark mood, and Thel sat down on the shipmaster's chair with a sneer. This was not Covenant standard; it was designed for Kig-Yar. It was an insult and an expression of their rebellious impulses. And even worse, it was an uncomfortable fit for the Sangheili. Nonetheless, it would be a good spot from which to oversee the destruction of the Rubble.

The sooner this mess was wrapped up, the sooner Thel imagined a more normal life would resume. Betrayals and intrigues were not his strong suit.

Sangheili were almost always more . . . direct.

Thel punched the console in front of him in frustration, shattering the screen and denting the metal.

CHAPTER 51

Peter Bonifacio unstrapped himself from the pilot's seat of the escape capsule. The long-burn engine had run out; he'd kept the thing maxed to get well clear of the damn Spartans that had hunted down *Distancia*.

Now he coasted toward Metisette.

What was that damn Kig-Yar's code? Bonifacio hunted through scraps of paper in his pockets until he found the tiny card.

He plugged the frequency into the escape pod's controls and transmitted the emergency.

Then he waited nervously until the speaker crackled with the sound of Kig-Yar voices. "Peter Bonifacio. Proceed."

"I need help," Bonifacio blurted out. "I'm in a capsule, headed toward Metisette. I need to be picked up!"

"And do you have our navigation data with you?"

"Is this Reth?" Bonifacio asked.

A moment as the question was transmitted, and then translated. "This is Reth," came the response. "Our data?"

Bonifacio swallowed nervously. This was indeed Reth, he told himself. He'd done a lot of business with the Kig-Yar. This was about business. And a partner like Reth would understand a setback. He was dealing with a trade-oriented species, just like himself. Reth would understand. "The data was stolen from me," Bonifacio finally admitted.

"Stolen? What use is this to us? Why did you bother even calling to admit this?" Bonifacio couldn't tell because of the delay and monotone of the translation device, but it felt to him that Reth sounded angry.

"I know where they will be taking the data," Bonifacio said quickly. "Please, if you come help me I'll help you get the data."

Another pause before the reply, then, "You are a useless lump of nothing that once glittered to us, Bonifacio. We gave you weapons to smuggle, and make a profit on. We gave you docking rights, and helped you in every way we could imagine. And all we asked is this one favor, for which you failed us."

"No!" Bonifacio screamed over the radio. He started babbling. "You can't just abandon me, you owe me. We worked well together. We were good together."

Only silence came from the other end.

"I'll tell you where they are taking it, if you do me this last favor," Bonifacio begged.

"Where are they taking it?" Reth asked.

"To the Exodus asteroid," Bonifacio said. "And if you do me the favor of picking me up, I'll tell you where it is."

Reth laughed. "I already know where it is, thank you. We will be taking it for ourselves soon enough."

Bonifacio's mouth dried with fear. He'd been wrong, he

realized. About the Kig-Yar. Probably about everything. But he still had his life to save. "But . . ."

"I will do you this last favor, Bonifacio," Reth said. "I will not come pick up your pod. Because right now, were I to pick you up, the last moments of your life would be horrible indeed. Good-bye, human."

The radio went silent.

Bonifacio was alone, floating toward Metisette, looking out the tiny portholes of his escape pod at the distant ruddy orb.

He wondered if the air would run out before the heater stopped.

CHAPTER 52

Somewhere near Charybdis IX

The Prophet of Regret stood in front of a giant screen that showed his fleet assembled in the far distance: tiny specks of light waiting to be flung through space wherever he wished.

He turned his chair about to regard the other body in the room: the Prophet of Truth.

Regret frowned as Truth rebuked him. "You are, as ever, too hasty."

"How is this?" Regret whined. "I have sent my hunters out to find the source of what I thought was trouble. I have hunted the humans. I have *acted*."

"You have not acted well. My plan was more elegant."

Truth, Regret thought, always did like working his intrigues. He shouldn't have been this surprised to find out Truth was behind the design of these smuggled weapons.

They were all just an attempt to furtively find the human home-world, Truth had said, without further fleet engagements. Never mind that Regret knew they could smash the humans, one world after another. Truth worried about the secret of humans, and their first encounter with them. Particularly since the three Hierarchs had worked so hard to hide that secret.

"Does it matter now what we have done?" Truth said. "There is a mess, and it needs cleaning. The fleet needs to return to this world. If the Kig-Yar have the location of the human homeworld, we can use it and the Unggoy quartered there. If not, then we destroy all traces of this . . . experiment."

"I agree," Regret said, finding himself once again following Truth's lead.

"The Jiralhanae who betrayed your Sangheili shipmaster, they will need to be destroyed. Their loyalty is commendable, but the knowledge of what they saw must die with them. We do not need any in High Charity speaking of this."

Regret agreed. "You will travel to this world with us, and watch the fleet in action?"

The Prophet of Truth bobbed his head. "I want to see this all concluded, yes. I have had my effects brought onto your flagship. We will have joint command. Together we will fix any problems. As we always have."

Regret turned and looked at the screen, with its live images of the fleet. Truth had platitudes, words about being brothers, now that his experiment had failed. But they were only brothers with a shared secret while the humans lived.

If they ever got rid of the threat humans presented, then Truth would have no need of Regret. More than ever, Regret realized, if he ever had the chance to destroy the humans first and keep control of his position in the Covenant, he would have to move fast in the future. Faster than Truth's intrigues.

Regret shook himself from his thoughts. "Then it is time for us to go there," he said. And using the controls on his floating throne, he keyed in a channel to the ship's bridge and gave the order for the fleet to make the jump.

PART IV

CHAPTER 53

Petya, near Habitat Tiago, The Rubble, 23 Librae

Delgado sat down in the cockpit of the Spartan's freighter, finding it strangely reassuring to be back aboard.

Keyes had joined the Spartans aboard the _Petya_, along with Markov and Delgado. The other ODSTs remained out on the docks, cleaning up after the firefight.

Things were happening all across the Rubble, Delgado felt. Juliana was off in some vast, spread out, processing mode that made it hard for her to focus on one small area. But she'd asked them all to get ready for a conference. So now they were just waiting, Mike running checks on the _Petya_, Jai and Adriana in the back examining his armor after the battle.

Keyes paced the cockpit, waiting for information, frustrated. Markov just stared at the metal floor, somewhat shell-shocked at the death of his commanding officer, Faison.

Everyone surged into the cockpit, though, when Juliana finally returned to manifest herself.

"I'm sorry for my absence," she said, appearing over the communications console. "I was verifying the data I had taken from the Kig-Yar ship. I'm also presenting this information to all members of the Rubble Security Council."

She faded away, and in her place the moon Metisette appeared. It zoomed large, until its clouds hung in front of the crowd in the cockpit. The image increased, until an irregular oval appeared on the rocky ground of Metisette's surface.

Another leap in perspective showed it to be the remains of a crater. Liquid covered the very bottom, filled by a river of some sort with a waterfall. Delgado looked at the shapes by the waterfall's edge. "Are those structures?"

"The Kig-Yar have created a natural home for hundreds of thousands of Unggoy," Juliana's voice said. "This structure, parked over a methane waterfall where the mists are thick enough with methane that the Unggoy can breathe out in the open, is called the Redoubt. Right now, as we speak, Unggoy are being readied for an invasion of the Rubble."

Juliana let that sink in.

"When do they mobilize?" Keyes asked.

"Within the next twenty-four hours," Juliana said. The image of Metisette faded, replaced by pictures of Kig-Yar ships moving out of orbit down to Metisette. "As soon as they pick up the Unggoy."

Those images faded as well, to be replaced by Juliana. She cocked her head, listening to someone else. "The Council wants to know what our Kig-Yar contacts are saying about all this."

"That would tip the hand of any defense the Rubble might need," Keyes muttered.

Juliana nodded. "May I offer another point of importance?"

"Please," Jai said from the cockpit's entrance. He'd removed his helmet, and his brown eyes were fixed on Juliana.

"The Kig-Yar know about the Exodus project." Juliana had dropped a bombshell, Delgado realized. Their most tightly held secret, something he hadn't known about, had been in the Kig-Yar databanks. It angered him. "And once Bonifacio had delivered the navigation data to them, the Kig-Yar were going to use the asteroid as a troop carrier to invade Earth."

Delgado felt vaguely sick.

Keyes looked confused, but didn't ask any questions for now. This was the first he had heard of the Exodus project, and while he could infer what it might entail from the AI's statement, he was hoping it would let something more solid slip.

Juliana waited for this, too, to sink in. "I'm unwilling to lose the Rubble. It's everything I exist for. I say we attack first. We use our mass drivers like MACs. We get Keyes and his men back aboard the *Midsummer Night*. If we start attacking them while their main force is on the ground, we have a chance of winning this."

Keyes fiddled with a pen as he looked around. "The *Midsummer Night* has the capacity to go up against that big Jackal ship, but we could get overwhelmed by sheer numbers with all these other craft they have parked throughout the Rubble. And then there's the other issue: have these Jackals been working alone? Because if not, all they have to do is call in support. One stealth frigate won't be much use against what the Covenant usually bring to a fight."

"I can't speak to that," Juliana said. "But now we have another problem. The Security Council is getting ready for a meeting. They're shutting me out. This isn't something I can override without drawing attention. Delgado, Maria was Diego's closest relative, and has been given a temporary seat on the Council to represent him. Can you get down there? I don't want us out of the loop here."

Delgado was already up. "Take me there, I'll go in."

Jai and Mike looked at each other. Jai shook his head. "We don't want to risk taking *Petya* into the heart of the Rubble. We're already exposing ourselves enough with the AI and Delgado aboard."

"I'll take tube cars," Delgado said.

Outside of the tall faux-marble columns of the Council Chambers, Maria Esquival looked over at Delgado. The chambers were buried deep in the heart of Korrah, one of the first Rubble habitats, and he had rushed to get there. "You got over here quickly." She looked like she hadn't slept in days, with bags under her eyes. She pushed a stray wisp of hair aside.

Delgado broke protocol and gave her a long hug. "I'm so sorry about Diego."

She let go and looked up at him. "They said that bastard Bonifacio is in an escape pod somewhere with the Kig-Yar?"

"As far as we know, yes. When this crisis is over, I will personally hunt that cockroach down."

Maria cleared her throat. "The Security Council just had an emergency meeting to figure out what to do next. I stood in for Diego. I had no voting rights, but I could talk if needed."

"I know. What can you tell me?"

"The summary is that we're grateful for all the risks you've taken, though I think half the Council is ready to string you all up for releasing the UNSC prisoners without locators, or without authority."

"We didn't have a lot of time to confer or ask permission, and Juliana was helping."

"That disturbs them almost as much as anything. You know the AI is well past her useful age."

Delgado nodded. "She's unpredictable. But I think, deep down, what she cares about is the Rubble. What is the Council going to do?"

"You're not going to like this."

"Really?" Delgado raised an eyebrow.

"They've called the Kig-Yar. They want to see if there is any negotiation to be done."

Delgado stared at Maria. "They *what?*"

"Understand—from their position, the Kig-Yar have only helped. And don't lecture me about the destruction of Madrigal. The fact is, you know a lot of people trust the Kig-Yar here. They've worked with us to build the Rubble. They've traded with us. They consider them allies."

"They really did it?"

"Yes. We're waiting for a response."

Delgado walked away, shaking his head. "We've completely tipped our hand."

Maria looked down at the ground. "I don't know. Maybe not. We're just asking for meetings. I'm not sure what else we can do except get ready to defend ourselves. We have a Council, it's the way the Rubble works. They've spoken."

"But they were wrong," Delgado snapped.

"What would you have us be?" Maria asked. "We're ruled by representatives, and by our votes."

"This is a disaster."

"Maybe not." Maria grabbed his arm. "Again, all we've done is ask for meetings. We haven't asked why. Certainly with all the recent activity around the Rubble it would make sense that we're jumpy."

Delgado looked at her. "I really hope so."

CHAPTER 54

Reth lay in a soft collection of pillows in an approximation of a nest. His skin had been bandaged, cuts and bruises covered with medicines that stank, and he was giddy from pain medication. The damage the Sangheili had done to him still throbbed, but he was beginning to feel like the worst of the pain was over now that a Kig-Yar healer had spent time with him.

The soft sound of air fans lulled him near the edge of sleep when the door to his room opened.

"I was not to be disturbed during this sleep cycle," Reth snapped, his eyes still closed.

"It is the humans." A lesser Kig-Yar groveled by Reth's feet. "They keep contacting us, requesting meetings."

"About what?" Reth opened his eyes. The room was decorated with bits and pieces of art from around Covenant space randomly piled in corners and hanging off shelves in random chaos and clutter. All were pieces stolen or traded from all the species the Kig-Yar dealt with—a riot of shapes, colors, sizes, and function. It may have looked like random junk, but any Kig-Yar in the room would know it was Reth's hoard. In the corner was a handmade Sangheili practice helmet, carved out of a hard wood and painted black. Reth's most prized piece of the collection.

Sangheili didn't part with their handmade gifts easily. Reth had to work hard to pilfer that particular item.

"They won't say," the Kig-Yar by his feet said.

Reth sat up, wincing as split skin on his shoulder recracked and started bleeding again. "Send word to all Kig-Yar in the Rubble to pull out. Have them stand ready to act as our front wave. The humans may be getting wind of our plan, somehow. Let's not leave our brothers sitting within easy reach of the aliens."

"Yes, lord. But . . . we have worked with these humans for so long. We have built good things with them. Are you sure we must destroy them?"

Reth sighed. "Any day now the Hierarchs will arrive. Do you wish to look like you were helping heretics? Our task is to fetch the location of Earth, and destroy them. Now we are to do this."

Time was growing short, Reth felt, if the humans were getting antsy. He was going to have to launch Kig-Yar ships against the Rubble before the Unggoy were even on their shuttles for the invasion.

No matter, he thought. That would just soften up the Rubble before he took it.

Once he had the Exodus asteroid, Reth thought, all these stolen baubles in his room would be meaningless compared to that fat prize.

CHAPTER 55

Petya, Just off Habitat Tiago, The Rubble, 23 Librae

Keyes turned to Jai at the back of the cockpit. "You and your team should leave. The Council seems to think things are unchanged; they might even fight to prevent us getting back aboard the *Midsummer Night*. I don't see the sense in us weighing you down."

"I don't see the sense in leaving either," Jai said.

"I could make it an order," Keyes said.

"You do outrank me. You may well order me to do it." Jai looked at Keyes. The unspoken second half of the sentence in the air was that Jai would refuse.

Keyes raised an eyebrow and drew in a breath to ream the Spartan out, but from behind him Mike spoke up. "Say what you will about Spartans, Lieutenant, one thing we don't do is leave fellow soldiers behind to die."

Jai raised a finger. "With us at your side retaking your ship will

— 318 —

not be hard to do. With *Petya*'s navigation charts and the computers synchronized—"

"We won't be leaving citizens behind to be *massacred*," Keyes interrupted. He already had to live with leaving Charybdis IX on its own. He couldn't bring himself to run away from yet another fight.

"The Rubble has no love for the UNSC," Jai said. "They are mostly Insurrectionists."

Keyes wondered if the Spartan was really that cold, having been trained to do nothing but kill Insurrectionists, and unable to shake that training. Or if Jai was somehow testing him.

"There are children, Spartan, and citizens. They will be slaughtered. I will offer my services to them, and we will be ready to fight for the Rubble."

Jai folded his arms. "Look—"

"The Jackals are moving out of the Rubble," Dante Kirtley shouted.

Keyes snapped his head up in interest. "They're moving out?"

"He's right. Take a look." Up at the front Mike tapped one of the many screens before his seat.

Jackal ships all eased their way out from the Rubble, according to the contacts on the radar and reports from all over the Rubble. "Like rats from a sinking ship," Keyes muttered.

Jai moved in for a closer look himself. "Does the Council know? Where's Juliana? Get that damn AI here, she has to have spotted this."

Keyes stepped back. The Spartan sounded agitated.

"My, my, temper, little Spartan," Juliana said. She'd appeared at their sides.

"Time is short!" Jai said. "We don't have the time to sit around and debate things. We need to move quickly."

"What's going on?" Keyes asked, realizing that Jai's frustration mainly came from leading a small team, alone, and now being part of a committee trying to figure out how to defend an entire community.

Jai was somewhat out of his element.

Keyes, on the other hand, had expected something to happen. The Rubble was basically a very large, slow ship, and it was constantly making course corrections.

"I come bearing news," Juliana said. "The Council has re-thought their approach based on this behavior. I had them recast their votes. They're willing to consider our plans. Second: aboard that Kig-Yar ship I stole some encryption keys. I've been tracking their chatter. We're in even more trouble than just the Kig-Yar attacking—according to the Kig-Yar, they're expecting high ranking officials from the very top of the Covenant hierarchy, and possibly a Covenant fleet, to arrive shortly."

"When?" Keyes asked.

"Even they don't know. Just . . . soon."

Keyes looked at Jai. "Still think we can even make a stand now?"

Jai slowly shook his head. "A whole Covenant fleet? Not without some minor miracle. These people are all doomed."

Keyes felt he had to agree. It was a chilling feeling.

"The Council agrees," Juliana said. "They have decided to launch the Exodus habitat and evacuate the Rubble."

"The Exodus habitat?" Keyes asked. "You mentioned the name before. I need to ask, what is it?"

Jai turned back to look at him. "Right, you need to get caught up a bit."

CHAPTER 56

Thel stalked across the bridge. "*All* the Kig-Yar ships are leaving the Rubble?"

Zhar exhaled through his mandibles in an audible sigh of happiness. "Yes. Now we won't have to worry about firing on them. One less reason the Prophets may seek to damn us when they arrive."

"Contact Reth," Thel ordered, tamping down his annoyance with Zhar's obsession about the wills of Prophets. They were Sangheili—noble warriors. This dithering didn't bode well. "It is time we spoke since his escape."

Zhar bowed his head and fiddled about. Thel ignored Zhar's mutterings with distant Kig-Yar, moving his way up the chain of command, until Reth's long face appeared on one of the screens.

Thel faced the image. The Kig-Yar still wore bandages over the wounds Saal had inflicted on him.

"Shipmaster," Reth said, the words dripping with fury. "You have stolen *Infinite Spoils*, the pride of my fleet."

Thel ducked his head. "I am not here for recrimination, Reth. You will do what you have been asked. I can only do the same, for we are both soldiers of the Covenant. I have offered to stay away from your main target, but I am also going to start attacking the humans."

"Do what you wish. Keep them occupied, Sangheili. The longer their eyes aren't looking toward this moon, the better."

The Kig-Yar's image flicked off. Thel looked around at the nervous Unggoy, and the now petulant Zhar. "That Kig-Yar will do his best to assassinate us with words to his Hierarch," Zhar said. "Why talk to him like this, Shipmaster? It serves nothing but to remind him that we're here."

Thel ignored Zhar. "Prepare this ship's weapons." He walked over to a screen showing the image of their first target, a small asteroid on the edge of the Rubble with mining equipment on it.

The long-barreled mass drivers could sling ingots of metal across the Rubble to wherever they were needed. The larger machines could send these slugs across the entire system, from planet to planet.

They made effective antiship weapons in a pinch, Thel knew. He'd encountered a few repurposed mass drivers in the service of canny humans before.

"Destroy it," he ordered, and watched as several balls of energy barreled their way across the empty space between them to plow into the asteroid, ripping it apart in fiery destruction.

Normally his heart leapt when dealing fire to his enemies. In this case, Thel felt as if he was merely going through the motions.

He had no idea what the Prophets would think of all this. But he had to do his duty.

And Sangheili knew all too much about duty and nobility.

It ran in the blood.

CHAPTER 57

Petya, Habitat Tiago, the Rubble, 23 Librae

The first attack on the Rubble came from the *Infinite Spoils.*

Keyes had Mike put the information up on one of *Petya's* larger screeens.

"They're going after the mass drivers," Juliana reported.

"They realize they're damn good weapons," Keyes said. Another blow. He'd hoped that the Jackals hadn't realized the defensive potential of the mining equipment. It would have been a useful surprise.

Delgado joined them, out of breath from running across the dock to get to the *Petya.* "They're starting the attack?"

"The Council is calling for the Rubble to evacuate to the Exodus habitat," Juliana told him. "There are ships moving in to defend the mass drivers and the most populated habitats while the evacuation proceeds. Exodus is being moved toward one of the limbs of the Rubble, so that civilians can get to it by tube car. I'm initiating emergency routing, all cars are one way."

"How long will it take to get everyone evacuated?" Keyes asked.

"A million citizens, once Exodus is docked, will take twelve hours. With me presiding. But then there is another question," Juliana said. She turned to look at the Spartans. "The Exodus can hardly go anywhere without the right data."

"The Cole Protocol is absolute," Keyes said. "We cannot risk handing that over."

"Not even to save a million lives?" Delgado asked.

"Because it risks billions more," Keyes said. "Don't even look at the Spartans, you turn and look at me. I'll carry the weight here. We cannot turn risk back on whole planets."

Juliana practically hissed her next sentence. "I have not held onto the edge of rampancy for *years* trying to save all this, just to watch the UNSC walk away from it."

Keyes closed his eyes. The weight of the entire million lives felt as if they were crushing his skull. He wanted to find a way to help. Anyway. But . . . "Juliana, there are hundreds of thousands of trained Grunts getting ready to board Jackal ships, and a suspected Covenant fleet getting ready to hit this system. You calculate the odds: what would you do if you were me?"

Juliana paused for a moment, running through simulations and possibilities, no doubt. "Give us something, Lieutenant. According to the records on your ship you're known for thinking outside the box. Now would be a good time, Lieutenant Keyes, to do some serious out-of-the-box thinking."

"We need your help," the AI whispered. "A last stand isn't what's needed. They need to be saved."

Keyes sat heavily in a seat. He looked at the images of Unggoy Grunts lining up amid the large structures on the waterfall of liquid methane.

He started flipping through the Jackal ship numbers. Hundreds of them perched on the ground on Metisette, except for the handful that had just withdrawn from the Rubble and were targeting mass drivers, as well as other weapons-like systems.

He tapped his pen against the screen, missing the heirloom pipe he usually held. It was still back on the *Midsummer Night*, with all his other effects. "Juliana, the habitats and asteroids, the parts of the Rubble—you keep them all aligned, correct?"

Keyes looked up and saw the AI nod.

He looked back down at the Covenant forces. They were all on the ground.

Vulnerable, if you had the right weapons.

Or something close enough.

Keyes stood up, and the eyes of everyone in the cockpit tracked him. "The Exodus is not the only habitat with engines—the entire Rubble can move. Juliana is constantly keeping the entire structure of the Rubble aligned. Which means they all have engines. Which also means, given enough time, the Rubble can be used as a weapon itself as it's emptied and abandoned."

Juliana hadn't seen it, Keyes realized, because it was almost a form of suicide. The AI lived for the Rubble. It was a part of her.

But it was lost to them. The Exodus was how these people would survive. So why protect the Rubble anymore?

Keyes pointed at the forces marshalling on the surface of Metisette. "The Covenant has destroyed us from orbit. Why not return the favor for once?"

He looked over at the Spartans, and was surprised to see a trio of grins.

Gray Team was in.

CHAPTER 58

Jai realized there was excitement building in the air. They'd gone from looking defeat in the eye, from contemplating a million lost lives, to realizing that Keyes had come up with a seed of a working strategy.

Juliana was glowing, abstract figures flowing faster and faster over the holographic space of her body. It was as if she was breathing faster and faster, as if having a panic attack, and then she slowed.

"I . . . I think I see what you're thinking, Keyes."

Jai saw that Keyes had been watching her closely. "Juliana, can you help us do it?"

"It . . . it won't be easy," she said.

Jai and Keyes exchanged glances. This was their best opportunity. If the AI stood in their way, it could all fall apart.

Jai moved close. "Juliana, they all need you now more than ever."

She focused on him, as if seeing him for the first time. "Ah, Spartan, are you worried about me?"

Jai blinked, not sure what to say, and Juliana laughed. "You're worrying about me, aren't you? It's flattering, Spartan. So flattering. But what I meant was that it's going to be hard to dodge the Jackal defenses and sensors."

On one of the screens three large structures were highlighted, then picked out of the picture and zoomed.

"Item number one is the central processing unit for their sensor grids. A big building. Kill that, and you take out their ability to see anything coming.

"These other two are Covenant antiship weapons, mounted to keep their Redoubt safe. They'll be firing at any non-Covenant ships coming in. You'll be dodging them to land. Not only that, they may be powerful enough to strike at any pieces of the Rubble that I throw at them."

Jai studied them. "We'll have to jump right into the heart of the attack to disable these?"

"Do that," Juliana said, "and I'll rain Armageddon down on them, I promise you."

Keyes leaned over and looked as well. "For this you'll need ODSTs. Can we get the Council to let us back aboard my ship?"

"I'm sure they'll be cooperative at this point," Juliana said.

"You'll need to be moved," Keyes said. "I can offer you space aboard *Midsummer Night*; we have the processing power for you. That is, if Exodus does not have the power yet. I know it's not completed."

"I'm not going anywhere, I'll be staying with the Rubble," Juliana said. "To hit Metisette and the Redoubt from here will require tricky calculations. I need to ride the pieces down where I can make instant adjustments for the best effect."

No one said anything for a moment.

Keyes looked at the hologram. "Are you sure about this, Juliana?"

"I lived for the Rubble. What am I without it? And who else can do this? You all know I'm approaching rampancy. I certainly know I am." Juliana chuckled. "How many get to choose how they will die. And how few in such a poetic manner? Besides, you can't get away with *all* the heroism here."

The words hung in the air as everyone let that settle in. They were all taking similar actions, and could well share the AI's fate.

Jai touched the lieutenant's arm. "The Exodus. What do we do?"

"Have the *Petya* stand off by the Exodus with the navigation data. If we fail, *Petya* makes a run for it. The moment we're successful, though, I think we should take a risk, don't you? We give them the navigation data, to be handed over when the 'all clear' goes through. *Petya* and *Midsummer Night* can pair up and cover the Exodus as it launches off to . . . wherever it's going to go. We go our own way. They head off into the depths of the galaxy, far from the Covenant, using random jumps."

"We'll still face a court-martial," Jai said, curious to see what Keyes's reaction would be.

"We'll still have saved a million lives," Keyes said. "I think it's worth it. We keep with the Exodus, long enough to make sure it's well clear."

Jai stood fully up from their quick conference. "So now we move."

Adriana stepped forward. "I want in on dropping to Metisette."

"Adriana . . ."

"You took on the Jackal ship alone. You're asking me to sit this one out as well?"

Mike stood up, and Jai shook his head. "*Petya* needs its pilot. We can't afford to lose the ship." The three of them hadn't worked as a team in combat since all this trouble erupted in the Rubble, but then, their missions always seemed to be a by-the-minute sort of thing.

And Jai didn't relish the thought of trying to even stop Adriana this time out, now that she knew there was a big fight ahead on Metisette.

For as long as he'd known her, Jai knew she was actually looking forward to it.

CHAPTER 59

Midsummer Night, Leaving EL Cuidad, the Rubble, 23 Librae

Delgado had offered his services as a pilot, and Keyes had accepted. Now Delgado trooped his way aboard the *Midsummer Night*, surprised by all the tight corridors, low bulkheads, and lack of confusion in the flurry of returning people on deck. Everyone had a mission: get the *Night* on its way toward Metisette at the highest possible speed.

When he got to the bay of the *Midsummer Night* Delgado was shown a Pelican.

"We lost a damn good pilot back on Charybdis IX," a grizzled fellow pilot with blond hair and a strong jaw said. His uniform had a patch naming him as Finlay.

"I'm sorry to hear it," Delgado said, walking around the long-tailed machine.

"Damn Insurrectionists," Finlay said. "Shot him right out of the sky."

Delgado looked over at the blond pilot. "Is there a problem?"

"Yeah." Finlay threw a punch to the gut that doubled Delgado up, coughing. "I don't like Insurrectionists. You sons of bitches have cost us enough—now we're covering your asses on some suicide mission?"

Delgado staggered back, and Finlay stepped forward. Delgado planted his feet and head-butted the man in the face. Finlay staggered back, hand on a bloody nose. "You goddamned—"

He didn't get any further. Pilots and an officer surrounded him, pulling him away.

"I'm not a damn Insurrectionist," Delgado said as he walked by him.

One of the other pilots joined him. "He's a bit strung out by all this. He and Jeffries hit it off pretty quickly."

"Jeffries was the one who was killed?"

"Yeah. Nice guy. Great pilot."

Delgado stopped. "I'm sorry to hear about it. But I didn't kill him."

The other pilot nodded. "I know. Come on. They're going to get Finlay patched up and calmed down. For all his testiness, you can trust him in the air, you understand? But we still should give him some space."

Delgado nodded and followed the pilot away.

The plan was to have the *Midsummer Night* come in fast at Metisette's upper atmosphere, then decelerate by aerobraking. Once the friction of the atmosphere had slowed them down, the ODSTs and Spartans would be released.

Then *Midsummer Night* would boost up and out again, and loop back around to settle into orbit so that her Pelicans could retrieve the ground forces.

But there was a good chance, Delgado knew, that even if they were successful, if the Spartans and ODSTs took too long they would all still be on the surface as the evacuated parts of the Rubble came down.

Then Delgado wouldn't be needed at all.

The deck of the *Midsummer Night* vibrated. The ship had left its berth in El Cuidad, and was accelerating toward Metisette.

Here we go, thought Delgado.

CHAPTER 60

Midsummer Night, En Route to Metisette, 23 Librae

Keyes was back on the bridge of the _Midsummer Night_, but this time he sat in the Commander's chair. He hadn't thought about Zheng in a while. Too much else going on.

But as they thundered toward Metisette, he wondered what thoughts would've run through Zheng's mind in this same predicament.

Zheng had been feared as a suicidal leader, one willing to throw his ship against the Covenant. An unfair assessment, Keyes knew. And ironic. Because here Keyes was now throwing his own ship and crew into a mission that might well have the same result.

He'd promoted Dante Kirtley to Ops. Rai Li remained on weapons. A junior officer, Lieutenant Second Grade Jason Burt, managed communications.

And Keyes had navigation rerouted to the Commander's chair, because what they were about to do was beyond tricky.

"How are you doing on your end, Juliana?" Keyes asked.

"Slinging mass and burning fuel, Lieutenant." All throughout the Rubble docking tubes had been severed as the last of the occupants pushed their way through.

Deputies with bullhorns shouted and directed traffic toward the Exodus habitat, but so did every computing device in the Rubble. They'd all been taken over by Juliana and were blaring the need for evacuation. She'd shown Keyes some of the organized chaos.

"I just took out the five Kig-Yar communications relays," Juliana reported. She'd used the last of her mass drivers to fire hyperkinetic slugs of metal at each of them. Now Kig-Yar comms were down to line of sight.

"And here comes those annoying Kig-Yar ships that have been hovering around."

Keyes smiled. It was a small trap for the Jackals. Knowing that they would move in, Rubble ships with missiles were lurking around the mass drivers to ambush them.

Juliana fed Keyes grainy video showing sparks of fire and tracers lighting up the vacuum, and the resulting return fire of plasma as Kig-Yar and Rubble ships fought it out over the mass drivers.

"Where's the *Infinite Spoils*?" Keyes asked. That was the one he was nervous about. That Jackal ship could match his frigate, from what he'd seen while aboard it.

"Keeping back. You said there were Sangheili aboard it?" Juliana asked.

"We saw Elites, yes," Keyes replied. "While we were retreating." A screen popped up on the arm of his chair, showing him a diagram of where that ship lurked. It was moving toward several of the large habitats, now thankfully abandoned.

The screen jumped to video showing plasma ripping apart the large asteroids and boiling rock as clouds of air burst out along with slagged metal.

Hopefully destroying those parts of the Rubble would keep that monster at bay until Keyes was done.

Then he looked forward to engaging it.

He shut the views down and brought up Metisette.

"Good luck, Juliana," Keyes said. The decoupled habitats that Juliana commanded were trailing far behind *Midsummer Night* on a seperate trajectory.

The Rubble trailed behind Hesiod in the same orbit around the sun as the gas giant. And Metisette orbited Hesiod. That meant that soon Metisette would disappear behind Hesiod from the point of view of the Rubble. Keyes was rushing to catch Metisette even as this happened. His signal to Juliana, a direct line-of-sight signal, was failing even now as Hesiod's stormy atmosphere began to get between them.

Juliana's trajectory was different. The pieces of the Rubble under her command were much slower. She was moving them forward from their trailing point behind Hesiod to a point where Metisette *would be* when it came out from behind Hesiod in its orbit.

To be strict about it, the Rubble wouldn't rain down upon Metisette. Instead, Metisette's orbit would swing the moon around Hesiod at breakneck speed right into the pieces Juliana had jockeyed into place.

The effect, however, was the same.

The Redoubt would be destroyed.

If they all did their work.

Keyes had the frigate moving so fast it was shaking. The reactor could be close to overheating, yet no one breathed a word about how hard they were pushing the ship. They all knew they needed each additional second.

"ODSTs ready?" Keyes asked.

"Standing by," Lt. Kirtley reported.

"Aerobraking in four minutes. Everyone strap in and hold on."

The *Midsummer Night* was in the shadow of the moon now, streaking toward it like an arrow toward a bull's-eye. Keyes could see the swirls and outlines of the moon's clouds.

It grew over the next minutes until it filled the cockpit with its strange orange- and red-hued light. Keyes was aiming his ship deep into the thick atmosphere, counting on the immense friction to slow *Midsummer Night* down.

He'd timed this down to the millisecond, run it by Juliana, and now all he could do was let the ship's computers continue with the course . . . and hope.

They'd picked up Jackal contacts, but they'd approached too fast for them to engage. They'd run right through the cordon before the Kig-Yar even realized they were there.

"Aerobraking!" Keyes shouted.

They hit Metisette's atmosphere and the ship began to buck and pitch. A junior officer standing by was thrown clear across the bridge.

"I gave orders to strap in, damn it," Keyes snarled as the young man grabbed someone's chair, his arm bent at an impossible angle, his face bloodied. "You're endangering the bridge crew."

The man crawled away and got himself to a safe place and strapped in, moaning loudly due to his injuries.

A fireball grew around the frigate, heating up as they continued to thunder through the high atmosphere of Metisette. Deck plates creaked and groaned as they readjusted. Keyes glanced at the readouts. They were losing speed. Dramatically.

They were also losing hull integrity. The friction was burning off plates every second.

Keyes tapped the screen. A second set of preloaded routines sprung into effect. Thrusters fired, slowing them down even further.

He glanced at the topographical map of Metisette that Juliana had uploaded to his computers.

"One minute!" Keyes shouted. They were closing in on the Redoubt.

They would be moving fast when they shot the ODSTs out. He could only hope the pods and their bodies could handle what came next. He didn't know of anyone who'd attempted dropping ODSTs in a maneuver like this.

The seconds ticked by as he waited. A hull-breach alarm sounded, and Keyes looked over at Kirtley.

"Hull abrasions, no serious structural damage, within expectations," the lieutenant reported. The aerobraking had lost them a lot of hull, but the ship would hold.

"The ODSTs are go in ten," Keyes said. He tapped the console to give authorization.

The *Midsummer Night*'s computers took care of the rest, spitting the ODSTs out from a bay like bombs being dropped on an enemy city.

Keyes watched them fall away like dangerous, black spores on another screen, then looked up as emergency klaxons went off.

"Covenant antiaircraft fire!" Rai Li shouted.

Teardrops of contained plasma rose to meet their ship.

Keyes turned off the thrusters and slammed on the main

engines. All ahead full, he thought with a grimace, as plasma grazed the sides of the ship.

The *Midsummer Night* shuddered and clawed its way along, struggling to escape the moon's gravity and get back into orbit.

"Come on, girl," Keyes found himself muttering quietly to the ship. "You can do it."

CHAPTER 61

Jai felt the SOEIV slam against him as it fired rockets to reach a sane velocity right before it slammed into the ground. The front popped off, and Jai stepped out onto the surface of Metisette with his battle rifle up.

Four SOEIVs had already hit the ground around him. Two ODSTs stumbled out; one fell to his knees.

"Shit, I can't even see straight," he muttered over the comm channel.

"Can the chatter," Jai said. They'd had a brutal launch from the ship and a rough journey down filled with Covenant antiaircraft fire picking them off. And even Jai had been slightly rattled by the whole experience.

But they were in enemy territory right now. They needed to get sharp, and quick. They had four hours of air strapped to their backs with rebreathers and tanks. They needed to get this mission wrapped up as fast as possible.

The air was thick and red, and a similar eerie red fog covered everything around them. Jai continued looking around. They'd landed within a mile of their target: the spirelike building along the banks of the methane river that housed the sensor equipment capable of spotting the Rubble.

On Juliana's map it hadn't looked so imposing, Jai thought.

"We launched with three Shivas," Jai radioed. "Tell me at least one of them managed to make it down." He glanced at their ID pips briefly to get their names.

Mutuku was yanking on the front of an SOEIV. The front popped loose, and a fully-suited ODST fell out.

"Jones ate it."

The other Helljumper, Adams, yanked the other pod open. "Your bomb, sir."

Jai ran over. Good. He glanced around. The other SOEIV pods must have landed all over the damn place. They were the only ones out of fifteen supposed to hit here.

They'd have to do.

Jai dragged the Shiva free from the pod. A foldable frame with wheels came loose as he yanked on it.

"Form up." Jai grunted from the strain of shoving the frame under the large missile. Once underneath it, he pressed a button, and the wheels deployed.

With the two marines covering his flanks, Jai started pulling the nuclear warhead toward the building.

Mutuku opened fire. Jai looked over to his right to see two Unggoy tumble to the ground, dead.

Ahead, more materialized. Jai gunned them down, realizing that they were only lightly armed.

"We caught them off guard," Mutuku observed. "They're carrying pistols."

"Good for us, then," Jai said. "Keep moving."

More Unggoy Grunts came, a fast frontal assault in two waves of ten. Jai picked them off as Mutuku and Adams held off attacks from the sides.

They sprinted for the building's door, which Jai kicked down. He threw a grenade inside and ducked as a cloud of debris flew out over him.

Three Kig-Yar hid behind energy shields in the far corner of the room. Jai left the Shiva behind and took cover around the nearest corner.

Mutuku and Adams got the Jackals' attention with a burst of rifle fire; Jai threw a grenade behind them. As they turned around to shield themselves from the blast Jai picked them off.

"We need to clear the building," Jai said.

"We'll hold the door," Adams said.

Jai ran down the hallway that the Jackals had come from. He turned a corner, and found himself face-to-face with another. He swept the butt of his rifle up without a second thought and caught it in the chin. The alien flew backward in a spray of purple blood.

Jai barely slowed down his run.

He got up a set of ramps without anything getting in his way, but as he started moving from room to room he found plenty of Grunts inside.

They were armed with plasma pistols. Jai hardly bothered keeping a count. He just moved from room to room, a gray killing machine.

Within fifteen minutes he'd swept the entire building. The rest of the upper floors looked to be just equipment. If any Grunts were hiding up there, they were cowering away and not going to present a problem.

He sprinted back to the foyer where the two Helljumpers waited. "How are we looking?"

Adams sighted down his rifle. "A handful of Grunts made a run on the door. We dropped them. But I think there are a lot more out there gearing up to come our way."

The building was half a mile upstream from hundreds of thousands of Grunts waiting to board hundreds of Jackal ships. Jai curled his lip at the thought of so many Grunts attacking. They wouldn't need weapons, they could just throw themselves at the team. "There'll be more," he said.

Satisfied they had the situation under control, he pulled the Shiva down the corridor. He'd spotted a thick door leading to what looked like a maintenance room.

He kicked the door open and smiled. A whole room of Covenant junk—consoles, chairs, screens.

He wheeled the Shiva into the heart of the room and pulled the cart out, smashing it to uselessness so the Shiva couldn't be easily moved.

"Jai, they're pressing hard," Mutuku radioed over the sound of plasma fire striking nearby. Battle rifles clattered. "Maybe a hundred Grunts this time."

"On my way soon," Jai promised.

He shoved Covenant junk up against the Shiva after checking the readout on the front. The timer said they had two hours before Pelicans would be back to rescue them.

Once he had the Shiva covered he left it, closing the heavy door behind him.

"Stowed our present away?" Adams asked from the side of the entrance.

Jai held his rifle up and scanned the murk outside. A lot of dead Unggoy lay out in the mist. "Safe for now."

"Now we stay put until the antiaircraft guns go down."

An explosion in the distance made them jump.

"Well, there goes one," Jai said, checking his ammo with a sense of satisfaction.

CHAPTER 62

Adriana opened her eyes inside the HEV. How long had she been out? The HEV had slammed into a building before the retro-rockets had finished their full burn, bringing it to a near stop. It had bounced down the side and hit the ground head-first, crumpling badly. She'd been knocked out by the impact.

In the dark she couldn't tell if her vision was okay, but she had a raging headache and what felt like whiplash.

She slapped the cover-eject switch and the explosive bolts on the cover thudded. It hardly moved an inch, but now streams of orange light came in from around cracks between the cover and the pod.

The HEV was facedown on the ground.

Adriana swore.

She pulled her knees up, forcing herself back against the restraints and padding, compressing it to get her feet under her.

The knees of her armor ground and scraped against the cover, but she finally planted her feet.

Then she pushed the entire HEV up, lifting it onto her shoulders. She heaved it off to the side where it landed with the restraints facing the sky. It would have been a lot easier had it landed like that, she thought.

She looked around.

"Oh . . ."

Tens of thousands of Grunts turned to face her, ripples of activity passing through their ranks like wind through tall grass. Since nothing had initially popped out of the pod, they'd ignored it and continued to line up to board the giant troop carriers that awaited them in this plaza.

Adriana was supposed to land outside the Redoubt, close to one of the antiaircraft emplacements. Not here.

". . . shit." She dove back into the HEV as plasma-pistol shots struck the sides.

The HEVs held a little bit of rocket fuel to allow soldiers to use them to easily hop over to a new location. But that required them to be standing up, in the position they were designed to land.

Adriana triggered the emergency burst with the HEV lying flat anyway, and the HEV took off across the mile-long plaza. It plowed through Grunts who flew overhead in sprays of bright-blue blood, constantly thumping and shivering as it made its way through the tightly packed mass.

The engines finally sputtered, then stopped, and the HEV ground to a halt over the icy rock.

Adriana vaulted out and ducked behind it with her battle rifle in one hand, yanking a rocket launcher out with the other. She was out of the main mass of Grunts. Those still hovering couldn't decide whether to chase her or continue boarding their vessel. A massive, purple-stained gap in the center of the Unggoy formation indicated the path the HEV had rocketed through.

Some hundred Grunts finally peeled off to make a run at her. Adriana fired in short, controlled bursts, watching wave after wave of Grunts tumble forward and die.

There were so many.

She was quickly running out of ammunition, and now hundreds of outraged Grunts had drawn their pistols and started a second assault on her position.

Just not enough ammo, she thought, checking her heads-up display. And she didn't want to use the rockets. Those were her last resort.

Screw it, this *was* a last-resort situation; it was her against a moonfull of Grunts. She popped up with the launcher on her shoulder and unleashed everything she had before ducking back for cover.

As the plaza boiled with rocket fire, she looked for blips on her heads-up display. Some of the signals were of HEVs that were weapons caches, dropped alongside the regular HEVs. She needed one right now.

She spotted one half a mile away.

Adriana threw the empty rocket launcher away and dashed from the large open grounds of Grunts before they could regroup.

She grinned as she approached a larger, bulky HEV that had struck into the side of one of the many tall structures that ringed the plaza. The Jackals had just grounded ships and turned them into buildings, by connecting them. Almost as ramshackle and bizarre as the Rubble, she thought, as she ripped the cover off the HEV.

A quad bike almost fell out onto her.

"A Mongoose?" she whispered. Useless. The four-wheeled ATVs just meant you were a biking target.

Several Grunts rounded one of the arches of the building. Adriana picked the Mongoose up by the handlebars, using it as a shield, and then ran into the small group, slamming the Grunts into the ground with it.

The Mongoose worked well as a weapon, a giant four-wheeled hammer that she used to crush three more Grunts in explosions of purple blood, until the wheels had all bounced off, the chassis warped, and finally snapped.

Adriana tossed the ruined machine away. Her muscles would pay for that later, but for now, there was too much adrenaline for her to notice.

In the distance, a long line of Grunts moved through the mist and buildings at her.

She checked her ammo and prepared for the onslaught, just as a distant explosion caught her attention.

They needed all the antiaircraft emplacements knocked out. They needed it more than they needed some extra dead Grunts. No matter how many she killed, they just kept coming at her. She needed to think smarter.

Adriana sprinted for the distant river of methane, visible by the fog banks created by the waterfall as it hit the warm grounds of the Redoubt.

Plasma fire hit the rocks near her, kicking up steam and molten splashes that stained her armor. Adriana ran faster than she ever had before in training, or in battle.

This was staying smart. She needed to find a way to rendezvous with the ODSTs trying to take out the second emplacement.

In the dense fog she had to slow down a bit, but it gave her a chance to catch her breath. The motion tracker in her heads-up display, overwhelmed up to this point, cleared, and showed friendlies.

Four Helljumpers were pinned at the riverbank behind their HEVs by Grunts.

Adriana ran up behind them. "What's the situation?"

"Two Jackal snipers. Lots of Grunts. Every time we try to break out of the fog and make a run at the antiaircraft gun they pick us off."

"You have the charges ready for the antiaircraft gun?" Adriana asked. "Who's placing them?"

One of the Helljumpers raised a hand. "Dobey took one in the head on the third attempt. But I can place them."

"There were supposed to be sixteen of you." Adriana pulled out the near-empty magazine on her battle rifle and slapped a fresh one in.

"Ten of us made it down—we lost six trying to get up to the damn thing."

Adriana looked out into the rolling banks of orange-lit mist. Large boulders of ice and rock on the edge of the Redoubt made for good hiding places, both in the mist and outside of it.

"Let's stop at five attempts to charge that gun, shall we? I'll take point." She wasn't sure how much longer she could keep this pace up. She could feel her blood pounding since the moment she'd stood up, surrounded by a sea of the enemy.

She realized now that she almost went out in a blaze of glory, until she'd spotted the river and came to her senses.

But she was still struggling to think clearly and not merely react.

She took a pair of large stones and threw them out right where the boundary of the mist ended. Two sharp bursts of plasma vaporized them.

That was enough for Adriana to pinpoint where the shots came from.

Adriana tossed a pair of grenades in a high arc, one right after the other, using her strength to get them higher than any normal human toss could.

She counted off two seconds, then radioed, "On me!"

The sprint through the mist took another several seconds. She dodged waist-high pieces of rock as she made her attack. Just as she was about to burst out of the mist, a good fifty feet ahead of the Helljumpers struggling to keep up with her, two grenades exploded behind the pair of boulders where she figured the snipers were taking cover.

It was all the distraction she needed to cover the ground to the first Jackal's boulder. The Jackal was already turning to face her when Adriana brushed the long Covenant weapon he held aside and struck him.

Adriana grabbed the Jackal by its feet, whipping it around, until she found a boulder and bashed him against it. The Jackal died in a spasm, its spine pulverized against the rock, its suit leaking air.

Rock exploded around her, and she dove behind another boulder.

Three Grunts rounded on her, and Adriana used the last of her precious ammo for three head shots, taking a deep breath before each one to center her aim. She hardly noticed their grazing plasma fire.

A grenade explosion from the other sniper's position got her attention. Adriana sprinted around another boulder, rifle up and at the ready, and found a Helljumper finishing the sniper off with a handgun.

The silvered faceplate turned to look up at her. "All clear," the Helljumper radioed.

One of them had gotten hit by the sniper as they'd rushed the position. But the Helljumper with the charges was still on his feet.

Rising over the haze and boulders by the river were the large tripod legs of the Covenant antiaircraft battery.

Adriana pointed. "Get that thing rigged ASAP, soldier. You two, follow me, we're creating a perimeter. He rigs it, we hold it."

She bent over the dead Helljumper for his extra ammo magazines, and before she stood back up, tapped his helmet.

"Okay gentlemen, let's do this. We have an hour before the Pelicans return."

They fanned out into the boulders, watching for more Grunts and Jackals.

CHAPTER 63

Delgado avoided looking over at his copilot. He didn't want the UNSC pilot seeing the pale look of fear on his face as they bucked and kicked their way through the thick atmosphere of Metisette.

Keyes had come at the moon fast, used its soupy atmosphere to burn off their speed, then sped back up into orbit to loop back around and drop the Pelicans off.

Several smaller Kig-Yar ships had come after them, but most of the troop carriers that had lifted off Metisette were staying well clear of the UNSC frigate.

The Kig-Yar ships attacking them were small, but then so was Keyes's frigate. Keyes was drawing them off, away from the drop zone.

It was mostly working.

As long as the antiaircraft guns didn't fire when Delgado and the five other Pelicans came in over the Redoubt, this insane, highly fragile plan would work.

Delgado watched as the clouds parted, and slammed his Pelican hard right to avoid a massive Kig-Yar troop carrier climbing up and away from the complex.

He wobbled back on course, looking over to the right to see another Pelican with a sheered tail diving and tumbling its way toward the ground.

"That was Finlay," someone radioed.

Delgado came in low over the remains of the antiaircraft emplacements with a smile, and touched down in front of the large spirelike building. The other Pelicans made similar flare-outs and landed in a row.

He fumbled for a second when trying to find the switch to lower the ramp, but the copilot was on it. The moment the ramp hit the ground, boots stamped their way up and into the Pelican.

Delgado turned around to see both Spartans standing behind him. Their armor was hardly recognizable: dented, carbon burned, peeling and flaking from heat and plasma and abuse.

They looked as if they'd fought through hell itself, Delgado thought.

Helljumpers snapped themselves in along the sides of the bay. Several hung out the back of the Pelican, firing back at a solid mass of Unggoy who started to flood the area. Plasma filled the air and slapped the sides of the Pelican.

The Spartans looked back, then tapped Delgado on the shoulder. "That's everybody. Go go go," he heard Jai yell over the radio. "The Shiva has ten minutes."

Delgado had the time up on a counter in his heads-up; he knew damn well how much time they had.

He rammed the engines up full and pulled out over the

Redoubt, moving upriver as fast as he could as Helljumpers fired their last few bursts from the closing ramp.

Once well clear of the Redoubt, and with the cabin repressurized, Delgado began a slow spiraling climb with the other four Pelicans.

A giant flash of light filled the inside of the Pelican. In the distance the Shiva went off. As the initial blast faded, they could see the plume of the explosion reaching up into the sky, slowly turning into a giant mushroom.

Then Delgado's slow spiral took it out of sight.

CHAPTER 64

The Redoubt, Metisette, 23 Librae

Reth sat at a table as a healer checked him over. He'd been inside a command center when the massive explosion occured, and since many of the Kig-Yar ships grounded to make the skeleton of the Redoubt were fighting ships, he was therefore well shielded. He'd been safe.

But he'd gotten a high dose of radiation.

The healer left him with pills to take, and Reth stalked his way up to an enclosed balcony carved out of a large airlock. The Redoubt was a mess. It was a good thing they were moving out to take the Rubble, he thought. Rebuilding this would be expensive.

There were Unggoy leaders wanting to see him, shocked by the damage the humans had done and wondering what it meant for the timeline they had in mind for their continuing development of Metisette as a world for themselves.

Reth growled.

Humans.

When the Prophet set him on this task, Reth had done it to raise his profile, and that of the Kig-Yar. He'd also enjoyed the guilty pleasure of working with the humans. Their profit-minded goals and Kig-Yar-like love of trade and smuggling and piracy had meshed. He'd been slightly disappointed to have to destroy the humans throughout the Rubble as the endgame of this grand experiment.

Now though, he wondered if the Prophets weren't right. The humans were unconscionable reprobates, too dangerous to let live. The Prophets' call for their extermination was starting to make sense to him.

Reth looked forward to taking the Rubble. Even more so, to getting the Exodus and the location to their homeworld on it.

He'd happily burn it all for the Prophet, now.

Reth left the balcony and donned a long cloak, his air supply for the walk across the plaza, and a pair of plasma pistols. He walked out in the plaza where droves of terrified Unggoy stood.

They'd all been dosed with antiradiation meds. Many had died in the blast, but Reth had had those bodies bulldozed away, and cleared the way for Unggoy waiting in the lower warrens to line up and get aboard the troop carriers. He had only lost a few thousand to the bomb, thankfully, as the communications and scanning station was miles upstream of the core Redoubt plaza.

It was time to repay the humans for their deeds, he thought, as he walked toward his shuttle and several of his senior Kig-Yar officers.

Unggoy were shaking and looking up into the sky. It was growing brighter.

Reth stopped and looked up. Giant fireballs were streaking down, growing larger and larger.

The humans had taken out the antiaircraft batteries and his ability to *see* . . . to see *this* coming. He ran for his shuttle, shoving frightened Unggoy aside.

"Go!" he screamed at his pilot in the cockpit. "Get off the ground!"

The shuttle fired its engines and started to rise, and Reth saw the first giant mound of rock slam into the Redoubt.

But where had they come from? he wondered, as the shock wave threw his shuttle aside and dashed it against the side of one of the large buildings.

The wreckage of the shuttle slid to the ground as debris and rock rained down on it.

A dazed Reth looked up through the cracked glass of the shuttle; he stared directly up at one large fireball that plummeted right at him.

It was irregularly shaped, he thought, with large docking collars sticking out of one side, melting away into slag as the heat deformed them.

A piece of the Rubble, he realized just before it struck, vaporizing everything in an immense release of hyperkinetic energy and destruction.

CHAPTER 65

Thel looked at the glowing, cratered remains of the Redoubt from orbit. "Nothing remains of Reth's fleet. There is no sign of Reth himself, either."

A stillness descended on the bridge of the *Infinite Spoils* as both Zhar and Thel contemplated the destruction the humans had wrought on Metisette.

"And now what, Shipmaster?" Zhar asked. "We have destroyed prime targets in the Rubble; the rest has dashed itself against Metisette."

Thel looked at the Unggoy working for them, and thought about Saal, brooding somewhere deep inside the ship.

"Some might say we have done our mission well, Zhar. Do you think the Prophets will believe it when they arrive?"

Zhar looked at him, his mandibles flexing slightly as if tasting the air for clues as to what Thel might want as an answer. His once proud mind had become erratic in the face of the idea that the Hierarchs may have had differing goals, and that they'd gotten caught in the middle of some machination between the Prophets of Regret and Truth.

Thel knew that Sangheili honor demanded they rise above it. He cleared his throat. "Reth's invasion fleet is in disarray. The Hierarchs will not be happy if we stand here and let the last of the humans escape with the location to Earth and the only chance all these loyal Unggoy have to live."

Thel looked at the Unggoy on the bridge as they paid close attention to him, without looking directly at him. So maybe Sangheili *could* play politics, Thel thought to himself, or at least set aside the desire for direct combat for a bit, despite the fact it coursed through their blood.

"What do you mean?" Zhar said.

"The Hierarchs want loyal subjects and true believers," Thel said. "I cannot imagine what would happen to all these surviving Unggoy if they do not try to take that asteroid in which the humans are trying to evacuate the system."

Unggoy eyes balefully watched Thel pace the bridge now.

Zhar coughed. "Their lives would all be forfeit."

Thel nodded. "They would indeed." He turned to the Unggoy in the room. "Tell your surviving brothers to board the Exodus asteroid. We will provide cover for the action, but then stand clear. That human ship is too much of a match for this ungainly Kig-Yar boat."

He walked over and shut off the screen showing the ruins of the Redoubt. "The Unggoy will take the asteroid, or die trying."

If the Hierarchs were to let any of them live, there was no other option.

Zhar got up and walked over to Thel. "If the illustrious

Hierarchs cannot agree on these things, what else do they disagree on, and what else might just be Prophet manipulation, Shipmaster?"

Thel grabbed Zhar's arm, and Zhar growled. But Thel looked his fellow Sangheili in the eye and whispered, "Such thinking lines the path to heresy. Do not indulge in it."

Zhar pulled free and left the bridge.

CHAPTER 66

From the moment the evacuation protocols had blared into life, Karl Simon's day had been a blur of tubes and long lines, waiting to board a habitat he'd never heard of until today. And it was a habitat that was going to jet them toward a new system. Away from home.

A home that was under attack.

It reminded him of the day the Covenant attacked Madrigal: the same nervous lines of people, hushed rumors, and fear that hung in the air.

At the very end, Karl had been shuttled to the Exodus in a cramped supplies freighter. He'd looked out the pilot's windows and seen the craters and pitted surface of what looked like a tiny moon.

The Exodus was six miles of potato-like asteroid, with a diameter of two miles. The freighter was a fleck of dust next to it, and the Exodus filled the windows as far as they could see as they approached it.

We did this, Karl had thought with a momentary flash of pride.

He'd been hustled to what felt like a stadium near the core of the ship, moving through miles and miles of corridors, following instructions on a card that had been handed to him in the shuttle.

A hundred thousand other refugees, their murmuring echoing around the walls and ceilings, all had assigned chairs that matched numbers on their cards.

But now, the moment Karl sat, an usher appeared. "Karl Simon?"

"Yes?"

"Volunteer for the Rubble Defense Force?"

"Yes." Karl had signed up during the early days of the Rubble, when they'd been looking over their shoulders every day, expecting the Covenant to return.

"Come with me."

The usher led Karl out of the rows of chairs with restraints where everyone else was being ordered to buckle in. Outside, the usher pointed down a corridor. "Follow this all the way to the end. They need you there."

It was a mile, which Karl walked as fast as he could, slightly out of breath when he reached an open bay near the front of the asteroid where thirty men with rifles and handguns stood, guarding the entrance. A grizzled old miner looked him up and down. "Volunteer Defense?"

"Yeah."

"You have certification in hand-to-hand combat and firearms training?"

Karl nodded. The minder handed Karl a datapad and a handgun. "We have an estimated three thousand Unggoy who've managed to get inside, more expected. You're drafted. The doors behind us lead to the control center, the bridge, of the Exodus. The aliens do not get past here. Understand?"

"Yes, *sir*," Karl said, and took up position just as the floor started to shake.

"What the hell is that?" one of the other men shouted, holding a machine gun up as a seven-foot-tall man in gray armor turned the corner.

They all stared as the half-ton, armor-clad human walked up to them.

"I have something the bridge crew needs," he said, and held up a small black chip casing in his gauntleted hand. "Mind letting me through?"

The Rubble Defense Force stepped aside, one of the large miners politely holding the door open for the giant, armor-clad soldier to step inside.

CHAPTER 67

Midsummer Night, near Habitat Exodus, 23 Librae

The bridge crew of the Exodus habitat hailed the *Midsummer Night*. Keyes looked over at Lt. Burt on the comms. "Patch them through."

Midsummer Night had been covering the slow flight out to the edges of the system to prepare for a slipspace jump for almost a day now. Unggoy and Kig-Yar fighters had dogged and harassed them the whole way, pockmarking the surface of the asteroid and occasionally scoring hits on the frigate, but unable to stop them. The desperate Grunt boarding parties left Keyes nervous. He'd had to make a snap decision to have the Spartans hand over the nav data, but all indications were that the Rubble Defense fighters were keeping the Grunts pinned down. And more importantly, well clear of the cockpit. The Grunts, with their methane tanks and nowhere to go once the Exodus entered slipspace, would eventually choke to death. Keyes had decided the million lives were worth the small risk. There'd been enough Colonist deaths by the Covenant so far. It was time to rescue some of them. He had no idea of what trouble might lie ahead for him from this decision, but the lives saved would be worth it.

They were now far enough out to enter slipspace.

An engineer appeared, his overalls dirty, bags under his eyes. "Lieutenant Keyes, I apologize, but the Security Council insisted I contact you."

The Rubble's Council. Keyes had almost forgotten about them. "What's wrong?"

"The Exodus will not be able to make the trip. We don't have the range and engine power. We expected more time to bring more engines online. With a Covenant fleet supposed to arrive, we have to go with what we have now. And what we have now, well, they'll burn out, or if we make lots of small jumps, it will literally take centuries to cross the galaxy away from where Covenant or UNSC people would ever dare venture, as we originally planned."

The man looked defeated.

"The Council knows?" Keyes asked.

"Yes. They're debating what to do." The engineer looked down at the floor.

"But the Exodus can make a journey, just not as far as origi-nally intended?" Keyes confirmed.

The Council didn't want to return to the colonies. Would they be hardheaded enough to risk Exodus and everyone in it to try and leave the Covenant and colonies behind anyway?

"Yes." The engineer met his eyes. Keyes realized the engineer was worried about the same thing.

"Put me through to the Council," Keyes ordered. He thought about the last time he'd given a speech.

Forget trying to sound stirring, he thought. Just lay it out. His duty was to convince the Council to head toward the Inner colonies. It was their best bet for survival.

The screen filled with the members of the Security Council. The Rubble wasn't working as a technocracy right now, not while being herded into their spots all throughout the Exodus asteroid.

This was their leadership. And Keyes had to influence it.

"Hello, I'm Lieutenant Keyes, of the *Midsummer Night*," he said with a faint grin. He locked his arms behind him. It was a classroom habit, and it would keep him from reaching for the pipe which he'd found sitting in his belongings, thankfully untouched. "I'm a fighting man, but as commander of this ship, I know something about holding people's lives in my hands. I won't bullshit around. You have enough engine power to reach an Inner Colony quickly, where there will be some measure of protection, and access to resources. The other option is to risk a slow, long journey out to a destination that has neither, but in which you retain your own power.

"I don't know what the UNSC will do, and I can't guarantee that all of you with Insurrectionist ties will be given a pass. But remember, you have a million lives you're deciding for. A million lives who could make a difference in the future fight against these bastard aliens who destroyed the Rubble. Unless you choose to let the Covenant win."

Keyes looked at them all, and Maria Esquival stood up. "We took a vote," she said, "before you called."

Keyes sucked in his breath.

She quirked a faint smile. "We're aiming to reach the 18 Scorpii system. If you would escort us, Lieutenant."

"Of course," Keyes said. "Make random jumps out, until we clear the asteroid of Grunts. We want to make sure not a single one remains alive before we turn toward the Inner Colonies." His after-action report was going to be damning enough. Showing up with an asteroid full of evidence . . . well, Keyes figured he'd be spending time behind bars again soon. But he couldn't turn his back on a million lives. He couldn't leave them for the Covenant. Not again.

Maria nodded. "We have teams combing Exodus thoroughly."

Keyes waited until the screen flickered off, then looked around at his bridge crew. "It's still tricky," he said. "Don't let those breaths out. We have to hope *Petya*'s computers can keep us in sync."

"Actually," said a voice from the back of the bridge. "We ditched *Petya*."

The Spartan at the back pulled his helmet off. It was Mike. He held out a chip.

"This what I think it is?" Keyes asked.

"Navigation charts." Mike sat down by Keyes's old console. "I ran simulations on syncing our two ships. The odds weren't good. Made more sense to dump the freighter. I pressed your crew into service; we off-loaded a lot of the more useful cargo into your bay. We also cut loose a couple of Pelicans to make some room."

Keyes raised an eyebrow. "And I authorized this when?"

Mike plugged the navigation data in, dumping star chart information into the ship's computers. "I took some liberties. Time was short when you showed up. Jai and Adriana lent a hand; they're still stowing things. A good price for the data, losing just a couple Pelicans, Lieutenant Keyes, don't you think?"

Keyes straightened out his back, holding in his private smile. "Don't ever try to run my ship for me again."

The Spartan did not reply, but plugged in a random vector out of the system. "We're going in the same direction. I carried these personally on a disk from their ship to this one. Can't be intercepted. Will you give the order?"

Keyes looked out into space through the windows of his bridge. "Send them the signal. Engage slipspace drives."

All across Exodus engines flickered to life, and the asteroid struggled its way into slipspace, ripping and clawing its way into a hole in the universe.

It was ungainly, but the asteroid managed it, and *Midsummer Night* followed, leaving behind the remains of the Rubble.

CHAPTER 68

Bonifacio drifted in orbit around Metisette. The batteries on his pod were close to dead, and condensation dripped off the portholes.

He'd seen the destruction of the Redoubt from orbit, the asteroids raining down into the atmosphere.

Since then things had been quiet.

The air was getting thick inside the pod, and it was hard to breathe. Occasionally he heard Kig-Yar voices on the radio and sometimes fast Unggoy chatter, but none of them would respond to his calls for help.

Not even calls back to the Rubble had been answered. He'd pleaded and begged, even offered rewards, but gotten only static.

He sat in place hugging his chest, when a loud pipping sound caught his attention.

Bonifacio moved over and looked at the scans.

A bulbous-headed ship had appeared in orbit nearby, expertly dropping out of slipspace in a way no human ship could.

Another flashed into space behind it, then another, and another. An entire Covenant fleet materialized in front of Bonifacio.

This would be a new group of Covenant. Ones who hadn't shut him out, Bonifacio thought. He moved to the radio. He'd surrender. Yes, he'd be a tool of the Covenant, a slave to them, but he'd live.

Yes, he'd live.

He grabbed the microphone and hailed the large cruiser moving nearby, and kept calling it until he saw it change course.

Bonifacio's heart skipped.

He'd done it. He'd survived. He was going to get picked up. He smiled as he watched the cruiser pick up speed, and then frowned.

It was still picking up speed. It was moving so close that he could see it from the windows of his pod, growing larger every second.

A ball of energy gathered underneath the ship. Bonifacio screamed and put his hand up against the slimy, wet porthole as if to ward off the plasma that lashed out and struck his tiny pod.

The massive Covenant cruiser plowed through the vaporized remains as it adjusted its orbit.

CHAPTER 69

Thel got to his knees and bowed to the pair of Hierarchs before him on the bridge of the *Infinite Sacrifice*. An honor guard of five Sangheili guards arrayed themselves around their floating chairs.

"Rise," the Prophet of Truth said. "You ordered the Unggoy to storm the human vehicle after the Kig-Yar Reth's death?"

"Yes, Hierarch," Thel said. "It was a chance to get the location of their homeworld. But we know now the Unggoy and any Kig-Yar that were with them have failed."

"How is that?" the Prophet of Regret asked.

"Their air would have run out by now."

The heavy crowns of the Hierarchs bobbed as they considered that. "Indeed," Truth said. "We are left only with Kig-Yar who imagined they were helping humans, at Reth's orders. Potential traitors, all of them. And these Unggoy as well, breeding outside the law. Traveling without permits."

Regret shook its head. "A mess."

"A mess that revealed much," Truth hissed.

For a moment, an uncomfortable silence hung in the air. Then Regret nodded at Truth. "We will destroy all the traitors."

Thel felt his neck tighten. He'd failed to appreciate the situation, and now he would pay the ultimate price for his mistakes. The Hierarchs would have his head.

Vadam would suffer. His lineage would be suspect.

The floor beneath his feet felt as if it wavered, and then Thel stiffened. Zhar was moving forward.

The Sangheili warrior had drawn the bar of his energy sword, but not yet unleashed it.

"*Zhar,*" Thel hissed, horrified. Zhar seemed to be struggling with himself.

"So you will kill us too, Shipmaster?" Zhar cried out. "Like animals? After all we served. How can I suffer such a dishonor? My line's dishonor?"

The honor guard drew their energy pikes, the ends shimmering with contained blue plasma.

Zhar took another hesitant step forward, and Thel pulled out his sword and turned it on. "Zhar?"

His old friend looked back at him. "I have already drawn," he said. "I will not stand and let them dishonor me."

"I have drawn as well," Thel said sadly.

Zhar leapt forward, but Thel jumped as well, slamming into his side and spearing Zhar through the throat with his sword. It sizzled and spat Sangheili blood.

Thel threw Zhar against a wall, then decapitated him with a swift swipe.

He stared at the mess of blood and Zhar's body, then turned back to the Hierarchs, setting his sword down on the ground away from him.

What else could he have done? Thel wondered. Zhar had forced him into it. To step toward the Hierarchs with a sword in hand was madness.

Regret looked shaken, but composed himself and piloted his chair out of the large bridge. "What madness Sangheili honor can be," he muttered as he left. "They should be careful, lest they lose their way."

But Truth looked at Thel with analytical eyes. "Tell me your name, noble warrior."

"Thel 'Vadamee," Thel said.

Truth moved closer, the honor guard moving with him. "You live. Say nothing of what happened here."

"Yes, Hierarch," Thel said.

"Report to the shipmaster—he will find you lodging until we return to High Charity." Truth also left the bridge.

Thel waited until they were well clear, then stood. He didn't look at Zhar's body as he walked to the large, Sangheili shipmaster to get his instructions.

This mission was over, and Thel was grateful. He wanted a ship to command that was part of a fleet, not off on its own. But leading a mission, away from the Prophets where his decisions could or could not risk their wrath . . .

Thel 'Vadamee never wanted to be in that position again.

CHAPTER 70

Commander Arthur Resnick of the frigate *Ready or Not* was enjoying a routine patrol at the edge of the system of 18 Scorpii. The slow pace gave him time to catch up on paperwork, and he was scrolling through a datapad full of reports when his navigation officer suddenly stiffened.

"Sir?"

Resnick glanced at the screen. "What the hell is that?"

The report showed something . . . huge. It was bearing down on the system in slipspace. The scan had been forwarded to them via an early warning sensor net and station farther out-system.

"That's gotta be Covenant," he said. "None of us have anything *that* heavy." The mass was off the charts.

"It's six miles long," the navigation officer said. She sounded shocked. "Whatever it is."

"Send the warning." The planet of Falaknuma would need to

gear up as best it could. There wasn't much in the way of UNSC Navy here. Falaknuma mainly served as a base for a section of the ONI Prowler Corps, and a handful of frigates.

They were going to get overwhelmed pretty quickly, if past Covenant encounters were anything to judge by.

Resnick cleared his datapad. "Get the MAC ready. Bring the reactor up to full operational power—"

"Sir." Comms stood up. "It's broadcasting a UNSC friend-or-foe tag. The *Midsummer Night*."

Resnick looked over at Navigation. Lt. Onika frowned. "There's another signature in there. About the right size to be a frigate."

"Could be a trap."

"Standby, but wait for my order to fire," Resnick said. "We stand off and watch this. For a moment."

Then the massive object dropped into real space and they finally got a read on it.

A six-mile-long asteroid, trailing debris, one engine misfiring and a UNSC frigate trailing it.

"Comms, open a channel," Resnick ordered.

On the screen a man with Navy-short salt-and-pepper hair appeared. "*Ready or Not*, this is Lieutenant Keyes, of the *Midsummer Night*. We're all friendly. Do not fire." Keyes grinned. "The asteroid is full of refugees from behind Covenant lines. They're all civilians from what was once Madrigal. About a million of them. Their air is getting stale, the asteroid has been holed from being shot at, and the engines are critical. We need to get these civilians off the moment they get into a stable orbit."

The bridge crew of the *Ready or Not* stared at the large asteroid moving by them.

Someone from the back of the bridge uttered what was on everyone's mind:

"Holy shit."

Resnick snapped around. "Alright, let's get to it. Comms, we need to bump this up the chain of command and to the Colonial Administration Authority. Let's get cracking—there are people's lives at stake."

The bridge exploded into motion as the rescue effort began.

PART V

PART V

CHAPTER 71

===========

High Charity

"We lost much," the Prophet of Regret said.

Truth looked at his fellow Hierarch. "No. We purged Kig-Yar and Unggoy who might have caused trouble, due to their inclinations to work with humans. And thanks to the modified weapons, we have found two more worlds of theirs to attack."

"Neither of which will be their homeworld," Regret grumbled.

"It is progress," Truth said.

From their throne room, high up in High Charity, they looked out over their subjects. Streams of other San'Shyuum wobbled around the city in the air in large rings, barges of Unggoy flew from point to point, and pilgrims from all throughout the Covenant worlds thronged the streets.

"We need to be more careful about the Sangheili," Regret said. "Honor and nobility might one day get in the way of orders."

— 379 —

Truth glided away from the city scene and into the heart of the chamber, where golden streams of light flashed through a gentle drug-smoke haze. "Maybe," he said. "But some of them seem fiercely loyal, and very useful. I value loyalty."

Regret grunted. "I value results."

"Then it is good we work together," Truth said. "For the good of the Covenant."

Regret picked up one of the bowls and inhaled. "For the good of the Covenant, yes. In all we do."

The two hierarchs had resolved the moment of bad blood that had grown between them. Their plans were back in synchronization.

For now, Regret thought. For now.

CHAPTER 72

Vadam Keep, Yermo, Sanghelios

"The Fleet of Particular Justice?" Lak 'Vadamee asked. The old Sangheili walked along the keep's walls with Thel. Thel had a new shipmaster's cloak that tugged and kicked at him in the cold mountain wind. "I have never heard of it."

"It is a new reorganization of the fleets. Against the Sangheili Councilors' desires. They have given me a cruiser to command within this fleet."

"A strange new age, Kaidon."

Thel looked out over Vadam valley, out toward the distant sea. "Stranger than I can dare speak. Even when I add my lines to the family saga."

"But our nobility rises, does it not?" Lak asked.

"For now," Thel replied. "But I have seen humans as strong and as fast as any of ours. And I have seen what happens to those who disappoint the Prophets."

"We are Vadam," Lak said. "We shall persevere."

Thel started to say something, then paused. Lak had trained Thel when he'd been among the keep's young. He'd bruised and kicked Thel, toughened him to be the warrior he was today. He'd taught him the histories, made him learn sagas, and taught him to reason. If he couldn't trust Lak to be a close advisor, then Thel had no friends and was alone in this universe. "You must never repeat this, but I saw the Hierarchs argue with each other, and it cost the lives of many souls," Thel finally said. "Is it heresy that I cannot shake the worry that gives me?"

"There is heresy, and then there is heresy," Lak said softly.

Thel rested his hands on the stone in front of him. "What do you mean by that riddle, elder Lak?"

"Long ago our ancestors believed without a doubt that the Forerunner artifacts we found scattered on our world were objects of veneration. We could study and worship them, and imagine transcendence. But that was it. To destroy, even take them apart, was heresy.

"Then came the Prophets, who wanted the artifacts to study. They wanted to violate them and explore them. So we fought to prevent this heresy, and both Prophets and Sangheili almost perished in the fight. Now we let the Prophets do what they will and study these artifacts. Might made heresy change. But what is the true truth? Who knows?" Lak shrugged.

"That is close to heretical," Thel said, looking over at his old master.

"I am an old Sangheili," Lak said. "I have been hit on the head too many times, and am easily confused. What do I know of theology?"

Thel grumbled. "We shall persevere then, elder, heresies or not, and strive to follow the path. I might even rise above just shipmaster."

"That is the attitude to take, Kaidon. Enjoy your moments of triumph now. The future will come soon enough; there is no reason to dwell too much on it. Then you will end up an old creature who has spent far too much time worrying."

Thel followed Lak down the stairs into the warmth, where the elders of the Vadam waited to congratulate him on his success and promotion.

There was living to do, Thel thought happily. And the warmth of a productive and virile keep to enjoy.

CHAPTER 73

Keyes saluted and stood ramrod-straight in front of the two men at the table in front of him.

Admiral Cole waved at him to sit down.

The other man, an ONI agent, slowly flipped through the pages of a report with exaggerated care while Keyes stared at *the* Admiral Cole, the Hero of Harvest and the man who'd dedicated his life to taking the fight to the Covenant.

Keyes realized that the slow page turning was theater, but it was working. Keyes *was* nervous and sweating under his full dress uniform.

This was the part where they busted him back to the classroom.

And yet, as he played back all his actions in the past few weeks, he found in himself few regrets. He was at peace with himself. In some ways, he'd managed to banish the guilt of not being able to help his sister, dead or trapped somewhere out in the Outer Colonies, by rescuing these million.

"Lieutenant Jacob Keyes," the ONI agent said in sibilant tones. "Quite a return from your mission."

Admiral Cole tapped the table. "To begin with: navigational hazards."

The Exodus asteroid had been falling apart as it came in, shaking itself to pieces due to resonances the engineers hadn't anticipated from trying to drive a six-mile-long asteroid through slipspace.

Once in orbit around Falaknuma the emergency scramble to evacuate the nearly one million ex-Rubble residents had been a success. But the asteroid had disintegrated shortly after. Falaknuma now had a ring of debris around it, and the UNSC was using frigates with MAC guns to blow the larger chunks into small enough pieces to burn up in Falaknuma's atmosphere.

But that now meant impediments to getting on and off Falaknuma until everything had deorbited and burned up, which according to experts would take years.

"Then there is the matter of your dumping an unknown number of Insurrectionists on the population. Some have slipped away from the camps. Who knows when that will start to come back to bite us," the ONI agent said.

Keyes stared straight ahead. "Yessir."

"And I've lost one commander," said Admiral Cole.

"I see, sir."

Cole fiddled with a pen. "Why, Lieutenant?"

Keyes looked at him. "A million civilians, sir. Behind enemy lines. I had a duty to do *something*. Anything. Sir."

"A good argument," the admiral said, much to Keyes's surprise. "At ease, Jacob. You did the best you could under some damn horrendous circumstances. You did good. A lot of those million civilians are people with experience in dealing with the Covenant, which ONI is already putting to good use through debriefing. Seems this Rubble group is full of pilots. We're getting some recruits out of them. And getting people back from behind the lines—damn it, that's a victory in my book any day."

Keyes couldn't help but be stunned. "Thank you, sir."

"Most important, I see you worked damn hard to keep my protocol in effect."

"Yessir."

"Good job, then, *Commander.*"

"Thank you, sir." Keyes took the compliment, then paused and looked back at Admiral Cole, who chuckled and pushed a set of bars across the table at him.

"You're promoted, Commander Keyes. We can't let someone who thinks like you get away from us, can we? A few more maneuvers like that stunt at Metisette and you'll be *in* the textbooks, not ever teaching them again."

"Thank you, sir."

"*Midsummer Night* is getting a refit, Keyes. You have time to take some leave, get back to the home system and see family. Get healed up and ready for the next round."

Keyes was dismissed.

Outside he found Jai, Adriana, and Mike.

"I thought you were all under a different branch?" he said.

"We're here to ask for a Prowler," Jai said. "Think they'll give us one? We need to get back to work."

Mike sighed and folded his massive arms. "I say we just take one now, ask for forgiveness later."

Keyes smiled. "There's going to be more lurking around behind Covenant lines?"

"Couldn't tell you," Adriana said. "Have to kill you if we did."

Keyes smiled, and Jai stood up, towering over him, and extended a hand. "It was a pleasure working with you, sir," Jai said.

They shook hands, all of them, and then Keyes stepped out.

CHAPTER 74

UNSC Local HQ, Falaknuma, 18 Scorpii

Admiral Cole turned to the man next to him. "Men like him will save us, you know. We need more like Keyes."

The ONI agent, one Commander Hadley, did not disagree. He looked down at the paperwork in front of him. "The Spartans want another Prowler. They seem to lose their own on a regular basis."

It was Cole's turn not to comment. Eventually Hadley turned back to his paperwork.

The door creaked open, and a ton and a half of gray-armored Spartans walked in. The three of them stood impassively before the table.

"We're giving you the Prowler," Hadley said. "And you're going back in. Deeper, this time."

He tossed them a binder that included the details of their next mission. "It doesn't get any easier, and you'll be even farther from our lines."

The three Spartans were poring over the documents. "That's the way we like it, sir," the team leader said. "We're Gray Team."

Cole imagined them all smiling with the excitement of heading back out over enemy lines.

CHAPTER 75

I gnatio Delgado, formerly of the Rubble, now sat slouched in front of a heavyset Navy recruiter in his full Navy dress uniform. They'd been trading barbs, Delgado getting more bored and irritated with the process. Questions about his background, lineage, political affiliations, ideals . . . it was a lot of bullshit really, Delgado thought.

He'd come back from a funeral for Diego, attended by Rubble refugees living in tents and temporary housing on Falaknuma. He'd held Maria as she cried.

And halfway through, made a decision to come here.

He saw the datapad the recruiter had on the table. "Trouble with authority" had been written down.

The recruiter was going through the motions now, not interested in Delgado unless he was looking to become a marine. They'd give him a gun and some boots, sure. But not a ship.

It seemed like it was too late to kiss and make nice with the recruiter, Delgado figured. He was wasting his time now.

"We'll process this application as soon as possible, then," the recruiter finally said, sensing Delgado's desire to leave.

But before he could turn to the next person in line, a man in a black uniform sidled up beside the recruiter and flashed identification.

"Commander Hadley, sir. What brings an ONI agent out to a simple recruiting station?"

Hadley looked down at the recruiter, then at Delgado. "He does." He pointed at Delgado.

He picked up the datapad and tapped on the screen. "Mr. Delgado has no love of the Covenant, do you, Mr. Delgado?"

Delgado shook his head. "No, no, I don't."

The ONI officer smiled. "Welcome to the Navy then, Mr. Delgado. You'll be picked up from the refugee camp here in two days. Get your effects in order by then."

The recruiter's mouth was open. It shut. "Sir, this man's background check came back with ties to known Insurrectionists!"

"How many recruits do you get who've fought one-on-one with the Covenant? Or ship to ship?" Commander Hadley asked the recruiter.

"But his psyche profile . . ."

"Oh, I'm sure Mr. Delgado will have a life-altering experience while at boot camp. In fact, I already have an instructor in mind for him. And if Mr. Delgado doesn't wash out, well then, there's an ONI Prowler with a spot on it for him. You won't wash out, will you, Mr. Delgado?"

Delgado looked up at him. "It would make too many people happy for me to even consider it."

Commander Hadley laughed. "So why are you joining, Mr. Delgado?"

"I'd like to shoot down some Covenant ships, Mr. ONI man."

Hadley turned to the recruiter. "See? He's perfect. I like him already."

"I'm not in the Navy until I sign, right?" Delgado said.

"Right," the recruiter said.

Delgado slowly flipped the ONI officer the bird, then pressed his thumbprint to the datapad.

"Be seeing you around, Mr. Delgado." Hadley walked away.

"Bet on it," Delgado called after him.

CHAPTER 76

When Keyes opened the door to his apartment on Luna, he found Miranda inside watching a hologram of an old naval battle. He'd radioed ahead to tell her she could leave the dorms and head home before he got there.

Tall, square-rigged ships lumbered around the center of the living room, battered about by raging seas, trying to line the sides of their ships up for the best cannon shot.

Miranda was studying the battle from various angles, rewinding it, and had alternate simulations of it running in different sections of the apartment.

Keyes set his luggage down inside the door, walked over to her, and grabbed her tight for a long hug.

"Geez, what's that all about?" she asked. "You're not normally that clingy."

He let her go. "Nothing. Just glad to see you." He realized he was a bit of a cold Navy father figure, urging her to study, keeping her on the straight and narrow. So much so that a hug caught her off guard, even though he'd been away for weeks.

"Is this homework?" Keyes asked, looking at the battle.

Miranda froze it all. "No, just something I'm playing with."

"I was hoping to tear you away, walk down Armstrong Alley, get an ice-cream cone."

"Okay."

Outside, as he locked the door, he refused to look up through the clear lunar dome at the night sky and the stars.

For Keyes, stars were no longer distant, amazing things. Now they were filled with the threat of the Covenant, bearing down and moving ever closer, always. An implacable foe.

Tonight, he kept his head straight ahead, walking down past the bronzed statues of lunar rovers and centuries-old busts of astronauts who'd first landed on Luna oh so long ago.

They might even enjoy a nice Earthrise by the decks.

Because tonight he was just a father, out with his daughter, enjoying the simple treats of life.

ACKNOWLEDGMENTS

First of all, my big thanks to my very patient wife, Emily. Not only for putting up with hours of me playing *Halo* (particularly when I was replaying all the games with the excuse of "but *this is* work, honey," but also for putting up with me while I was in the throes of meeting the deadline.

My next thank you goes out to my good friend Josh Smith, who insisted I get an Xbox 360 when my old PlayStation died, thus turning me into a fan of *Halo* when I got my hands on the games.

I'd like to thank the folks at Bungie for such a great game, and for bringing me into the fold and letting me play in this cool universe with *The Cole Protocol*. Special thanks to Frank O'Connor and Robt McLees for edits and suggestions and general brainstorming, and to Frank (again) and Brian Jarrard for general brainstorming of the core concepts of the book. I'd also like to thank Eric Nylund and Joe Staten for welcoming a nervous author into their ranks. Thanks to Alicia Brattin and Alicia Hatch at Microsoft Game Studios for coordinating the project and welcoming me aboard.

I'd also really like to thank my editor on this book, Eric Raab at Tor, for being right there in the mix with me with suggestions, revisions, edits, shared stress, and talking me off the ledge when needed.

ABOUT THE AUTHOR

Called "violent, poetic and compulsively readable" by *Maclean*'s, science fiction author Tobias S. Buckell is a *New York Times* best-selling writer born in the Caribbean. He grew up in Grenada and spent time in the British and U.S. Virgin Islands, and these places influence much of his work.

His Xenowealth series begins with *Crystal Rain*. Along with other stand-alone novels and his more than fifty stories, Tobias has been translated into eighteen different languages. He has been nominated for such awards as the Hugo, Nebula, Prometheus, and John W. Campbell Award for Best New Science Fiction Author.

His latest original novels are *Hurricane Fever*, a follow-up to the successful *Arctic Rising*, which NPR says will "give you the shivers," and the acclaimed *Halo: Envoy*. He currently lives in Bluffton, Ohio, with his wife, twin daughters, and a pair of dogs. He can be found online at www.TobiasBuckell.com.

Build Beyond™

MEGACONSTRUX.COM

XBOX
OFFICIAL
GEAR

gear.xbox.com